Beautiful Eyes

In Their Eyes Book Two

by

Gabbi Black

This is a work of fiction. Names, characters, places, and incidents are either the product of the author's imagination or are used fictitiously, and any resemblance to actual persons living or dead, business establishments, events, or locales, is entirely coincidental.

Beautiful Eyes

Contact Information: info@thewildrosepress.com

Cover Art by *Diana Carlile*

The Wild Rose Press, Inc.
PO Box 708
Adams Basin, NY 14410-0708

Visit us at www.thewildrosepress.com

Publishing History
First Edition, 2021
Print ISBN 978-1-5092-3866-8
Digital ISBN 978-1-5092-3867-5
Published in the United States of America

She needs redemption.
He needs to demand it of her.

Alessandra was sliding bonelessly to the ground, so he stepped forward and scooped her up. Hefting her into his arms and looking down, he recoiled as a jolt ricocheted through him. He'd been right about her eyes. They were a deep, dark-brown chocolate, like fudge on the sundae he treated himself to once in a while. Pure indulgence. They were eyes a man could get lost in.

Damn, her eyes were glassy and unfocused. Mood-altering substances were banned from the club, although that didn't mean people didn't sneak things in or imbibe before arriving. But if she'd been acting drunk at the door, she'd never have gained admittance.

"The man with the beautiful eyes." She mumbled the words just before *her* eyes rolled upward.

Dedication

Sara Blaze
Cheryl D.
Shaun and Jenn—for more than thirty years of
friendship

Chapter One

Was he hallucinating? Smith did a double take and looked again, just to be sure, because the lighting in the club was low. No, definitely Alessandra Soriano. Who the hell had cut off her beautiful, long, blue-black curls with a weed whacker? Barely an inch long, the ends stuck out in every direction. Her eyes weren't visible, but he hadn't seen them the last time, given her sunglasses. Of course they'd be unique, just like the woman.

He'd obsessed over her for six months—ever since their brief meeting at the baby shower for Gage and Rielle. She left abruptly five minutes into the party.

Gage tried to soften the blow by suggesting a pseudo-blind date to get the two of them together.

But the mysterious Alessandra disappeared.

Gage kept him apprised of the situation when Smith peppered him with questions, demanding updates. How did a woman just disappear?

When she hadn't shown up at work for several days, someone called the Mission City police. Her car was in her driveway. Entering through her unlocked front door, the officers located her keys, cell phone, and wallet on the front hall table. Nothing in the house was disturbed. No signs of violence. Nothing was out of place. No clues to explain why a thirty-five-year-old woman picked up and left her life.

The police classified her as a missing person because no proof existed that she'd been taken against her will. Her body hadn't turned up. She'd just vanished.

Smith took another long look to make sure he wasn't just seeing what he wanted to see. What he longed to see. Despite their brief acquaintance, he felt oddly connected to the woman.

No, it *was* Alessandra. He reached for his cell phone to call Gage but paused. His friends had been frantic all this time. A jolt of anger shot through him like a bullet because the woman didn't seem like she had a care in the world. After everything she'd put her friends and colleagues through, the least she could do was look…well, something other than the way she looked right now.

Understandably, the scene in front of them mesmerized her.

Club Kink was Vancouver's premier BDSM club, and Spike was a regular. The talented man was a whiz with the whip, always drawing attention to himself and his partner du jour. The weird hairdo, bare chest, multiple tattoos, and pierced body parts only added to the mystique. The showman scened with a few select women, even though his talents were constantly in demand.

Ending with a flourish, Spike coiled his whip and dropped it to the ground before beginning aftercare for his bottom.

The woman was probably well into subspace—that place Smith always tried to get his women to but sometimes found it hard to achieve. A submissive had to let go of everything around her and focus on the sensations he was eliciting.

The latest woman descended the platform into the waiting arms of another woman.

Spike stepped forward. "I need another volunteer."

Alessandra's hand shot up.

Before Smith could intervene, Spike led her onto the stage. Barely breathing, Smith stepped forward to stop the scene but halted in his tracks when Spike peeled the spandex away. She was not—surprise, surprise—wearing a bra. He'd seen plenty of breasts before, so this display shouldn't be affecting him so profoundly. Each pair was distinctive, appealing in unique ways. Unlike most men, however, he didn't have a preference in size. High, small breasts he could suck entirely into his mouth were as nice as ones that filled his palms. No, the size wasn't making his cock twitch.

Oh, those nipples. Color never mattered—although the difference of hues fascinated him—but he adored responsiveness. Nipples hardened to points as sharp as diamonds were as enticing as any twenty-year-old scotch. Of course, nipples hardened because of chilly air was one thing, but when a woman's chest was flushed with arousal and her nipples taut, calling for his notice, his cock would come to full attention, like now.

He couldn't definitively discern color in the club's dimness, but Alessandra's appeared to be a dusky rose. Hard as rocks. He needed every ounce of willpower not to stride over and pay them the homage they clearly deserved. He swallowed the saliva pooling in his mouth, clenching his jaw to try to dispel the desire to suckle, lick, and then bite.

Spike's stubby fingers twisted the nipples so

forcefully that Smith winced. *What the hell?*

She didn't react. No pulling away, no leaning in. Nothing changed in her expression—her eyes were still closed, and she emitted no moan of pleasure or squeak of pain.

Hearing something as faint as a moan over the beat of the house music would be hard, but he was connected to her and convinced he'd hear anything that might escape those soft lips.

She still had no reaction as Spike attached her wrists to the manacles hanging from the ceiling.

Smith's gut churned as Spike positioned Alessandra with her arms wide above her head, tight enough it forced her up onto the balls of her feet.

The position couldn't have been comfortable, but she was secure and hadn't complained. Some bottoms enjoyed the surrender of choice. For them, the power exchange, even if only in the context of a scene, could be more powerful than whatever came next.

How often had he reveled in making a woman helpless, completely at his mercy? That the women enjoyed the bite of the whip, the slap of the paddle, or the thud of the flogger was a secondary consideration.

When Spike hit the ground experimentally with his whip, a collective gasp rose from the audience, but no reaction from his target.

Smith leaned forward…should he intervene? She didn't look right. She looked…altered.

The first lash cracked across her back.

She screamed.

Not a scream of distress—but something more primal. Her eyes didn't open, and she swayed. The next lash had her pitching forward, her arms straining against the restraints. Had she set up a safeword with Spike? Would she use it? Was she even capable?

Smith cursed under his breath. He had no right to interfere. He'd seen this kind of show many times, and submissives had admitted to him just how good it felt to be on the receiving end of Spike's attention.

Painfully hard, he watched Alessandra at the mercy of another man. This was more than voyeurism. His desire to possess her, to own her, was more powerful than anything he'd ever endured. His fingers itched as if covered in mosquito bites, but he forced himself not to scratch them. His pants were tight, but at least he'd worn the wool trousers instead of the jeans he normally donned when he came here.

After what seemed to be an interminable amount of time but was probably more like ten minutes, Spike coiled his whip and let it drop to the floor. The audience dispersed, and Smith pushed forward.

Spike released one of Alessandra's arms, and her body immediately transferred its entire weight to the other.

The man'd better be careful, or she might dislocate a shoulder.

When he released her other arm, she began to crumple to the ground.

Spike caught her but barely. He wasn't a big man. Good thing she was a petite woman. Taking her by the elbows, he guided her to several chairs behind the platform and out of the way.

With little finesse or grace, Spike shoved her arms into her catsuit.

Smith bit back a growl at the way the younger man's hands lingered on her breasts as he pushed them under the spandex.

After the suit was in place, Spike leaned in for a kiss.

Smith nearly gagged at the sight of him thrusting his tongue into her mouth.

She barely stirred.

Leaving her as she was, Spike headed back to the platform to retrieve his whip.

He was stepping from the stage when Smith grabbed the man's arm. "You call that aftercare?" He spat out the words through gritted teeth. "You're responsible for her."

Spike wrenched his arm free. "I did my part. If she didn't enjoy herself, it's not my fault."

While Smith uttered an oath, the uncaring fool sauntered away.

Alessandra was leaning forward, barely able to sit up.

Even as he stepped toward her, Mistress Gigi bustled past him. She reached Alessandra and was pushing the younger woman's shoulders back when whatever had been holding her up fled her body.

Alessandra was sliding bonelessly to the ground, so he stepped forward and scooped her up. Hefting her into his arms and looking down, he recoiled as a jolt ricocheted through him. He'd been right about her eyes. They were a deep, dark-brown chocolate, like fudge on the sundae he treated himself to once in a while. Pure indulgence. They were eyes a man could get lost in.

Damn, her eyes were glassy and unfocused. Mood-altering substances were banned from the club, although that didn't mean people didn't sneak things in or imbibe before arriving. But if she'd been acting drunk at the door, she'd never have gained admittance.

"The man with the beautiful eyes." She mumbled the words just before *her* eyes rolled upward.

Smith tightened his grip on the raven-haired beauty. He glanced over at Gigi and raised an eyebrow.

She frowned in return. "I need her out of here, now."

"That I can help you with. My apartment is just a couple of blocks from here. I'll take her there until she sobers up. Unless you know where she lives."

"I'll call a taxi."

****

The cab ride was relatively uneventful, and Alessandra stirred, took in her surroundings, then closed her eyes again.

He wasn't thrilled, bringing a drunk woman home to his condo, but the only other choices were the drunk tank at the police station or the busiest hospital in downtown Vancouver, and neither seemed necessary, although he'd keep his options open.

The night security guard, Tarah, was there to hold the door for him. "Good evening, Mr. MacLean." She eyed the drunk woman dubiously but said nothing.

"Could I impose upon you to come up and open my door? I'd hate to drop the lady."

She nodded and went for her keys. He was pretty sure she mumbled something about Alessandra not being a lady, but he put her comments down to the fact he was carrying a woman in a spandex catsuit who wore four-inch stiletto heels.

The ride in the elevator was brief, and ever efficient, Tarah had his suite unlocked in no time. As he stepped through the threshold, Alessandra stirred.

She placed her nose against his throat and sniffed. "You smell good."

The last thing he saw before the door closed was the concierge rolling her eyes. He'd have to make sure he gave her a good Christmas bonus. On the other hand, Tarah was friends with Gage and his wife, Rielle, so the young woman probably wasn't ignorant of what went on in this condo. Smith'd escorted a few young, nubile women over the past few months, trying to blot out the image of a more mature and sensual woman—the woman who was now stirring in his arms.

Entering his spare bedroom with his unexpected houseguest, he flipped on the light with his elbow. Bright, but not enough to wake her. Although he laid her on the bed on her back, she instantly curled onto her side. He slipped her shoes from her feet. She couldn't possibly have been comfortable, so why the hell wear stilettos like these? Sure, they gave her height, and perhaps she might feel she needed it, but he'd liked her when she wore sensible pumps. These shoes showed off her legs and thrust her tits forward, but good posture could accomplish the same thing.

He pulled the duvet over her. As uncomfortable as she might be in that catsuit, peeling her out of it would likely prove impossible. He put the trashcan within close proximity before flipping on the bedside lamp that provided barely enough wattage to read by, then turned off the overhead light. Leaving the door open, he made his way to the kitchen.

Twelve thirty in the morning.

Gage and Rielle had a six-month-old baby so were probably dead-to-the-world tired. No, too late to call. He'd send Gage a text and let him know Alessandra was safe.

That simple task completed, he contemplated what to do. He'd planned on staying at Club Kink until closing, unless he'd gotten lucky, of course. Having a woman passed out in his spare bedroom definitely didn't qualify as lucky, no matter how beautiful she was.

Time to pour a nightcap.

****

He awoke suddenly with a jolt.

"Fuck, fuck, fuck, fuck, fuck!"

Well, Sleeping Beauty was awake, was she? And probably had to go to the bathroom. Popping out of bed, he rushed to meet her in the hallway. The lights were on so she'd be able to find her way by herself, but that was beyond her capability at the moment. If her current posture was any indication, she'd stubbed her toe.

She glanced up when he stepped in front of her. "What the fuck are you looking at?"

He just managed to prevent a full-on smile. "Do you need a hand?"

"I need a fucking bathroom."

Stepping aside, he pointed to the end of the hall. "It's down there."

She took one step, then staggered against the wall.

He scooped her up.

"Put me down, you shit. I've had enough of you carrying me. I can walk on my own."

"I'm sure you can." His reply was smooth as he carried her to the bathroom. "But since I don't want a puddle of urine on the hardwood floor, I'll give you a hand." He plopped her down rather unceremoniously on the closed toilet seat. "Do you need help undressing?"

9

His question was rhetorical as she was already struggling out of the suit.

Just as she was about to pull it down over her breasts, she paused. "Could you leave?" Her voice was almost begging.

"Of course." His grin was unrepentant. "I'll be right outside if you need me." With that, he shut the door. *Hmm*, just how close did he need to stick to the door? *Forget it*. He'd go ahead and put on a pot of coffee.

That accomplished, he made his way back to the bathroom. *Ah*, the shower was running. After going to his closet, he grabbed the terry robe he kept for guests of the female persuasion. She'd left the bathroom door unlocked, so he slipped it open and placed the robe on the counter where she'd be able to find it.

The scent of coffee wafted through his place as he rummaged for food. The first traces of morning light were coming through the blinds in the living room, so he opened them. A stunning pink, purple, and red combo streaked the sky. He might live in a concrete jungle, but at least he could still see the sky.

"It's beautiful."

He turned to face her. *Okay, don't tell her she's beautiful because not only is it completely inappropriate, but she probably wouldn't believe you anyway.* But now that she was scrubbed clean of makeup and away from the haze of the club, he could really see her.

Her eyes, which last night had been unfocused, now gazed softly at him. Once heavily gelled hair now lay limply against her scalp, clean and shiny. She was tugging the lapels of the oversized robe together as if trying to hide.

He held her gaze for one more beat before speaking. "Coffee?"

No genuine enthusiasm in her nod. She was wary and had every right to be. When he passed her to go into the kitchen, she shrank back from him.

"Do you think you can handle some toast?"

Her "no, thank you" was barely audible.

Since he was hungry, he put some bread in the toaster. He grabbed both mugs of coffee and placed them on the table in the dining room where she'd already seated herself.

Her head rested upon her propped arm.

She was the epitome of misery, and his empathy tugged just a little bit. Then he remembered how perilously close to disaster she'd come last night. "Milk, sugar?"

"Both, please."

He grabbed them along with a glass of water and some aspirin and placed them in front of her.

Without a word, she put the pill in her mouth and chased it down with the water.

"Drink the whole glass."

"Yes, Sir." A rude mumble.

"What did you say?" Brusque and sharp, he couldn't help his reaction.

Her movements were slow, but she eventually raised her head and met his gaze. "I said, *thank you very much*."

Before he could say anything, someone started pounding on his door, and he jumped.

She put her hands over her ears. "Jesus Christ."

He was already on his way to the door. *Let's not*

wake up my neighbors at eight thirty on a Sunday morning. He opened the door but barely had time to register surprise when someone pushed past him.

"Where is she?" Rielle demanded.

"At the table." He didn't know why he replied since Rielle was already heading in that direction. Turning back to Gage, he held open the door. "Where's Cara?"

"Babysitter. We would've been here even sooner, but I insisted we wait until the decent hour of seven. I was up with Cara when my phone vibrated last night. I would've called, but I didn't want to try to get an explanation in the middle of the night. Of course, when I told Rielle, she was ready to pack up the baby and drive right over."

Gage's inky hair was still rumpled, and Smith would swear more silver threads had appeared in the last six months or so. His gray eyes were bloodshot, but he still stood tall and strong. Alessandra's disappearance had hurt both of his friends. Maybe, now that she'd returned, the damage could be mitigated.

"We appreciate your patience. In fact, we just woke up." He led the way into the condo with Gage on his heels.

Rielle had pulled Alessandra from her chair and was now patting the woman—cheeks, shoulders, upper arms, hands, and then her head. "Your hair." Rielle patted Alessandra's scalp. "Your beautiful hair."

Stiffly, Alessandra reached up and touched it. "I always wanted short hair." Her voice was hoarse, her excuse lame.

Tears brimmed in Rielle's amber eyes as she stared. "Did you hit your head? Did you have amnesia?

Did someone kidnap you? Oh, God, did someone hurt you?" She began another pass over the other woman.

Gage stepped forward and pulled his wife away from all but groping their missing friend. He handed Rielle over to Smith and then embraced Alessandra. "Thank God you're all right." Even though he whispered the words, his voice was thick with emotion. "Thank God."

Smith was sure God had little if anything to do with it, but he shared the sentiment. The relief of his friends was ten times what his had been, and his had been staggering. "I'll just go start some breakfast."

"Why don't we go out?" Rielle gestured toward the door. "Then Allie can tell us what's going on."

Alessandra shot him a look.

Right. She didn't have any clothes except a spandex catsuit. That was hardly appropriate for Sunday morning brunch, even if they were downtown. "I'll just whip up some eggs. Easier to stay here, I think. Privacy and all."

Seeming to get the message, Rielle moved toward him. "I'll help."

They retreated, leaving Gage and Alessandra alone.

He reluctantly followed Rielle into the kitchen. Although he trusted Gage implicitly, Alessandra was another story. He didn't trust her not to rabbit again. Sure, she wore only a robe, but he wouldn't put it past her to find a way to escape again. He was being completely irrational, but now that he'd found her, he wasn't prepared to let her go. The touch of a hand on his arm pulled him back.

"Trust that they'll make it through this. He's not going to let anything bad happen to her again."

He heard the words, even understood them, but didn't accept them. "How can you be so certain?"

Rielle smiled.

The smile was slightly strained but there nonetheless, and the first one he'd seen from her in a long time. Except when she held her daughter, Cara.

"Because now you've found her, you're not going to let her go. And Gage will do everything in his power to take care of her. We'll show her how much we've missed her, and we'll make sure she never goes away again."

So simple. Just like that they'd magically convince Alessandra not to disappear again. Great in theory, but they still didn't even know what had happened.

Rielle squeezed his arm. "I'll scramble some eggs and make toast. Do you think Allie can eat?"

Of this, he was certain. "Absolutely no eggs, but some dry toast might work."

She scrunched her nose. "I hate dry toast. Why…?"

Before she could leap to any conclusions, Smith said simply, "Hangover." Although he'd never seen Rielle imbibe, that didn't mean she couldn't empathize.

She nodded again. "Dry toast, then." She pointed to the entry between the kitchen and the dining room where Alessandra and Gage were located. "I know you're curious, and I can make breakfast on my own."

The suspense was killing him, and he needed to know what was being said. He pressed a gentle kiss to her cheek and crept to the dining room, careful to stay out of the line of sight.

Gage had his arm around Alessandra's shoulders, having pulled her close.

She clung to his shirt and shook.

Finally, she retreated, sniffled, and whispered in a choked voice, "I'm sorry."

Gage's hand slid to her shoulder, and he drew her toward him again, pressing a kiss to her temple. "We'll get through this, Allie. Whatever this is, we'll get through it."

We won't. Gage and Rielle definitely didn't need to be dragged down further than they already were. They had a baby to care for and jobs to tend to. He, on the other hand, had time to spare. Well, maybe spare was a bit of an exaggeration, but he at least could take time to find out what'd happened.

This woman drew him. Some might see her as too much work, but he didn't. And he had no business feeling jealous of his best friend. Yes, she was Gage's former submissive, but that relationship had ended when Gage's first wife, Cara, died more than three years ago. As much as his friend cared for Alessandra, Rielle was the one who'd captured his heart. They had a familiarity and comfort Smith probably would never share with this complex woman. He didn't tend to revel in the soft and comfortable.

"I have toast." Rielle breezed past him as if she didn't care he'd been eavesdropping.

At Rielle's words, Alessandra leapt from the chair like a jack-in-the-box being sprung. One hand pressed to her belly while the other covered her mouth.

She bolted.

Gage moved to follow her, but Smith waylaid him. "I think between the hangover and your arrival, she's probably not in a good place. Let's give her some time, okay?"

The three sat at the table and began to eat their

food, but clearly their hearts weren't in it.

"I didn't ask." Rielle interrupted the silence. "Where did you find her?"

"Club Kink." That would open a can of worms.

"Shit." Gage spoke succinctly. "She was drunk at Kink?"

Smith nodded. "And participated in one of Spike's shows, but she never should have. She was already three sheets to the wind by then."

Rielle placed a hand on his. "But you were there. You took care of her, and you brought her here. She's safe now."

"Which reminds me, I have to leave a message on Gigi's machine to let her know Alessandra survived the night unmolested." He stood and started gathering the dirty dishes.

Rielle swatted his hands away. "We can do this. You go call Gigi." She glanced at Gage with a sly smile. "And tell her Rielle and Gage say *hi*."

Almost sappy, the look that passed between them, but Smith said nothing. He entered his bedroom and raised his brows at Alessandra standing in the middle of it. Okay, so she hadn't stayed in the bathroom.

She turned when he entered the room. "I'm sorry." Her voice was barely audible. "I just couldn't face them."

He wanted to tell her she had nothing to apologize for, but that wasn't technically true. She'd put them through six months of hell. "I'm not the one you should apologize to."

Guilt flared across her face. "I told Gage I was sorry. And I am. Sorry," she clarified. "I never meant to hurt anyone."

"Then why did you go away?"

Now the flash across her face was something much deeper, much darker—a mix of abject misery and desperate despair.

If only he could gather her in his arms and take away the pain she was so clearly encompassed by. Instead he shifted his stance. "Do you think you can face Gage and Rielle?"

Her response was quick. "No. Tell them I'm sorry…but I just can't right now."

"Do you think you'll ever be able to?"

"Ever is such a long time." A plaintive tone in her voice. Plaintive, but not whiny. She was begging for understanding.

"I'll talk to them." He laid out his stipulations. "But then you've got to commit to talking to me."

Her face changed from sorrow to mutiny in a heartbeat. "I don't have to talk to you." She sputtered. "I appreciate what you did for me last night. If you could just call a cab for me, then I'll be on my way."

"In stilettos and a catsuit? Where's your dignity? Your self-respect?"

"That went out with the trash a long time ago." Her bluster was gone as quickly as it had flared. "If you could just let me pass, I'll get changed and get out of your hair."

He stepped aside.

She headed back to the bathroom with as much dignity as she likely could muster, given her position.

After making a call to the club and leaving a message, he returned to his friends who sat on the couch, holding hands, heads bowed together.

Rielle's long blonde hair veiled her face.

If Smith didn't know better, he might've thought they were praying.

When he stepped into view, Gage stood, drawing Rielle with him. "She won't talk to us, will she?"

Smith shook his head. "She's too overwhelmed. Maybe give her time…"

"Time? I have to go to the police and the prosecutor's office and tell them she's alive. That she's not 'disappeared' anymore." Rielle took a breath. "There are people who care about her. People who've grieved for her. She owes them. She owes us. All those months…"

Although he couldn't fault a single one of those assertions, he still felt the need to defend Alessandra. "We don't know what happened. Can you give me some time? A few days? Maybe a week?"

Gage glanced at Rielle and then back to him. "What are you going to do?"

"Ask questions, get answers."

"You make it sound so simple."

"It is," Smith assured his friend. "She just needs someone to…guide her."

Gage understood the unspoken message behind the words. "You know she and I were there before…"

"I do." He shrugged. "And there's no guarantee she'll go there again, but I have to try. Something's got to give, and it won't be me."

For the first time, a genuine smile crossed Rielle's face. She reached out, then pulled Smith into a hug. "Just bring her back to us."

He squeezed her tight. "I'll do my best." When Rielle eased back, he guided his friends to the door. "Rielle, you might want to give Tarah a call. She got an eyeful last night."

"Probably no more than she did the night Spike brought Rielle back here." Gage's contribution.

Smith didn't bother to hide his surprise. "You and Spike?"

Rielle shuddered. "For all of five minutes. That man is a sadist, and believe it or not, I'm not a masochist."

She didn't enjoy pain simply for pain's sake. Good to know.

Gage held the door for his wife, and they stepped into the corridor.

Rielle turned. "Oh, hello, Mrs. Wannamaker."

Poking out his head, Smith looked at his slack-jawed older neighbor. Two men and one woman at eight thirty on a Sunday morning. The old woman had to know they weren't heading for church.

She shook her fist. "You stay away from her."

Gage smiled. "Too late for that." He put an arm around his wife's waist and guided Rielle toward the stairs.

Weird. Well, they already knew where the elevator was since the condo had been Rielle's home for four years. She'd been living here when she met Gage—at Club Kink.

Smith and Gage hadn't seen each other for years and would have remained out of touch if not for Mistress Gigi. When she heard Rielle was moving in with Gage out in the suburbs, she knew Rielle would be ready to sell the condo. Smith happened to be in need of a place to live, and voilà, a deal had been done.

He wasn't crazy about not living on a higher floor and enjoying the accompanying prestige, but the master bedroom in this condo more than made up for that. The most telling thing about Alessandra had been her lack of discomfort in his bedroom. He couldn't imagine Gage or Rielle had ever told their friend about Rielle's old place.

About the dungeon.

He smiled to himself as he secured the deadbolt on the front door. Nope, Alessandra Soriano hadn't batted an eyelash in his private domain. Stopping by the guest bedroom, he snagged her shoes, then made a detour to the walk-in closet in the master bedroom. Selecting a blue-checked shirt that was one size too big for him, he held it up. It would swamp his guest's frame and hang down to her knees. Hopefully people would be too busy gaping to notice the spandex underneath.

Nothing he could do about the shoes, though. Hopefully she had enough equilibrium to wear them home.

He knocked on the bathroom door, and she opened it immediately.

"They're gone."

She let out a long breath. "Thank you."

"Don't thank me yet—you're not off the hook." At her questioning gaze, he simply passed her the shirt and her shoes. "Put these on. We'll take the elevator to the garage, and I'll drive you home."

"I can take a cab—"

"I'm sure you can"—he cut her off—"but you're not going to. Now put these on. We're leaving in five minutes."

He expected her to argue, but she took the proffered items and closed the door again.

Going to the master bedroom, he grabbed his keys,

wallet, and cell phone. He flipped off the lights, and the room plunged into darkness. Rielle's former Master had converted the master bedroom into the dungeon Smith now owned. The windows had been walled over, soundproofing installed. A woman could scream at the top of her lungs, and no one would hear.

Except maybe Mrs. Wannamaker. Even if the old woman couldn't hear, she must've figured out what was going on in this place. Not his problem. He really didn't care what people thought about him. He lived the way he wanted to and left others to do the same.

So why was he so concerned about Alessandra? If she didn't want to be found, what business was it of his? Then the image of Rielle practically molesting her friend, terrified to let go lest Alessandra simply be a figment of her imagination, popped into his head. No, she owed it to the people in her life to either reclaim said life or say *goodbye* permanently.

"Smith?"

He turned. *Huh*, the first time she'd ever called him by his name. He liked the way she said it, just a little bit breathy—with a slight catch in her voice.

She stood in her heels with relative stability, thank God. He didn't want to be spotted carrying her again if at all possible. Good, the shirt went down to her knees. "Ready to go?"

She nodded. "I hung the bathrobe on the hook on the back of the door."

"It's fine. Everything will be fine."

Chapter Two

Heart beating a devious rhythm, Allie directed Smith to a building a few blocks from his place. Instead of just letting her out of the car, he parked and came around to the passenger door.

Busted.

When she didn't exit, he opened the door and dropped to his haunches, looking up at her. "Now are you going to tell me where you really live?"

"How did you know?" Unnerving he already knew her so well. But then she'd always been told she didn't have a poker face.

"Call it a gut instinct." After closing her door, he rounded the car to get back into the driver's seat.

She briefly considered running, but how far could she possibly get in her heels? She let out a lengthy sigh when he started the engine.

"Now which way?"

Despite being only about three miles from Smith's condo, her neighborhood was almost a different city. The Downtown East Side of Vancouver was the polar opposite from the soaring concrete buildings where Smith belonged.

She was living in what could be generously called a rooming house. At least she had her own room. Of course, she shared a bathroom with six other people whose hygiene was highly questionable. But they didn't care about her, and she didn't care about them. That was what she craved and what this flophouse gave her—anonymity.

Impossible, now, not to see it through Smith's eyes. The grass was overgrown, and no one had mowed the lawn...well, since before she'd arrived in late spring. Summer had long given way to autumn, and as she stepped from the car, she hunched against the wind. They should've condemned the dilapidated building years ago, but that'd mean an inspector would have to come down here. All the houses on the street had peeling paint, sagging roofs, and uneven walkways.

Smith had stepped from the car and met her in front of the house.

"Well, thanks for the ride." She forced cheerfulness into her voice.

"Let's go inside." Not a request.

Anger radiated from the depths of those beautiful azure-blue eyes. Eyes now disdainful and showing something even more elemental—something akin to rage.

She stared back into those critical eyes. He had no right to judge her. How she chose to live had nothing to do with him, so he could just suck it up. "No, you're not coming in. I don't *want* you to come in."

He took a breath. "Let's be clear, Alessandra. I don't care what you want. Now is there a key, or do I simply break down the door?"

Little effort would be required to break down the door. A very nasty drug dealer had done just that the first week of June. The landlord had finally fixed it himself—in August. The repair job wasn't just shoddy—it was shitty. But this was her home, and she wasn't going to let Smith break the door. Again.

She bypassed the broken step and got a secret thrill when Smith stepped on it and almost took a tumble. It served him right, and she hoped at the very least it mussed his blond hair. Better a broken leg, but then he might sue the landlord, and that'd bring down an entire world of hurt on her. Hurt she neither wanted nor needed.

Reaching into a hanging basket of what had at one time been flowers, she snagged the key.

"Fuck me, Alessandra, you keep your key in a plant?"

Instead of answering, she stuck the key in the lock. It gave on the second try, for which she was grateful. Usually it took four or more jiggles before the mechanism gave up the fight. She entered the dim hallway and immediately climbed the stairs, not waiting to see if he was going to follow her. Of course, he did.

She ignored the smell of stale cigarettes and marijuana, but it permeated the house. Accustomed to the gross odor, she was already breathing through her mouth. Smith's pretty leather coat was going to reek.

Just her luck, one of her roommates stepped into the hallway and headed for the bathroom. She tried to remember his name but gave up. Clifford? Carlton? Something starting with a *C*. At least she thought it did. As usual, he wasn't wearing a stitch of clothing. In fact, she'd learned to put down a handkerchief before she sat on any of the communal furniture. Not an issue, since she could count on both hands the number of times she'd done that in the past six months. She kept to herself and stayed in her room.

After turning the door handle, she stepped into her

room. She'd left the window open last night to get some fresh air, planning to close it when she came home from the club. Instead, it'd remained open all night, and the temperature in the room was near freezing. When Smith came up behind her, she whirled on him. She was exasperated that he followed her into her private space—the space she never shared with anyone.

"What, no heat?"

"There's heat." Well, sometimes the heat worked, and sometimes it didn't. She had a wool blanket to use when it got cold. She'd been lucky, though, to this point. It'd been a mild autumn. If it got cold this winter, she was in trouble.

Again, she tried not to see the room through his eyes. A small cot was pushed against the wall with a mattress of questionable origin. Since she hadn't bothered to make the bed yesterday, blankets were skewed everywhere. She'd also gone through several outfits before picking the catsuit, so discarded clothes littered the bed and what floor space there was.

And there wasn't much.

A rickety, old desk with a broken leg was being held up by three phone books, and the chair had seen better days. A cassette player rounded out the furniture, if it could be called that.

The closet door was broken, and he looked in, obviously careful not to touch anything.

Humiliation washed over her. She would never have brought anyone back here in a million years.

"You can't stay here."

She frowned at him. *What?* "I'm sorry?"

"I said, you can't stay here." He looked around. "Find a suitcase and pack what you need, and then we're leaving."

"I live here." *Duh.* "This is my home."

He rounded on her. "You call this a home? You call this living? This place isn't fit for rats, let alone human beings."

Good thing he hadn't seen the kitchen.

"Look, Smith, you did your good deed. You picked me up when I fell down, watched out for me, and then brought me home. I thank you for your time, but you can take your Good Samaritan act and play it with someone who gives a damn. I promise you it's not going to be me."

He took two steps toward her, and if she could've, she would've stepped back. Except she had nowhere to go. A room that normally felt cozy now felt positively claustrophobic. Even pulling herself to her full height plus the four-inch heels, she had to crane her neck back. Damn, why couldn't she be taller than five foot three?

The steel in his eyes was intimidating, but she forced herself to straighten her spine and stare back at him.

"Get it through your thick skull, Alessandra— you're coming home with me. Now put your belongings in a suitcase, and let's get out of here before we catch something."

"I don't have a suitcase, and even if I did, I wouldn't follow you anywhere. Get it through your thick skull." She mimicked him. "I'm not leaving, and you can't force me."

His face darkened, and this time she did shrink down an inch or two. Maybe three.

"I have a proposition for you. We're going to pretend, just for a moment, you have some say in this.

Either you come with me or we go down to the closest cop shop, and you explain where you've been for the last six months. I'll tell them I've found a missing person. Maybe I'll even get a reward."

She laughed mirthlessly. "No one would care enough to offer a reward for me."

He snaked out his hand, grabbing her wrist. "I'm going to pretend I didn't hear that. Now are you bringing clothes, or am I just hauling you out of here as you are?"

A frisson of terror ran up and down her spine, and her hands became clammy. Until now she'd counted on Smith being a gentleman. He was a friend of Gage's, so he couldn't be a threat to her. She looked into the depths of those azure eyes. *Uh-oh*, that fine line she was walking was getting thinner. He was keeping his temper in check—barely—and this wasn't going to end well. Somehow, she couldn't picture Carlton or whatever his name was calling the cops if she started screaming. No one in this neighborhood would bat an eyelash if someone shoved her into their car and drove away.

Okay, time to try a different tactic. "Look, Smith, I know it may not look like much, but it's all that I have. If I leave here, if I don't pay my rent, then I'm out on the streets. That might not mean much to a man like you, but it means a hell of a lot to a woman like me. Please, don't make me go back there."

"Back where? Were you living on the streets?" He arched his brow like he couldn't believe what he was hearing.

Shit.

"I was being...figurative, not literal." *Please let him buy that.*

27

"I'm not going to call you out on being a liar this time, but there will be consequences the next time." His tone was mild, but his body language wasn't.

She believed him. "Look, please just let me go. I'm asking you because you're an honorable man. You can walk away."

His bark of laughter hit her in the gut.

"Honorable is not a word people often associate with me. My patience has run out. My place or the cop shop?"

This was no joke, and she needed to defuse this. "I don't have a suitcase." Possibly the lamest excuse she had, as if it would make an ounce of difference.

Smith turned and left the room.

She took her first breath of crappy-smelling air and reveled in it. It might not be much of a home, but this was her home. She'd even hung a picture she'd scrounged from a dumpster, of a dog. Actually, several things in her place came from dumpsters. Amazing what the well-to-do in this city threw out.

She was closing the door when Smith stomped up the staircase. Well, maybe not stomping, but something close. She tried to slam the door, but he simply reached out to prevent her. *Damn*, he was strong, and momentum pushed her back into the room. Her heel twisted, and she landed on her bed in a heap.

He dropped a pile of garbage bags on the desk. He grabbed one, snapping it open. "This is for the trash." He knelt, unceremoniously pulled the stilettos from her feet, and dumped them in the bag.

Protest died on her lips when he turned to face her.

Without looking, he snagged another garbage bag and snapped that one open. "And this is for your

28

belongings. I'll make this simple. I hold something up, and you tell me which bag it belongs in. No answer means garbage. Noncompliance has consequences."

Before she could answer, he stepped toward her again, and her neck snapped back.

"Or we go to the cop shop, and you explain why you vanished off the face of the fucking planet."

He picked up a pair of sneakers she'd found—surprise, surprise—in a dumpster.

He all but threw them at her. "Put these on."

"I want to get changed."

"I don't give a flying fuck what you want. Everything we take with us is going to be deloused before you get within ten feet of it. My washing machine has a sterilization feature. I think we'll put it to good use." He took a breath. "I saw that fucking kitchen. It's amazing you haven't all died from food poisoning, E. coli, salmonella, or some other shit." He turned to the closet and pulled out a pair of jeans. Saying nothing, he arched an eyebrow.

She considered, for one brief moment, trying to be defiant but suddenly couldn't bring herself to care. Would it kill her to spend a few days in a luxury apartment? Would it be so bad to eat wholesome food? Soak in a bathtub rather than rushing through a shower because of the earwigs? Let someone else carry the burden of her existence for just one week? "Keep."

Chapter Three

Smith wasn't surprised Alessandra crawled into bed and fell asleep when they arrived back at the condo. He would've preferred her to select *his* bed but could worry about that later.

As promised, he set about doing her laundry. Although he was tempted to drop all of it off at a local dry-cleaning service, the store stymied him by being closed on Sundays. He was chilled that all Alessandra's belongings had fit into two garbage bags with room to spare. She'd consented to almost nothing being thrown out. Not surprising since she hardly owned anything. Everything she did have had seen better days. That was the first thing he was going to change. She couldn't stay with him and wear clothes like these. He'd prefer for her to be naked the whole time, but that probably wouldn't work either.

Along with the two garbage bags they loaded up had been a trash bag Alessandra insisted on packing herself. When he carried it, it'd been heavy. Like full of books. Plus she'd probably included her little stereo, which should've been relegated to the scrap pile in the '80s.

He put in the second load of laundry and was about to settle down with a beer to watch a game of play-off baseball when the woman herself came out of the spare bedroom. Sans catsuit, she now wore just the flannel shirt.

"May I have my jeans?"

No need to specify which pair as there had only been one.

"They're in the dryer, should be ready in about an hour. Are you cold? I can get you some sweatpants."

She shook her head. "No, I'm not cold. I just feel naked."

He cocked an eyebrow. "You're wearing something far less revealing than the skin-hugging spandex you wore last night."

A flush came across her cheeks. "That was different."

"I don't see how, but if you want to believe it, go ahead. I've put some chicken in the oven, and I thought we might have potatoes and broccoli."

"With cheese?" Then, as if having caught herself, she gazed around the room, obviously attempting nonchalance.

He'd seen it, though. Longing. When was the last time she'd had a nutritious meal? The one time he'd seen her before, she'd been wearing slacks and a blouse, and he thought he'd glimpsed some luscious curves. Last night she'd looked bony. Less curves, more angles. She'd also been light in his arms. Insubstantial.

"You can have all the cheese you want."

She rewarded him with a flash of gratitude.

"You can have some now if you would like. Otherwise, dinner should be ready in about ten minutes."

"How long have I been asleep?"

No need to consult his watch since he'd been

watching the clock closely, worried she might still be suffering from lingering effects of the alcohol. "About four hours."

"I never…I never sleep that long."

"Well, I guess you needed it." He pointed to a chair.

She sat, pulling her legs under her.

She probably had no idea how much thigh she was showing or how much he was reacting to it. *Too long.* He'd been too long without a woman. "Can I offer you something to drink? Coffee, tea, or water?"

Alessandra pointed to his beer. "I'll take one of those."

"No, you won't." No room for equivocation or misunderstanding. "Coffee, tea, or water?"

Her face scrunched in a precious look of annoyance. "I'll get myself some water." She pushed out of the chair, flashing a glimpse of her cleavage.

Too damn long.

He was trying to calculate just how long it'd been when she returned.

Sitting, she took a sip of her water. "What're you looking at?"

"You." Simple and concise. "I'm looking at you."

She eyed him warily. "And what do you see?"

"Do you really want me to tell you, Alessandra, what I see? Think carefully before you answer that."

She swallowed convulsively. "Probably not."

"Probably not." He nodded. What had that admission cost her? She wasn't ready yet for the unvarnished truth he'd be forcing her to confront.

"Now, aside from your landlord, is there anyone who will miss you? An employer? Welfare?" In other words, how was she surviving?

"No one will miss me. But I need to get my rent to my landlord."

Smith inclined his head. "I have taken care of it."

Her eyes narrowed. "You tracked down my landlord and paid my rent?"

"No, you won't be returning there. When our time is concluded, I will find you suitable accommodations."

A snicker. "I won't be able to afford your *suitable accommodations*."

"You needn't worry about that."

Her jaw clenched.

Give her more. "After our month together, I'll set you up in suitable accommodations. To your liking and your approval—"

"A month!" She leapt from her seat. "I never agreed to a month."

"Didn't you?" He unfolded himself from the couch and rose as if he had all the time in the world. "You agreed to come with me under my terms. My terms are thirty days. No less."

She shook her head. "Never. I never agreed to that. A day or two, I thought, maybe a week. You can't expect me to live here for a month."

"Oh, I do, and you will." Not open for debate. By the look on her face, she realized it as well.

****

Alessandra probably would've called the dinner *strained*, but Smith enjoyed himself. His dinner companion did not have a poker face. Every emotion she felt was as visible as a neon sign. Gage wasn't good at hiding things either. The guy had taken Alessandra's disappearance hard, despite how much he tried to put

33

up a good front.

She was going to pay for causing pain to those Smith cared about. Sure, he'd only been back in Gage's life for a year, but their connection was as tight as it'd been while they were attending the university. His friend had graduated and gone on to teacher's college, but Smith had gone over to Hong Kong to work for a financial company. He'd worked his way to the top quickly, then decided he wanted to work for himself. That was fifteen years and about a billion dollars ago. No one knew how rich he was, and he planned to keep it that way. His company owned a whole bunch of smaller ones in a variety of industries, but Smith's involvement was not widely known to the public—just the way he liked it.

When Alessandra put her knife and fork at the five o'clock position, he frowned. "You haven't eaten enough."

"But I'm full." Her chin jutted out.

"You didn't eat breakfast or lunch. Now you've barely touched half your food."

"You put too much on my plate." She glared at him. "Maybe you should've asked me first before piling it on."

He tilted his head. "Possibly, but I'm not known for consulting with others. I do things the way I want, and people do things the way I want them done."

"Sounds a little autocratic to me."

"Possibly even oligarchical, but let's not argue semantics. I noticed you ate all the cheese off the broccoli but didn't finish the greens. Do that, and I'll be happy."

She gaped. "What am I, a child?"

"Act like a spoiled brat and get treated like one. You're trying my patience. Eat your broccoli."

"And if I won't?"

"Then you won't get your clothes."

Her eyes nearly bugged out from her head. "You can't do that."

He leaned forward. "I can do whatever I want, Alessandra—you need to get that into your head. You're here for a month in my home and living by my rules. If you don't like it, then we go down to the cop shop."

"Are you going to threaten that every time I object?"

"Yes."

She began to speak and then stopped. Her mouth opened, and then it snapped shut. "Bastard." She spat the word.

"So my mother tells me, but that's none of your business."

That telltale flush crossed her features. "I didn't mean—"

"I know you didn't, but watch your words."

The diminutive woman shifted in her seat. "Look, why don't you just give me my clothes and let me go? I'll just disappear, and no one will be the wiser."

Ignoring her, he rose and picked up the dishes.

"I could help."

"Sit."

She muttered something about not being a dog, but he didn't really care. She had a stubborn streak a mile wide, this one. But then she'd had to, hadn't she? She'd survived living the last six months in that hellhole or somewhere worse.

Cleanup took very little time, and when he returned to the dining room, she'd changed into her own sweater and jeans. Her chin jutted in defiance, but he knew it to be bluster. She'd disobeyed him, and there'd be consequences.

He put a piece of paper in front of her along with a pen.

"What's this?" She eyed him warily.

"You can read, Alessandra, so I'm sure you can figure it out." He retook his seat at the table and watched the emotions play across her face as she picked up the paper and perused it.

Finally, she dropped it back to the table and shoved it toward him. "I'm not signing that."

"You will."

"I will not." Her expressive brown eyes shot daggers.

God, he loved it when she was riled. Would she be a spitfire in bed as well? *Get your cock under control.* He gave her a long, icy look. "You will, Alessandra, or we find the nearest police officer."

"Fine, then let's go." She stood and crossed her arms against her chest.

He stood and began to walk toward the door.

"Wait." No mistaking the tremor in the whispered word.

He stopped and pivoted to her.

The arms previously crossed in defiance were now wrapped around her waist. "Why are you doing this to me? What are you expecting from me? What are you getting out of this?"

All valid questions. "I'm doing this to you so you can face your actions. You're expected to abide by the terms of the contract for one month. I get the satisfaction of knowing you're in a safe place."

"Why do you care?" Her voice was barely audible.

"Good question, but not relevant." He stepped toward the table, picked up the paper, and handed her the pen. "Sign."

"This is a slave contract."

He considered her assertion. "This is not a slave contract. This is a behavior contract. You behave in a certain way, and I will reward. Misbehave, and there will be consequences."

"I'll just leave when you go to work."

"Didn't read the contract, did you? You won't have access to clothing when you're not in my presence. Misbehave enough, and you lose all clothing privileges."

"I'll just, just…"

"Call the cops? See, you think you're an equal here, Alessandra, but really you're not. One month." He tried for a conciliatory note. "Even you can obey for one month."

Her eyes flashed.

Ha, he'd pushed the right button.

"Gage told you, didn't he?"

Smith smiled. "Yes, Gage told me, but that was long after you'd left. I knew the moment I laid eyes on you, Alessandra. You're a born submissive. I'm giving you a month to try being one twenty-four seven. I'm offering you a chance to be the person you were meant to be."

"You're awfully sure of yourself, aren't you?"

The words were bluster, and he knew capitulation when he saw it. "Sign the contract, Alessandra."

She swallowed once, twice. Then she bent over the table and signed it with a flourish.

Without warning he smacked her on the bottom.

She yelped, dropping the pen and scattering the papers, and then reached to rub her ass. "What was that for? I signed the fucking contract."

He reached for her wrist and twisted her around. Before she could protest, he bent her over the table and landed another good smack on her ass. Then he pulled her back against him and whispered into her ear, "Care to make it three?"

She shook her head and wisely kept silent.

He encouraged her to sit, and she complied. Retrieving the papers, he placed them in front of her. "That's the last time I pick up after you. You will not treat my home like you did yours." That was a dig for the disaster area of a room that she'd lived in.

"Yes."

"I'm sorry, I didn't catch that."

"I said, *yes*."

He placed one hand on the table by her arm and the other on the back of her chair to cage her in. He leaned in so close he smelled her scent, and he knew she could feel his breath on her cheek. "It's *yes, Sir* or *yes, Master*." He let that sink in for a moment. "Are we clear?"

"Crystal."

Like a shot, he stood. "Get up."

She looked around, eyebrows raised. "But you just told me to sit. You told me to read the contract."

"And I told you how to address me, and you haven't done that either. Now stand."

She scrambled to her feet.

"Now take off the sweater."

"But…I'm not wearing a bra."

"I should hope not. That thing was so stretched it wouldn't hold up lemons, let alone the nice grapefruits you have. I'm not going to repeat myself. Take off your sweater."

With a flash of defiance in her eyes, she reached down, grabbed the hem of the sweater, and pulled it over her head. She dropped it to the floor and covered herself.

"What did I say about picking up after yourself?"

She bent and snagged the sweater.

Each of her vertebrae and ribs was distinct.

She folded the sweater and put it on the table, then crossed her arms across her breasts.

"Again, I'm not getting the respect I deserve."

"Sorry, Sir," she stammered.

He paused. "No, I think you were right when you called it a slave contract. It'll be *Master* for the next month."

"Yes, Master," she said through gritted teeth.

He'd let that one slide. "Now how about a movie?"

She gaped at him as if he'd taken leave of his senses. "I'm not wearing a shirt."

"I'll give you a blanket."

She looked around the room, took in the furniture, and shrank back.

Hmm, chrome and black leather probably didn't look all that inviting to a woman with bare skin. He was not, however, going to yield. "What do you want to do?"

"I'm going to go to my room and read."

"Fine." He waited a beat and then pointed. "Jeans."

"Smith, this is getting out of hand."

He reached for her wrist and pulled it toward him.

Faced with the choice of letting go of her chest or getting bruises, she relented.

Little effort was required on his part to get her to follow him to the dungeon. Capitulation. Either that or he was giving her what she had wanted all along. He could read her, but he couldn't read her that well. Yet. By the end of the month, he'd know everything there was to know about Alessandra Soriano.

Including why she'd walked away from her life.

Chapter Four

She'd stepped in it the moment Smith's name had slipped from her mouth. All she'd had to do was call him *Master*. And give him her fucking jeans.

But she'd done neither, and now there'd be consequences.

The dungeon was dark when she entered it, the tyrant by her side.

He flipped on the lights—medieval-looking torches strategically placed around the room.

She hadn't really looked around this afternoon because she'd been so shocked. Sure, she'd been inside Gage and his deceased wife's—now Rielle's—playroom, but this was just so much more.

Every implement of torture and pleasure was laid out against the wall, hung with loving care like stockings on a Christmas hearth. Whips, paddles, floggers, clamps, plugs, dildos, vibrators, spreader bars, collars, handcuffs, and ropes all adorned the space. A St. Andrew's cross sat in one corner while a medieval torture chair sat in the other.

Smith glanced around. "It's pretty much the way Rielle left it. Well, the toys are mine, and I had to get a new cross built. Rielle and Gage took the old one."

"He didn't have one before." Why did her voice sound so breathy? Was it wistfulness? Loneliness? For Gage and what had been or for something more?

Something she might actually have today?

"Maybe in here you'll remember to stick to protocol." Smith gestured. "Now jeans."

This time she didn't hesitate. The jeans slid easily off her hips because she'd lost a good fifteen pounds since she bought them. She'd worn them the day she left home. Pushing that thought from her mind, she reached down to scoop up the jeans, folded them, and put them over the back of a chair. She returned her arms to her sides. "What would Master like me to do?"

Standing there in nothing except her underwear, she was still trying to hold on to some form of dignity. Why did she waste the effort?

Smith's gaze raked over her from head to toe and back again, lingering on her breasts.

Almost against her will, her nipples tightened. When he smirked, she gave him a look. "It's cold." After a pause she added, "Master."

"I won't tolerate lies, Alessandra, least of all in here. Now try again."

"I…" Her voice failed her.

"It's easy. You say, *I get turned on when you look at me, Master*." He met her gaze. "Now you try."

She swallowed. Once, twice. Then she took a deep breath. "I get turned on when you look at me, Master." Warmth started at the top of her chest, raced up her neck, and bloomed across her face.

"Better, but I want complete honesty."

She looked at him in confusion, afraid to speak.

"Say, *I'm wet for you, Master*."

Surely he couldn't tell. She was, but that was beside the point.

"Alessandra." The warning was clear in his tone.

If only the earth would open up and swallow her. Or maybe the ceiling would crash down on her. How about an earthquake? She wished God would strike her down. Anything but admit the truth. And yet it came, unbidden. "I'm...wet for you, Master."

"Was that so hard?" His tone was quiet and reasonable.

"You'll never know," she muttered, then slapped a hand across her mouth. "Shit."

"That's going to cost you your last vestige of cover." His smile was broad as he held out his hand. "Panties, Alessandra, now."

She debated doing a little striptease, but he might take it in the sarcastic way she meant it. Instead, she pulled her panties down, and with as much dignity as she could muster, handed them over. To her infinite embarrassment, he smelled them before placing them over the back of the chair.

"Don't ever try to hide from me, Alessandra. I can see right through you."

Not everything. I still have some secrets.

But for how long?

He was looking at her pointedly, and she realized she'd missed what he said.

"I'm sorry, Master—could you repeat that?"

"I was asking you to select your punishment, but your lack of attention will also need to be addressed." His look was serious, a scowl marring his handsome face. "I need you fully present. That's why you don't get beer. Or anything else that might create a repeat of last night."

She shut her eyes, trying yet again to block out the memories from last night. If only she hadn't passed out

43

in his arms. If only she hadn't gone up on stage with Spike. If only she hadn't gone to Club Kink. If only she hadn't done vodka shots. If she had to be punished, let it be for that rather than any other transgression. Six months of living with guilt should've been enough. But it hadn't been. It never would be.

"Open your eyes."

His tone was gentle, entreating, so soft she felt compelled to comply. Seas of azure flowed across her blurry vision. She was startled when the first tear slid down her cheek.

He snagged a piece of silk from the wall and pressed it to the dampness.

His gentleness only increased the flow as it hit a place deep inside her. A place she'd believed shriveled up and dead.

Her heart. It still beat. It still lived.

God, that scared her more than anything else in the world.

He placed his hands against her jaw and tilted her toward him.

His face neared hers, and her eyes drifted shut. He gently kissed away the tears, which only caused her to shed more. When he pulled her into his arms, she went willingly, clinging to him as if he were a port in the hurricane of her life.

For just one treacherous moment, she felt safe.

Chapter Five

Smith forced himself to hold her securely in his arms even though his world had shifted. He'd been planning to curb a bit of that feisty defiance, but he never intended to break her. What had been the proverbial straw breaking the camel's back? The power in this room had shifted. How in the hell did he take command again?

She stepped out of his arms, wiping furiously at her tears. She ducked her head as she spoke. "I'm so sorry, Master. That was..."

He tipped her face toward him and handed her the scarf. "Blow," he ordered.

She obeyed, if a little noisily.

When she tried to hand it back to him, he simply pointed to the chair. Five-hundred-dollar Hermès scarf reduced to the status of a Kleenex.

She placed the scarf on the seat of the chair and then returned to her position, arms at her sides, head down.

"You may go to the bathroom and then go to bed."

Her head snapped up. "But I thought..." She looked around frantically. "I thought I'd be punished."

He hesitated, which wasn't like him. "I think we've done enough for tonight. Unless you want to be punished."

"No! I mean, no, Master. I mean—"

"The truth, Alessandra."

She brought her hands to her face and scrubbed. She met his gaze head-on. "Yes, Master, I want to be punished. I deserve to be punished."

He heard the truth in her words. She *needed* him to punish her, to exert his authority. To right the ship that had veered so far off course. Despite feeling gentle toward her in this moment, he'd have to make this count. This was going to be their first time together, so it had to be good. "Stand by the wall. Press your face against it."

She bobbed her head and went to the wall. Not actual stone, but it had both the texture and temperature of the authentic thing. Planting her feet toward the wall, she leaned forward, pressing her chest in and resting her cheek against it.

Hmm, better revise his plan to offer her a choice of implement—that didn't suit this moment. Grabbing the flogger, he ran the leather across his palm as he turned the handle in his hand. The weight was reassuringly familiar, even if the current of electricity was not. He'd brought many women to this room, but never had he felt uncertain, not about what they wanted nor his ability to give it to them. Hesitation wasn't like him.

Taking a breath, he swung, letting the first strike hit her across the ass.

She didn't move.

Normally he liked to warm up his submissives, perhaps showing his prowess with Florentine flogging, but they weren't doing a scene tonight. In fact, none of this had been properly negotiated. Still, she'd agreed to this, if only tacitly. So he increased the strength he put into the swing, aiming for more sting than thud.

This time she rocked up onto the balls of her feet and let out a strangled sound. After the next hit, her hands curled into fists by her head, but she said nothing.

He pulled back on the next one, letting gravity pull it downward, hitting the tops of her thighs. She rewarded him with a yelp—of surprise more than pain, probably, he'd take it. Several more hits were administered before he returned the flogger to the wall.

She still held herself erect, as if afraid to move.

Walking toward her, Smith examined his handiwork. A nice crisscross of marks across her back and ass matched the parallel stripes left by Spike's whip. Nothing that'd cause any undue discomfort. He wanted to reach out and touch, but that hadn't been in the contract. *Damn*, how could he have left that out? On the other hand, hadn't he already touched? He'd held her, comforted her.

One touch.

Just one. He allowed himself to press a finger to her back and trace one of the marks.

She reacted instantly to his touch. But instead of pulling back from it, she leaned into it. Then her pelvis flexed, and her ass stuck out.

Had she really read the contract? He could probably add a thing or two without her noticing. Because she was seeking, her body was reaching, pleading for something.

One touch.

He reached between her thighs and pressed his finger to her clit.

And she ground against him for about twenty seconds before she climaxed. Hard.

Had he ever brought a woman to orgasm so quickly

and with so little effort? If he had, he couldn't remember it.

Her breathing was harsh and ragged. She sighed as she tried to catch her breath. Finally, with monumental effort, she pushed away from the wall, eyes downcast, and turned to face him. "You did me great honor, Master, for which I am grateful."

"You bore your punishment well, Alessandra. Now I want you to clean up and go to bed. We have a big day planned for tomorrow."

Instead of asking, instead of questioning, instead of arguing, she nodded and fled the room.

What the hell had just happened? One of the shortest scenes followed by one of the swiftest orgasms. Hell, he hadn't even had time to get properly aroused. His cock might be a little stiff, but not a full-fledged erection by any means. His body tended to associate the infliction of pain with the eventual physical relief of an orgasm. Tonight, none of that had happened for him.

Although he could have easily put in several hours of work in his home office, he needed a good night's sleep. He stripped, and when he was sure she'd gone to bed, he slipped into the shower.

The multi-heads provided a constant and pleasant stream of water, but he couldn't relax as usual. Instead, images flashed through his mind. Alessandra standing naked before him, desire written all over her body. Alessandra flush against the wall as she received her punishment.

Alessandra pressing her pussy to his hand as she orgasmed.

Not surprisingly, he grew hard during his trip down memory lane. He'd love nothing better than to sink into her, but that wasn't going to happen. Instead, he fisted his cock, seeking the rhythm that'd bring release. He tried to prolong it, revel in it, but he was too far gone. His semen shot from him, mixing in the spray of scorching water. His breathing was almost as ragged as hers had been when she'd come.

Invigorated instead of drained, he might as well put in a couple of hours of work. First thing he was going to do was manipulate the contract. She hadn't really read every page, so slipping in another one shouldn't be a problem. Every element of the plan was wrong, and his conscience screamed, but he couldn't forget her reaction to his touch. Normally he'd never consider such a devious plan, but Alessandra's situation was not normal. It required more finesse and, perhaps, a deeper connection between them. She wasn't new to D/s relationships, so this wasn't a stretch. And if she balked, then he'd let it go. He needed an active and eager woman, and after tonight he was sure she'd be such a partner. Conscience be damned, he'd follow his gut instinct on this one. Safe, Sane, Consensual. If her flesh was willing, who was he to deny her?

Or himself.

Chapter Six

Lying awake, Allie tried to identify the constellations on the ceiling. When she'd first turned off the lights, she'd freaked out. Children's stickers that evidently absorbed light during the day and then glowed at night completely covered the ceiling. Planets, stars, moons, and even a shooting comet lit the room with an eerie green glow. Had Rielle put the stickers up, or had there been a child living here once? Did Smith even know they were there? She'd bet her last dollar he never slept in there.

Of course, her last dollar wasn't worth much. When she packed her toiletries, he'd given her a modicum of privacy. He hadn't seen the stash of bills in her box of tampons. All fifty-five dollars. There'd been closer to a hundred before she went out last night and hit the bar before heading to Kink. Now she had just her measly savings and no way of making more.

She rotated to her side. At least he let her bring her books. She'd turned her back to him when she packed them, so he hadn't seen everything. Still, he had them with him right now—probably under lock and key—so she couldn't get to them. And what would she do if she could? She sighed. Maybe she'd fall asleep reading because it didn't look like she was going to go into la-la land any other way. He let her sleep for too long today, and now she was paying for it.

Well, not entirely *his* fault, but it felt better to blame him.

What a clusterfuck.

She didn't have any other choice. Nope. No way was she going back to Mission City. No way was she going back to social services. No way was she going to face her old life. If that meant a month with Smith MacLean, then so be it. The only wrinkle in the plan was Gage and Rielle. She needed to get Smith to convince her friends they needed to forget they'd ever seen her—that they needed to walk away from her as much as she needed to walk away from them.

Unbidden, the warmth of Gage's embrace came to mind. The feeling of Rielle's soft hands against her cheeks filled her consciousness. Telling Smith no one would've put up a reward for her safe return might've been speaking a little hastily. Her only comfort was that he obviously didn't need the reward money.

This condo wasn't ostentatious, but downtown Vancouver was a pricey proposition. Clearly he had some wealth. How much, she didn't care to speculate. Money had never had any real meaning to her because she'd never had much. She grew up with a single mother, who'd died six years ago, dropping dead of a heart attack at the cleaning job she'd held for Allie's entire life. When Allie finished her education—financed entirely by scholarships—and landed a good job, she'd tried to convince her mother to retire and move in with her.

Gina Soriano was stubborn, saying she would retire at age sixty-five. She had been almost ten years shy of that magical date when she'd collapsed. She'd been working alone on the night shift and hadn't been found until morning. An undignified death for a woman who'd always held her head high.

Allie's father had died in an industrial accident when she was just a baby, so it'd been just her and her mother. She'd been closer to her mother than to anyone else in the world. Except perhaps Cara. Cara had been there to offer support when Allie's mother died.

One night, when the two women had imbibed far too much, Cara confided what she and Gage were involved with—kinky sex, submissive behavior, punishments, and a whole bunch of other things. Allie'd been intrigued instead of shocked. Cara offered to talk to Gage about maybe sharing what they had with her. Desperate for human contact, Allie'd been looking forward to exploring new things.

The couple had never exploited her loneliness, only offered her much-needed solace. Allie had never expected to find such nirvana, but she had. At least one weekend a month, she spent playing with her friends. Oh, that first time she'd stripped naked for them—the first time Cara had touched her, kissed her. The clear delineation was Gage could look, but he couldn't touch.

But when Cara had gone down on her, Allie had closed her eyes and imagined Gage's mouth was bringing her to an orgasm that singed her to the tips of her toes. That he was the one providing the loving aftercare each time he'd taken the whip to her. She kept imagining he loved her as much as he loved his wife.

He hadn't, though, and their sessions had ended abruptly when Cara died from a brain aneurysm. There had never been another session. About a month after his wife's death, Gage offered to help Allie find another Dominant, but she'd only ever have room for Gage in her heart.

So why had she reacted so…violently to Smith? Not just that he was a good Dom. He said he'd known she was a born submissive, and she'd probably have recognized him as a born Dom had their first meeting not been aborted. Five minutes had not been enough time to get to know one another. She'd been called away and—

Wrong thought.

Instead of dwelling on the past, Allie turned on her back again and pressed herself into the mattress. That way she could better feel the marks left so callously by Spike and so lovingly by Smith.

She smiled as she drifted off.

Chapter Seven

When Allie awoke, a tidy little pile of clothes sat on the desk next to her. Her jeans, a blouse, socks, sneakers, and a jacket. Clearly they were going out. Wait—no bra or underwear. Kinky. And not in a good way. Despite her affinity for the lifestyle, she never went without undergarments. Her breasts might just be grapefruits—whatever the hell that meant—but she didn't enjoy swinging free.

With a sigh, she slipped into the clothes. She'd need a few minutes with a comb and water to sort out her hair, but she could do that in the bathroom.

Smith was sitting at the dining room table, reading a newspaper.

Did people really do that anymore? She ignored him, walking to the bathroom. Everything was digital these days. Maybe he just liked the feel of paper, the sound it made when it crinkled.

After using the facilities, she searched the cupboards and sighed. When he'd done the laundry, he'd brought her toiletries into the bathroom and put them away as if it were the most natural thing. Breath caught in her throat, she checked the box of tampons and found her money. Snagging her comb, she rooted around for her hair gel, but couldn't find it. Shit, she'd spent three dollars on the stuff, and as bad as the crap was, it was still better than nothing.

Ruthlessly, she pulled the comb through her hair and then tried to use her fingers to get some semblance of a style. Not for the first time, she regretted having cut her hair. But those long black locks would have been easily spotted, and she'd wanted to disappear. And although that hadn't been the main reason for cutting her hair, changing her hairstyle had gone a long way toward altering her appearance.

But Smith had recognized her. She'd spent all of five minutes in his presence over six months ago, but he'd seen her and remembered. Just like, even in her inebriated state, she'd recognized him the night before.

Looking as good as she was going to, she left the bathroom. Smelling the coffee, she made her way to the kitchen. After she poured a cup, she sat. Smith pushed a bowl of cereal and, *ugh*, soy milk in front of her. She struggled to not wrinkle her nose.

"I didn't know if you were lactose intolerant. If it's really so repugnant to you, then you may have oatmeal."

That sounded just as repugnant, so she poured the soy over the organic cereal. Her usual breakfast had been an extra-large latté from Starbucks. Her mouth watered at the memory. Six months was a hell of a dry spell. Maybe she could convince Smith to take her to a café so she could indulge. Just once, of course. This would only last a month, right? Well, twenty-nine days, if she was being technical.

The first bite wasn't as gross as she expected, and she was hungry, so she continued to eat.

Smith hadn't looked up from his paper.

"What happened to my hair gel?"

"It's *what happened to my hair gel, Master?*"

So *that* was how the relationship was going to be.

Smith folded the newspaper and looked at her. "That product you call hair gel, which was really just shoe polish, went in yesterday's trash. Clever girl, by the way."

She looked at him quizzically.

"Hiding your cash in the tampon box."

A blush crept across her cheeks. *Get a grip.* This man's hand had been against her clit last night, so not like she had any reason to be embarrassed about natural body functions. Still, she felt inexplicably shy. "Thank you for not taking it, Master." She tried for just the right tone of appreciation so he wouldn't mistake genuine gratitude for something else.

"I debated doing it, but I knew the distress it'd cause you, so I left it. Now are you ready to go?"

"Yes, Master."

She rose from the table, and before she could clear the dishes, he placed a hand on her arm, fingers curling around her wrist. He encircled it as gently as he'd been rough the night before. She fought to keep her heart rate under control.

"When we're out today, we're vanilla, okay?"

Unable to formulate a response, she simply nodded.

****

The first thing Allie noticed about the office Smith took her to was that unlike all the others, no nameplate appeared on the door. The *Private* label gave her a sinking feeling. She couldn't put a finger on the reason, but when she followed him into the space, she knew she wouldn't be happy. "I don't need to be here." She tried to pull away, but his grip only tightened.

"Alessandra, if you think you're living in my home without doing this, you're sadly mistaken. I'll lock you in your bedroom naked for a month if you prefer, or you can do this."

The receptionist hadn't batted an eyelash at his speech, said loudly enough for all to hear. Anger flashed and then died just as quickly as she became resigned. No way would she be locked away alone for a month. "Fine. Just superb." She hissed the words, grabbed the clipboard offered by the woman, and flounced into the nearest chair. Smith took his time joining her. She flipped through the three-page questionnaire before turning to him. "What kind of doctor am I seeing?"

"He's a…specialist."

"You mean Kink friendly." She cringed at the questions listed. Her skin grew hot from her chest to the root of her hair, but she didn't care.

When was the last time you had anal sex?

When was the last time you participated in an orgy?

When was the last time you used a dildo or vibrator that was not your own?

"Jesus Christ," she hissed.

"I'm sure he appreciates you using his name in vain—now fill out the damn answers, and for fuck's sake, be honest."

A hard swallow. "Is this how you see me? As a sex toy?"

He turned on her. "Is that how you see yourself? Christ Jesus, Alessandra, I have no idea what you've been doing or who you've been with for the last six months."

57

"You didn't know from before then either." *So there.*

"Maybe not, but I somehow don't see the local social worker getting so sloshed she'd do anything to get laid with any cock that comes along."

Closing her eyes, she prayed the world would swallow her up whole. Shame cramped her gut. "I didn't…I mean, I haven't…not since…"

"Fine." Smith snagged the clipboard from her grip. He stood and stalked over to the receptionist. "Is he ready to see us?"

Beautiful plump lips curved into a smile. "Of course, Mr. MacLean. First door on the left. Anthony will be in shortly."

Allie was smart enough to be on her feet when he got to her because he'd just haul her up anyway. She followed him in silence to the appointed room. The space was lush and spacious with comfortable chairs, but all she could focus on was the metal table with stirrups. When she tried to back away, he simply propelled her into the room.

The room was spacious compared to the cramped exam room of her family doctor's office. A leather couch and two comfortable chairs sat at one end while the exam table with stirrups was at the other. She eyed it warily.

"Sit, Alessandra."

This isn't going to end well.

But did it ever? She always seemed to get the short end of the stick.

She sat on the table. Well, more like perched. Smith stood by the door and never took his gaze off her. After holding his gaze for what felt like forever, she finally looked away. She didn't have his fortitude. She didn't have his determination. She didn't have his strength.

The door opened, and despite her pique, she smiled. Whatever she'd expected, this wasn't it. If this was Anthony, he was seventy if he was a day. Still upright, but the lines on his face told of a life well-lived.

He stepped forward, taking Smith's hand. "Good to see you, my friend."

"It's been a while," Smith admitted. "This is Alessandra. She needs your services."

The doctor gave her a once-over and turned back to Smith. "What did you have in mind?"

"Full sexually transmitted infections panel, blood work, urinalysis, pelvic exam, and pap smear."

She just closed her eyes, wanting to die of embarrassment.

Anthony moved closer to look at her. "When was the last time you had a physical?"

She was so startled at being addressed she hesitated.

Before she could utter a word, Smith spoke up. "Do the whole thing."

"Okay." He turned to Smith. "You're going to have to leave."

She expected an argument, but he merely nodded. Meeting her gaze, he said, "I'll be right outside." Without another word, he exited the room.

"Time for you to get undressed." Dr. Anthony handed Alessandra a sheet and gown, but knowing he'd be poking and prodding didn't help. Yes, he seemed like a nice old man, but he was one of Smith's friends.

Gabbi Black

Yes, medical information was supposed to be private, but how much privacy would he afford her? Hopefully a lot because otherwise he risked his license.

That being said, who was she going to complain to if he did tell Smith everything? She didn't even have a proverbial leg to stand on.

The doctor had her lay down and thus began an hour-long odyssey. No question unasked. No place that wasn't poked, prodded, or pored over. Whether by happenstance or by happy nefarious plan, the doctor left the intimate parts for last. He had her raise her arms above her head and began the breast exam, palpating carefully. "Do you do monthly exams?"

"Sure." A bald-faced lie. She'd stopped caring months ago about her health or anything else that might be important.

"Alessandra."

His voice was mild, but the warning message came through loud and clear. "No, Sir, I don't. I just don't see the need…" She took a breath. "I just don't see the point."

The doctor tsked and then reached for one of her hands. He placed it on her breast and guided her through the process. "You're feeling for lumps and bumps, anything that wasn't there before. You also look for any discharge or change in color in the nipple."

Somehow, despite her most fervent wishes, the floor did not swallow her up.

"You can put your arms down."

She did just that, crossing them over her breasts to hold on to a modicum of dignity.

"Now scoot down."

When the doctor sat on his stool with wheels and

rolled up to her nether regions, she closed her eyes and sought her happy place. The place where a man in a white coat wasn't feeling around inside of her. Where no one was pressing a speculum into her. The place where she couldn't feel the scrape of the…what was the name of the thing they used to scrape up cells?

Never mind. Go to your happy place.

"Your IUD is in place," the doctor said. "And you have a nice healthy cervix."

Who gives a fuck?

She wanted this all over with.

She just didn't care anymore. She'd hit rock bottom.

****

Smith was waiting for her right outside the door. He and Anthony exchanged a handshake, and although no words were spoken, Allie imagined an entire silent conversation in those brief nods.

She followed Smith obediently to the lab in the basement of the building and subjected herself to the blood and urine tests. What did it matter? These results weren't going to change anything between the two of them. No clean panel was going to induce her to give herself over to him.

But knowing the results of the tests?

Don't go there.

"I'm ready."

He glanced up from the six-month-old magazine he was reading. "Okay." He stood. "Now we go shopping."

She shrugged.

When he held out his hand, she took it, although with great reluctance.

"I don't want to go shopping." The words were whispered, and she hated her cowardice. "I just want to go back to your place."

His jaw dropped, and he stared at her. Undoubtedly he was accustomed to women who loved shopping. Who enjoyed purchasing trinkets and treasures, baubles and bling. Well, she didn't. Couldn't stand shopping. Least of all right now after she'd endured such humiliation.

"Your choice."

"Yes." Quiet and sure. "My choice."

Taking her hand in his, he led her to the elevator. She continued to hold on to him and even leaned against him. When they went out onto the street, he halted. He took her chin between his thumb and forefinger, tipping her head back. "Did you not sleep well?"

"I never do when I'm not in my own bed." Petulance? Perhaps. He deserved her ire.

He snickered. "That crappy excuse for a mattress at your old home could hardly be called a bed, and you should've been more concerned with your safety since the room didn't even have a lock." His glare lessened a fraction. "Perhaps you can take a nap."

"That was my problem yesterday—I slept too much during the afternoon. I just want to go back to your place."

"Why don't we have lunch first?" He steered her toward a bistro.

"If that would please you." Her response was listless. She wasn't hungry and wouldn't eat, but if this would get him off her back, she could survive. In truth, she had no choice.

He slowed his pace and turned to look down at her. "Maybe we can stop by Indigo on our way home, and you can select several books."

The joy was instantaneous. "Really? Oh, that would be wonderful. I haven't had a new book in—" She halted, catching herself.

"Six months?" He completed the sentence.

She nodded.

"Well, eat a full lunch, and maybe we'll add a couple more."

Maybe a meal wouldn't hurt. If that meant she got a book, maybe it'd be worth it.

Chapter Eight

Later that afternoon, Allie sat on her bed, resisting the urge to bounce like a kid on Christmas. Instead of books, Smith had bought her an e-reader. They'd had to go to an electronics store so he could buy her a laptop to attach to her e-reader. He'd insisted she needed a cell phone she could use to hook into the laptop to get online so she could download e-books. She was pretty sure she didn't need this much tech. But then he'd bought her a thousand dollars in gift cards so she could buy any book she wanted. And a whole bunch more.

For the first few purchases, she'd tried to protest. She'd pointed out how silly the entire thing was. In response, between stores, he'd all but pushed her into an alley. Follow his lead, or she wouldn't be able to sit down for a week. He might just do it anyway, he mused. She'd grown damp when faced with the naked desire in his eyes. In that moment, she was just a little desperate. If he'd crushed her to the wall with his body and taken her right there, she probably wouldn't have even put up a token protest.

Except he hadn't. He took her hand and, with great solicitude, led her into the next store.

She scanned the books by a favorite author. Wow, the woman had released three books since she'd gone to ground. Grinning madly, she bought all of them and waited with great impatience as they downloaded. Was downloaded the right term? He'd explained all this, but it'd gone right over her head. Her only experience with computers was word processing for reports and the occasional spreadsheet. The internet had been for searches related to work. Books were her escape from everyday life.

That had been an unfilled void for the past few months. When she went to the library sometimes just to sit and read, she'd selected short stories or poems because she didn't want to leave in the middle of something. She hadn't gotten a library card because that required showing ID and would've left a trace. She needed to be invisible. Untraceable.

But now, with a laptop and internet stick, she was traceable. The plan was to download as many books as her e-reader would hold and leave everything else behind when she left. She couldn't afford to do anything else. A laptop could be traced. She didn't know if an e-reader could be, but she was willing to take that risk.

For now she could do other things with the laptop. Pulling up a word processing program, she began to type.

****

She was still working away when Smith knocked on her door, then entered before she could respond. "Alessandra, it's seven o'clock. I think it's time for you to come out and eat dinner."

Her head snapped up. "I've been at this for how long?"

"Over five hours. Have you even moved?"

She shook her head.

Removing the laptop from her lap, he held out his

hand.

Uncrossing her legs was simple, but when she tried to stand, she staggered. She smiled up at him, trying for contrite amusement. "I promise I didn't get into the beer."

He didn't look amused. Instead, he ran his hand down her spine, pressing here, nudging there.

She winced. "That hurts."

"Nothing less than you deserve, stupid woman."

"I just…" Words failed her. Okay, she'd been stupid and deserved the criticism. Then she caught a whiff of something. "Garlic?" His look told her he knew what she was doing but would let it pass.

This time.

"Lasagna with Caesar salad."

Her taste buds went into overdrive, and she salivated. "I'm hungry."

"Well, you barely ate anything for lunch, so this is hardly a surprise."

Yeah, now wasn't the time to point out that between the morning's adventure into the world of kinky medicine and her excitement about the prospect of getting books, food had been the last thing on her mind. Now that she had her sea legs, she smiled up at Smith. "Can we eat now?"

He touched the tip of her nose with his finger. "Yes, silly girl, we can eat now."

Her smile faltered for just a moment. The gesture felt so intimate…yet so right. In that instant, she wanted him to kiss her. To brush his lips to hers. To demand access which she'd readily give him. He'd masturbated her but hadn't kissed her.

Then the moment was gone, and he gestured for

her to walk in front of him, out of the room.

****

Dinner was no less strained than it'd been the previous night, but for completely different reasons. Instead of stress, sexual tension reigned supreme. After the morning's debacle, she doubted she'd ever see him in a sexual way again, but that resolution had lasted for as long as it'd taken him to offer her a book. What did that say about her, that she was willing to grant him full access to her body in exchange for the written word?

Because the written word was all she had. Her mind was all she had.

"I said, have you had enough, Alessandra?"

Damn, her mind had wandered again. She needed to stay focused on him. On his instructions, his needs, his desires.

"I've had enough, thank you for asking, Master." She laid her cutlery down at the appropriate place. "May I clear the table?"

He nodded with obvious approval.

It warmed her just a bit. A frisson of anticipation ran up her spine at the look he'd given her. It offered just a hint of promise. She'd hang on to that.

When she returned to the dining area, he rose and offered his hand. The desire snaking through her at the thought of going to the bedroom fizzled when he led her to the bathroom.

"We came home six hours ago."

He offered the explanation she didn't necessarily deserve.

"I'll wait here. Be naked when you come out."

At least he let her close the door.

Of course he led her to the dungeon after she came

out. The room was warmer than it'd been the previous night. Or maybe the need thrumming through her body was raising her temperature.

"Present yourself."

She stood with her spine erect, arms hanging loosely by her sides, her feet together, and her chest pressed forward.

He did a lazy circle around her, inspecting her, evaluating her.

Thankfully, she felt more like she was receiving a loving caress than being subjected to some kind of fault-finding expedition.

When he was in front of her, he grasped one of her breasts. He palmed it, framed it, seemed to weigh it. "My grapefruit comment caught you off guard. A compliment, I assure you. I've had enough of melons, and lemons have their place, but I like breasts to be substantial enough to hold on to."

She tried to push away the flash of the doctor's hands, poking and prodding her breasts that morning.

"Let it go, Alessandra."

She didn't ask how he'd known. Undoubtedly written all over her face. Instead, she let her eyes drift shut and focused on his hand against her breast. His palm was smooth, but the pads of his fingers had slight calluses.

Then he tweaked her already pert nipple. He did it a second time and then a third, this time with some force.

She winced but said nothing.

"I think you liked that."

Her hesitation was momentary. "Yes, Master, I did enjoy that."

"The question is, what am I going to do with you?"

"Master?" Her uncertainty laced her voice.

"You were disrespectful to me today. I suspect you were disrespectful to my friend as well."

Somehow she couldn't picture Smith and Dr. Anthony hanging out, but what did she know? Not much. And she hadn't really been disrespectful to Anthony. More…indifferent. She doubted Smith would see the distinction.

"I didn't mean to be disrespectful either to you or your friend. Your friend was very kind in making sure I'm healthy."

"Because you've been neglecting your own health, haven't you?" She started to speak, but he continued the thought. "That makes you a bad girl. And you know what happens to bad girls?"

Don't shake. "They get punished?"

"Alessandra, was that a question or a statement?"

Don't back down. "Both?" Was her voice wavering? Again? *Seriously, get your shit together.*

Smith chuckled—that wicked chuckle she was quickly becoming acquainted with. "Now I want you to go stand at the side of the bed."

She complied immediately.

He picked up the chair, brought it over, and placed it directly in front of her. Then he came right up to her, standing toe-to-toe between her and the chair. Grasping her shoulders, he urged her back until her knees knocked against the mattress, and she had no choice but to sit.

She was looking directly at his crotch.

"Scoot back."

Uh-oh, where was this going? She complied out of

sheer self-preservation. She'd only made it about a foot when Smith ordered her to stop.

"Lie back."

Face warming, she complied, her legs still half-hanging over the edge of the bed. When he reached for her ankles, things became evident.

He bent her knees and placed the soles of her feet by her ass cheeks. Then, with just the gentlest of pressure, he pushed her knees apart.

She tried to snap them together but encountered strong resistance.

"Work with me, and this'll be a lot less painful."

Conceding defeat, she placed her hands on her abdomen, let her knees fall, and closed her eyes. Her most fervent wish was to hide herself, but that'd only lead to more punishment, although what would be worse than this? Time spun out, and instead of focusing on him gazing at her labia, she chose to think about all the books she planned to download. All the fictional worlds she planned to visit. All the horrible things she'd do to him if she ever got her hands on his balls.

"You're a beautiful woman, Alessandra."

She tensed, waiting for him to touch, anticipating and dreading it at the same time. *Breathe. Just remember to breathe.*

When he pushed the chair back, she relaxed. Whatever was going to happen would be sooner rather than later. His footsteps were barely audible as he walked over to the wall. She resisted the urge to watch. If he wanted her to look, he'd order her to do so. When he came back, she worked to find that place of calm again, but that proved impossible.

"You may open your eyes now."

She did so but only looked at the ceiling.

He pinched her inner thigh. "You know I meant look at me."

She tilted her chin toward her chest and looked at him.

In one hand he held a bottle and in the other a dildo. He held up the bottle first. "This is a brand-new bottle. I always use a new bottle with a new woman."

I so do not want to hear this. Just get it over with.

Then he held up the dildo. "This is also new. Again, a different one for each woman."

"You must own shares in the company."

His pupils dilated.

She silently cursed her stupid mouth. All she had to do was lie there and subject herself to this. He was going to do this, but she just didn't understand why. What was he going to get out of this? Seriously, was her humiliation to be total and complete, or might there be some respite? A reprieve? Closing her eyes, she dropped her head to the mattress. Clearly her attention was no longer required.

The cap came off, then plastic was squeezed, far louder in her imagination than in reality. Still, she jumped when he began to lubricate her—first her clit and around the opening of her vagina.

Two fingers covered in cold gel pressed inside her. "Relax, Alessandra, and this will go so much easier."

He pushed in even farther and hit her G-spot, causing her to nearly buck off the bed. This entire time she'd been telling herself she wasn't turned on, but that'd been a lie. From the moment he had brought her into this space, she'd been wanting something. Needing something.

He pulled back, and she whimpered. When he pressed the dildo into her, she keened.

He twisted, he pushed, he withdrew, and then he started all over again.

It felt like it took forever for him to seat it fully, but by the time he had, her flesh was sensitive and stretched. Then the wicked buzz of a vibrator started. It might be small, but when he put it against her clit, she screamed.

He must have six arms. Her legs were pinned, the vibe was pressed against her, and a pressure held her hips in place. Pressed against already tender flesh, the sensation was exquisite torture. She wanted to hold back, if only because of her righteous anger. Wasn't happening, though, because her body was poised to orgasm. Her body needed this, and if she was honest, so did her soul. Despite her valiant effort at self-control, she was cresting.

"I'm going to come." She didn't try to hide the desperation in her voice.

"Don't you dare." His voice was cold and cruel. "You don't come unless I tell you to."

He must be joking. The first orgasm hit. Wave after wave pulsed through her, and even as she fought against them, still more threatened to engulf her. She was wrung out and sated, but he still held the vibe to her clit. The second climax came right on the heels of the first as her inner muscles clamped. The dildo slipped out, but he ruthlessly thrust it back in.

Her breathing had barely returned to normal when her body began to climb again. She tried bravely to fight it but again lost the battle. This one so ferocious her back bowed off the bed. Collapsing back, she fought her way through the fog, through the ecstasy, through what was quickly becoming agony. "Okay," she whimpered. "Enough." She was one of the very few lucky women who were multi-orgasmic. Even Gage's Cara hadn't been up for so much in a brief period of time. Allie was.

"You're going to come again, Alessandra."

She snapped her eyes open. Shit, he was serious.

"I told you not to come without permission, and you've done it three times. Your punishment is a fourth."

Tears filled her eyes as her sensitive flesh continued to be bombarded with stimulation. "I can't, I just can't. Master." She added the honorific as an afterthought.

"You can and you will. You didn't fight the pleasure before, so now you can let yourself give in to it."

Except it didn't feel like pleasure anymore. It felt like work. But she knew how to work. Mind over matter. So she let the motion of the vibe soothe rather than sting. When he shifted the dildo and it raked her G-spot, it ended in a matter of seconds.

Chapter Nine

Smith withdrew the dildo.

Alessandra turned on her side and curled into the fetal position. Tremors still shook her body, and little whimpers and mewls still escaped from her throat. She covered her face with her hands and wrapped her arms around her knees, pulling them up to her chest.

He placed the instruments of tonight's torture on a towel. As he pulled a comforter across her prone form, a tenderness enveloped him. He shouldn't have been so affected by the scene. He also shouldn't have punished her for being so responsive.

Going around to the other side of the bed, he then sat by her head and pried her hands back.

Tears streamed down her face.

Tears of pain or tears of regret? Maybe they were tears of joy. He pulled her head into his lap, and she came willingly, her sobs easing as he smoothed back her hair.

"I'm very proud of you, Alessandra. You saw you needed punishment, and you submitted to that punishment." She huffed, and her warm breath seeped through his pants. She'd get snot and tears on them, but he didn't care. That was what dry cleaners were for. "Now, since you were a good girl, you get to choose your reward."

She turned her head to look up at him. "I thought

74

Master's gifts to me were my reward."

"They were your reward for having blood drawn and donating urine."

As he hoped, she laughed.

"But I'm talking about tonight. Despite what you might think, I am very proud of what you did. I know this isn't easy for you."

The thoughts flitted across her face as she obviously tried to discern his meaning. "Master?"

"Yes, Alessandra."

"You said I could have anything I wanted?"

"Within reason, and before you ask, letting you walk out the door isn't an option."

Shit. By the look on her face, he'd read her wrong. She hadn't been thinking that at all. Now it probably was all she could think about. "What was your first impulse?" He continued to stroke hair so short the shape of her scalp was prominent.

When she struggled to get up, he helped her into a sitting position. She pressed her palms to his cheeks. He stared at her.

"Will you kiss me?"

Wait, what?

A kiss? When was the last time anyone had requested a kiss from him? He was obscenely wealthy and could've given her just about anything, and all she wanted was a kiss? It felt like too much and not enough, all in one breath. He pulled her into his lap. That she came willingly was a nice touch. Then he tipped her chin toward him and settled his mouth on hers, planning to take it slow.

Evidently, she wanted none of that.

She threw her arms around his neck, dragged him

toward her, and opened immediately, welcoming him in.

He eased his tongue into her mouth, delving into the crevices, thoroughly exploring. Her garlic flavor was just a touch erotic.

She slipped her tongue into his mouth.

Nice, a woman who knew what she wanted. The feistiness was something he rarely experienced. The women he normally chose as bed partners were more reserved—not wild she-cats.

Alessandra sucked, she nibbled, she parried. She gave back as good as she got.

He hardened. The moment she stilled, he cursed his own body. *Damn it.* The kissing had been pleasant—hot and demanding alternating with sweet and tender. It'd been everything a kiss might be, and now it ended.

She drew back and met his gaze.

"It's just an erection, Alessandra, nothing for you to worry about."

Her lips curved into a smile. "Master, may I ask for another reward?"

"You can ask, my little one, but you may not get what you want."

Her eyes twinkled. "May I service my master?"

His cock twitched painfully, but he held himself in check. "As tempting an offer as that might be, you may not serve me."

Her eyebrow shot up. "But I thought…I mean, doesn't every man want…?"

Progress—all those emotions flitting across her face, embarrassment being the most prominent. "I didn't say I didn't want. I said you may not. There's a distinction."

Confusion was writ large in her eyes.

"Until I know where you've been, what you've been doing, and who you've been doing it with, you're not getting anywhere near me. You should demand the same thing from me."

Realization dawned, and then she turned crimson, a color he'd never seen on her, and that said something.

She leapt from his lap like a scalded cat and backed away. "You son of a bitch."

Smith shot off the bed, reaching her in one stride and grabbing her wrists. "I may be a bastard, but I am not a son of a bitch. I warned you, Alessandra, about choosing your words very carefully. I'll not have you impugning the woman who gave birth to me."

He pulled her toward the bed and sat down heavily, dragging her so she sprawled over his lap. She tried to struggle, but his grip was too strong for her to win the fight.

"Hold on to my pant leg, Alessandra, because the more you squirm, the more smacks you'll get." He laid the first blow in the middle of her ass, leaving a nice handprint. The next three came in quick succession.

Although she no longer struggled, she tried to cover her butt with her hands.

"I said to hold on to my pant leg, and I meant it."

Instantly, all struggling stopped, and she took a vise-like grip on his pants.

He landed four more good ones before he stopped.

Suddenly the room was very still.

She was trying to stifle her sobs, and it ate away at him. Carefully, he eased her from him and helped her to stand. "Go to bed." He needn't have bothered. She'd fled before he even uttered the last syllable.

He wasn't surprised to see his hands shaking. He'd never hit a woman in anger, yet somehow, for some reason, he'd done it. It hadn't been punishment as correction, it'd been punishment for its own sake, and he was furious at having lost control, even for that instant. Of course, when Alessandra had called him a *son of a bitch*, she hadn't really been talking about his mother. But that, on top of her brazen carelessness for her own health, had pushed him over the edge. He should go to her and apologize. He'd been out of line, and he owed her words of repentance.

Yet he remained seated. Remained rooted to the one place that brought him the most pleasure. God, he could still smell her musk. Her juices were all over his sheets. Her tears were still damp against his thigh. Her sobs were still ringing in his ears. He wasn't going to apologize, so he'd have to find another way to make amends.

There had to be a way to make this right.

Chapter Ten

Smith was reading the newspaper when Alessandra appeared.

She wore the blouse and pair of slacks he'd put in her room about six that morning. She'd been curled into a ball, hands tucked under her chin.

Wondering if she was cold, he'd turned up the temperature several degrees. He'd have to watch that if he was going to keep taking away her clothes. Of course, if she'd just behave, then he wouldn't have to mete out such punishments.

The previous night flashed in his mind before he ruthlessly pushed it aside. When she sat with her bowl of cereal, he handed her some papers.

"What are these?"

"My latest STI results. They were done a month ago, and I haven't been with anyone since." No need for her to know he hadn't been with anyone for a while before that.

She didn't even pretend to look at the results. "Thank you for that, but since we won't be exchanging any bodily fluids, it doesn't really matter, does it?"

He inclined his head. "A month is a long time, Alessandra."

"Twenty-eight days," she corrected. "It'll go by in a heartbeat."

He was about to respond when a knock came. After

rising, he stepped to the door. Opening it, he smiled at the welcome sight. "Mme Veronique, I couldn't be more pleased to see you, but you didn't have to come in person. I thought you might delegate this to someone."

"I never delegate my favorite clients."

Her voice was deep and rich with the slightest trace of an Eastern European accent he'd never been able to pin down.

She shook her head at him. "Now I have three assistants, so where may we set up?"

"We might as well set up in the living room since it's just us today." Smith stepped aside and let the woman enter.

The already uncommonly tall woman wore three-inch heels. Her midnight-black hair with elegant silver threads was swept up in a twist. She was class and sophistication with a spine of solid steel.

Her professionalism was always impressive, but the woman did scare him just a little bit.

Three women followed Mme Veronique, all pushing trolleys full of boxes and bags. Probably overkill, but he hadn't been able to give many specifics over the phone. He secured the door and followed the troop into the living room.

Alessandra had risen and was now looking at Mme Veronique who was, in turn, looking her over.

When he entered, the elegant woman made a sweeping gesture. "This is a beautiful place you have, Mr. MacLean."

Despite his numerous requests that she call him by his given name, she stood on ceremony, so he'd do the same. "Mme Veronique, may I present Alessandra Soriano, a very dear friend." He stepped forward.

"Alessandra, this is Mme Veronique. She's…" Words failed him. How would he describe her? She worked at the high-end hotel where he'd stayed many times before deciding to buy his condo. She was a fixer, but that term seemed rather vulgar.

Veronique rescued him by stepping forward and offering her hand. "I am also a friend of Mr. MacLean's, and he asked me to help you out. I understand you recently lost your belongings and are in need of a few necessities."

If looks could kill, he would've been struck dead by the thunderous glare Alessandra shot him. But he was counting on her inbred manners to be more important than anything she might utter out loud. Returning her gaze, he offered a warning of his own. *Fight me on this, and there'll be hell to pay.*

So she pasted on an expression that fooled no one and turned to the guest and her entourage. "It's so kind of you to help me out. I just need a few things to tide me over for the next twenty-eight days."

Mme Veronique beamed, appearing extraordinarily pleased. "A month? Oh, my dear, I hope I've brought enough things." She turned toward the first of her assistants. "Simone will take you into the bedroom and get you fitted for undergarments. Meanwhile Jeanne, Kelci, and I will organize the first few outfits."

Alessandra hesitated, and he fought to tamp down the panic. Then, as if knowing how much trouble would come to bear, she led the woman toward her bedroom. The threat had been implied, though. She'd almost led poor Simone into the dungeon. The younger woman probably wouldn't have batted an eyelash, but Smith wasn't willing to take that chance.

"Will you be staying or leaving?"

He turned to Mme Veronique. "I have a report to read, and I thought I'd sit on the sofa to do that. Is that acceptable?"

Her smile was demure and serene. "I think your presence will be most desirable. Your opinions are always welcome, and you have excellent taste." She looked toward the closed door of Alessandra's bedroom. "I trust that everything is as it should be."

Tell her the truth or just what she wants to hear? "The lady has had trouble in the past, but I'm hoping to guide her away from that and on to better things."

Veronique nodded. "She is lucky to have you."

"You'll have to tell her that, because she sure won't listen to me."

Chapter Eleven

Allie was exhausted. She was tired of fighting, she was tired of arguing, and she was tired of not being listened to. She was especially tired of pretending everything was okay when it so clearly wasn't. The closet in the room where she was staying had been stuffed. Dresses, blouses, jeans, pants, and shoes. Lingerie, bathing suits, and nightgowns. A bit of a joke, those were, since Smith only let her sleep naked, but she refrained from comment.

She kept her mouth shut the entire time because one look from him had warned her this was a hard limit. Not wanting to seem churlish and ungrateful, she'd allowed the four women to pamper her.

Jeanne was a stylist, Kelci a makeup artist, and Simone was a professional dresser. All of them worked in the movie industry.

While Allie remained stubbornly mute, Smith peppered the women with questions, and each preened under his attention and praise.

Well, maybe preened was too strong a word. In fact, acted surprised might be more appropriate. From the brief comments made, Allie gleaned not all rich boyfriends hung around for the hard work.

He, however, reveled in the show, insisting she try on every outfit. The women had left just after noon, and he'd prepared sandwiches. Then he forced her to carry all the clothes from her room to his, where he might keep a close eye on them.

On the face, ridiculous. All she'd had to do was tuck some jeans and a shirt under the sheets when he wasn't paying attention. But she hadn't thought of that until after she had finished the transfer, so she was shit out of luck.

Hopefully, once she departed, he might donate them to the closest homeless shelter. Of course, sexy teddies, fashionable lingerie, slinky satin dresses, ornate silk blouses, and designer linen trousers probably wouldn't help anyone, but she sure as shit wasn't taking them with her.

Today had been an exercise of him putting her in her proper place. He'd tried to prove he could buy her.

More fool him.

She'd been ready to go to the living room and have a hissy fit. And she would have, except then she'd laid eyes on her e-reader, and all her thoughts of animosity had fled. That had been a genuine gift—a gift from the heart instead of the pocketbook.

A knock on her bedroom door pulled her from her reverie. At least he was knocking instead of just barging in. She rose from the bed, walked the three steps, and opened the door a crack.

"Yes?" She didn't try very hard to hide the animosity in her voice.

"I have a gift for you."

Unable to help herself, she gaped. "You just bought several thousand dollars' worth of gifts."

"More like tens of thousands, but who's counting? Those were necessities." He paused for dramatic effect. "This is a gift." He held up a bag with the name of a high-end jeweler.

Rolling her eyes, she relented and opened the door, which he could have easily pushed ajar himself.

He stepped into her space and surveyed the room. "I'm pleased to see you're keeping the room clean, Alessandra. That's very respectful of you."

She laughed. "I don't have any personal items to leave around. You take my clothes every night and bring me fresh ones in the morning." She hesitated. How to proceed? Obsequiousness wasn't her style, but a bit of gratitude would likely hold her in good stead. "But I'm following your instructions on how to care for the electronics, and I thank you for them."

"Your gratitude is unnecessary, but it brings me back to the reason for my visit." He presented her with the bag. "Although this is also a gift, I'll stretch the truth and call it a necessity."

Intrigued, she pulled the long case from the bag. Let it not be some obscenely expensive necklace, an image of Richard Gere and Julia Roberts flitting through her mind. She didn't want to be bought. She…

"Open it," he entreated softly.

She couldn't help it—she let out a gasp of delight. The watch was the most exquisite she'd ever seen. Delicate twists, silver in color, were braided and intertwined from the catch to the face. The face had a pearl-like, iridescent sheen and changed hues from ivory to pale pink when twisted under the lights. She peered closer. Oh…the braided twists were tree roots with tiny delicate animals etched in.

She watched with rapt fascination as Smith slipped the watch around her slender wrist and closed the clasp.

"Waterproof. You can wear it in the shower. In

fact, you never have to take it off."

And she didn't want to. The watch was the most precious thing she'd ever seen, let alone received. "It's too much." Her voice broke.

"You need a watch, Alessandra. You're always losing time and then looking at your wrist, expecting something to be there."

"I had a watch." She shrugged and dropped her gaze. "It broke about a month ago, and, as you can probably deduce, I didn't have the money to get it fixed."

Smith put the bag and case on the desk. "This one comes with a lifetime warranty. The receipt is in the bag, and before you go getting any ideas, it's a gift receipt, so you won't know the price."

"It wouldn't be hard to track down that information."

His look turned contemplative. "Maybe not, but it'd be tacky and would make you look ungracious. You're not ungracious, are you, Alessandra? You'll take this necessity in the spirit in which I am giving it, won't you."

A statement, not a question. He'd hit a tender spot, though. Of course she didn't want to refuse the gift. She loved it. "Did Mme Veronique select it?"

He shook his head. "No, and before you ask, I gave her directions on the clothes. More than just your bra size, I'll have you know. I want you to be comfortable in the clothes I've selected for you. Now I need you to come with me."

Intrigued, she followed him to the dungeon. A play session now? Her watch showed the time to be nearly five o'clock, and her stomach rumbled.

When they stepped across the threshold, he closed the door and flipped on the lights.

She reached for the hem of her sweater and pulled it over her head.

"Eager, are we?"

As she undid the snap of her jeans, she shrugged. "I want to get this over with. I was disrespectful this morning—again—and I was, as you put it, ungracious. I should've been kinder to those women who were just doing their job. Not their fault they were doing your bidding." The jeans slid down her legs. She stepped out of them, bending automatically to pick them up. When they were neatly folded on the chair, she reached behind herself to unhook her bra.

Smith raised his hand to stop her. "We're not going to play right now. In fact, we're going out to a business dinner."

She was struck dumb, and her heart started racing. A business dinner? He expected her to join him for cocktails and then a meal? She was still trying to breathe normally when he returned from a quick trip to the walk-in closet.

He held a powder-blue suit with an ivory blouse in one hand and a pair of matching pumps in the other. "Normally I like to 'prepare' my dates before we go out, but I want your mind on business tonight."

Nope, didn't want to know what those preparations were. She took the proffered items.

"You have forty-five minutes to shower and change. I'll bring you a pair of nylons and fresh undergarments while you're in the shower." He raised an eyebrow. "Questions?"

She shook her head. "None, Master."

He gave her one of those penetrating stares that bored right through her. "Tonight we're on equal footing. I expect you to be attentive and to contribute intelligently to the conversation. After we're home, I expect a complete debriefing from you as well as your insights and opinions. Now go get ready. And your makeup this evening can be subtle and understated. I'm bringing you for your brains, not your beauty."

Giving him one quick nod, she took her bundle of clothes into the bathroom. Brains not beauty? She didn't feel like she had either at the moment.

****

Allie didn't recognize the restaurant Smith selected, but her shoulders relaxed a bit at seeing the crowd was mainly business class and her attire was appropriate. Not that she would've expected anything less from him.

A hostess led them to a more secluded area with an empty table set for four.

He ordered water with a slice of lemon for each of them.

Once the waitress, Isabelle, departed, he said, "I hope you don't mind—there won't be any alcohol tonight."

Don't be embarrassed. But the shame came every time he casually referred to the night they'd met at Kink. She offered a tight smile. "I like a little squeeze of lemon with my water, and that's more than adequate. Whatever you might think of me, I am not a drinker. Saturday night was an aberration. It hadn't happened before, and it won't happen again."

"In my presence, it certainly will not." His tone was level. "Order whatever suits your fancy for dinner."

He evidently caught something from the corner of his eye, and he placed a hand over hers. "You'll be fine, Alessandra. Don't worry." He rose.

Unsure of the protocol, she stood as well. The couple making their way over were a study in contradictions.

The older woman, with short silver hair, was buxom and curvy, nails matching her dark-red dress.

Her smile radiated comfort, and Allie had to fight the urge to step into the woman's arms. She ruthlessly tamped down the strange sensation.

The younger man in the wire-rimmed glasses was tall, gangly, and...awkward. His light-brown hair was desperately in need of a cut, unless he was aiming for the unkempt look. His corduroy pants, plaid shirt, and cardigan sweater should've looked out of place, but he pulled it off.

He reminded her of her professors from grad school except he was probably thirty years younger, maybe no more than twenty-five. Any family resemblance to the older woman? No, probably not her son.

Introductions were made, and Allie resettled with Smith on one side, Dr. Hamish McAllister on the other, Agnes Strongman across from her. She just managed to keep her jaw from dropping when she heard that Hamish was a doctor. Not like she could judge or make assumptions about anyone.

By mutual consent, they skipped hors d'oeuvres in favor of going straight to dinner. The two guests ordered chicken dishes, Smith ordered steak, and she opted for shrimp linguini.

Agnes began a conversation with Smith about

whether or not he was seriously thinking about acquiring JEAP. Soon they were involved in intricacies that had no meaning to Allie, and her heart began to race.

"Let them go at it." Hamish's voice was soft. "They'll forget we're here, so we should endeavor to do the same."

Allie turned toward him. "You're right. So what is it you do, Dr. McAllister?"

"Hamish, please. I'm the clinical director at JEAP."

"JEAP?"

"Johnson Employee Assistance Program. We offer counseling services to employees of some of the biggest corporations in Canada. I don't know if you're familiar with how EAP services work?"

Yes, but she wasn't sure how to respond.

Obviously reading her indecision, Hamish smiled. "We provide counseling services over the phone for employees in crisis and referrals whenever needed. It's all confidential, but we still have to work hard to convince employees of that. We try to do as much outreach as responding when approached."

"Do you do crisis counseling?"

Hamish nodded. "One of our clients had a workplace incident where a former employee came in and stabbed six co-workers. Two died."

"I heard about that." She gulped and shifted. "That must have been difficult."

"I led the crisis team." He smiled at her expression. "Yes, I'm young. I got my PhD in clinical psychology at twenty-four and saw my first patient that year. I may be young, but I'm good at what I do."

"I would never question that." Yet she had to ask. "Just how old are you?"

Hamish chuckled. "Thirty-seven. It's in the genes. My younger sister still gets carded, and she's twenty-five. We all find it greatly amusing—her, not so much."

"How many of you are there?"

"I'm one of five. All of us have doctorates."

"Those are some genes." Who couldn't be at ease with this unassuming man?

"My mother was the head of the Health Canada Infectious Diseases Lab, and my father sequenced a genome for a rare blood disorder. I'm only a clinician. Because I haven't made any genuine discoveries, I'm the disappointment of the family." His serene face belied any true hurt.

She arched an eyebrow. "Helping people is incredibly important. One in four people will struggle at some point. That's a staggering number."

"And I see the manifestation of that all the time." A heartfelt nod. "But it doesn't get me down. We do evaluations after each intervention or referral. We get good feedback."

"There must be bad as well."

"Of course." Hamish sighed. "We can't always have a happy outcome. Sometimes we're brought in too late to help. Sometimes people are too far gone. Terrible things happen. We've lost patients to suicide, which is always the worst outcome."

No, there are worse ones than that.

Obviously picking up on her disquiet, he became solicitous. "I do go on, don't I? I just get really involved in my work."

"As you should." She respected the hell out of him

because she knew what it took to put oneself out there day after day, trying to help those in need. It could exhilarate, but it could also drain.

"So what is it you do, Ms. Soriano?"

That brought a smile to her lips. "It's Alessandra, but my friends call me Allie."

"And am I a friend?"

From anyone else that might have been a come-on, but from Hamish obviously an earnest question.

"Yes." A grin. "I think you're a friend."

"So, Allie, what is it that you do?"

Cringing inwardly, she cursed that she hadn't thought this evening through with greater scrutiny. She still wasn't sure why she was there, let alone what Smith might've told these people about her.

"I'm freelancing right now. I have several projects I'm working on."

Hamish nodded, not calling her out on what was so clearly an evasion. The lie was probably written all over her face, and with his clinical experience he likely saw through the whole thing.

"And how do you know Mr. MacLean?"

"Smith? We met through mutual acquaintances." At least there she didn't have to equivocate. She shifted to the side as Isabelle, their server, removed her dinner plate. Hopefully desserts would be refused so she could get out of there as quickly as possible. She was comfortable asking questions, but not so good at answering them.

"Alessandra is a social worker."

Smith's tone was light and conversational, and she wouldn't have heard it if there hadn't been a lull in her conversation with Hamish.

The doctor turned to her. "Where's your practice?"

Don't falter. "I took some time off. I'm not sure when I'm going to go back to practice."

If ever.

Hamish's gaze was unwavering.

The back of her eyes burned. She stood.

Hamish and Smith did as well.

"If you gentlemen don't mind, I'll be back." She was about to step away when Agnes stood.

"I'll join you."

Pasting on the most genial smile possible, she said, "Of course." With that, the two of them made their way to the ladies' room.

Fortunately, Allie really did need to use the facilities, so she ducked into a stall. She detested the concept of public restrooms although they were a necessity. As much as she wanted to sit on the toilet and feel sorry for herself, that wasn't an option. She left the stall, washed her hands, and pulled the lip gloss from her purse—also provided by the helpful Mme Veronique.

Kelci, the makeup artist, had taken time to show her how to create the look Smith favored, and she'd endeavored to replicate it. The soft bronze color of eye shadow emphasized her big brown eyes, and the light dusty rose of blush emphasized her delicate bone structure. She looked more sophisticated than she had in her entire life. Her old job had demanded professionalism with no room for niceties. Even when she'd prepared to be with Gage and Cara, she'd never felt this...alluring.

The mirror showed Agnes watching her intently. "What is the lipstick you use?"

Allie handed over the container.

The older woman lifted a brow. "I've heard of this company."

"Let me guess—they're very expensive."

Agnes gave her an odd look. "Actually, I was going to say they're the leading advocates of products not tested on animals. They've set a new standard in the cosmetics industry."

Allie took back the tube with as much dignity as she could muster, trying not to show how flustered she was.

Agnes pointed to the watch. "May I...?"

Just because she wanted to churlishly say no, she held out her arm for inspection.

"This is exquisite."

Damn blush. "A gift."

Agnes eyed her. "Whoever your beau is, he has excellent taste." She smiled. "Now any chance you might put a word in Smith's ear about acquiring JEAP?"

"I...I'm not sure I'm qualified to give him an opinion about it. Why? Are you hoping he'll buy you out?"

"We're growing too rapidly. Either we're going to have to turn away paying clients and those who need us, or we need a huge influx of cash. Our reserves aren't there, but the business is. Companies are starting to see the importance of mentally healthy workers."

"I can see where you're coming from. Is it a public company?"

Agnes shook her head. "I started it twenty-five years ago with four employees and eight clients. It's time for me to let go and retire. I have a new grandbaby on the way, so I figure the time is now, or I'll get dragged into another ten years, you know?"

Instead of trying to formulate an articulate response, Allie merely inclined her head. "We should probably rejoin the men."

The older woman smiled. "They're probably making some kind of comment about women in the ladies' room, but I've found very important business can get done in unusual places."

Given the places she'd endured as a social worker—including a jail, a psychiatric facility, and a drug dealer's home that should've been condemned—Allie couldn't help but agree. Sometimes work got accomplished in very odd places.

****

"Why did you tell them I'm a social worker?" Allie was proud of the fact she'd waited until they arrived back at Smith's place before asking.

"Alessandra, I would like to take my jacket off and get a beer first if that's okay."

Contrite, she opted not to press the issue. "I would like to get out of this outfit as well. I'm surprised I didn't spill any food on it at dinner."

"Are you in the habit of wearing food?"

"Only every time I wear something expensive." She swept her hand up and down her body. "Especially white. It's like a magnet for food, especially tomato sauce."

He chuckled. "I would never have believed that, but I'll take your word for it. There's a pair of pajamas in the closet. Let me get them for you."

Maybe he'd let her keep them for the night. She'd been cold the past two nights, and although tempted to beg, she held back. She still had some modicum of pride. Not much, but that was all that she had.

Going into the bathroom, she removed the clothes and put them into a pile. Smith kept his dirty clothes in a hamper in the dungeon, so she couldn't sneak out in dirty clothes. A knock on the door had her opening it a crack and thrusting out her hand. Soft flannel was put into her grasp.

Amazingly, they were white with little, pale-blue snowflakes and accompanied by a pair of thick socks. She didn't remember those from that morning, but even as she shrugged, Smith's thoughtfulness touched her. After dressing, she washed her face, almost sorry to wipe away the traces of sophistication. Nothing to be done about it, though. She was no longer the erudite and classy Alessandra, back to being just plain old Allie.

She followed the hallway lights out to the living room, finding him at the windows, looking at the building across the way. Who knew what he saw? She'd been surprised to find him living on the third floor until she discovered the dungeon. That explained a lot. She briefly wondered if he'd ever participated in a threesome with Rielle and Gage. Better not ask. No point in garnering punishment over idle curiosity.

Hey, two bottles of beer sat on the coffee table. "Is one of those for me?"

He nodded but didn't turn around. "You earned it."

Somehow she'd acquired a taste for beer while attending the university. Although she'd never had more than one or two at a time and had never gotten wasted, she liked the taste. Taking a long pull from her bottle, she smiled. Granville Island Pale Ale, one of her favorites. Sipping it slowly, she sat in one of the chairs.

Time spun out as she nursed her precious beer. She'd have to make it last because in all likelihood she was only going to get the one. The challenge was to enjoy the beer while the drink was still cold and not flat, but not drink it so quickly she missed out on the taste. She'd just about mastered the art of drinking beer.

Finally, after what seemed like hours but was probably only a few minutes, Smith turned.

"What did you think of them?" He picked up his bottle, moved to the sofa, and sat. His throat worked as he took his first sip.

How was she supposed to answer that? She still hadn't figured out why he'd invited her.

"It sounds like they're running a wonderful organization. Providing psychological counseling services is challenging, and they rely on outside providers to do the actual work, so that's always a risk. They're based here, but their clientele are from everywhere in Canada, and they're looking to expand into the States. The question is sustainability. You have to prove to companies that good value is being provided for the money being spent. That's challenging. How do you prove a negative? *You're not having problems with your employees because they are using our confidential services, so you should keep using our services.*" She paused. "Agnes is friendly, but she really wants this deal to go through. Hamish cares less about the business side and more about the actual clients. He chose his profession to help people and derives great satisfaction from that."

"And you? Did you derive great satisfaction from helping people?"

Pain lanced through her, sharp and sure, before she could school herself. "We're not talking about me. But since you brought it up, why the hell did you tell them I'm a social worker?"

"Are you not? Were you sanctioned? Did you have your license revoked?"

She dropped her gaze to the floor and shook her head. *Jesus, anything but this.* "They should've done all those things, but they didn't."

"What happened, Alessandra?"

A neutral tone. Not demanding, not pleading, just a disinterested tone as if he couldn't care one way or the other. It didn't mean anything to him, but it meant *everything* to her.

She closed her eyes and downed the rest of her beer. "Thank you for the treat. I'm exhausted. May I keep the pajamas?"

A nerve-shattering pause.

"You may."

She waited for him to dismiss her but was forced to endure through another interminable silence. Finally, she looked up to meet his gaze.

"Know this, Alessandra—I will find out what happened. If I must, I'll start asking questions myself. Something happened six months ago. I think it'd be better if I heard about it from you, but if you choose to remain silent, then that's to your own detriment."

The arrogant tenor reminded her who really held the power in this relationship. She rose and took her bottle to the kitchen. Making one last visit to the bathroom, she peed and brushed her teeth. Only when she lay in bed did she realize he hadn't touched her once all day.

Chapter Twelve

The next morning, Smith was having trouble concentrating on the news in the paper. Alessandra had been dozing fitfully when he gave her clothes for the day. He always felt like a voyeur when he did this daily ritual, but he enjoyed doing it, so he'd continue to do so. Since she seemed resigned to his terms, he could probably be freer with her clothing privileges, but he liked picking her clothes. He enjoyed anticipating what she'd look like, even in just jeans and a turtleneck.

He glimpsed her as she went to the bathroom, a blur of white. Virginal white pajamas. Mme Veronique certainly had a sense of humor. The other clothes were elegant, even the lingerie. Smith didn't like slutty stuff. He liked sleek classic lines in sophisticated color palettes. Mme Veronique had ensured he'd be very happy over the next month.

Maybe even longer.

Another blur passed, this one in cream jeans, a gray turtleneck, and a scarf. The scarf was black with accents of gold and platinum. Platinum like the watch he'd given her. She hadn't hidden her look of unadulterated pleasure from him. Her reaction assured him his instincts were good. He was learning more about her as time went on.

He'd also begun discreet inquiries into anything that happened six months ago in Mission City in which she might've been involved. People didn't just decide one day to walk out the door and never come back. Even if she'd had a mental breakdown, there should've been indicators. No one had seen this coming—not her co-workers, not her friends. Gage said she had no family, and Smith was inclined to believe him, but he still would verify that. He'd hoped she'd fill in the blanks, but last night showed him he was going to have to force the issue.

What was the best tactic? Aggressive? Passive? Passive aggressive? Sit back and wait for her to come to him or force her hand?

He turned the page when she sat, cursing that he hadn't absorbed a single item from the previous page. Not a big deal, really. He employed a woman on his payroll solely to find media stories that might interest him and send him a daily email. She could also text him if urgent.

"Don't you have to go to work?"

He folded the paper. "Looking to get rid of me so you can bolt?"

"You'll just take my clothes before you go, so that's not really the point, is it? I just mean, how can you afford to take this much time off work?"

He offered her a smile. "I am in a position to work as much or as little as I choose. I have the best people working for me, Alessandra. People who have the ability and the permission to do what they see is best. My presence is not required, and if I dropped dead of a heart attack tomorrow, things would continue on as they had been."

"Will you?"

"Will I what?"

"Drop dead from a heart attack tomorrow?" She frowned. "Don't you need some kind of succession plan?"

Her intelligence impressed him. "My workers will be provided for. The board of directors have the authority to take the company public, and there is a team in place to run operations until they can name a CEO." He chuckled. "Good enough?"

She nodded. "I guess so."

He passed a pile of papers to her. She didn't even look at them.

"Those are your test results."

"I guessed."

"Aren't you going to look?"

"Nope."

He suppressed the quick flare of annoyance. "Aren't you even the least bit curious?"

"Nope."

"Alessandra." He said it softly, careful to add just the right inflection of warning.

"Fine," she spat out. "But I already know what they're going to say." She took the papers and scanned them.

Her shoulders lowered. She'd had no idea what they were going to say. She'd been scared but bluffing.

Well, well, that was more revealing than anything she might've said.

She placed them down with a flourish. "There, I read the fucking papers. Like I said yesterday, since we won't be exchanging any bodily fluids, I don't see why it would possibly matter."

"Do you have a death wish?"

Her head snapped up so fast a vertebrae cracked.

Yet she didn't respond. She just kept looking at him.

"Keep sleeping with every available cock, and you're going to catch something. It's not a matter of *if*, Alessandra—it's a matter of *when*." He tried to keep his voice reasonable when all he wanted to do was lunge across the table and throttle the damn woman. She'd been clean, but that appeared to be more because of the horseshoe up her ass than from any responsible behavior on her part.

Still, she just kept looking at him. Who would blink first? Because he could sit here all day and do this. Of course, emotions had already flitted across her face—shock, anger, annoyance, discomfort, pain, anguish, desolation, and then some vain attempt at neutrality. Where was she going to go next? Then she looked away, toward the windows.

She took one breath, then another. As if she was having to force herself to breathe rather than it being an autonomic response. Almost like she was having to force herself to choose life rather than fading into oblivion. Was this how she'd been when she walked away? He desperately wanted to ask, but she looked like she'd shatter if a breath of wind touched her.

"Your cereal is getting soggy."

She turned to him with unfocused eyes. "I'm sorry?"

"I said, you need to eat your cereal."

Looking down at it like she hadn't even known it was there, she pushed the bowl away from her with slow deliberation. "I'm not really hungry."

He'd let that slide. For now. "Well, let me know when you're ready to start."

She frowned. "Start what?"

Rising, he took the breakfast dishes to the kitchen.

"I should do that." Her voice was meek and quiet, with barely any energy.

"You may bring your own dishes and help with cleaning up, but then we begin."

The look on her face said she was expecting a set of corrections, a punishment of some kind. She seemed to troll through her memories to find her transgression. Finding none, she seemed to resign herself to accepting whatever punishment he meted out simply because he wanted to.

What would she think of his choice for the day?

He turned on the dishwasher as Alessandra wiped down the counters. They worked in companionable silence. Well, he'd call it companionable. She might call it a whole other thing.

When they finished, she presented herself but with downcast eyes. "What is my Master's pleasure?"

To fuck you senseless. He doubted that'd go over very well. Those test results were like permission. Permission to touch. Permission to taste. Suddenly, he was very greedy.

It would have to wait until she was in a more amenable mood.

"Follow me." Not a command, but a request. That she obeyed pleased him immeasurably.

He led her to his office and ushered her into the room. Although he worked from there a lot, the space was orderly. Everything had its place, and he liked it that way. He sat at his desk and pointed to the chair across from him. Her hesitation was brief but noticeable.

Then she sat and crossed her legs.

Was she nervous? She had no reason to be because he wasn't pushing her too far today. *She can handle this, right?*

"You know I'm considering acquiring JEAP."

The resigned woman nodded.

"They've sent me plenty of reports showing the viability of the business model, and I can see there is tremendous potential for growth."

"But you have reservations."

"Of course. Service industries can be much harder to quantify. Salaries make up the lion's share of the costs, and those can be unpredictable. Maybe more people use the services around Christmastime, for example. But patterns and analyses only go so far. It's the human element that sometimes eludes businesspeople like me."

"Oh, I think you have the human element all figured out." Her gaze was steady. "And I suspect you're perfectly capable of reading and analyzing reports. So why am I here? Do you need a secretary?"

He smiled. *Hmm*, Alessandra flouncing around in a too-tight blouse, short skirt, and no underwear. She'd wear sexy glasses, fire-engine-red lipstick, and give him blowjobs whenever he wanted.

"No." He cleared his throat and adjusted his crotch. "I don't need a secretary. I need a guinea pig."

Now he had her attention.

"Their business is all done over the phone. People call in with their problems, and they're referred to services. If it's an emergency, they can speak to a counselor right away." He pointed to his laptop. "I can get all the procedures and manuals I want, but that's theory. I can read all the feedback reports, but those can be skewed. People who were helped might not bother to fill out the survey because they're happy. People who weren't helped might not fill out the survey because they don't think it will make any difference."

"Have you considered using an outside service? They can call to follow up…" Her brow furrowed, and she waved her hand in front of her face. "Never mind, stupid idea. Confidentiality precludes that. And some people won't fill out the survey for the same reason. There can't be a hint that someone's identity might be revealed because that discourages use of this service."

She still had it. It was still there. She was just afraid. Why? No point in demanding an answer, he wasn't going to get one. Instead, he nodded. "I need someone to call JEAP and be a client. I need someone who can evaluate their response. I need someone who can pretend to be in distress."

"Hire an actor."

He'd expected resistance but hoped she'd at least contemplate helping him. "I don't want an actor. Privacy laws dictate I cannot tape the calls, nor can a third person listen in." That wasn't strictly true, but she didn't need to know that. "I need someone who can evaluate with honesty and integrity." *Don't lose your shit. Don't beg.*

"Hire a real social worker."

"Alessandra, I want you. I trust your judgment—"

"Well, you shouldn't." Her response was terse. "I tried to warn you last night."

Was he doing more harm than good? No, she needed to be stretched. He then pushed ahead anyway, heedless of consequences. "Let's make a deal."

"What is this, a 1970s game show?"

He chuckled. "Call it whatever you like. Aside from leaving here, what do you most desire?"

And again—abject misery. She wanted to erase the past. He'd do it in a heartbeat if he could, but that was beyond his powers. Money could buy a lot of things, but alleviating such clear anguish wasn't one of them. Then the moment passed, and her expression lightened.

"Donate ten thousand dollars to the Healing Horses Ranch. Do that, and I'll be your guinea pig."

Had he heard correctly? "You have nothing. You have no money, no possessions, and a whole fifty-five dollars to your name, and you want me to donate money to a charity?"

Her chin tipped up. "They do outstanding work there. They have funding sources, but Kennedy Dixon needs to repair some fencing and would never take away money from the patients to do the repairs."

"And where is this Healing Horses Ranch?"

"Mission City."

Smith nodded. "I'll do it. I'll contact Ms. Dixon—"

"Doctor."

"Sorry?"

"It's Dr. Kennedy Dixon. She's a psychologist."

He held up his hands in acknowledgment. "I'll call Dr. Dixon and make the arrangements." He paused. "But you should be the one to go out and inspect the work. I want to make sure they put my donation to excellent use."

The refusal formed on her lips.

"In fact, if you'll go, then I'll donate a hundred thousand dollars. I'm sure there are other repairs they can make."

The look of misery was back. "Those clients, those

patients, those kids and mothers and…and…" She sputtered. "Do you know how much good they could do with that kind of money?" Standing, she paced. "I know you said I can't call you a bastard or a son of a bitch, but you're pushing me. I have buttons. You know I can't go back. You're asking too much."

"Am I?" He kept his tone mild, but he was very interested in her answer.

She sat back down, braced her hands against her knees, and leaned forward. "I agreed to the thirty days precisely because I can't go back. Kennedy and every one of her staff know who I am. If I show up, there'll be questions. Recriminations. I walked away for a reason, Smith, and I can't go back. Ask anything else of me, and I'll do it."

"You'll do anything so I donate a hundred thousand dollars to the ranch?" That look of eager anticipation and wariness threatened to distract him. "You're expecting me to make some kind of sexual proposition, aren't you?"

Her gaze lowered to the ground, and then she looked back at him. "I'll do it. Whatever you want, I'll do it."

He saw red. "Is that what you've been doing for the last six months? Trading your body for favors? For money?"

She looked like she'd been slapped, but she didn't respond aloud.

"Let's agree on ten grand and a guinea pig. Now I suggest you leave without saying another word before I really lose my temper."

She scrambled out of the room as fast as she could. He let her go.

Chapter Thirteen

Instead of the pages in front of her, all Allie saw was the unadulterated rage on Smith's face when she offered him her body. It'd been a gut instinct. After all, he'd said he'd give the money if she agreed to do anything he wanted. All she had was her body, and, despite any protestations he might make, he liked her body. She wasn't oblivious of the glances, the lingering looks. Despite her discomfort with flirting, she was quickly learning to read the signals he did and didn't say. Since going back to her profession had already been off the table, she had no other choice. What could a woman in her position offer a man like Smith? She had nothing. She was *worth* nothing.

So what if it made her sound like a prostitute? Kennedy Dixon was truly doing something good in the world, and Allie just wanted to help. She should've just kept her mouth shut, agreed to be the guinea pig, and not asked for anything else. Or she could've asked for something as impractical as the watch was. Beautiful as the watch was, she'd have to leave it behind. People on the Downtown Eastside had been mugged for a lot less than a watch bought from Birks.

Knock, knock. Her treacherous heart lurched in her chest. He'd come after her. Not that she'd wanted him to, of course. She wasn't a manipulator—she wasn't one of those women who'd run, expecting to be followed and groveled to. But even so, the knock at the door was welcome.

She rose and opened the door.

"Put this on."

She barely had time to grab the plain, black, one-piece bathing suit and robe before he was gone. Okay...that was why he'd purchased it yesterday. The building must have a swimming pool. It'd just serve Mr. Arrogant right if she didn't know how to swim. But she did, so she put on the suit. She checked herself in the mirror. Oh, good, the marks from a few days ago had faded. Nothing like shocking the neighbors by bringing a guest with whip marks across her back.

There had also been a bikini, basically three triangles of fabric. She rolled her eyes as she slipped into the robe. Where the hell did he think she was going to wear that? Just more things she'd have to leave behind when she left. For now, however, she'd get some physical activity, no complaints about that.

****

An hour later, she definitely had a few complaints. She'd envisioned doing a few laps and then treading water in the deep end. Nope. He'd had her do lengths for five minutes, rest for five minutes, swim for five minutes, rest for five minutes, and so on until an hour had elapsed. Once upon a time, she'd been in shape. She used to walk two to three miles a day for stress relief. But she hadn't walked more than a few blocks in all these months, and her lack of physical exercise was evident. Smith'd been displeased every time she wheezed and gasped her way through her five-minute rest periods. He hadn't even joined her in the pool. Instead he'd stood over her like a taskmaster.

At least she hadn't complained. Yes, she'd muttered a few oaths under her breath and again thought about creative things to do with his balls, but she'd sucked it up.

Now, as the hot spray of the shower enveloped her, she massaged sore muscles. Although she wanted to prolong the shower, her legs wobbled. With some regret, she exited the shower and reached for a towel. Drying off was a quick process, and she didn't even bother with a comb for her hair. By the end of the month, she'd need to take the scissors to it again. Maybe Smith had a pair she could borrow before she left.

She slipped on her robe and was leaving the bathroom when she bumped into him. "I'm sorry," she muttered and tried to step out of his way.

"No bother, I was waiting for you."

Uh-oh. That didn't portend well. Without even having to be asked, she followed him into the dungeon.

And groaned.

"I see we're in agreement on this one, Alessandra."

"I'm not sure agreement is the word I would use, but I can see what you think I'm going to do."

Smith tsked. "Not *think* you're going to do, my dear. This is what you're *going* to do. Now take off your robe."

He'd jacked up the temperature in the room to a very pleasant level. There went that excuse. She slipped from the robe, placed it on the chair, and then stepped to the little circle of carpet. At least she wouldn't be standing on the hardwood.

He'd unhooked the manacles attached to the ceiling and lowered them.

Silently she raised her arms so he could shackle her. Just enough give that she could plant her feet on the floor. Was that a good thing or not? Feet...arms...they were all going to ache, so what difference did it make?

When he went to the wall and grabbed the spreader bar, she suppressed a groan. There would be no way for her to stretch her muscles or find any relief. She gritted her teeth when he attached it because she wasn't going to say anything. She could be strong. She could endure this. She'd endured far worse.

Once he had her well and truly trussed, he sat in the chair, propped his feet up on the bed, and began to read another damn report.

"You're staying?"

He looked up, startled. "Of course I'm staying. What kind of Dom would tie someone up and leave them alone? Was Gage ever that irresponsible?"

"Of course not." *How stupid are you? Of course he'd never leave you alone. How to be a good Dom 101.* "I just thought you might have something better to do."

He held up the report. "I have plenty to do, but maybe you're on to something. Maybe we should have a discussion."

Looking desperately at the report, she sought divine intervention. "I'm quite sure you have important work to do. I'm just going to, um, hang here and be quiet."

The laughter came out as a bark. "You, Alessandra, do not know how to be quiet. Besides, you've reminded me we have yet to establish protocol."

"Protocol?" *I don't like the sound of this.*

111

He eased his feet from the bed, stood, and then meandered over to her. "For example, you never told me your safeword. Very wrong of me to scene with you without a safeword."

She lifted her chin. "I don't need a safeword."

"Really?" He said the word casually as he circled around her.

He stopped when he was behind her, and she couldn't look over her shoulder to see him. She tried to shift, but the spreader bar held her in place.

"How are you feeling?"

"Fine," she answered quickly. "I feel fine."

"Would you tell me if you weren't?"

Good question. "Well, of course I would."

"But how am I supposed to know the difference between you simply complaining and you really needing help?"

"My words, I guess. I'll tell you if I need help?"

"Sounds very reasonable, Alessandra, but what happens if I release you and you didn't really need help? What if I find out you didn't push yourself hard enough?"

Hard enough? Her knees were going to buckle, her shoulders felt like they were going to be pulled out of their sockets, and her head ached. What was hard enough, anyway? What did he mean? "I thought slaves didn't get safewords."

"You're very wrong about that. There always must be a safeword. No matter how much a slave can endure, things can go wrong. The body's reactions can be anticipated and monitored, but it's still an unpredictable thing. Add the mind to that mix, and there are limits."

He still stood behind her. *Damn it.* She wanted to

turn. Wanted to see what his facial expressions might give away. Not likely much, admittedly. Smith played his cards very close to his vest, and discerning his emotions was a challenge. Except when she really pissed him off. In those all-too-frequent moments, he let his anger show. On purpose, no doubt.

"And speaking of limits, we haven't discussed those either. Or wish lists for that matter."

"I have no wishes."

"I have no wishes, Master."

Shit. "I have no wishes, Master."

Still, he didn't move.

"But you do. Aside from the little monetary gift you asked for this morning, you have other desires. There are things you want to do to me and things you want me to do to you." He chuckled. "You want the structure I can bring to your life. You want to be corrected when you make a mistake and praised when you succeed. Everyone needs those things."

"Who corrects your mistakes? Who praises you? You're invincible, and you make no mistakes." She spat the words out. "You wouldn't know what to do with someone who told you what to do."

A lengthy silence. "I always did what my mother told me to do, Alessandra. I was lucky to have her in my life to guide me and to teach me right from wrong. I learned ethics from her. I learned that how you treat those who are weaker than you is even more important than how you treat those stronger than you."

"You're lucky to have a mother like that."

"Was lucky," he corrected. "My mother was in a car accident when I was twenty-five. I was overseas at the time and came home as quickly as I could, but I wasn't fast enough. She died without me telling her how much I loved her."

"I'm sure she knew." Why was she trying to reassure him? "Mothers…they're good like that." When he didn't respond right away, she again tried to look over her shoulder. Unsuccessfully, of course, and now she had a crimp in her neck.

"Where is your mother?"

She fought the lance of pain. "She's also gone."

"And your father?"

"I never knew him. He died in an industrial accident when I was just an infant." Flexing her abdominals caused nothing good to happen.

"I never knew my father either. When my mother told him she was pregnant, he conveniently remembered he was already married, with one child and another on the way. He offered to pay for a back-alley abortion. My mother bought a one-way ticket out of that town and never looked back."

"That was brave of her."

"No braver than your mother raising you after your father died. Do you have any brothers or sisters?"

Her wrists ached. "I was an only child."

"So was I. You see, Alessandra, we have a lot in common. We would never have discovered that if we hadn't taken the time to talk." He paused. "But we've veered off topic. What is your safeword?"

Just a few minutes longer. Just hold out a few minutes longer.

"I don't enjoy repeating myself, so let's have it."

"Bilbo." She said it in a broken whisper.

"I'm sorry—you'll have to repeat that."

She curled her fingers into fists and then relaxed

them. "Hobbit is my slow-down word, and Bilbo is my safeword."

"I'm sure it amused Gage."

"Actually, he made the suggestion. We were watching *The Lord of the Rings* trilogy, and I fell asleep."

Smith snickered. "He had two beautiful women at his beck and call, and you were watching Peter Jackson movies?"

She shook her head and then suppressed a gasp at the pain shooting down her spine. "That was before…before we started playing together."

"And after?"

"Fewer movies," she admitted. "We had other things to occupy us."

"Gage must have incredible stamina. All those weekends with two beautiful women."

Good God. "We didn't have *that* kind of relationship. Gage and I…we never touched. Not like that, anyway." She closed her eyes so he wouldn't see her pain, forced the words past her tight throat. "We had boundaries, you know. He could do anything he wanted to me except…touch me down there."

"Down there? You sound like a virgin. You say, 'He didn't have permission to touch my vagina and my clitoris.' "

She gulped. "He didn't have permission to touch my vagina and my clitoris just like I didn't have permission to touch his penis."

"But you wanted to, didn't you? You ached to give him that kind of service. Just like you were aching for him to touch you. Cara was a good surrogate, but not enough. You wanted him. All of him."

No way could he know that. She'd never told a single soul, and no way would Gage ever have betrayed her…if he even knew. Since his feelings for her weren't romantic, just as likely he'd never known about her feelings for him.

"How we touched, or wanted to touch, is of no relevance."

"That's where you're wrong, Alessandra. If your only experience as a submissive was with Gage, then there's an entire realm of experiences you haven't been exposed to."

"Who says Gage was my only Dom?" Her tone was insolent, but she didn't care. Her vision was now blurry with black spots in the middle.

"Are you saying he wasn't? I asked it before, Alessandra, and I'll ask it again. Where have you been for the last six months, what have you been doing, and who have you been doing it with?"

She bit on her lower lip so hard she tasted blood. "I yield, Smith. I give up."

"Say the word, Alessandra."

She shook her head and this time didn't bother to hold in the gasp of pain.

"One word, Alessandra, and this all ends."

So tempting, but she couldn't do it. She wouldn't be the one to give in. Instead, the tears began. At first just one and then another. But then the dam burst, and she began crying. "I yield." She gasped. "You win."

Smith appeared in her vision, but she closed her eyes again. He was saying something, but she couldn't hear him. Her own sobs echoed around the room and in her head. She could've given in, *should've* given in. But she hadn't, and now she was going to pay for it. Then she closed her eyes and gave up the fight.

****

She was warm. Warm and wet. A womb would feel like this. Splashing and then her muscles were being rubbed down. It felt good. She wanted the feeling to go on and on and on. A straw was pressed against her lips.

"Drink this."

Recognizing that voice, she wanted to balk. She wanted to keep her eyes closed and revel in the steam.

"Alessandra, don't try my patience. You have a buildup of lactic acid in your muscles, and you need to flush it out. Now drink."

If…whatever the hell he had said, whose fault was it? Not hers. She hadn't strung herself up. She hadn't stretched muscles that weren't meant to be stretched. She hadn't extended joints beyond their capacity.

But she hadn't safeworded either, so she took a sip.

"That's a good girl." No encouragement, though, no praise. No positive tone that went along with the words.

Since the straw was still by her mouth, she took another sip. Then she took longer pulls. Wow, was she thirsty. Imagine, surrounded by all that water and she was thirsty. Finally, the straw was gone, and she sank just a little bit farther into the tub. Maybe if she sank all the way down and submerged herself, she could drown. If she drowned, she could escape the pain. Not just the physical pain—although that was bad—but the emotional pain. She was so tired of fighting.

And just like that, tears that'd dried began anew. Unchecked, they fell in rivulets down her cheeks, her throat, and then into the water. Water to water. Ashes to ashes. Dust to dust.

"Let go, Alessandra, let go of the pain."

"I can't." Another broken whisper. "It won't go away."

"Just because it has its talons in you doesn't mean you can't break free. You may tear flesh, but flesh can heal. You may break bones, but bones can mend. You've survived this far, Alessandra—give yourself credit for that."

She couldn't. She was alive when she had no right to be.

Chapter Fourteen

He was losing her again, and he hunched in desperation. What'd begun as an object lesson had quickly disintegrated into something ugly. All he'd wanted to do was show her limits and safewords existed for a reason. Her capitulation, both physical and emotional, had happened so quickly it caught him off guard. He should've been watching her more closely. He knew better.

Never had he pushed a submissive so far, but then he'd never had a challenging submissive like Alessandra. She enchanted him, beguiled him, infuriated him. She was at one moment innocent and then the next world-weary. Every time he thought he had a read on her, she'd change the script, throw a monkey wrench into his nice ordered existence.

The water was cooling, so he pulled the plug. She made no argument when he lifted her from the tub and set her on the toilet. With great care, he dried her, tended to her, coddled her, cosseted her. She deserved all of that and more after what she'd endured. Her eyes were still shut, but her breathing told him she was present.

When she was as dry as she was going to get, he slipped her into her bathrobe. He lifted her again, and she looped her arms around his neck.

She sniffed and sighed. "You smell good."

He couldn't help it—he chuckled.

After carrying her across the condo to her room, he pushed the door open with his shoulders. Her pajamas were neatly folded on the pillow, just waiting for her. He put her down and was happy when her eyes opened. Keeping an arm around her waist, he reached for the pajamas.

"I can dress myself." She pulled back from him.

He didn't want to let her go. She might be fine, but he wasn't. Fine line. He was walking a fine line. "Well, while you do that, I'll order some pizza. Any preferences?"

She squinted at him for a long moment. "No, I trust you."

He wanted to believe her, but that seemed too incredible after what he'd just put her through. He left her for only as long as it took him to make the call, and when he came back, she was perched on the bed, looking lost. At least she wore clothes.

"I feel like I should know the time, but I don't. There's no natural light in this room, so I can't tell if it's daytime or nighttime. I don't remember eating lunch, but it feels like bedtime."

"Did you try checking your watch?"

She squinted at him, and then her face broke into a grin. "I have a watch." She held up her arm. "You gave me a watch."

If he didn't know better, he'd swear she'd gotten into his liquor cabinet. But he knew better. He pulled the chair so he sat at eye level with her. "How do you feel?"

Her eyes sharpened. "Like you give a shit."

Ah, so she *was* in there somewhere.

"Do you know what today's lesson was?"

"I have no fucking idea." She squinted again. "I mean Master, Sir, I have no fucking idea."

He suppressed amusement because he had to get through to her. "Well, you haven't been taking care of yourself, have you?"

She looked like she was going to argue but then nodded.

"You know physical fitness is important, right?"

Her head bobbed.

"I was showing you that you need to exercise." She ducked her head, but he reached out to snag her chin and guide her gaze back to his. "But you needed to learn a more important lesson, Alessandra. One I want you to remember for the rest of your life."

He had her full attention.

"You must always be with someone who respects a safeword. You should never get involved with someone who doesn't ask you for your safeword."

"I got involved with you, didn't I?"

Damn, she had him there. "And you paid for that, didn't you?" Her raised eyebrows and slight "oh" told him she hadn't seen it in that light.

"You said you trust me, Alessandra. Did you mean that?"

Slowly but steadily, she nodded.

"You need to choose your Dominant very carefully. I'm basically a good guy, but I could have really hurt you today."

"Lesson learned." Her voice was quiet, and she seemed appropriately chastised. It looked like she was going to say something else, but a knock at the door sounded.

"That'll be the food." He was just about to leave her where she was when he realized he couldn't. He held out his hand. "Come with me?"

She nodded, took his hand, and allowed him to help her rise.

Her hand was tiny and insubstantial when engulfed in his own. He urged her to the sofa when another knock sounded. Fishing for his wallet, he then moved to answer the door. He gave the older man a hefty tip and balanced the salads on top of the pizza as he took everything to the kitchen.

Surprisingly, Alessandra was there pulling down plates. "What would you like to drink?" She didn't make eye contact.

"I'll have a water." He waited for her to ask for a beer.

She simply nodded. "I'll have one as well."

Within about a minute, they were settled at the table and eating.

They were almost finished when she looked up with an odd expression on her face. "You never answered my question."

"Which question?"

"I asked the time, and you never gave me an answer."

He tilted his head. "When you asked, two o'clock. Now it's two thirty."

Her pupils dilated. "That's all? I feel like it's about ten. I feel like it's time to go to bed."

"Extreme physical activity can confuse you. Your body is telling you it needs rest, so you'll rest."

"But it's mid-afternoon." A distinct whine in her voice. "I can't go to bed. I don't want to go to bed."

Her tone and not the words were important. "What's wrong, Alessandra?"

Her gaze dropped to her plate as she pushed it away. "I don't want to be alone."

The words were quiet, their meaning clear. He rose and went to her. When he held out his hand, she reached for it, wrapping her hands around it. He helped her up and then lifted her into his arms, heading to her bedroom.

When he laid her on the bed and stepped back, she whimpered.

"I'll return momentarily—just give me one moment." He strode across the condo to retrieve his report and then returned as quickly.

She'd twisted herself into a ball, hands over her face.

He placed the papers on the bedside table and then crawled into bed behind her. He pulled her back against him, curling his body protectively around hers. Putting his arms around her chest, he imprisoned her arms, holding her as tightly as he dared. "You had a very intense experience, Alessandra. You need to let go."

"If I let go, I'll fly apart."

Whispered words.

Within moments, though, she did let go. She slowly relaxed and then fell into something resembling sleep.

****

He identified the exact moment she moved from sleep into awareness. He'd extricated himself enough to prop up against a pillow to read the report.

She'd turned in her sleep and placed her head on his chest.

Unable to resist, he'd given in to the absurdly ridiculous gesture of kissing the top of her head and then let her snuggle against him. His arm looped around her shoulder, and he grasped her upper arm. Now, however, instead of being pliant and soft, she was rigid. Her hand, which had been lightly curled, resting against his chest, was now stiff, fingers extended.

What was she thinking? He almost asked, but he wanted her to be fully awake before questioning her.

"What time is it?"

He should have seen that coming. He glanced at his watch. "Almost six."

She made some inarticulate noise he was incapable of interpreting. He doubted she expected him to anyway.

"Was it a dream?"

"No. Not a nightmare either."

This time, the sound came a little louder.

Laughter? "What're you thinking?"

"That we're sharing a bed and both of us are fully clothed."

Ah, it had been laughter. "You asked me to stay." His tone was a little dry.

"I did indeed." Then she snuggled into his embrace. "And I thank you for doing so."

"My pleasure, Alessandra."

"Why do you call me that?"

His brow furrowed. "It is your name, is it not?"

The hand on his chest relaxed. "It is, but everyone calls me Allie."

"I am not everyone, Alessandra. You should know that by now." He paused. "Do you want me to call you Allie?"

She shrugged. "I guess it doesn't really matter. It's just that Alessandra feels very formal. It feels like we're colleagues rather than friends."

"You mean friends like you are with Dr. McAllister?"

"Hamish?" She chuckled. "Yeah, like that. Gage and Rielle call me Allie."

"Maybe I should come up with a pet name just for you."

She shuddered against him. "I'm not a dog, thank you. I don't need a pet name."

He put the report on the nightstand. "May I ask you a question?"

She snickered. "You've never asked permission before, and it hasn't stopped you, so have at it." Her face still rested on his chest, her gaze toward their feet.

He couldn't even tell if her eyes were open. "What are we to each other?"

Her hand, which had relaxed, stiffened again. "I'm here on your good graces, Smith. I'm here because you blackmailed me into it. I'm here because I don't have any other choice."

"But what if you had a choice? What if you hadn't been called away that day last spring?"

Her body went still. "We can't go back. We can't change what has happened."

"I know that, but that's not what I'm asking. I'm saying if I'd asked you out, would you have said yes?"

She struggled to rise, and he let her. She pushed away, crawling back so she was almost sitting at his feet.

"Would I have let you be my Dominant? That's why you were there, wasn't it? Gage had told you about me, and you were checking me out. Taking me for a spin." A hedgehog had fewer spikes. That defensive barrier rammed into place.

"I told you, I didn't know about you until later. I meant it when I said I had you pegged the first time we met, but as an instinct, not knowledge. The question is would you have consented to a D/s relationship with me?"

"We'll never know." She ended the discussion. "I have to go to the bathroom."

Order her to stay and answer the question? Did he really want to hear her response? Instead, he nodded, and she scooted off the bed.

He got off the bed and snagged the report. Informative, to be sure, but he still wanted more data. No, data was the wrong word. He had spreadsheets, pie charts, and graphs. Everything looked wonderful, but he still wasn't feeling it in his gut. His gut had served him well over the years, but that didn't mean that he hadn't made mistakes. Sometimes acquisitions hadn't panned out, or he occasionally failed to invest in opportunities that generated huge buzz or revenues. Of course, he hadn't gotten where he was by being conservative.

Sighing, he went back to his office. Unlike Alessandra's room, his home office had soaring windows letting in plenty of natural light. Now, however, dusk had arrived. The sun had set behind the next building, throwing the condo into inky shadows. Still, as he sat at his desk staring out the window, he resisted the urge to close the blinds and turn on the lights. He wanted to continue to hold on to the last vestige of daylight before the gloaming set in.

A knock on the open door pulled him from his

reverie.

She looked uncomfortable and uncertain.

"Yes?" His tone was a little sharper than it should've been.

"I'll be your guinea pig." She clasped her hands together—almost white, they were so tight. "Just tell me what you want me to do."

Not wanting to give her a chance to change her mind, he waved her into the room. Flipping on the light as he shut the blinds, he urged her to sit, but instead of sitting back behind the desk, he grabbed a file folder and then came around to sit next to her, pulling up a chair. They were close but weren't touching.

He handed her the folder. "These are the top ten requests or issues JEAP deals with. They're standard things, as you can see."

She scanned the page.

"I would like you to call and pretend to be someone in one of those scenarios."

She inclined her head in acknowledgment but kept her eyes on the page. "You mean pretend I have a family member with a substance abuse problem? Pretend they have diagnosed me with an illness? Act like I've just lost a loved one?" She took a breath. "Make believe I'm suicidal."

She didn't phrase the last one as a question but as a statement.

"Yes, that's exactly what I'm looking for. I want to know how the intake representatives deal with someone in crisis. If you talk to a counselor, I want to know if they're doing what needs to be done."

Finally, she looked at him, penetrative and disconcerting. "I'll do this, but how will they know to help me?"

He held out his hand for the folder. She gave it to him, and he noted she was careful to not touch him. He shuffled some papers. "I own a company that has employed the services for several years now. I've had good feedback from our people, but, like I said, it's anecdotal. I want something more concrete. Anyway, you'll pretend to be different employees. I've set up fake employee files for you, all female but with varying ages. I leave it to you to decide which scenario you want to use. I'd prefer you not use the same one all five times, but you can if you want. Write the name of the intake rep and the counselor, then give me a summary of their performance."

She looked at him uneasily. "You want their information? Are you going to fire them if they don't do a good job?"

He shook his head. "That's not my goal. This isn't about any one person. That's why I'm asking you to make five calls. I'm only asking for names so we can ensure there isn't overlap. Odds are you won't speak to the same person twice, but if you do, I need to know."

She didn't look particularly appeased.

"It's the process and quality I'm looking at, Alessandra. I want to know they're doing what they claim they are."

Her shoulders relaxed. "When do you want me to make these calls?"

"They operate twenty-four seven, so anytime is fine. I'll leave it to you to determine the best approach. I defer to your judgment, and you can present your report however you wish."

"Do I have a deadline?"

He nodded. "I'd like to have this wrapped up in the next week or so. Does that give you enough time?"

"To make five phone calls? Yeah, I think I can manage that."

"Maybe, but I'm concerned there might be an emotional toll for you."

She snickered. "I'm just acting, Smith—it won't be that big a deal. Pretend, right? I can do that."

Her offhand response disconcerted him. He didn't buy her laissez-faire attitude for a moment. Still, he couldn't compel her to share her feelings with him, so he returned the folder to her.

With a curt nod, she rose. He reached out to take her wrist, and she turned back to him, meeting his gaze.

"I'll make the ten-thousand-dollar donation, Alessandra. I'll do it anonymously so they'll never know you had anything to do with it."

Her eyes betrayed nothing. They were steady and still, penetrative—like she was searching for some way into his soul. Since she wasn't going to get more than he was willing to give, he released her wrist.

She lifted her head like she was going to say something but then turned and slipped from the room.

Damn woman. Every time he might have a read on her, she did something unpredictable. After this afternoon, he'd expected to have to push her to do the work, maybe use more inducements.

He'd donate a hundred thousand, but she didn't need to know that. After she mentioned the ranch, he'd done research. The program exposed patients to animals as a way to encourage them to open up in counseling. It sounded a little far-fetched, but the data showed a high rate of success. He'd also looked at the financials of the ranch. Although solvent, more money would allow them to take on more clients. He'd request they fix the fence first and to earmark the rest of the money for the counseling services.

Now that the JEAP file was advancing, he could start looking at some other issues he'd delegated. First, he'd tackle his email. He glanced at the screen. Yep, he'd have plenty of work to occupy him.

****

A knock pulled him from his work. Alessandra stood at the doorway, looking uncertain. He beckoned her in, but she didn't move.

"I just wanted to let you know that it's nine and I've made some dinner. Would you like some, or should I wrap it up, and you might eat it later?"

Chuckling, he stood. "It seems you're not the only one who can't tell time. I'll join you, unless you've already eaten?"

Shaking her head, she watched him as he crossed the room. "I made stir-fry." She spoke tentatively. "I hope that was okay."

As they walked to the kitchen, the scents assailed him. "I'm pleased you made yourself at home, but you needn't cook for me. I could've heated some pizza."

She stopped just short of the kitchen. "Are you displeased?"

"Not at all, but I didn't bring you here to cook for me."

That seemed to appease her, and she gestured for him to sit at the dining room table while she heaped the food onto the plates. She served his food with a beer.

"Would you like one yourself?"

After a moment's contemplation, she shook her

head. "Thank you, but I still feel...odd. I don't trust myself right now."

He waited until she returned with her plate of food before he took his first bite. "This is fantastic."

"You sound surprised."

"No, not surprised, grateful."

"Grateful I'm not trying to poison you?"

Unable to help himself, he laughed. "Am I so terrible?"

She paused, then finally gave him a tremulous smile. "When I was attached to the ceiling, I might have thought a few nasty things."

"About that—"

"But then you held me." She continued as if she hadn't heard him. "You didn't leave me alone."

"You were in no state to be left to your own devices. I owed you that and more." Debating whether to reach out and take her hand, he ruthlessly tamped down the urge. He searched for the next words. "I think we should talk about what happened."

She frowned at him. "We've already done that, and I don't want to be reminded. You were teaching me a lesson. I'm a quick study, and you made your point very effectively."

"Or not. I told you we needed to establish protocols. Soft limits, hard limits, wish lists."

"Why would we bother to do that?"

"Before we scene again, we need to be clear about boundaries."

Her brow furrowed. "Are we?"

"Are we what?"

"Going to scene again." Her eyes were inky pools, wide with question. "I thought this entire farce was just one big scene for you and I'm the butt of the joke."

His first instinct was to reprimand her, but he held his tongue. Were they in perpetual play? Had this all started the moment he'd seen her at Kink, and they were just going along with it? When she suddenly put down her fork, he scowled. "You haven't finished your dinner."

She bowed her head. "I lost my appetite."

"Well, find it." He snapped out the command.

She raised her hand but hovered over the fork. Just when it looked like she might pick it up, her hand dropped listlessly to the table. "I'm sorry, Master. I can't do it."

"Then you can leave the table."

"But I—"

"Go to bed, Alessandra."

Her head snapped up. "It's only nine thirty, and I need to clean the kitchen."

"I'll clean the kitchen. You go to bed." When she began to speak, he raised his hand. "Now, before I lose my patience."

"Yes, Master." Her tone made it clear what she thought of his order, but she rose and headed toward the bathroom.

He took another few bites of food, but his own appetite had waned. The food had been flavorful and colorful, full of healthy nutrition. It'd been better than anything he could've put together himself, although he was an adequate cook. He just didn't spend a lot of time in the kitchen because he lived alone, and what was the point of cooking for one?

Her bedroom door closed, and he rose from the table. Cleanup only took a few minutes as she'd been very efficient and made little mess. He grabbed his beer and headed into the living room. No game on, but the national news was beginning. Not exactly a stimulating evening, but he wasn't going to go back to the office, and he wasn't going to beg Alessandra to join him. Hadn't he just sent her away? Already, he missed her company. It frustrated him, knowing she was steps away and he could do nothing about it. He had a beautiful woman in his condo, and he wasn't getting any.

His own damn fault. She'd offered, and he'd refused.

The news was unremarkable and much of it depressingly bad. One positive story was about a possible medical breakthrough in the fight against cancer, but it'd be years before it might see fruition. What was the point of the story? Flipping off the television, he turned off the lights. He hadn't closed the drapes, so the lights from the nearby buildings and streetlamps filtered into the room, throwing an eerie, yellow-and-pink, neon glow. They called it light pollution, but he was used to it. He thrived being in the center of the city, living off the vitality, the energy.

He was contemplating going to bed when Alessandra's door creaked open. Figuring she was heading to the bathroom, he was about to call out. Once he realized she was heading for the front door, he became intrigued. She opened it, and a heartbeat too late, he realized she'd fled.

Fast as lightning, he was up and heading for the door. By the time he hit the corridor, she was nowhere in sight. He strode to the stairs and listened, not hearing any footfalls. Maybe she took the elevator? The door down at lobby level closed. Hightailing it down the stairs, he emerged in the main foyer.

He made it to the lobby just as Alessandra requested the security guard to call her a taxi. "That won't be necessary, Tarah, as Ms. Soriano will come back upstairs with me."

Alessandra whirled, gasped, and pressed her fingers to her lips. She turned back to the concierge. "Please, Tarah, I need a taxi."

He closed the distance and reached for Alessandra's wrist. "Not necessary, Tarah, but thank you."

Tarah eyed them both warily, clearly torn. When he tugged on Alessandra's wrist and she balked, Tarah stepped forward. "Mr. MacLean, sir, I have to ask you to desist."

The steel in her voice brought him up short. *Damn.* What must this look like to her? Alessandra was standing in the lobby asking for a cab, wearing flannel pajamas and wool socks. He was physically manhandling her.

When he released her wrist, she reflexively reached with her other hand to rub it. Inhaling deeply, he tried to reason with her. "Alessandra, if you would come back upstairs with me, perhaps you can put on clothes and shoes before you try to leave again."

Tarah drew herself up to her full height, only a couple of inches taller than Alessandra. "Ms. Soriano, are you being held against your will?"

He frowned.

Alessandra gasped, evidently realizing the seriousness of the situation. She took a breath. "I am not being held against my will, Tarah, and silly of me to go out without shoes and a coat. I…" She struggled to come up with some kind of explanation for her behavior.

"Ms. Soriano just wanted to get some night air. I'll take her out on the balcony once we're upstairs. If she still wants to come out after that, we'll let you know."

Tarah didn't look convinced. "If he's hurting you—"

"That's enough, Tarah. Ms. Soriano is not—"

"I don't care if you try to get me fired, Mr. MacLean—I have to say something." She looked into Alessandra's eyes. "There are places you can go. People you can talk to."

Silence descended. Smith held his breath, waiting for Alessandra to act. This was her chance. If she wanted to leave, then this was her out. Panic encroached as he rifled through all his options. He didn't have many because if she wanted to go to a shelter, he could do nothing about it.

He sighed. "Ms. Soriano can stay down here with you, Tarah. I'll go upstairs and pack a bag for her and bring her some shoes." He took a step away even as his heart broke.

"No."

Alessandra's voice was so soft he might have imagined it.

Then she pressed a hand to Tarah's arm. "Thank you for caring. I am not being abused, nor am I being held against my will." She laughed, but the sound was more choked. "I was just being silly, you know? Just a silly minor disagreement." She turned to Smith. "I'll go back upstairs with Mr. MacLean, and we'll call it a night."

Tarah did not look convinced, instead reaching for a business card. "Call this number if you change your mind." She glared at Smith. "He doesn't have the right to lay a finger on you without your permission."

That's right, the only other time Tarah saw Alessandra had been the night he brought her back after being at Kink. "I didn't drug her, Tarah, or get her drunk."

Alessandra groaned, closing her eyes. When she opened them, they were wide and bright. "What happened the other night—that was on me. Mr. MacLean has never been anything but solicitous and kind." She took the card. "I'll call if I need help."

Tarah appeared to be suppressing a snort, and she gave a curt nod.

Smith held out his hand, and Alessandra placed hers in his grasp. She let him guide her to the elevator where they rode up in silence. She entered before him and was halfway to her room before he had the chance to lock the deadbolt. "Alessandra?"

She didn't stop.

He covered the distance in three strides and barred her entrance to her room. "We're going to talk about this."

She looked up at him, then started to rain blows onto his chest.

Her hands were tight little fists, and she packed a punch. Utterly confused, he let her continue for a few moments before he reached for her wrists to stop her. She continued to try to hit him, so he spun her around, wrapping his arms around her and pinning her arms to her sides.

Her knees gave way, and she caught him off

balance, almost dragging them to the ground.

She let out one long, keening wail like a woman in the throes of intense grief.

What the hell? "Alessandra," he hissed into her ear. "This room isn't soundproofed."

She didn't respond as she continued to emit an otherworldly sound.

Having no other option, he scooped her into his arms and carried her to the dungeon. She was rigid in his arms, and as soon as he placed her on the bed, she was scrambling up and heading for the door. He was quicker and slammed it before she could get to it.

"You don't understand." The wail had become a howl of anguish. "They'll kill her if I'm not there. It's Wednesday night. I have to be there on Wednesday night, or they'll kill her."

Had he heard her correctly? "If you're not there, they'll *kill* someone? Jesus, Alessandra, you're not making any sense."

She whirled on him, eyes pleading. "Please, it's just for a few hours. I'll come back, I promise. I just have to go for a few hours. Then I'll come back."

"Well, if it's so fucking important, I'll take you."

Her eyes went wide and wild with fright. "You can't." She clung to his shirt. "You don't understand. I have to go by myself. No one knows I go. No one knows, and I'll never say anything. I go and she lives. I don't and she dies."

"You were willing to walk out of here in pajamas and socks to go somewhere in the dead of night? What the fuck is going on?"

"If she dies, it's on you." She pounded her fist on his chest—just once this time—then whirled away from him. "Maybe if I call..." She let out a howl of frustration.

Smith pulled his phone from his pocket. "Here's the phone, Alessandra. Call whomever you want."

Then, as if she were a balloon and all the air had been let out, she deflated. She dropped to the bed and clutched her head in her hands. The tears started. Her sobs echoed around the room.

He shook his head, rocked on his heels. Finally, he moved to the closet and pulled out jeans, a sweater, and some running shoes. He dropped them on the bed next to her. "I'll give you cab fare to wherever you want to go. Get dressed, and I'll call the taxi."

She didn't move, didn't even acknowledge he'd spoken. Instead, her gut-wrenching cries continued.

Well, what the fuck was he supposed to do now? Since he didn't know what was wrong, he as shit sure didn't know how to fix it. He dropped to the bed next to her. Awkwardly, he put his arm around her shoulders.

Time spun out until, finally, her sobs abated. Eventually she wound down to just sniffles. "I want to go to bed." Her whisper was that of a broken soul. "Please let me go to bed."

"Fine." He cringed at the abruptness of his tone. What he wanted was an explanation, but it looked like he wasn't going to get that. "Why don't we go to your room, and you can give me the pajamas?"

She rose, then stripped them off right in front of him. Leaving them on the floor where they had dropped, she whispered, "I'm taking the socks," then left the room.

Smith scooped the pajamas up and put them in the clothes hamper. He'd bought several other pairs, so not a big deal.

He stripped himself and crawled into bed. What had just happened?

Chapter Fifteen

When he put her clothes in her room around seven, Alessandra had been sleeping soundly. He sighed as he glanced at his watch. That'd been over four hours ago. After answering an urgent email, he headed from his home office to her bedroom.

He knocked, but no answer came. He cracked the door open. The room was still dark. "Alessandra?"

She barely stirred.

"Alessandra." This time, not a question.

She finally stirred. Opening her eyes, she shielded them from the harshness of the overhead light he had flipped on. "What time is it?" Her voice was muted and scratchy.

He banked down the urge to tell her to check her watch. "Time for you to come and eat."

Shifting the hand that blocked the light, she covered her eyes before falling back to the bed. "I'm not hungry...I don't feel well."

"Are you sick?" He could've injected some concern in his voice, but annoyance was at the forefront.

She took a breath. "I don't think so, but I don't feel well. Could you just let me sleep?"

The sound of her tremulous voice hit him in the gut. He'd replayed the scene from last night over and over, but to no avail. He still had no idea what'd happened. "I'm making some soup," he said decisively. "If you come out and eat it, then you can"—he made a sweeping motion she couldn't see—"wallow in here all day."

"I'm not wallowing." Her voice was quiet, but a hint of petulance pervaded. "I just want to be left alone."

"Well, that's not going to happen. If I have to, I'll force-feed you."

That had her rolling onto her side. She was almost up to a sitting position before she paused. "Do you think you can give me some privacy?" She glanced up at him. "I'm not wearing any clothes."

As if he didn't know.

He yielded. "No problem. You do what you have to do. I'm serving the soup in twenty minutes." With that, he left. He searched his cupboards until he located a can of soup. Following the instructions on the label, he added water and then set the pot on the stove. He dug out saltine crackers and put the kettle on for tea. He did not, for one moment, believe she was physically ill. However, her physical distress was undoubtedly caused by her emotional crisis last night.

When she passed the kitchen heading to the bathroom, he glimpsed enough to see she'd put on the clothes he'd set out for her. He'd gone for jeans and a turtleneck, thinking they might go out later in the afternoon. He doubted that would happen now.

At the appointed minute, she slid into a kitchen chair. She gave him the briefest of thanks when he put the food in front of her.

He sat across from her and watched her while he waited for the soup and tea to cool.

Alessandra reached out to snag a cracker and ate it mechanically, as if by rote.

"I was thinking about us going out for a walk later today."

She glanced at him. "You can go ahead, but I'm going back to bed."

"If I go alone, then you'll have to strip and return the clothes."

She only shrugged.

"I think you need the exercise. Unless you would prefer to go swimming…"

The look she shot him told him exactly what she thought of that suggestion. Feeling enough time had passed, he tried the soup, finding it the perfect temperature. He was more than halfway finished before she ventured to take her first spoonful. "Is it to your liking?"

She looked at him warily. "It's chicken noodle soup from a can, so yeah, it's to my liking. You could feed me sawdust right now, and that'd be to my liking."

"Alessandra—"

She stood up and pulled the hem of her turtleneck from the jeans.

"What are you doing?"

"Stripping, you fuck, so I can go back to bed."

Before he had a chance to argue, she did exactly that. In just her undergarments and socks, she stalked back into her room and slammed the door. Unperturbed, he finished his soup and then cleaned up. He took her clothes, folded them carefully, and put them back in the dungeon. Instead of going for a walk, he took his laptop out to the balcony and sat in the light, working until the sun dipped.

As the temperature dropped, he went back into the condo. As he found no sign Alessandra had done anything, he went to her room. Not bothering to knock, he opened the door.

In the dark, she was huddled under a pile of blankets with her nose at her e-reader.

Good thing he got the function that allowed it to be read in low—or no—light. He suppressed the urge to sigh. "Good book?"

She glanced up at him, blinking. "Yes, thank you for asking."

"You're feeling better."

She blinked again. "Yes, thank you for asking."

"Will you be joining me for dinner?"

She hesitated. "Yes, thank you for asking."

"One hour," he barked out, then left the room, all but slamming the door. Truth be told, he wasn't in the mood to cook. He pulled out the flyer for the local Greek restaurant and placed an order. If Alessandra didn't like what he selected for her, then it was her own fucking fault.

Fuck. She'd truly looked awful. Sallow with a gray pallor, eyes deep and haunted. Should he have let her go out last night? Where in the hell had she planned to go wearing only socks and pajamas? She hadn't even asked him for clothes, just said she wanted to go as she was.

Crazy woman.

He startled at the knock on the door. Pulling out more than enough to cover the bill, he handed over the money and brought the food into the condo. It smelled delicious, and after having sorted out the spread, he knocked on Alessandra's door. "The food is here. Come out so you can eat while it's hot."

He heard something muffled, which he chose to interpret as assent. He sat at the table and was about to begin when she joined him.

Her nose was in the air as if she were deigning to grace him with her presence, all the while wearing only a bra, panties, and socks.

"I'll go get you some clothes," he offered.

"Don't bother. This won't take very long." Then, as if it were perfectly normal to eat while scantily clad, she dug into her food.

Since she showed more interest in said food than she had with the soup, he let it go.

She ate everything on her plate. "May I clean up the dishes?"

"Not necessary. Would you like to watch a movie this evening?"

She shot him a look that was pure venom. "I would like to go back to my room."

She would be shitty company anyway, so he waved her off.

This time, she didn't strive for dignity. She scrambled away as fast as she could.

As she passed, he saw her goose bumps. Well, served her right. He would've given her clothes, but her obstinacy prevented it.

He cleaned up the remnants of the meal and headed back to his office. Might as well put in another few hours before he went to bed.

After a few hours, though, he admitted his concentration was shot. He kept thinking about the enigmatic woman in his spare room. Going to his bedroom, he stripped and tossed his clothes into the hamper. Although barely ten, it felt like three in the morning. Often he'd stay up working until late, pushing himself so he wouldn't have to face the fact he was lonely. A month with Alessandra had promised companionship with a woman who was whip-smart.

Then he pushed aside those thoughts and reviewed all the things needing to be done the next day. The list was getting longer since he'd spent time on Alessandra that hadn't been planned for. She was proving to be a distraction and not in a good way.

He could cut her loose. Get her a place to live, give her an allowance, and walk away. That was what he planned to do in twenty-six days anyway.

He wouldn't. She might be a tough nut to crack, but crack she would. He was going to put together the events in her life since the night they'd met. If it took him an entire month, he'd piece together this jigsaw puzzle.

An image of her flashed in his mind—Alessandra, shackled, hanging from the ceiling, her beautiful thighs forced apart by the spreader bar. God, she'd looked lovely. When he walked around her, it'd taken a lot of self-control to look and not touch. When he stood behind her and looked at her perfect ass, he'd wanted to take her right then and there. Maybe that was where he'd gone wrong—he'd been so obsessed with getting in her that he missed what was going on with her. No, he wouldn't let the end ruin what'd been an interesting journey. He liked the way her mind worked, and their verbal sparring had been fun.

Bilbo? Hobbit? The woman had a wicked sense of humor.

His cock twitched. The way she'd looked when he

laid her across his bed and masturbated her with a dildo and a vibe. *Ha*, he'd given her three orgasms in rapid succession. She'd been flushed and panting, begging him to stop, and she'd then allowed herself to have that ultimate climax. Had he ever seen anything so magnificent? If he had, he couldn't remember it.

He used one hand to stroke his cock while the other grazed his balls. What would it be like to have her touch him? Have her lips envelop him? She'd be good, if only because she'd want to please him.

Using his precum as lubricant, he slicked his shaft. His pace increased as he thought about how beautiful she looked, all creamy skin contrasting with her black hair, those chocolate brown eyes with flecks of gold, the lean and trim body. He was even getting accustomed to the choppy haircut. The look was growing on him.

Without much work, his balls drew up, and he let go.

Chapter Sixteen

She'd done it again. Slept all day and now she lay wide-awake at night. This was all Smith's fault. If he'd just let her go last night, then she wouldn't have been so worried. If she hadn't been so worried, then she would've slept last night. If she'd slept last night, then she wouldn't have needed to sleep during the day today.

And on it went.

Surely they wouldn't hurt Denise because Allie hadn't shown up last night. She hadn't called, but they might think she was sick, right? Maybe they'd think she had the flu or something. Maybe they wouldn't even notice her absence.

She scoffed. Her absence would be noted, and when she returned, they'd punish her for the transgression. There'd be hell to pay, and there'd be retribution—of that, she had no doubt. So where did that leave her? Naked, cold, and scared. She could've told Smith, of course, but *that* cost would've been even higher. He would've tossed her out on her ass with only pajamas and socks and without a second thought. If her own behavior disgusted her, how would he feel?

He'll never find out.

A vow she intended to keep.

Smith MacLean.

She closed her eyes and pressed them with the heels of her hands. She should be angry with him. Yes, damn it, she should be livid with him. He'd pushed her physically and emotionally, forcing her again to face her weaknesses. His obsession with her past was chasing the demons further and further to the fore. How easy would it be to tell him the truth? Tell him why she ran. Tell him what she'd done to survive.

Not his business. If she gave in even an inch, he'd take more than a mile. He'd demand complete and total surrender. The problem was she wanted to surrender, wanted to give herself over to him. And that scared her more than anything—perhaps even more than the truth.

She'd hold herself apart until the month was over. Protect herself and fight the good fight to hold on to whatever dignity remained.

Reaching for her wrist, she touched the watch like a talisman. If he knew her well enough to pick something so intimate, it stood to reason he'd eventually ferret out the truth. Letting out a long sigh, she reached for the bedside lamp to turn it on. The watch confirmed the witching hour had come and gone.

Sleep was an impossibility, so she got up and went to the computer to write again. Since arriving back at the condo, she hadn't found the right time to ask Smith for the trash bag of her things, and she hoped he hadn't thrown them out. Hidden among the books was her journal. Nothing incriminating in there, just some odd thoughts and observations about what she'd seen over the past six months. She'd also recorded ideas about how the problems might be solved. Pie-in-the-sky kind of solutions.

Now she needed to put down the thoughts swirling around in her head. Again, nothing incriminating, but still… How had she come to this?

Nothing.

No words were forthcoming.

She was getting nowhere. Her gut churned with stress, and her head hurt from worry. Not a stretch when she told him she hadn't been feeling well.

A memory flashed. The JEAP counselors were available twenty-four seven. She quickly contemplated various potential scenarios and settled on one that might suit this hour. Grabbing the file folder, a pad of paper, and a pen, she settled cross-legged on the bed, pulling a blanket over her shoulders. With nimble fingers, she dialed the number and let out a quick breath before pressing send.

Answered on the second ring. "Hello, this is Marianne, and you've reached Johnson Employee Assistance Program. How can I help you tonight?"

Allie swallowed. Easy to pretend to be nervous because she was. "Hi, Marianne, my name is Lucinda. I work for Triptych Technologies. I got a pamphlet from them telling me about you guys. This is private, right? I mean, I don't want my boss to know I've called."

"Lucinda, you have nothing to worry about. We will notify human resources someone is using our services, but they have no way of knowing it's you. Now, if it's okay with you, I'd like to open a file. I need to ask you a few questions. Is that all right?"

She nodded, even though Marianne couldn't see her. Then she cleared her throat. "Yes, that would be fine."

"We are a crisis line. Are you or anyone around you in a situation requiring immediate counseling or assistance?"

"Uh...no."

"Great, thank you for telling me that." The woman's voice was cheerful yet soothing. "May I ask you some questions now?"

"Yes, thank you."

Marianne took her through a series of noninvasive questions to verify she worked for the company. At the end, she asked the question Allie had been both dreading and anticipating.

"And why are you calling today?"

"My husband lost his job a month ago, and things have been tough. I mean, financially we're probably okay for another few weeks because we have some savings and I work for a great company. I make good money, and that makes him mad. Everything makes him mad."

"Okay, Lucinda, it sounds like you're in a tough situation. I'm glad you called, and I want to get you help. We have several things we can do. I have a counselor working tonight if you need to talk. He's a good guy, I promise you. Also, we can arrange for a referral so you can speak to someone in person." She paused. "I think that's important because this must really worry you."

Allie smiled, then schooled her features. "I hope it's okay that I called."

"That's why we're here, Lucinda, anytime. Even after the referral, if you're in crisis, you can always call."

"I appreciate that," Allie said quietly. "I'd like to speak to someone now, and I will take the referral."

"Okay, let's get started."

Within fifteen minutes, she had her referral with the name of a therapist just down the road from her fictitious address. Then she was transferred to Ian.

"I understand from Marianne that you're having a tough time these days. What can you tell me about it?"

Allie repeated the story pretty much verbatim.

"You said your husband isn't dealing with it very well, which is understandable. Is he taking out his anger on you or the kids?" Lucinda had two young children.

"No, well, maybe. He's been making snide comments about me and my work. I work really hard, and it's important to me."

"So he's not being…abusive?"

"Oh no," she rushed to assure him. "He'd never hurt me or the kids. It's just I want to be supportive but don't know how. Do I push him to find another job? Should I just be a shoulder for him to lean on?"

Ian took her through more questions, and although he never told her what to do, he guided her to some answers on her own, based on her *relationship* with her husband.

"Now, Lucinda, are you going to be okay tonight?"

"I think I will be, Ian. Thank you for your help. I've got that appointment with the counselor. Hopefully, things will work out."

"We're here to help you if you need it."

Unable to help herself, she smiled. "Thank you, I appreciate it. I should be able to sleep for the rest of the night."

Disconnecting the call, she picked up her pen and furiously scribbled notes. She'd remember if she spoke to Ian or Marianne in a future call. Both had been empathetic and understanding, not making her feel silly for having called in the middle of the night.

By the time she finished her notes, her eyelids were

drooping. She still had the report to write, but it'd keep. Deciding on a quick trip to the bathroom, she padded her way on socked feet across the condo. Her pale reflection was stark in the harsh lights of the bathroom. Hardly surprising since—she glanced at her watch— two in the morning had come and gone. Although she was fatigued, she was also restless. How was she going to fall asleep?

She opened the door, and her heart jumped. Smith stood on the other side.

Immediately, he snagged her chin and eased her face up toward him. "Are you all right?"

She frowned. "I had to go to the bathroom, hardly cause for concern."

He let go. "I just thought maybe you needed something."

You.

"Stay where you are." He issued the order, then went into the bathroom.

Baffled, she did as bade, belatedly realizing Smith had been naked. She replayed that moment in her mind.

His blond hair had been ruffled, his eyes sleepy. His body, however, was something to behold. The hair that lightly dusted his chest was slightly darker than that on his head. Muscles in both his arms and abs. He was a man who took pride in his body and worked out. Even naked, he had a commanding presence. Oh, and he was hung like a horse.

Despite herself, she giggled. She'd always wondered about the expression, and now she knew what they'd been talking about. Smith would probably make very good money at a strip club…if his business empire ever fell on hard times.

"What's so funny?"

Okay, look Smith in the eyes—those amazing eyes—so I don't sneak another peek at his cock. Lying would only get her in trouble, so she opted for the truth. "I think you're hung like a horse, Master."

Twin spots of color crossed his high cheekbones. He blinked, and then his eyes narrowed. "That's very impertinent, Alessandra."

She shrugged. "I guess I'm feeling impertinent."

"Have you slept?" A demand.

Shaking her head, she grinned impudently. "Nope. Couldn't."

"Did you break into the liquor cabinet?"

Now her humor fled. "I might be a little giddy, Master, but I'm not drunk. I know what the consequences would be, and I'd never be that foolish."

"Glad to hear it." He spoke the words smoothly, as if he hadn't just insulted her. "You lied to me."

She shook her head violently. "I swear I didn't touch the booze. You can smell my breath. I'll do a breathalyzer."

"That wasn't what I was referring to."

Squinting, she tried to discern what he was saying. "What did I do?" Confusing. She always seemed to be stepping in it with him.

"I asked if you might need something, and you answered in the negative."

"Actually, if you want to be accurate, I didn't answer at all. You told me to stay here." She paused. "I did, by the way. Obey you, I mean."

Smith nodded solemnly. "So I'll ask the question, and I expect the truth. Do you need something?"

She couldn't lie to him. Didn't want to lie. "I want

153

my Master."

Surprise flittered across his face, quickly replaced by something darker. Something intense and a little bit frightening. "How do you want me?"

"Anyway I can get." The words spilled out before she had time to consider them. She was heading toward the deep end of the pool and might, at any moment, drown. She knew how to swim, but these were shark-infested waters. He might just pull her down for the kill.

"It's two in the morning." He wiped his hand up and down his face vigorously. "The question is will you feel the same way in the morning, or will you have regrets?"

"My regrets will come if I don't tell you the truth." *Please believe me.* "Two at night or two in the afternoon, it doesn't matter. I want, hell, I *need* you."

A slow sardonic smile flitted across his face. "At last, we're in agreement about something." He paused and stared at her. "The question is what are we going to do about it?"

Attempting for nonchalance while every nerve ending came to high alert, she shrugged. Would he? His choices were to send her away or invite her in. She knew what her choice would be if he asked her.

"You're eager for this, aren't you, my little one?"

Damn her inability to hide anything. Or maybe she should be thankful, because it meant she might get what she wanted. "Please." She didn't bother to hide the need in her voice. "Don't send me back to my room alone."

His hand snaked out to grasp her wrist, his long fingers easily encircling it. He pressed two fingers against her wrist and appeared to count. "Your pulse is strong."

"I'm not going to fight." Her heart kicked into overdrive with the contact. "I'll take whatever you're willing to give."

He chuckled. "You might come to regret that offer."

"Never." Of this, she was sure. "There's nothing you can do to me that'd be worse than sending me back there without you."

He tugged gently on her wrist, and she followed without hesitation. The dungeon was dark, so he flipped on the torches. The light was low, casting shadows across the room.

"What I really want to do is take my time with you, but I'm not sure that'll work."

For the first time, her gaze dropped so she could ogle his crotch. *Ah*, that's why slow might be a problem for him. Looking up into his eyes, she waited for the signal. At his quick nod she dropped to her knees. She'd wanted this, had waited for this, but she wanted to make it good for him.

First she licked his length, paying special attention to the vein running along the underside. A drop of precum already leaked, and she swiped it with her tongue. The salty taste hit her tongue, and she swirled the tip in his slit.

He moaned.

She took his head in her mouth, sucking gently. An intimacy suffused this gesture where she was offering up herself even as she was pleasing him. With every pass, she took him farther and farther into her mouth, his musky scent filling her nose and overwhelming her senses.

He groaned.

"Fuck this." He brusquely snagged her cheeks. In one quick motion, he flexed his hips and plunged into her mouth.

She couldn't help it—when his cock pressed against the back of her throat, she gagged.

"Breathe through your nose, Alessandra." He pulled out just a bit.

Hard to take breaths through her nose because snot filled it, going with her watering eyes, but she did her best.

Once her breathing normalized, he began a slower, but no less demanding, pace.

Slowly, inch by aching inch, she took him in. Then he started to fuck her face, and she lost all sense of balance, all sense of time, and all sense of place. All that mattered was Smith and what she could do to him. What she could do for him. When his release finally came, she was ready and swallowed hungrily, almost greedily. This was something she could do to show how she really felt. Proof she was willing to give herself over to him.

As his cock shrank, she gave his balls a brief squeeze for good measure.

"That was good, Alessandra." A hitch in his voice. "You did very well, my little one."

"Thank you, Master, you do me a great honor to let me service you." And it meant something to her because his rejection just days ago had stung. Now, as she pressed her face against his hip and snuggled against his pubic hairs, he rested his hand on her head.

"Stand."

With both grace and speed, she rose.

"Strip."

An edge to his voice advised her to move swiftly and efficiently. Since she wore only bra, panties, and socks, she dispatched them quickly and presented herself.

"You're a little too thin, Alessandra. I'd like to see you gain about five or ten pounds over the next month."

She opened her mouth to argue and then closed it again, looking down at her body. Losing those fifteen pounds hadn't been kind to her as she'd been slender to begin with. Most women didn't want to put on weight, but there might be benefits.

"I'm going to watch your food intake and exercise carefully over the next month, and we'll see where you get to. About a pound or two a week and I'll be happy."

Nutritious food had been one of the reasons she'd yielded to his demand she come here with him. "I'd appreciate your guidance, Master."

"That's my good little one. Now go lie on the bed, legs open."

Heat rushed to her core as her body anticipated pleasure. She hadn't thought herself to be so lucky. Now she'd brought him to orgasm, she assumed he'd send her back to her room. Lying on the middle of the bed, she placed a pillow behind her head.

"Close your eyes."

Since he coaxed rather than ordered, she obeyed. When the mattress dipped, she smiled. When he pulled back her nether lips, she sighed. When he nipped her engorged clit, she screamed.

"It's a good thing they soundproofed the room." Amusement laced his voice.

"Sir is very good at what he does." She said it through gritted teeth, her voice breathy. Then he laved her, and all rational thought fled from her mind. Heat suffused her, and sweat broke out on her brow. She hadn't been kidding when she'd complimented him— he was definitely proficient. Desire strummed through her blood, and she gave in to the sensations he elicited. With each swipe, each pass, her resolve weakened.

"Give in, Alessandra."

She greedily took that permission and did exactly that. Easy to yield to the pleasure. The crest was a gentle one, the waves coming in steady beats. Her breath hitched, but she didn't lose control.

He ruthlessly thrust her knees up and out, flexing her hips, and then he drove into her.

She snapped open startled eyes to face dark-blue ones staring back. She hadn't expected him to recover so quickly, but this was Smith, and she should know by now to expect the unexpected.

He urged her higher, using his hips to seat himself fully. Then he began to piston.

She struggled against the demanding rhythm, with it, and then against it again. His hips snapped as he kept slamming into her. Her nerves fried, singed, and flamed. Clawing at his back, she searched for purchase and found none as his back was smooth and sweat-slicked.

"Give in." He issued the demand as he pressed her thighs even farther apart.

She was afraid he might dislocate a hip, but he wasn't hurting her, simply pushing her higher. When she crested, it was hard and fast. She clamped down around him, and when he thrust his tongue into her mouth, she sucked, nipped, and parried, all at the same time.

Unrelentingly, the next orgasm ripped through her, not waiting for his command. Her eyes rolled back in her head as she shut them against the onslaught. His hands were rough, touching—demanding one moment and then gentle, soothing, relaxing the next. Every nerve in her body sang as she acquiesced both to his demand and the needs of her body. Giving in meant leaving the confines of her dreary existence and moving into another realm altogether. A place where pleasure reigned supreme and misery was banished, if only for that moment.

"One more."

He gave the order, ignoring her groan of desperation. Apparently he liked things in fours, so she endured more thrusts. She was sore, but his unrelenting torment barraged her senses and pushed her higher and higher. When he ground against her clit, however, she was a goner. This was the most terrifying orgasm, and its intensity robbed her of all breath. He held himself still and then collapsed against her, assuring her that he'd climaxed as well. She breathed a sigh of relief.

"Jesus Christ." He whispered it harshly in her ear.

She returned the sentiment wholeheartedly. When he went to roll off her, she wrapped her legs around his thighs and held her arms around his neck. "Just a minute more," she begged. "Just stay with me a minute more."

He chuckled. "And here I was afraid I'd broken you."

"On the contrary—" She pressed a kiss to his neck. "—I think you might have fixed me."

Chapter Seventeen

Allie awoke disoriented. The room was completely dark, no night sky overhead to illuminate the space. She was in the dungeon. When she reached for Smith, his place was empty and cold. So she'd been alone for a while. Groping for the bedside lamp, she nearly knocked it over before switching it on.

The room was eerie with just the single bulb to illuminate it. Still, she rose from the bed and walked to the wall of torture. At least, that was what she called it. She pressed her hands against the leather of the whip and the flogger. Lazily, she drew a finger along the cold rubber of the various dildos and plastic of the vibrators, remembering how relentlessly he'd pleasured her. She lovingly grazed her knuckles to the handcuffs, imagining how it would feel to be bound at his mercy. Would he push her into a different realm? A world where she existed only for him and he for her?

Folly. She was a diversion for him—something to keep him amused for a month. A plaything to be brought out when convenient and shut away when not.

Pulling away from morose thoughts, she scooped up her pajamas and headed for the shower. A good twenty minutes in the multi-head sprayer was a pure joy she wouldn't take for granted.

Twenty-five more days.

Shrugging on a silk dressing gown after drying

herself, she chanced another glance in the mirror. She saw a well-rested and sated woman—which she was. According to her watch, she'd slept for almost eight straight hours. Decadent, to sleep in sturdy arms that protected as well as comforted. That luxury she wasn't used to and would have to make sure she didn't get addicted to.

Walking through the apartment to her room, she noticed the quiet. Smith was probably in his office. She'd make sandwiches for lunch and surprise him around noon. Earlier she'd spotted a tin of shrimp in the pantry. Add mayonnaise, hot sauce, and lettuce, and she could make a decent sandwich. The kitchen had few provisions, just lots of single-serve meals. She'd have to ask for permission to either go to the grocery store or maybe place an order for supplies from one of the companies that delivered. She really hated shopping, even for groceries, so those services were a godsend.

Nice, a pile of clothes sat on her bed. Jeans, a blouse, and a cardigan, probably in case she should feel cold. A pair of socks anchored a sheet of paper. She picked it up.

Stunned, her knees buckled, and she abruptly sat on the bed.

Smith had to go out for the day, an emergency with one of his companies that had to be dealt with in person.

She should eat whatever she wanted, do whatever she wanted. Even a key in case she wanted to go swimming. Distractedly, she noted the bathing suit was on the desk.

Surging to her feet, she all but ripped the gown from her body and slid into the underwear and bra in record time, pulled on her jeans and blouse. *Hmm*, what could she take with her, and what would she have to leave? There'd been a knapsack and suitcase delivered with the clothes. Did she dare fill them, or would it be too noticeable when she slipped from the building? Maybe she could go out through the garage to attract less attention.

Reaching for the sweater, she spotted the watch on her wrist. The breath in her lungs whooshed out. He'd offered his trust, and she was about to betray it. He'd known when he left this morning her first instinct would be to run. Maybe he even wanted her to run. Maybe after yesterday he'd decided she was more hassle than she was worth.

Yet if pressed, she'd say the opposite. They'd come to a new understanding the previous night, finding a place where they could be comfortable with each other.

And then the minor matter of JEAP still existed. She'd given her word she'd finish the project. He'd made it the only way to secure the funding for Healing Horses Ranch.

Despondency threatened to overwhelm her. They really did need some repairs to the fence, but Kennedy would never spend money on anything so frivolous if patients were in need of counseling. Maybe…maybe Smith might donate the money anyway?

Not likely. She dropped to the bed, leaned forward, and let her head droop even as tears formed. She was stuck. She was right where he wanted her—she could go and live with her conscience, or she could stay here and live by his rules.

Twenty-five days.

Time to enjoy the company of someone who wanted her for her and not for what she could give him. Time to be with someone who respected her intellect and not just her body.

The tears fell freely. He'd set her up. He could've dragged her out of bed and locked her in this room without clothes. But no, he had something far more sadistic in mind. He was leaving the decision up to her. She'd tried to flee once, so he had to know she was likely to do it again. Still, he'd left her.

"Fuck you, Smith! Fuck, fuck, fuck you!" She was bordering on hysteria as the sobs wracked her body. The indecision was literally pulling her in two. She wanted to rail against the Fates who'd brought her to this place.

One little decision. She'd made one little decision six months ago, and it still tore her apart—pushing her to the brink of insanity whenever she thought about it.

Without rational thought, she ran to the dungeon. She threw open the door, stepped inside, and slammed the door shut. There, in the dark, she let out a scream so primal it would've raised the hairs on the back of someone else's neck, had there been anyone to hear it.

Soundproof, he'd said.

The next scream was so intense it brought her to her knees. She dropped like a stone, heedless of the pain shooting up her thighs to her hips. She deserved the pain, deserved to feel grief so intense it ate her up inside. Her guts twisted, and nausea roiled.

One decision. One fucking little decision and four lives had been ruined. Four lives had been lost. Five, if one counted hers. But she didn't count. Her life meant nothing in the grand scheme of things. She was worth nothing, and her grief wouldn't—couldn't—fix things. Oh, Christ Jesus, the agony. Wrapping her arms around her waist, she let out another keening wail, wishing the earth would swallow her up whole and take her to purgatory. That was nothing less than she deserved.

Falling forward, she barely caught herself before face-planting on the hardwood floor. She rolled awkwardly onto her side, laying her cheek on the ground and pulling her knees to her chin, as if she could somehow hold on to the grief at the same time as trying to let go of it.

She'd told Smith if she let go, she'd fly apart. She'd been dead serious.

Time had no meaning when she fell into this abyss.

She didn't register temperature, sensation, discomfort, or any of those things that signaled to a human being a problem might exist.

And so she lay.

Eventually, she slept.

Chapter Eighteen

Smith glanced at his watch as surreptitiously as he could, tamping down his annoyance. One of the financial analysts he employed had played fast and loose with his recommendations to invest in a company that'd looked solid. Another advisor hadn't done his due diligence to discover the company had been in trouble. An infusion of cash from Smith's company had allowed the other company to limp along for another few months, but they hadn't made any changes in management, and the company had folded. Not so much the money he'd lost that annoyed him. Easy come, easy go. What hurt was thirty people were out of work when it hadn't been necessary. If he'd known about the issues, he would've gotten rid of the president and his minions and brought in his own people. He could've turned it around, as the company had a niche market but hadn't figured out how to exploit it.

Oh, and the fact that the financial analyst had been the president's cousin? The advisor had missed that as well.

He could've asked one of his managers to handle this, but it required a strong response with a light touch. He'd fired the analyst, of course, and then reprimanded the advisor for failing to perform due diligence. Smith had asked several people in various human resources departments in his companies to see if they could find work for those who now faced unemployment. It looked like they could slot several people in, but there just wasn't room for all of them. Smith ran a tight ship, so fat was always being trimmed.

What he had done was step in with generous severance packages. He'd keep it hidden that he'd personally been behind it, of course. Obviously, the president and his minions would receive none of his largesse.

Goddamn, his head ached. He'd been at this for more than seven hours, and every minute, his attention had been split.

Would Alessandra be there when he got home? He'd taken an unbelievable gamble today and was prepared to face the consequences. If he came home and found an empty apartment, he'd call Gage and Rielle and tell them he'd done his best, but Alessandra was beyond help. That she didn't want what they all were willing to give to her. That she knew they cared about her, but they were better off letting her go.

Did she know he cared about her? Not just her safety and welfare as he had in those first days, but something more. Something less definable. Something ethereal.

Goddamn it, when was this day going to end?

"I think we're good, Mr. MacLean."

Smith glanced at Chandra, the vice president of human resources. She'd been with him for over ten years, working her way up the ladder and steadfastly refusing to call him by his given name. He had four vice presidents, two of them women, and all were capable and competent. He'd been serious when he told Alessandra the company would survive the loss of the president, should it ever happen. Not that he planned to step in front of a bus or drop dead of a heart attack anytime soon.

"Thanks for this, Chandra. You've done a really good job."

"I just wish I could do more."

He nodded. "So do I, but sometimes we do what we can and cut our losses. Those workers will have a couple of months to find other work."

"That was very generous of you." Her gaze was steady. "More than you needed to be."

"I'm not without sympathy for those who did nothing to deserve what happened to them." Before Chandra could say more, he held up his hand. "Go home to the kids and your amazing husband. You can clean up the rest of this on Monday. Do not"—he pointed at her and shook his head—"come in on the weekend. I'm not planning to take this home, and you shouldn't either." She would, however. Just like he would, even if he had...diversions. Of course, if Alessandra had left, then he'd be happy for the distraction.

Chandra nodded and stood, scooping up her laptop and papers. "Good work today, boss."

She wouldn't call him Smith, but she'd call him boss.

He stood, also collecting his things. "I will probably be working from home for the next few weeks"—*fingers crossed*—"but you know how to reach me."

"Of course. Maybe you should consider taking a holiday. Even I took a vacation this year." With a wry smile, she left the room.

A vacation? Honestly, he didn't take vacations. He didn't need time to recharge his batteries although he insisted that those around him do so. Their three weeks were mandatory and not up for negotiation. For himself? He got a natural high from working.

What if he took a few days off—or even a week? He and Alessandra could fly to Mexico for some fun in the sun. Or they could go to New York and see some Broadway plays. They could fly to Hawaii and... What did people do while in Hawaii? He honestly had no idea.

Those plans would only work if Alessandra was still in the apartment. If she'd fled, then all was for naught. He should've locked her in. Shouldn't have taken the risk. He took the elevator down to the parking garage and strode to his car. He only lived eight blocks from work and often walked, but not today. Today he'd wanted to get to work, resolve the problem, and then get home as soon as possible.

The elevator ride down from his penthouse office suite was interminable.

He couldn't remember the last time he'd had a reason to want to go home.

Never, if he was honest.

So he'd hold his breath until he discovered if Alessandra had stayed or left.

After getting in his car, he let his mind wander.

Alessandra had lain curled contentedly in his arms and slept like a baby, but he hadn't been able to get her words out of his mind. He'd been a mindless brute with her, taking as much as he could. Sure, he'd given her pleasure too, but that'd almost been secondary. He'd been so single-minded in his focus to take all he could get. She was a selfless lover while he felt like a selfish one. Did that make them a good pair or destined to failure?

He'd done things with her that he rarely, if ever, did. Although he enjoyed giving orgasms, he rarely went down on a woman. He tended to shy away from such a private and intimate act. Not to mention, he was also letting her sleep in his bed. Usually he'd encourage the woman to either go home or sleep in the white room. That was what Rielle had called it when she'd given him a tour—the white room. Even without natural light, the room was as bright as the dungeon was dark. He would encourage his partners to get a *good night's rest* in that room, claiming he was a restless sleeper and would keep them awake. Most women accepted that lie without question. Maybe they wanted to get away as badly as he wanted them to go.

He pulled out of the underground garage and merged into the chaos on Howe Street. Late Friday afternoon and traffic was a crawl as many people fled the city for the suburbs. He was one of the lucky ones who could afford to live in downtown Vancouver. Alessandra had lived mere miles from here in abject poverty while he lived in the lap of luxury. And the women in his life? Certainly none like Alessandra.

Most of his partners had been for play or for sex but nothing more. He rarely chose women with the highest IQ as intelligence wasn't necessary for him to take his pleasure, and they rarely had a conversation about business matters or world events. Of much more interest was how a woman screamed when he whipped her or how she writhed when he forced her to orgasm or how she moaned when he was inside her.

With Alessandra, those things weren't enough. He wanted more from her. She was the most educated woman he'd dated in a while, which shamed him. But it went both ways. Women tended to pick him because of his money and what he could give to them. He was always generous with gifts but stingy with his time, and most women tired of him. He'd give them a gracious parting gift and, often as not, wait months before going out to look again.

This amazing woman was different. Her responses were spontaneous and electrifying, leaving him wanting more. He wanted to push her to her limits and maybe even beyond them.

He needed to do better and vowed to do so as he maneuvered his car into the garage at his building. He parked, grabbed his briefcase, and booted his ass to the elevator, tapping his toes as he waited. It arrived, and he stepped in, quickly scanning for the close-door button even as a voice rang out.

Fuck.

He stuck his hand in the door to stop it and reached for the open button.

A woman pushing a stroller managed to get it in the elevator car with a toddler in tow. "Thank you so much." Her cheeks were flushed, and she was breathless. "I'm running late. My mother-in-law is coming to babysit, and if I'm not there, she's liable to just take off."

Didn't sound like a patient woman, but Smith's own patience was stretching to its limit. "Which floor?"

"Oh, uh, fifteen." She smoothed her hair back.

"Mommy, who's that?"

Smith glanced down at the young boy. What, four?

Five? He was no good with kids, and although he was looking forward to getting to know Gage and Rielle's daughter, Cara, she was an infant. This child was an ankle biter.

The bell dinged, and relief flooded him. Thank God he lived on the third floor and didn't have to endure the entire trip up to the top. He tipped his head. "Smith." He stepped out.

"Thank you, Mr. Smith." The woman offered a harried smile.

As the door was shutting, he mumbled, "Just Smith."

Nothing to be done now.

When he tried the door to the condo and he needed his key, he felt a surge of hope. Of course she might've used his spare to lock up and then left it with the concierge. That would be just like her, considerate.

When the door closed, he stood for a moment. The sun had been bright and beautiful again today, but his condo was now in shadows. Silence hung in the air, mocking him. So she had left. It shouldn't have surprised him, but still, it stung just a little bit.

Deciding he wasn't ready to face the dungeon and the memories from last night, he went to her bedroom. As he suspected, pajamas lay on the floor, the robe lay carelessly tossed on the bed and—

He did a double take. Her computer and e-reader were still present. Surely she wouldn't have left without them. Then he spotted her shoes. Maybe she'd raided the stash in the dungeon and picked one of the pairs of boots. Still, he couldn't suppress the surge of hope.

Forcing himself to remain calm, he went to his office. Untouched as far as he could see. That left the kitchen, the bathroom, and the dungeon. No, if she was in the kitchen, he would've heard her. Maybe she was in the dungeon. But why get dressed and then go back there?

Only one way to find out. *Suck it up.* Whatever happened, he'd deal with it. Steeling himself for what he might find, he opened the door.

Nothing. The lights were off, and he found no sign of anyone having been there. He was just about to back out when the dim light of the hall hit something shiny.

Alessandra's watch.

He flipped on the light, and his heart stuttered. She just lay there, curled into the fetal position, tighter than he'd imagined possible. Dropping to his knees by her head, he reached for her shoulder and shook her, too panicked to be gentle in his approach.

Her head lolled, but she stirred.

And what if she hadn't? Sure, he knew CPR, but he would've been way too late for that. Had she taken something? Alcohol? Drugs? He only had a bottle of ibuprofen, but if she'd taken all of them, it'd cause an overdose.

He shook her again, this time with more force. "Alessandra." No significant visible reaction. Should he get her medical attention?

What the fuck do I do?

Then she stirred again. Her hands, which had been curled under her chin, began to shake.

When he touched them, they were freezing. And why not? She'd been lying on the floor for a while, by his estimation. But how long? With her penchant for losing time, she might've been here all day.

Gently, he rolled her over and into his arms.

Awkward, but he settled onto the bed with her in his lap. She was as cold as he'd suspected, and suddenly she started shaking. Afraid she might unbalance them, he whispered, "Put your arms around my neck."

To his surprise and infinite relief, she did exactly that. Her hands were icy against the back of his neck, but he didn't care. She was alive, and that was all that mattered. Everything else was just icing on the cake. She hadn't left when he gave her a choice. She'd chosen him over freedom.

Or maybe not. Maybe she'd been coming in here to get her clothes and had suffered a seizure. What if she'd hit her head and been unconscious? One wasn't supposed to move someone who might have a head injury. What if he'd done her harm?

Get a grip, MacLean. He wasn't going to help Alessandra if he didn't keep a clear head. Cradling her closer, he held on tight, rocking her. Difficult, and maybe a little childish, but she seemed to respond to it. He couldn't see her face, so he had no idea what she was thinking.

Then, just like that, the dam burst, and she started sobbing. Nerve-wracking, soul-shattering sobs in which her entire body convulsed.

He had to hold her even closer and tighter, for fear of dropping her. This was the fourth time he'd reduced her to tears, and just like the other times, he had no idea what he'd done. Maybe this had nothing to do with him. Maybe this was Alessandra exorcising her demons. God, he hoped so. Better that than something he'd done.

Then, just as suddenly, the sobs stopped. She went limp.

For a panicked moment, he wondered if she'd gone unconscious. She still had a tight grip on his neck, though, so he didn't think that was the issue. He had to take another tack. "Alessandra, tell me what's happened."

She shuddered but didn't respond to his command.

He shifted her again because his legs were going numb. He wouldn't let her go, of course, so he'd have to do his best to stay comfortable. He was in this for the long haul. "Alessandra, talk to me. Tell me what's wrong." His voice was soft and coaxing. *You can do this. You can trust me with your deepest and darkest secrets.*

"They're…" She hiccupped. "They're all dead."

He swallowed convulsively. "Who's dead, Alessandra?"

"All of them." Her voice was hoarse, and it hitched. "And it's my fault."

He pressed a kiss to her hair, the only part of her he could reach. "Alessandra, I know that's not true. You're the gentlest person I know. You couldn't have killed anyone. You're mistaken. There's been a mistake." He racked his brain for a logical explanation. "Or maybe you just think you're to blame, but you're not really. Tell me what happened."

She went still.

He'd pushed too far. At least she'd shared this much. This was something he could work with, something he could research. People who'd died six months ago. Mission City was a small town, so surely he'd be able to track down deaths.

Maybe there'd been a drinking-and-driving crash. No, the police would've given that as a reason for her disappearance. Maybe it had to do with work? No, surely her co-workers would've stepped forward with that information. What if they couldn't? What if the reason was confidential information?

Too many questions and too few answers. *Just going to have to wait.* Right now, in this moment, he had her in his arms, and she was hurting. He had to figure out a way to ease the pain. She was still ice-block cold.

"Why don't I put you in the bath? So you can warm up?"

She shook her head.

"Will you get into bed?"

To his infinite relief she nodded. The bed was still unmade from the morning, so he easily laid her down. When he went to extricate himself, however, her arms tightened around his neck, and she dragged him into a kiss. Not a light peck, but a tongue-thrusting-in-mouth, toe-curling kiss. He was half bent over her, and things were awkward, but still he kissed her back.

When she let out a little moan, he ended the kiss.

"Make me forget."

That fierce, whispered demand he couldn't ignore.

"Help me go somewhere else, please." Her voice broke. "Please, Smith, take me away."

He could think of nothing he wanted more, but he didn't know how.

Then she spoke, answering his unspoken question. "I need you inside me right now."

Theoretically a simple request, but a logistical nightmare since they were both still fully dressed. On top of that, was this the right thing to do? If she was broken, might he break her further? Could he hurt her even more than she already was?

"I'll die if…" She hiccupped again. "I need…"

He placed a gentle finger to her lips. "I'll do it, Alessandra. I just need to figure out how to get you out of your clothes."

Like a gazelle, she leapt from the bed. She stripped without hesitation. Buttons were only a momentary impediment, her bra was an afterthought, and soon she slipped from her jeans and underwear. She reached for him, hands groping, fingers clutching. When things weren't moving fast enough for her, she reached out and cupped him through his trousers.

She rubbed him so hard he was likely to chafe. "Jesus Christ, Alessandra, I'll get there—just calm down."

"I don't want calm. I want passion. I want flames. I want to fucking forget."

"Then lie on the bed and give me a minute to get out of my clothes." She obeyed, and he undertook untying and removing his shoes. The room was only lit by the torchlight but bright enough to see her reach down and touch herself.

Her eyes drifted shut, her breath hitched, and her pelvis flexed as she ran a hand up and down her labia.

He momentarily stilled to watch in rapt fascination but then redoubled his efforts to get out of his clothes. As erotic as this was, he wanted to be the one to make her come.

He was about to settle on the bed when an inarticulate noise escaped her lips followed by a long sigh as she climaxed. He'd had no idea how close to the edge she'd been. Suddenly he felt extraneous to the entire process and was pulling away when she reached out and snagged his cock.

"I need you inside me, now." None of the previous pleading. Now her voice was all steel.

He was powerless to deny her. Growing harder as she stroked him, he then leaned forward to kiss her gently and thoroughly, but she was having none of that as her fingernails raked painfully down his cock.

"Fuck me now, Smith."

Self-preservation had him levering himself over her. Her thighs spread easily, her hips flexing to instinctively welcome him in. When he probed her entrance, she reached down between their bodies and guided him to her. She was well-lubricated from her previous orgasm, so he slid right in. Her legs wrapped so tightly around his waist he wondered absently if she was going to bruise him.

Then she rocked against him and grabbed his ass in her hands, encouraging him to press even farther into her. At this rate, he'd be able to feel her cervix.

"Fuck me." A broken whisper. A hitched voice. Her nails digging.

Christ, what had he gotten himself into?

At the first flex of his hips, she gasped. When he pulled back, she groaned.

Then he pressed home, seating himself fully. After that, just a matter of following the age-old mating ritual. He was male, and she was female. Two halves of a whole. His thrusts were rough, but her body demanded it. She didn't want finesse, and she didn't want tenderness. She wanted life-affirming passion, and so he'd give it to her.

An eternity seemed to pass before she began to crest, her body seeking some release, but it was probably only a few minutes. Enough, though, and he went right along with her.

He barely had time to draw breath when she pushed him off her. Obliging, although not entirely pleased about it, he rolled off. Usually he liked to slip out of his partner gently, rather than being unceremoniously thrust out, but he wasn't going to argue.

Once his hands were off her, she shot up and out of the room.

So much for the afterglow. Now that just sucked. After mind-blowing sex, he preferred to cuddle just a little bit. Enjoy the sensation of floating back to earth rather than being dropped like a hot potato.

Curiosity warred with fatigue, and he rose, following her path. He turned left. The bathroom door was closed. She deserved her privacy, but he had the right to know if she was okay. He raised his hand to knock, but she started retching.

Well, that was a first. He couldn't remember a single time when his lovemaking had sent a woman into the bathroom with the heaves. Unsurprisingly, the door was locked. He waited until it seemed she was finished, and then he knocked on the door. "Alessandra, open the door."

No response.

He wasn't surprised. He knocked again, this time lighter. "Allie, please let me in."

Chapter Nineteen

His use of the nickname Allie brought her up short. He never called her that. Maybe he was as scared as she was. Of course not. Men like Smith MacLean didn't get scared. Someone like her, though…she'd begged him to fuck her. *Begged* him. She'd felt desperate in a way that was utterly foreign to her. She'd felt like she'd die if they hadn't been joined at the pelvis in that exact moment.

Now the soul-searing shame and bone-deep weariness overwhelmed.

She rinsed her mouth with mouthwash and then unlocked the door. Who knew what she was expecting, but him pulling her into an embrace hadn't been it.

He pulled back just far enough so he could place a kiss on her forehead. Then he eased her back another step, his gaze raking across her face. "Are you okay? What the hell just happened?"

Tears welled. *Fuck.* No, she was not going to cry. There'd been an ocean of tears already today, and she wasn't going to let herself go there again. If she did, she might never come back. "I…I had a rough day, that's all. I'm sorry."

He pressed a hand to her cheek. "You don't have to apologize, just explain."

That brought her up short. "What if I can't, Smith? What if I can't give you an adequate explanation? What if I can't tell you?"

"Is this because of confidentiality? With your job? You know I'd never betray a confidence, Alessandra."

He was hitting just a little too close to home, but his use of her formal name straightened her spine. "I trust you—it's not a question of that. Look, I'm cold. I should probably go put some clothes on."

"Have a shower with me first." His voice was an entreaty. "We can warm each other up."

She'd already had one shower today, but the thought of those jet sprays pulsing against her cramped muscles was too tempting. Plus, his blue eyes were mesmerizing in their concern for her. She allowed him to put her under the spray and then closed her eyes in bliss.

Smith squeezed something plastic, probably going to shampoo his hair.

Then he cupped her breasts. She yanked open her eyes just as his mouth descended on hers. He nibbled on her lower lip until she granted him access. His tongue slid across hers as his soapy hands moved from her breasts to her belly and then around to the small of her back. His hands roved up and down her body, leaving her sensitized, tingling. Fingers hit that sensitive place where her ass and thighs met, and she gasped.

"Shush." He pressed his lips to her temple. Then his hand crept around her hip, and he cupped her.

She'd known this was coming, but still it startled her. She gripped his shoulders when he pressed two fingers into her.

"Shush," he said again when she began mewling.

Her body clawed, demanded, and she didn't fight

it. As his thumb did delicious things to her clit, she bored down on his fingers and came.

Now she needed him to hold her up, which he did. He did a passable job of getting them clean, but he'd forgone washing his hair. He placed her on the toilet seat and wrapped a towel around her. "I'll go get your pajamas."

"And a sweater?"

"And thick socks." His eyes shone in the light of the bathroom, and he stroked her cheek. "I'll be right back, okay?"

She nodded.

He was being considerate, and she felt contrite. Pained.

What must he think of me?

Hell, what did she think of herself?

She hadn't moved, and when he returned, she let him dry her. Her eyes were closed, but his touch soothed her. Lulled her. She'd begged him to take her away from this place, and that'd scared her more than anything.

"I was thinking about Chinese for dinner."

Food? Now?

Except she hadn't eaten all day, and her stomach approved of the suggestion. "We should finish the pizza from yesterday." Very practical. She was the queen of leftovers.

"Pizza it is. Maybe a movie?"

Her eyes opened, and she took him in. "I don't really feel like a movie. I can read—"

"No." His response was so swift it caught her off guard. "Something happened at work today, and I'd like to talk about it."

Okay, not what she'd expected. What could he possibly have to talk to her about? He worked in finance, and she counseled mothers on social assistance. Well, whatever. "I'd like that."

His grin was all the answer she received.

Chapter Twenty

Smith was pleased as the conversation took them through dinner and beyond. Alessandra appeared to be engaged in his story, adding comments and asking insightful questions. For a woman who'd never studied business, her instincts were solid. Of course, as a social worker, she knew how to read people and make good inquiries. She always asked open-ended questions, encouraging him to give lengthy answers.

Finally, though, he said what was really on his mind. "You didn't leave."

Her pupils dilated in surprise, and then her gaze dropped to her plate.

An empty plate, he was glad to note.

"Did you want me to?"

"That's a stupid question, Alessandra." His temper frayed. "If I wanted you to leave, then I would've shown you the door, wouldn't I?"

She nodded, still not meeting his eyes.

"Fine, now that we have that out of the way, may I ask why you stayed?"

She shifted on her seat.

He stifled the urge to order her to sit still.

"I gave my word." Quiet steel in her voice. "You said you'd let me go after a month, and I said I'd stay for that month. Plus, I really want you to give that money to the ranch, and that means completing the work on the JEAP project."

He'd already donated the ten thousand and obtained a guarantee from Kennedy Dixon she'd mend the fence. He'd made the donation through one of his subsidiaries, so no way anyone could trace it back to him. At the end of the month, he'd give the other ninety thousand as a going-away present to Alessandra. For the moment, however, he had her right where he wanted her and intended to keep her there.

"I made my first phone call." Unprompted, she volunteered the information.

Progress. "And how did it go?"

"It went well. I figured I'd make all five and then provide you with the written report."

"Of course. But you're always free to give me a preview."

She raised her head at that and offered a slight smile. "Well, I chose the scenario where my husband lost his job and it's been very stressful on our family. Very pertinent given the day you had."

Smith nodded, thinking of all the families in the same situation. "I feel like I haven't done enough."

"Was there more you could do? I mean, if you give them a job just for the sake of giving them a job without giving them something useful to do, is that any better than encouraging them to move forward?"

"You said it yourself it's very stressful for someone to lose their job. It affects the entire family."

"Smith, people lose their jobs every day. They pick themselves up, dust themselves off, and then find a way to move forward."

"Is that what happened to you? Did you lose your job?" He had heard nothing about that, but it'd explain a lot.

She shook her head. "No, I didn't lose my job. I should have, but I didn't."

"Who died, Alessandra?"

His abrupt question obviously caught her off guard. She shifted again, dropping her gaze.

He was losing her again. "Forget I asked."

She looked up at him, her face a mask of misery. "Does it matter? They're dead, and I can't change it. I'd give my life, you know, to bring them back."

"But the world doesn't work that way, does it? And you're smart enough to realize that."

"Which is why I left."

"To punish yourself." His voice was as flat as her expression. "You thought if you went far enough, you'd outrun this."

She nodded. "Except I didn't think it through. If I'd really thought it through, I would've gone farther than Vancouver."

"Where would you have gone?"

Shrugging, she dropped her gaze again.

God, this was frustrating.

"Seattle, Calgary…maybe Toronto. Or Montréal," she added. "I studied French in high school and probably could do a passable job."

"There's a huge English population in Montréal anyway."

"That's true." Her voice was barely above a whisper and without emotion.

"Just as long as it's a city big enough for you to get lost in." He knew he'd hit the nail on the head when she wiped an invisible crumb from the table.

"I guess Vancouver wasn't big enough."

"Oh, the city was plenty big. Your mistake was going to Kink. Believe it or not, I don't think anyone thought to look for you here in the city. They spent most of the time and effort looking for your body around Mission City."

She blanched, as he had expected her to. He wouldn't give an inch on this one. "They weren't sure if the disappearance was homicide or suicide."

"They thought..."

"The police were open to the theory you'd walked away from your life and become one of the vanished. Gage and Rielle, though, refused to believe it. They were sure something bad had happened to you because they couldn't fathom why you'd walk away from your life without a backward glance." He paused. "But something bad did happen to you, didn't it? People died on your watch." He was pushing again, but he needed more to go on. He needed to understand.

Standing abruptly, she almost knocked over the chair. "I'll do the dishes."

He opened his mouth but saw her expression. She was on the verge of...something. Did he really want to push her over yet again? Would she be able to survive it? Probably not today. So he let her remove the plates and waited for her to return. "Are you warm?"

His question seemed to catch her off guard, but she nodded warily.

"I thought maybe we could play tonight. If you're tired—"

"No. I mean, no, I'm not tired. I mean, yes, I want to play." She met his gaze. "Please, Master, I need this."

That was what she'd said last night just before

giving him one of the best blow jobs he'd ever gotten. She needed to play, and that was why he'd offered.

"Prepare."

She scurried off, and he smiled. He'd give her a few minutes to stew because he had a phone call to make. He made his way to the office and pulled out his phone. The call was answered on the first ring.

"Toby Driscoll."

"Toby, it's Smith MacLean."

"Smith, it's nice to hear from you. Do you need security?"

Right to business, just the way Smith liked it. "No security this time, but I need to put those investigative skills to use."

"Shoot."

"The woman's name is Alessandra Soriano. She was a social worker in Mission City for the department of social services. Six months ago she comes home from work one day and goes for a walk, never comes back."

"And you want me to find her?" Toby's voice was wary.

Smith chuckled. "I found her, quite by accident, and I've got her with me. She's safe for now. I have two questions I need answered. The first is why she left, and the second is what she's been doing for the last six months."

"Did you try asking her?"

This time Smith's laugh was rueful. "I've tried multiple times and in multiple ways." *Christ, that sounded dirty.* "The lady's not talking. I can text you the address where I found her, and I can tell you she thinks she was responsible for multiple deaths."

"Sure. Wait...what?"

"She said, and I quote, 'They're all dead, and it's my fault.' "

A nerve-shattering pause. "That's not a lot to work with."

"That's why I called you. You're the best, Toby, and I need the best. I've got less than a month to figure this out."

"What're you going to do with the information?"

He sighed. "I don't know. Once I have the information, I'll decide."

"What if she wants to stay gone? What if she had an excellent reason to walk away?"

"I'll cross that bridge when I come to it. I'll text you the address when we get off the phone. Standard rates plus a bonus if you get it to me in less than a week."

Toby snickered. "You don't ask for much."

"Like I said, I'm willing to pay for the best. Oh, and Toby, this must stay between us. Clean, you know? They can't be able to get to me through you."

"So the lady stays protected? Yeah, I'll be discreet. I'll give you an update by close of business tomorrow."

"Tomorrow's Saturday."

"Being a private investigator doesn't lend itself to regular hours. At the very least I'll check out her previous residence. Does she still live there?"

"Nope and she's not going back, so knock heads around."

"Done. Later."

The call ended. In mere moments he sent the text, and then he laid the phone on the desk. He wouldn't be surprised if Toby turned up something in less than twenty-four hours.

Now, however, he had a warm and willing woman waiting for him.

She was right where he expected her to be— kneeling buck naked on the rug beneath the hanging manacles in the center of the room.

He went to her and tilted her chin up so she could meet his gaze. "Not tonight, little one." He almost laughed at her hangdog expression. "I have other treats in store for you." Her look of anticipation was priceless. "I thought we might try a variation on the naughty secretary."

"Naughty financial analyst?"

He laughed. Really laughed. "Well, since the analyst was a guy, that probably won't work. I don't want to be thinking about him when I'm...playing with you."

Clearly she was almost salivating with anticipation, and he helped her rise.

"I want to play naughty psychoanalyst."

She blinked. "How does that work?"

"I'm the psychoanalyst, and you're the patient."

"Smith..."

Her tone of voice was exactly what he'd expected. "Do you trust me? As your Dominant?"

Her eyes were still wary. "Yes." Grudging.

"We set up protocol, and you trust me to follow it." He was trying to make it all sound very reasonable. The question was whether she'd accept it.

"Hobbit."

Slow down, she was telling him, and he heard her loud and clear. "I'm proud of you, Alessandra."

She looked confused.

"A test."

She started to speak, then closed her mouth. That mouth twisted, and she took a breath. "What kind of test?"

"I want to see how far you'll let me push you tonight, but you need to know I'm going to fuck with your mind as much as I'm going to fuck with your body."

She shifted from foot to foot, her arms wrapping around her waist. "You said something about protocol?"

He nodded. "Details from the last six months is off the table, but everything else is fair game."

"How do I know you'll stick to your promise?"

"Trust, Alessandra, it all comes down to trust." He took her chin between his thumb and forefinger. "Enough of this, it's time to begin." His tone brooked no opposition.

She nodded.

"As a patient, I think it's important for you to be comfortable. Usually one lies down during a psychoanalysis session, but I'll leave it up to you."

She looked between the bed, the medieval torture chair, and the regular wood chair. No matter what she picked, he had devious plans for her.

"I'll take the bed."

"Excellent choice. Now we just need to get you comfortable."

She quirked an eyebrow but said nothing, instead letting him guide her across the room.

"You need to lie down."

Nodding, she obeyed.

"I think we need to make sure you stay where you

are."

Again, another quirked eyebrow.

She was silent as he grabbed the four shackles attached to the bedposts. He was quick, and soon he'd secured her to the bed.

"Are we comfortable?"

"There's no royal *we* here, Mr. Psychoanalyst. I feel like a lamb heading for the slaughter."

He pinched the inside of her thigh, making her gasp. "You need to work with me to improve and get over your neuroses. And it's Dr. MacLean to you."

"Sorry, Dr. MacLean, I'm touched you're concerned about my comfort. I'm fine."

"Glad to hear it." He pulled the chair to the side of the bed and sat, never moving his gaze from her.

She stared up at the ceiling, wariness clouding her features.

He crossed his legs, wishing he'd brought a pad of paper and a pen. Not that he'd forget her answers, but he'd do well to jot down impressions and ideas. This game was as much about figuring out her soft limits and hard limits as actually playing. "Now tell me about your mother."

She shot him a glance.

They'd already talked about their parents, but he wanted more. He wanted to know about the woman who'd given birth to and then single-handedly raised this magnificent creature.

"My mother was…incredible. She cleaned office buildings at night."

"Did she leave you alone?"

"Of course not," she rushed to assure him. "I'd sleep over at a neighbor's house. I don't know how she did it—working and raising me. But she did an amazing job."

"When did you lose her?"

"Six years ago." She paused, closed her eyes for a moment, and then sighed heavily. "She died of a heart attack. I tried to get her to quit working, you know? I told her she'd supported me my entire life and it was my turn to take care of her. But she was adamant she needed something to do with her time. She said she might take it easy if I gave her grandbabies." Her voice hitched. "If she'd just held on a bit longer…"

"Were you just about to produce grandbabies?"

That pulled her out of her haze of pain. "No, Dr. MacLean, I was not then—nor am I now—in a position to have babies."

"Do you want to have a child?"

She sucked in her breath so abruptly she had to swallow before she could breathe again. "Since I can't have a child, it's a moot point."

"Why can't you have a child?"

She shook her head, and an interminable pause spun out.

Finally, he broke the silence. "Alessandra, answer me—why can't you have a child? Is it physical?" *Shit, what was going on?*

"It's not physical."

He waited.

"I can't bring a child into my world. How can I live in Downtown Eastside and have a baby? You saw where I lived. I will never do that to a child."

The first time since Sunday she'd mentioned her former residence.

"Let's say you had everything needed to bring a

child into the world—a lovely house in the suburbs, a dutiful husband, and all the money you could want. Would you choose to have a child under those circumstances?"

Her eyes shut, and she pulled against her restraints.

He didn't just have her naked physically—he'd laid her bare emotionally. How far could he push? What was her hard limit? Aside from the past six months, of course.

"Doctor, with all due respect, I'll never be living in those circumstances, so it's not a hypothetical worth visiting."

"What if you got pregnant?"

"Very unlikely with an IUD, but I know a kink-friendly doctor who'd probably give me a referral to someone who'd give me an abortion."

That stunned him into silence. Moments stretched out again as he contemplated how to move on from that admission.

She finally broke the silence. "Or I might carry the child and then give him up for adoption."

"Him?"

When she shrugged, she again pulled at the restraints. "Or her. Like I said, it'll never happen."

But it could. He'd done the research. IUDs had a failure rate of around one percent. Of those, most pregnancies were ectopic and had to be aborted for the health of the mother, but still a few succeeded. What would it be like to see Alessandra's belly swell with pregnancy? To see her bloom and flourish rather than wilt and flounder? Could a baby bring her back to life? Or was that an unfair burden to put on a little life? "So no babies."

"No babies." A strong affirmation.

"Where do you see yourself going?"

Her eyes snapped open. "I…I hadn't…I mean…"

"Simple question, Alessandra. Where do you see yourself in six months?"

"Dead."

A knife to the gut and for a moment he couldn't breathe. The mask dropped. "Are you dying?"

Responding to his change in tone, her head swiveled to him. "What? No, not like that. Not that kind of dead."

"There are different kinds of dead?" He was ghoulishly and perversely fascinated.

Her head returned to its previous position, her stare fixing on some point in the ceiling. "I mean there's dead like dying from cancer. There's dead like suicide. There's dead like…well, you know, just death."

He had absolutely no idea what she was talking about. "Alessandra, are you suicidal?" He held his breath.

"No, but neither do I want to live." Her eyes closed again, but that look of abject misery was back. "I have a death wish, but I'm too chickenshit to take myself out, you know?"

Weirdly, he got it. He'd never felt that way himself, but he could see where she was coming from. "So you've been doing everything in your power over the last six months to die without actually pulling the proverbial trigger."

"Exactly." She sounded pleased he understood what she was trying to say, and she didn't point out he'd broken protocol by mentioning the recent past.

"So what behaviors have you engaged in…?"

Her eyebrow quirked.

"Let me rephrase. What activities do you plan to engage in that will get you dead?" Appalling grammar, but nothing to be done about that.

He waited as she debated whether to answer. God, her face was so expressive. The war she was waging with herself was plain to see, so he'd be able to tell if she was lying to him.

She let out a long, deep breath. "Hobbit." A pain-ridden whisper.

Well, she hadn't used Bilbo, so that was something.

"Tell me why you picked social work. That's not an easy profession."

Her laugh sent shivers down his spine. "I had the misguided belief I could help people. Now I know better."

"But before." He *had* to get through to her. "Before...the people died." He hoped he wasn't stepping too far into this. "You were working for, what, eight years?"

"Nine."

"You must've done some good, Alessandra, or they would've fired you. But they didn't, did they? In fact, they promoted you."

There. Just a flash. But there.

Pride.

Gage had told him how much she loved her work and what a stellar reputation she had. She hadn't forgotten all the good. A surge of hope rose in his chest. "How did you meet Gage?"

"Actually, I met Cara first. She was the school guidance counselor who called me in on a suspected molestation case. Her instincts were bang-on, and after the student sat in a session with Cara and me, he admitted what was happening at home."

"He?" That caught him off guard.

"A soccer coach who was also a friend of the family. The man had been sexually abusing him since he was five years old."

"How old was he when you and Cara intervened?"

Alessandra smiled sadly. "He was fourteen. A teacher, Jenna Lee, saw…well, I'm not sure what she saw, but she knew. She went to Cara who came to me. We arrested the son of a bitch, and they sentenced him to twenty-five years. After the arrest, eleven other victims came forward. He'd been abusing children for more than twenty years, and none of them had the guts to step forward. He had threatened them. Told them he'd tell the world the relationship was consensual, that they were gay, that they'd enjoyed it."

"That's sick."

"Did you hear the story behind Cara, baby Cara?"

Smith shook his head. "I just received a birth notice. I hadn't even known Rielle was pregnant, but then they told me they'd adopted."

"The young woman, Katie, had been molested by her father for as long as she could remember. She got pregnant, and he was going to take her to get an abortion. She took a shotgun and killed him."

"Good for her." His response was simple and gut-deep. "I assume he was the father…"

Alessandra nodded. "Rielle was Katie's lawyer and Gage her principal. She asked them to adopt the infant, and they initially hesitated, but eventually they agreed."

"Why was there hesitation? I mean, not that you

have to tell me…" Confidentiality, he reminded himself. "How much do you know about Rielle?"

Now she shrugged. "I haven't spent a lot of time getting to know her."

"Because you're in love with Gage."

"I thought I was in love."

He was pleased she made that important correction.

"I think just infatuation for the man who introduced me to a D/s relationship. But you were saying about Rielle…"

How much to reveal? Alessandra would feel bound by her ethics to keep Rielle's secret, but she needed to know. "Rielle grew up with violence for the first six years of her life and then went into the system for the next twelve. She was determined, though, and made it through law school. She was doing okay until she met a man who was strong and powerful. A man who promised her the moon and took her to Hell."

"Why did she—?"

"I'm not finished."

Alessandra closed her mouth.

"She lived in a very dangerous situation, in this condo, for four years. She was a twenty-four-seven slave, and, although she told herself she was happy, she wasn't really. Then, without warning, he released her. She hadn't been prepared for life after slavery. That was when she met Gage."

"I wondered how they met."

"Club Kink. They were both grieving—Gage for Cara and Rielle for Mr. X."

Alessandra turned her dark-brown eyes to him and arched one eyebrow. "Mr. X?"

"That's what Gage calls him. I think he knows who

the man is, but he's never said. I'd be happy to do the man physical harm after what he put Rielle through."

"Did you know her back then?"

He shook his head, his eyes remaining locked with hers. "I abhor violence against women. I offered to go with Gage to teach the guy a lesson, but he'd moved on, and at that point so had Rielle. She's been in counseling."

"The bruises I saw that day...that horrible day a year ago when Katie Rhodes was arrested for shooting her father."

"Rielle's father. He'd been in jail for beating her mother to death. The prison released him, Rielle went to see him, and he tried for a repeat."

Alessandra sucked in a breath. "I didn't know that."

"And you might not have known Rielle has been in counseling. Gage wanted to make sure she wasn't submitting to him because of her being a victim of violence."

"Gage's conclusion?"

"Rielle has assured him she has chosen the lifestyle because it makes her happy. And it has. I think it's the only reason they've survived the last six months."

Her gaze narrowed. "Have there been problems with Cara?"

His ire rose, the mask of repressed anger slipping. "The baby has been their saving grace. Did you never consider your actions might have consequences? They lived every day in fear of you turning up dead. Do you not remember how fast they showed up here? The concern they showed? God, Alessandra, I know you believed you had good reasons to walk away, but you committed a very selfish act. If you had just left a note…"

She broke their staring contest and returned to looking at the ceiling. "I wouldn't have been capable of writing a letter. Smith, I never meant to hurt anyone, but I was desperate to escape. Maybe the act was selfish, but I didn't think anyone would miss me."

"That's a child's perspective, Alessandra, and I expected better from you."

She flexed her feet, pulling against the restraints, but didn't ask him to release her. "How do you know so much about Rielle?"

"After you walked away, she went to a bad place. Gage needed someone to talk to and, given his position as principal, needed someone outside his normal sphere. I went there one night when Rielle had taken to her bed. Gage got really drunk and told me everything."

"If you were told in confidence, why are you telling me?"

"Because you need to know how much you owe these people."

She bit her lip, obviously fighting whatever emotion churned in her gut. "They've seen me. Isn't that enough?"

"No, my dear patient, it's not. You're going to have to face them at least once more before the month is over, and convince them why they shouldn't go to the police. Why they shouldn't tell the world you're alive." He paused. "They're coming for dinner tomorrow night. You can tell them then."

"What if…? Can't I just stay in my room?"

God, but she was a tough nut to crack. "They're coming to see *you*. I've held them off for a week.

They're not going to wait a moment longer."

"I should've left today when I had the chance."

He chuckled and shifted, stretching his legs. "I suspect that more than once over the next month you're going to wish you had, but, as you say, you've given me your word. Your word has to mean something, or you'll lose your clothing privileges."

She sighed. "You have my word. Please don't take away my clothes."

"I won't." It'd been an empty threat anyway. She'd stayed when she could have run. "Are you uncomfortable?"

She shook her head. "I'm just not sure how much psychoanalyzing is going on."

"Well, I didn't study psychology and have never read the writings of Sigmund Freud. I just wanted a chance for us to get to know each other better."

She turned her head to face him again. "What's this 'us' crap? I haven't learned a single thing about you." She paused, her nose wrinkling. "No, that's not true. I've learned you're protective of the weak and a sympathetic friend to the Claytons. I appreciate what you did for them."

"They're kind people." Smith willed her to believe what he was saying. "And so are you."

A sigh escaped her lips.

"What made you doubt yourself, Alessandra? What mortal sin have you committed?"

Another sigh.

I'm losing her. "Well, I think our session is over."

Now she breathed a sigh of relief.

"I believe you've earned a recompense."

She rewarded him with a brilliant smile. "And what

does the doctor have in mind?" A hint of shyness in her expression.

"I was thinking a massage."

Her frown demonstrated what she thought of that idea. "I think I'm facing the wrong direction for that."

Standing, he walked to the dresser, opened the top drawer, and removed a bottle of lube.

Her eyes lit up. "Oh," she said reverently. "That kind of massage."

Not quite. At least, not at first. He moved to the side of the bed and put a large dollop of lube in his hands. This was going to be a messy proposition, and they'd have to change the sheets before they slept, but that'd be an insignificant price to pay for the pleasure they were about to indulge in.

Once the gel was warmer, Smith laid his hands on her chest, right above her breasts.

Despite his best efforts, the lube was still chilly, and she sucked in a breath.

"Close your eyes, little one." To his pleasure, she obeyed. And he began a very sensual journey. He massaged her chest, but not her breasts. Working his way down her sides, he then slid his fingers across her belly. He massaged her mound, but didn't reach between her thighs, despite the flexing of her hips as she offered greater access. Then he used some more lube to massage her breasts. He knew how to bring maximum pleasure with minimum pressure, and soon she was moaning softly and arching her back, pressing into his palms.

"Greedy little thing." But no chastisement in his voice. When he switched to using his mouth, she bucked.

She let out a lengthy sigh but then asked, "Doesn't that taste disgusting?"

"Nope." He lifted his mouth from her nipple. "Strawberry flavored." As he resumed his erotic examination of her nipple, she writhed beneath him.

"Please." She whispered the word that was also a demand.

He knew what she was asking for, and without breaking contact, he meandered lower. Belly, hips, thighs. Pretty soon, he stroked his hand between her legs. Since she was still slick from the liquid and had added her own juices, sliding two fingers in was easy. She ground against his palm to stimulate her clit, and he added another finger, stretching her. Fist her? No, she needed her legs unbound for that. Three would have to suffice.

Her body was winding up, so he sucked harder. Then, when she was right on the edge, he bit her nipple. Hard. Her hips arched against him even as spasms overtook her body. He could think of nothing he loved more than feeling the powerful contractions of an orgasm against his fingers. He let himself ride the journey of pleasure along with her, growing impossibly hard.

When the last of the climax passed, she opened her eyes, glassy with pleasure. "You do me great honor, Dr. MacLean. I hope we have more sessions in the future."

He did too, and not just because of how glorious she looked now that he'd sated her. He'd learned so much about her it staggered. It would've taken days to ferret out what he had in one *psychoanalysis* session. He'd given her the license to be open, honest, and free with him. That she'd taken him up on his offer spoke volumes about her own need to share. She'd held everything inside for so long she'd probably forgotten how to divulge secrets. If she'd ever known how. She seemed like the type to want to appear self-sufficient, unwilling to let others see her insecurities.

Had Gage seen them? If he had, he hadn't shared them with Smith. Perhaps he felt it would've been too much of an invasion of her privacy—too much of a betrayal. Today's conversation with him had been very brief. Gage had demanded to know what was going on, and nothing short of a dinner invitation would get him to back off. So they'd all have dinner tomorrow night, and Smith could see if Alessandra really was over her infatuation with his friend.

She had closed her eyes again and made no argument when he released her. The cuffs were leather shackles with fur lining, so no marks were visible. Still, he massaged each wrist and ankle to ensure the circulation was strong. When he released the last cuff, she turned on her side, curling into a ball. Good, not like before.

She wasn't trying to make herself so small so as to disappear. This was a curl like she was trying to cling to the pleasure she had endured. Her eyes opened to meet his gaze, and she snaked out a hand to press against his crotch.

Predictably, his cock twitched.

Her eyebrow arched. "We'll have to do something about that."

He'd planned to go jerk off in the bathroom. A few minutes spent remembering her in the throes of passion would do the trick. "Are you offering?"

She wrinkled her brow. "I'm pretty tired and not

sure I could keep up a pace to bring you pleasure."

"What if I told you to lay back and enjoy it?"

Alessandra's eyes lit with pleasure. "I like the sound of that."

"So get on all fours, ass over the side of the bed."

She groaned but rolled over obediently, positioning herself so he could press into her with ease.

With slow, deliberate motions, he removed his clothes, laying them on the chair. When he was naked, he reached for the bottle of lube and put a good dollop on his cock and then a good dollop on her asshole. She groaned again but didn't fight him as he worked his fingers into her. They hadn't discussed ass play, but if she had an objection, she didn't raise it. In fact, she pushed back against him. First one finger, then two. She was unbelievably tight, but that just made him harder. He'd have to be careful.

When he pressed the head of his cock against her, she tensed. He made long strokes along her back. "You need to relax, and this will go much easier." And, slowly, her sphincter muscles let go of their tension. He pressed into her. It took some work, but eventually he managed to get in, a little pop sound accompanying his success.

She made an inarticulate sound, her hands fisting into the sheets.

Then he seated himself. In and out, letting the lube do much of the work. He was big, and he didn't want to hurt her, but man, was she tight. When he was balls-deep in her, he stroked her back again, one hand seeking purchase on her shoulder while the other held her ass.

"It's time." He watched for a signal from her. She

nodded, and he rocked against her. Pushing in and pulling out, he let the friction do the work, reveling in the sensations she was eliciting. His thrusts increased in intensity, and her arms gave way, and she pressed her face to the mattress. He lessened the time between strokes, giving her less time to recover and purposely stealing more and more of her oxygen. As he was getting closer, he moved his hand around her waist and delved into that sacred spot between her thighs.

She ground her clit into his thumb, signifying she was close.

A few more thrusts and he found his release. He sped up the pace with Alessandra, and soon she fell over the precipice with him. Her contractions gripped her pelvis and squeezed his cock.

He slipped from her and then lay on the bed next to her, pulling her against him. Their feet dangled off the bed, and he had no idea where the comforter was, but none of that mattered. The pleasure still sang in his veins, and both of them still breathed harshly. He stroked her hair, not even minding those spiky bits.

"Thank you." Her voice was barely audible as she reached behind her to press a hand to his thigh.

"Um, you're welcome." It felt so inadequate. She seemed to have enjoyed it quite a lot, but he could have gone slower, been gentler. Except, gentle hadn't been what she'd needed. She'd begged for that life-affirming passion her soul sought. She was fighting her death wish with every breath, and he was unwilling to just let her slip away.

For now they had more pressing concerns.

"I think we need another shower."

"No." She murmured a protest. "I'm not moving

until morning."

He rose, found the comforter, and placed it over her. Within moments, she was asleep.

Chapter Twenty-One

When Smith shook her, Allie tried to push him away. "It can't possibly be morning." She would've looked at her watch, but her eyelids were too heavy, her wrist too far away.

"Nope." His confirmation was in a far-too-cheerful voice. "It's about ten o'clock, and you're going to have a bath. Now are you going to walk, or am I going to carry you?"

She was tired but could still move under her own steam, so she rose.

"You get into the bath while I change the sheets, then I'll join you."

She brightened. "A bath together? I like the sound of that." She did a little happy dance as she went to the tub. With a big soaker tub, two would be a tight fit, which just made her all the happier. She took a quick pee and then slipped into the warmth. *Wonderful.* Steam still rose from the water. She laid her head back and floated away.

When Smith shifted her so he could slip in behind her, she didn't even open her eyes. Instead, she let him pull her back against his chest and wrap his arms around her. He pressed a kiss just below her ear, and she shivered.

"Cold?"

She shook her head. "I didn't think it'd be possible,

but I'm turned on."

"Whore." The teasing was clear.

Yet still, she stiffened. *God, he couldn't know. No one knew.*

His arms tightened around her. "A joke, Alessandra, and a piss-poor one at that. Please accept my apologies."

He'd hit just a little too close to home because she felt like a kept woman here, in his space. *Take a breath and don't take his words to heart.* Just an expression, and it meant nothing. Time passed, and eventually she relaxed again.

When he touched her breasts, that relaxation abandoned her body. Gently, she removed his hand. "I'm sorry, Smith, but I'm not...turned on anymore."

He pressed a kiss to her cheek. "I'm the one who's sorry. I was out of line."

"Let's just let it go." *Please. Please God.*

She thought he was going to argue with her, but he didn't. Instead he cleaned her chest with clinical detachment. He eased her forward and scrubbed her back. She couldn't bite back the sigh escaping her lips. "It's so nice to have someone to wash my back."

"Hard to do it yourself, isn't it?"

She moaned in pleasure.

He pressed his lips to the upper curve of her ear and whispered, "I'm very proud of you, Alessandra."

"What for?"

"For your bravery."

She snickered. "I'm hardly brave."

"You could've given in, but you've fought on."

"Smith." She put a warning note in her voice. He was hitting too close to home, and she didn't know if she could keep her shit together.

He seemed to get the message since he said nothing, simply resumed his leisurely cleansing of her body. Knees, thighs, hips. Everything he had massaged before was now being touched again, sensitizing her skin. God, all it took was his touch, and a flame lit within her. Mindlessly, she reached for his right hand and guided it to her core.

"I thought…" His voice trailed off as she flexed her hips and let her knees fall to the sides of the tub. "What the lady wants, the lady gets."

His hands did wonderful things to her body, and she marveled at how close she was to the edge. Her body begged and wouldn't be happy until it yielded, and she did. She bit down on her lip to keep from crying out.

"Let go, Alessandra." He whispered the words into her ear. "Fly free."

She came, hard and fast, her cry echoing in the small, confined space of the room. When she expected him to pull back, he kept up the relentless pressure.

"I'm not going to manage four orgasms." She could barely get the words out.

"I'll settle for two." He brought his other hand down to slip inside her. An odd angle, but his fingers were long enough to hit her G-spot.

She groaned as the next climax hit her. This one was slower but no less powerful. She slumped back against him as his hands let her go. She floated along, allowing the water to seep into her muscles as they rode the glory his magical fingers had elicited.

She continued to float until she felt something very hard against her hip. "Hmm." She slipped her hand into the water, reaching behind her.

He yelped when her icy hand grasped him. "Alessandra..." Her name escaped from him, sliding the *S* and elongating the *A*.

She found it a challenge to find purchase in the water, but she was determined. "You got dirty and need to be cleaned," she informed him, even as she stroked.

He shifted her so her arm wasn't stretched so far, giving her tacit permission to have her way with him.

The culmination came surprisingly quickly, ending with one long groan from him. "Jesus." A reverential hiss. "I wasn't expecting that."

"Those are the best ones, I think." That was her opinion. "The ones that catch you unaware."

"I don't think I have another orgasm in me. It's been quite an evening."

"Are you complaining?"

"Fuck, no." His answer was quick, decisive. "It's just that I'm getting tired."

"So am I. I think I'll sleep well tonight." As the water was cooling quickly, she reluctantly rose from the bath.

"You dry off." He reached for a plastic bottle. "I'm just going to wash my hair."

She did as she was bade but watched him as she did so.

In the water, his hair appeared darker. He was proficient in his movements, quick and efficient. He was out of the tub before she was completely dry.

Reversing the afternoon's scenario, she pressed a towel to him. "Let me dry you."

He looked like he was going to argue but let his arms drop.

Taking a fresh towel, she started with his feet—big feet for a big man. His legs were lightly covered with the same blond hair that dusted his chest and crowned his head. His pubic hair was a shade darker but still well within the realm of golden yellow. His hips were lean, his stomach taut, and his abs rock hard.

He must exercise regularly, because this kind of body wasn't achieved by sitting in an office all day.

His arms were muscular, and his biceps flexed when he lifted his arms so she could dry under them.

Then she moved around to his ass. A very nice ass to be sure, and as she was drying it, she was tempted to grab. But she refrained, instead moving on to his broad and solid back. Reaching up to his shoulders, she was grateful when he bent his knees slightly so she could run the towel through his hair a couple of times. Just before she backed away, she stepped closer and pressed herself against his back, flattening her breasts and resting her cheek just under his shoulder blade. He reached behind with both hands to grasp her ass, bringing her even closer. She wrapped her arms around his chest and let out a ragged breath.

He was such a robust man. He'd told her she could tell him anything, and she believed him because she was within a breath of telling him everything.

When she sighed, he took her hands in his and quickly reversed his position so he could cradle her in his arms. "Let go, Alessandra."

"I can't, Smith." She said the words with conviction. "If I do, I'll fly apart."

When he reached for a towel to dry her hair, she let him. His hands were gentle and sure. Soon most of the moisture was gone.

"Let's go to bed."

Did that mean they'd be sharing a bed? She didn't care. No, to be honest, it did matter. She wanted to lie in those powerful arms and absorb all the comfort they were offering.

When they got to the threshold of the dungeon, he took her cheeks in his hands. "I'm asking you to sleep here, with me."

In that moment, she recognized vulnerability. Sure, they'd slept together last night, but that'd been after a bout of intense blow jobs, cunnilingus, and mind-blowing fucking. This was different. This was him asking her into his inner sanctum with them on even terms. As a man and a woman, not a submissive and her Dominant.

"Yes, please." She searched his eyes, dark in the dim torchlight. "I want you to hold me tonight, and I want to be able to hold you."

A momentary look of relief—just a flash—but she saw it.

He took her much smaller hand in his, leading her to the bed that was turned down, just waiting for them.

She lay down, luxuriating against the Egyptian cotton of some obscenely high thread count. When he slipped in behind her, she let him pull her close, fitting them together. Her back against his chest, his hips to her bottom, their thighs in union. His hand snaked around her waist, settling on the shelf under her breasts. His sigh was gentle against her nape.

She felt so safe she wanted to stay curled up there forever.

Within moments, however, she drifted away.

Chapter Twenty-Two

Awareness came in degrees. He kept the room in complete darkness. No clock radio. A clock, of course, but it emitted no light. And the alarm hadn't awakened him since it was Saturday.

Alessandra wasn't in bed with him. He had a vague memory of her slipping from bed, and the thought that flitted through his mind as he'd sunk back to sleep had been she was going to the bathroom. How long ago had that been?

Well, he was awake now, so he might as well go and find her.

The hallway had dull illumination from the sky, indicating the sun hadn't risen yet. The forecast called for another sunny day. They'd go for a walk, he decided as he took a piss. She needed the fresh air, and he needed the exercise. Their exertions in bed were all good, but they needed more.

He returned to the dungeon and dressed for the day in jeans and a sweater. He'd add a coat if necessary. Selecting a similar outfit for Alessandra, he also chose a nice pair of walking boots. Since she'd be breaking them in, he'd have to make sure she didn't get blisters. He added a wool coat and leather gloves. All were expensive but understated. Mme Veronique had impeccable taste, which was why he'd called her.

As he walked toward the kitchen, Alessandra's

voice sounded from the direction of the dining room. He was about to call out, but no, she wasn't talking to him.

"I found drugs in his room. I mean, he's been acting strange. He's my baby boy, you know? But he's been so moody and…distant. I thought he's just being a teenager, but then, when I was putting his laundry away, I found a baggie full of pills. I mean, where did he get all those pills? I never have more than Tylenol in the house, so they didn't come from me. Do you think he's addicted? How would I even know?" A pause. "Oh, I'm sorry for rambling on, but I'm just so scared." Another pause.

He could go into the kitchen where she wouldn't be able to see him, or he could give her privacy and go back to the bedroom. He shook his head with a small smile because he wasn't above listening in.

He headed to the kitchen.

"You think I should talk to him with a counselor? Can you help me with that? I mean, I don't want him to feel threatened, but I'm scared. What if he overdoses?" A pause. "That soon? Really? I thought it might be weeks, but just a few days? Oh, God, thank you so much."

Figuring the call was pretty much over, Smith set about making coffee.

"I know you're there."

He poked his head around the corner and tried to look innocent. "Me? I just got here."

She scowled. "I'm not allowed to lie, but you think you can bullshit me?" A twitch at the corner of her mouth gave her away. She smiled when he came over and planted one hand on the table, the other on the back of the chair.

He leaned in, and just a fraction of an inch before he reached her lips, he whispered, "Good morning, little one." He pressed his lips to hers. Gentle at first, then he moved to coaxing. Finally, he moved to demanding, seeking entrance. He moved his hand from the back of the chair and ran his fingers through her short, choppy hair. Why had she cut off that glorious mane? To try to hide herself, she'd said. He'd love to delve his hands into those thick black locks, but that was not to be.

She snaked her arms out to grip his shoulders.

He slipped his other hand into her robe. As he pressed his palm against her breast, he was pleased when the nipple came alive and perked up in his hand. He gave it one painful squeeze, and she squealed.

Pulling back from the kiss, he hauled her to her feet. He handed her the pile of clothes and then patted her on the ass. "Go get dressed like a good girl."

Her expression was mutinous.

God, he could've reached down between her thighs and made her come. Instead he had chosen the more prudent course. They needed food and fresh air before they went back to the dungeon.

She was halfway to her bedroom before she turned. "Smith?"

"Yes."

"Do you call me 'little one' as a term of endearment, a term meant to demean me and keep me in my place, or because of my height?"

It stunned him. "I'll say one thing, and you had better hear me clearly. I would never say something to demean you. It is, as you say, a term of endearment, not a term of condescension."

She held his gaze for another beat. "Okay." With that, she left.

He'd have to watch his words. She was intuitive about some things, but not with others. She was shifting ground with him, keeping him on his toes.

A quick search of the fridge produced eggs that hadn't yet expired and bread not quite gone stale. Scrambled-egg sandwiches coming up.

She was back before long, and they worked together in companionable silence.

Finally, he had to speak. "How was the call?"

"Let me guess—you hated waiting to open presents and were always trying to figure out what you were getting?"

"We had few presents." Sharp and perhaps too blunt.

"I'm sorry." She was contrite. "I should've known because the same held for me. It's just that you can be very impatient. Are you like this with everything?"

He shook his head, taking the plates in hand while she brought the mugs of coffee. "I'm able to wait and bide my time if necessary, and other times, I need to be ready to pounce. It's a delicate balance I don't always get right."

"It's the opposite for me. I always need be patient and let them come to me. If I push too hard, I could lose them forever."

Holding his breath, he kept his gaze down, looking at his plate. She was talking, and he sure as shit wasn't going to interrupt.

"They teach you that in school, but especially on your first few cases, you want to speed things up. You want to understand a problem as quickly as possible.

Instead you have to take a breath and work to build trust." She hesitated. "Trust is such a tricky thing. Hard to obtain and so easy to lose. When they made me supervisor, I had to show some of that patience and share my knowledge with new social workers. They were fresh out of school and had the same impatience I'd had. Teaching those new counselors was a powerful feeling but one that came with great responsibility, because the other thing I had to impart to them was how to keep their objectivity. It's so easy to get sucked in and want to fix everything all at once. It's so hard to separate the personal from the professional." Another pause. "I lost that objectivity, and I'm paying a high price for it."

"Too high." He strove to keep his voice level and quiet. "You hold yourself to such lofty standards—it's hardly a surprise you fell. If one of your workers had done the same thing as you, how would you have treated her?"

Her eyes had been focused on some point far in the distance. She snapped them to stare into his. "It's not the same thing."

"Isn't it?" He raised a challenging brow. "Would you have fired them?"

"No, of course not."

"But you thought you committed such a grievous mistake you deserved a harsher punishment than one you'd mete out? That's a double standard, Alessandra. What about objectivity? How about applying that to yourself and your situation?"

"It's not the same."

"The hell it's not." Anger coursed through his veins, and he spit the words out. "You're feeling sorry for yourself."

She jerked to her feet. "Fuck you. You have no idea what you're talking about."

"Sit down."

She shook her head wildly.

He stood and pulled himself to his full height. "You are going to sit down, and you will eat your breakfast. If you do that, we'll go out for a walk. If you don't, there will be serious consequences. Consequences you won't like. Make your choice, Alessandra, but make it wisely."

Mutiny was still in her expression when she dropped to her chair. Smith retook his seat and began eating as if the past minute hadn't happened. Who knew if she feared the consequences, wanted the walk, or was just hungry? She was eating, however, and he'd take that.

****

Smith was grateful Mme Veronique had provided sunglasses, because the sun was brilliant and strong. In the end, they opted to forgo coats, and the wind was brisk and refreshing.

"I thought we might go grocery shopping."

Alessandra nodded approval. "We're running out of food. What would you like me to cook for dinner?"

That brought him up short. He'd almost forgotten the Claytons were coming over.

"What were you thinking?"

"Rosemary chicken, mashed potatoes, and broccoli. For dessert, I was thinking of baking a fresh blueberry pie. They're in season now, and I heard the valley had a bumper crop."

He could all but taste the luscious blueberries.

Following her into the grocery store, he removed his sunglasses. "Do you think we could have a spinach and blueberry salad for lunch?"

Her smile came easily as she stuck her glasses on her head. "Yes, but you'll be pooping blue."

He bent and placed a kiss to her temple, then smiled. "I don't care."

"Fair enough, but consider yourself warned."

She seemed a little disconcerted by the PDA but didn't protest.

They used a cart but selected judiciously since they had to carry what they bought. In the end, they bought too much and used a taxi to get them home.

They put the groceries away together, but her moves were jerky, the easygoing attitude absent. She turned to him. "While you make the salad, do you mind if I go make another phone call?"

"For JEAP or personal?"

She shot him a funny look. "Who the hell would I call?"

Excellent point.

"Sure, you can do whatever might make you happy." She looked vulnerable, and he fought the urge to reach out and touch her. "You can use my office if you want privacy."

She nodded, parted her lips, but shook her head slightly and then simply slipped away.

As he washed the spinach, he mused on their morning. Highs and lows. That's what it always felt like with her. Like he was on a roller coaster. He was searching for purchase, for sure footing, yet finding none. She'd been forthcoming this morning, probably not even aware of how much she'd given him.

219

He sliced the cucumbers and grimaced. He shouldn't have challenged her. He should've just let her talk. Her assertion she deserved to lose her job, while admitting she wouldn't fire a subordinate for the same transgression, had been so ridiculous he hadn't been able to keep his own counsel.

As he washed the blueberries, he mused on their walk. It'd mostly been made in silence, but they'd held hands. In the grocery store they'd teased each other and then laughed at the jokes made by their cabbie. Smith had given the man double their fare just because he'd made Alessandra giggle. She had a beautiful laugh, sparkling and light—delicate like the woman. But she had strength behind that fragile exterior.

His stomach clenched at her assertion she wanted to die. Today, there'd been no sign of that woman. Yet last night, he'd had no doubt of the veracity or ferocity of her statement. Somehow he had to get through to her.

The salad was ready, so he brought it to the table along with a selection of dressings. He was just deciding between bacon ranch and Caesar when she returned, holding out his phone.

"It buzzed while I was on the landline. I would have brought it out…"

"No, it's fine." He waved dismissively. "Whoever can wait. Let's eat."

She nodded, letting him dish out her portion. The first few bites were almost mechanical, and she speared each blueberry, eating them one at a time.

"Tough call?"

Glancing up at him, she nodded. "My mother died a month ago, and I can't seem to deal with it. I keep crying at stupid commercials and when I see old women."

"That'd hit close to home."

"I suppose I could've made it my father or a sibling, but I wanted there to be some authenticity to it."

"As opposed to finding drugs in your son's room?"

That made her smile. "Clichéd, I admit, but there's truth in it as well. I counseled lots of parents in similar situations and worked with local family doctors to get kids into rehab. Imagine, rehab at sixteen."

"I didn't even sneak my first beer until I was seventeen."

"You were a respectful kid, then."

Smith shrugged. "I had to be. I didn't want to disappoint my mother. She sacrificed so much…"

"I felt the same way." She took another bite.

He was dying to ask about the call to JEAP, but she'd made it clear he'd have to wait. At least she was doing something productive. Maybe that would raise her self-esteem. People needed a purpose. What had her purpose been the last six months? Surviving rather than thriving, that was for sure.

The rest of the meal passed in silence. When they rose, she took the salad bowl and he the dirty dishes.

"If the two of us work together, how long will it take to make dinner?"

She paused. "Once the pie is ready to bake, it takes just under an hour. While it cools, I'll cook the chicken, boil the potatoes, and steam the broccoli. A couple of hours should cover it. Less if you help me."

"Oh, I'll help—you can count on that."

She leaned over to place the plates in the dishwasher. "I should probably turn this on…ow."

He'd pinched her ass. Probably didn't have the same effect because she wore jeans, but he had her attention. "Conservatively, we have three hours to kill."

She didn't turn to face him as she put the soap in the dishwasher. "And you have a way to pass the time?"

That earned her a smack on the ass so hard she went up on her toes.

"I'll take that as a *yes*."

"Go and wait for me."

Still, she didn't turn. "Yes, Master." She ducked her head and left.

Better to keep her occupied than let her dwell on the upcoming dinner. Her tension level had been ratcheting up as each hour passed, and he didn't need all his genius to figure out what was wrong.

He was about to head to the dungeon when he caught sight of his phone. Better to check for messages in case Gage was calling to cancel. Oh, a text message and not a missed call.

Toby Driscoll.

He glanced over at the closed door. The dungeon was soundproof, but he wasn't willing to take that chance. He strode into the office and closed the door. No way would she breach his inner sanctum without permission.

The call was answered on the first ring. "Toby Driscoll."

"It's Smith. Do you have something?"

"Yeah, and you're probably not going to like it."

"Look, Toby, I've imagined every potential scenario. Nothing can be worse than that."

A sardonic chuckle. "Ever heard of the Masters'

Club?"

"No."

"And there would be a reason for that. This club is beyond exclusive. We're talking the richest of the rich, most powerful of the powerful."

Smith bristled. He certainly wasn't poor… "What's your point?"

"Carl Jergen created it."

That caught Smith's attention. That was the name of one of the top members of the judiciary in British Columbia who was running to be the leader of the most conservative of parties. Smith had met the so-called pillar of the community a couple times over the course of the past year at political fundraisers, and the man had felt…off. "So what's the Masters' Club?"

"It's a BDSM club, but these guys are nasty. They meet at Club Kink. Exclusive, invitation only. I talked to one of the girls who used to work there, and she told me some of the shit that went down."

Time to proceed with caution. Some people thought Kink on a Saturday night was nasty shit, so all relative. "What else did she say?"

"The club only operates on Wednesday nights, so the girls have to earn enough to make it through the week or find a second gig. Trixie opted to get a second job rather than go for the works. Alessandra, it appears, was up for anything."

"Define anything."

"Whippings, beatings, chains, oral sex, sodomy, gang bangs. You name it, and she did it. Trixie says she was scared one of the guys would go overboard and really hurt Alessandra, but it never went quite that far. But they'd pass her around like a toy." Toby paused.

"You still there?"

"Yeah, I'm still here." Smith grimaced, trying to settle his churning gut. "Does Trixie want out?"

"She got out last month when Mr. Jergen himself almost choked a girl to death. She begged Alessandra to come with her, but the next Wednesday she heard from another girl that Alessandra had gone back for more." Toby let that sink in. "The thing is the Masters' Club is like Fight Club. The first rule is no one talks about it."

"Trixie did."

"True, but she did it at her own peril." Toby let out something that might have been a sigh. "She wants to blow town. She's thinking somewhere back East."

Now it was Smith's turn to sigh. "How much?"

"Five, ten large should get her out of town and keep her there."

"I don't keep that much cash here, but we can meet on Monday. Give her whatever you've got and tell her to keep her fucking head down until then."

Toby chuckled. "I gave her ten and put her on the bus myself. I figured you were good for it."

Smith let out a sigh of relief. "That's excellent work, Toby."

"I'm angling for my bonus. I'm heading to Mission City on Monday."

"Discretion, my friend."

"Always. I'll get people talking. If I have anything to report, I'll get back to you Monday night." A noise resonated in the background. "I've got to run. Later." With that, he terminated the call.

Smith stared at his phone as if it could provide some divination into the situation. He was disgusted and outraged, but not altogether shocked. He'd seen her scanning those STI results. She'd known the risk she'd been taking but had done it anyway. His urge was to barge in and confront her, but that wouldn't do. He needed her fully present for the soirée with the Claytons. He and Gage had a few surprises up their sleeves, and it would require her complete attention.

He dropped the phone back to the desk. *Focus, damn it.* He never played when he wasn't completely focused. Pushing aside thoughts of Masters' Club and Carl Jergen, he headed to the dungeon.

Chapter Twenty-Three

God, but he loved to make her wait. *Mind over matter*. She imagined herself lying in the sun, absorbing the light and the warmth. She usually loved summer. Slather on some sunscreen and laze about. Not this summer. She'd spent her time in her stifling, cramped, little room, trying to live with herself. Her past and her present had been swirling around her, hitting her in unrelenting blasts of conscience. Most days she'd just lie there, bathed in sweat, and try to find a way out of her life.

She'd been truthful when she told Smith she'd been too chickenshit to kill herself. For just a moment, her mind flitted to what might be. Not returning to her old life—that wasn't a possibility—but maybe she could be more than a whore.

Her eyes shut, and she shivered, not from the cold. He'd been right on the nose with that name, even if he only said it in jest. He didn't know—couldn't know—what she was, but it was her reality. She sold access to her body for money. If that wasn't a whore, then she wasn't sure what was.

The door opened, and she dropped her gaze to the ground. She was kneeling again, hands on her thighs, palms up. Offering herself up to whatever he was willing to give her. She needed this and understood why he was doing this. Not just for his pleasure. To provide her with a distraction.

"Stand."

With practiced grace, she rose. Gage had taught her that—how to kneel, how to stand gracefully, how to present herself. He'd been a taskmaster, but now she was grateful.

"You please your Master, little one. Go stand by the wall."

As she had the first night, she went to the wall by the manacles. The last time he hadn't shackled her. Might he this time? She put her toes to the wall, leaned forward so her breasts pressed flat, and then turned so her cheek lay flush. When he reached for her arm, she let it go limp. Ah, that little frisson of pleasure when he cuffed first one, then the other wrist to the wall. It left her arms outstretched, but not uncomfortably so. When he stepped back, she tested the restraints, making sure they'd hold her, then rolled her eyes at herself. As if he'd have anything that might not be sturdy. Or Rielle would have. No, this place was as durable as anything else she'd ever encountered.

He went to the wall of torture, but she kept her eyes closed. Sometimes she liked surprises.

The first hit had her rocking up on her toes and gnashing her teeth. "Shit, that hurt." She spit it out before she could marshal herself.

"I'm sorry—did you say something?"

"I said, thank you, Master, I appreciated that paddle."

"I thought that's what you said." He paused. "Now count." He laid this one across the top of her thighs.

"Two."

He tapped her lightly against her already sore ass.

"You don't know how to count, little one."

She shook her head in confusion. She was *sure* there'd only been two hits.

"The first one was to warm you up. Now we have to start all over again."

Shit. She didn't dare ask how far she'd have to count. She suspected she might run out of fingers and even toes by the time—

The smack caught her off guard. She needed to focus. "One, thank you, Master."

"That's a good little one." Then he hit her again.

In the end, he only hit her fifteen times, but that'd been enough for her to live in the pain instead of fighting against it. She wasn't even aware he was finished until she felt him naked and pressing into her. Her ass must have been hot against his hips, but her only thought was how fast he was going to make this.

"You're so wet, little one. Someone might think you enjoyed being paddled."

Too much talk. She flexed her hips to draw him in more fully.

In response, he pulled out.

She keened and gritted her teeth in frustration. Desire thrummed through her continuously, a marching band of drums.

"I'm sorry—did you say something?"

She shook her head. Nope, she wasn't going to beg again.

He planted his hands against her fiery ass and then squeezed.

Pain bloomed and spread.

"I said, did you say something?"

Oh, to hell with it. "Please, Master, fuck me. The

sooner, the better," she added, just in case he didn't hear the desperation in her voice.

He rammed himself into her. Thus began a battery of thrusts that had her pulling against her restraints, wanting to touch, wanting to scream.

"Let go." He bit her shoulder.

This time, she did scream.

Chapter Twenty-Four

As Smith released her, she sagged back against him, completely spent. He scooped her into his arms and carried her the few feet to the bed. When he laid her down, her breasts were red from him repeatedly slamming her against the wall. He'd been a brute. He wanted to obliterate the image Toby had planted in his mind, and instead, he'd debased her. Brought himself down to the level of those rich pricks.

He opened one of the dresser drawers and pulled out a tin of salve. With the lightest of touches, he applied the concoction, hoping he hadn't caused any lasting damage. He'd been so obsessed with being in her he'd forgotten all about tonight.

As her skin absorbed the salve, the red color diminished. Her eyes fluttered open. "I appreciate Master is taking care of me."

He bit back the sarcastic remark on the tip of his tongue and instead offered her a smile. "You were very good, little one. Your Master is just sorry he got a little overenthusiastic."

She reached out to snag the hand he'd been applying the salve with and pressed it to her chest. "Please, don't ever apologize."

His chest tightened. "Even Masters make mistakes, little one. And when we do, we must apologize and, in certain circumstances, atone." He offered a smile. "But since you seem to have forgiven me, we'll skip the atonement for today."

Her eyes drifted shut.

He leaned down to place a kiss on her forehead. "Sleep now. I'll wake you when it's time."

Rising, he pulled the comforter over her. He put the salve away, grabbed his clothes, turned off the lights, and closed the door.

Anger still churned in his gut as he made his way to the office. Did he have the right to pry? Even if he knew how to ferret out this Masters' Club, what would he do? It sounded like it all was between consenting adults, although when money was involved, things got dicey.

Still, she'd made her choice. The one question uppermost in his mind was how had she been recruited? A woman wasn't simply walking down the street, accosted, and then dragged to a BDSM club. Someone had to know someone.

He flipped through the contacts on his phone. The call was answered on the third ring.

"Mistress Gigi? We need to talk."

****

As he stared at the package of blueberries, the dungeon door opened. *Whew*.

Alessandra padded out, barefoot and swamped in his robe. She was trying to do something with her hair, which appeared extra-spiky. "You should've woken me."

Smith shrugged. "I figured with a recipe I should be okay, but I'll admit I'm a little lost."

She stunned them both by leaning over to place a kiss on his cheek. Eyes wide, she placed her fingers to her lips, as if trying to take it back.

He was having none of it, though. Reaching for her hand, he used it to drag her against him. He pressed a kiss to her lips that scorched them both.

Damn, if a pie didn't need to be baked, he'd take her right there on the kitchen floor.

She composed herself first. "Did you take the pie crust out of the fridge?"

She'd wanted to do the entire thing from scratch, but he'd put his foot down on that one. Nothing wrong with store-bought crust because it'd given them extra play time. Time, as it turned out, they'd both needed.

He took a steadying breath. "Crust out of fridge, got it."

They worked together, him following her carefully meted-out instructions. He wasn't accustomed to taking orders, but something in her crisp-and-clipped remarks stirred him. She was also generous in her praise when he got it right and quick to correct when he got it wrong.

When they hit a lull, he told her to go take a quick shower. "And put on the crimson silk dress. No bra or underwear."

Now her cheeks turned crimson. "We're having guests."

"Are you arguing with me?"

A vigorous headshake. "No, Master. Just making sure I understood you."

They both knew she was lying, but he'd let that one slide. When she left, he put his hands against the counter and took another steadying breath. Then he glanced at his watch and pulled himself up. All that was left to do was mashing the potatoes. She ran a very efficient kitchen. He set about unloading the dishwasher.

Then another image came, this one unbidden. She deserved more than what she had. He could see her living in the suburbs with some guy and having two-point-three kids. He'd lay even odds that'd been her dream before everything went to shit. Fallen apart.

Maybe, maybe not. She'd had a demanding career, and maybe that'd been enough.

No, he'd seen the look on her face yesterday when he asked her if she wanted a baby. Her denial had been too swift, too certain. The pain had been there, even as she'd tried to hide it.

"Smith?"

Her call brought him from his reverie. He followed the sound of her voice to the dungeon. "Yes, Alessandra."

She stood in the walk-in closet. As he'd asked, she wore the crimson dress. It hugged her body so tightly panty lines would've shown anyway, so she should be grateful for his thoughtfulness. But that didn't seem to be the problem. She was looking at the shoeboxes, turning to him when he was next to her. "Which shoes am I supposed to wear?"

The situation seemed absurd to him. Didn't women know everything about shoes? He pulled out the box with the strappy silver sandals. "These will do."

"Those have three-inch heels. I don't walk in three-inch heels. I'm liable to fall over and spill the blueberry pie on your lap."

Hadn't she been wearing heels that high when he'd met her at Kink? Well, she hadn't been steady that night either. "Then I carry and you serve. Honestly,

Alessandra, didn't Gage teach you to wear heels?"

Twin spots of blush appeared on her cheeks. "We, um, didn't leave the house very much. Or ever. Well, that's not true. As a threesome, we went out, but we had to be vanilla. Wouldn't do to have the local principal being seen with two women dressed in tight dresses, high heels, and no underwear."

He couldn't help it. He smiled. "Fair enough. Look, put on the heels, go barefoot—I don't care. Just help me make sure the pie doesn't burn."

That spurred her into action as she opened the box, took the shoes, dropped the box, and headed toward the kitchen.

He delivered a quick and hard smack to her ass.

She immediately reached out and rubbed it.

Good. She was still sore from this afternoon.

"What was that for?"

"For leaving me to pick up after you."

She let out a huff, returned, picked up the box, and shoved it back where it'd come from. "If we burn the pie, it's on you, not me."

The pie wasn't burned but emitted the most mouthwatering smell.

He wanted a quick bite, but she wanted to present it intact and then slice it at the table.

She'd also bought whipped cream to go with it.

He could think of a few things he wanted to do with that cream, but he held himself in check. Later.

****

Exactly at the appointed hour, a knock sounded at the door. Gage was nothing if not prompt.

The man himself looked good in a suit, and Rielle looked gorgeous in a soft, bronze-colored dress that

234

brought out the amber of her eyes. She looked very different from the last time Smith had seen her, when she'd been so distressed. The lines of worry, so prominent for the past six months, seemed to have eased. Damn Alessandra for what she'd put these caring people through.

Shaking away the morose thoughts, Smith held the door for them.

Rielle stepped forward first, her high heels clicking on the hardwood. Gage followed with a bottle of wine that he handed over.

A nice vintage, but how could Gage afford it? That's right, Gage had said something about Rielle having money. They hadn't been hurting after Smith had paid market rate for the condo. According to the papers, Rielle had owned it free and clear.

He stepped into the dining room where Alessandra was.

She stood behind a chair, using it as a protective shield between herself and the Claytons.

"Alessandra, come and greet our guests." He was careful to make it a command.

That snapped her to attention, and she stepped out from behind her chair. She took several halting steps.

Whether she was tottering from the shoes or the emotions, he wasn't sure.

Then she stepped into Rielle's waiting arms and began to sob.

Smith caught Gage's gaze and nodded toward the kitchen. When they stepped out of the hearing range of the women, he sighed. "I didn't see that coming."

"Neither did I. After the last time we saw her, we weren't sure what kind of a reception we'd get." Gage reached for the glasses when Smith opened the bottle of wine. "How's she been holding up?"

Smith shrugged. "She has her moments. A lot of highs and lows."

"I found it the same way when I first met Rielle. It takes time to get in sync, you know? To find that balance between dominance and nurturing."

"Ugh, that makes it sound like…"

The two men laughed.

"Yeah, but no matter how hard we try, Rielle and I are never twenty-four seven. The entire world changes when you have a baby. We want Cara to grow up and have a balanced perspective on relationships."

"And if she grows up to be a submissive?"

Gage cringed. "You know, that wouldn't be my first choice. Doctor, veterinarian, teacher, even a lawyer like her mama, but not a submissive."

"Isn't that a double standard?"

He pondered. "If, as an adult, she chose the lifestyle, then I'd encourage her to do what made her happy. Is she ever going to see the playroom? Not in this lifetime or the next."

The two men chuckled.

Smith sobered first. "Time to take wine out to the women?"

"Only one glass, of course."

"Yeah, about that…"

"You haven't changed your mind, have you?"

Smith shook his head. "Hell, no. But I haven't spoken to Alessandra about it. Did you talk to Rielle?"

"Before I called you. I didn't want her to be weirded out by the fact I'm going to be with my old submissive and my new one."

"And she was okay with it?"

Gage smiled. "She brought the nipple clamps with the extra-long chain."

Chapter Twenty-Five

Allie tried to play the perfect hostess, but she struggled. Her meltdown in Rielle's arms put an odd pall on the evening, and she was racking her brain on how to lighten the mood. Smith talked about the business deal gone bad, Rielle talked about her latest legal-aid case, and Gage talked about things from school. Allie had nothing to add. What was there to report? The kinky doctor? The huge shopping kerfuffle?

Then inspiration hit. During a lull in the conversation, she volunteered, "Smith bought me an e-reader."

Rielle's eyes lit. "I've had one for years. Have you seen all the erotica?"

Huh? "Um, no, I was just catching up on the latest bestsellers. I haven't ventured much beyond that."

"Well, I've got a list of authors you just have to read."

Gage nodded. "Make sure you give her the name of that book. The one I liked."

Now Alessandra gaped. Gage? Reading erotica? Wow, she hadn't seen that coming.

Smith nodded indulgently. "I gave her a gift certificate, but I should probably give her more."

She wanted to argue but then remembered the reader still had available memory. She wanted it full when she left. If she added some erotica to the mix, no one would be the wiser.

"Your thoughtfulness is appreciated."

She didn't add the *Master*, but the glint in his eyes told her the message had hit its mark.

"Now maybe you could get the pie?"

He gave her a look that promised retribution. However, he rose and without a word left the room.

"Not to be nosy…" Gage's nose twitched. "Why is Smith getting the pie?"

"Gage, that's incredibly sexist—to expect Allie to wait on us."

Allie laughed, surprising herself. She needed to do that more often. "Actually, it's because of the shoes. I told Smith if he made me wear three-inch heels, I was liable to trip and drop the pie on his lap. He told me if I wore them, he'd carry the pie."

As hoped, Rielle and Gage laughed.

Rielle placed a hand on Allie's arm. "High heels are the worst."

"Hey, you were wearing three-inch heels when we met." Gage waggled his brows.

"Actually three-and-a-quarter-inch heels."

"Smarten up, Gage." Smith reentered the room. "That extra quarter inch makes all the difference." He placed the pie in front of Allie. "You serve."

She didn't miss the steel in his voice, and it only made her smile. "My pleasure, Sir." Okay, maybe that was over the top, but he'd earned it.

She took the knife and cut.

Rielle held the plates as she dished. When she put the last piece of pie on a plate, her friend reached for her wrist and stroked the watch. "This is exquisite."

Cheeks growing warm, she stammered, "A gift from Smith."

Relinquishing the wrist, Rielle raised an eyebrow at Smith. "White gold?"

"Platinum," he smoothly corrected her.

Allie's flush deepened.

Rielle held out her wedding ring for Allie's inspection. "Platinum as well. It's a good solid material. Hard to scratch."

The wedding ring was stunning in its simplicity. Very understated and she could see why Gage had selected it. "It's lovely, Rielle. I'm sorry I missed the wedding."

"Oh, if you had been there, then you would've met Smith earlier."

Holding her breath, she fought against the memories of that horrible night when she'd met Smith. Meeting him had been great. What followed had been…

"Are you okay?"

Allie's eyes snapped up, and she found everyone was looking at her.

"Alessandra, why don't you get the whipped cream?"

She rose, smoothed down her dress, and offered a shaky smile. "Silly me. I'll be right back."

She saw the two baffled looks and the one of concern and had no answer. The whipped cream was on the counter. Obviously, Smith had taken it from the fridge and then forgotten it. One breath. Then another one. She had to hurry back, or someone might come after her. If someone came after her, she might just break.

The conversation had resumed by the time she reached the dining room, and everyone acted as if nothing odd had happened. Sometimes nice to be around people who knew her well enough to know when to leave well enough alone.

After they consumed dessert, they lingered over a deep discussion about the environmental impact the latest pipeline was likely to cause. Rielle firmly opposed the entire thing, but Smith pointed out they had to move the crude oil somehow, and that railcars crashed almost as often as pipelines ruptured. Rielle countered that only so much oil could fit in a tanker car, but a pipeline could pump out hundreds of thousands of barrels before anyone fixed the problem. Allie caught Gage's eye, and they shared a smile. They both believed in environmental causes, but not nearly as passionately as Rielle.

"Rielle." Gage evidently didn't care whether he was interrupting. If he hadn't, the debate might've gone on all night. "Why don't you get Allie to show you the dungeon? I hear Smith has made a few additions."

Rielle's eyes lit. "Oh, that's a splendid idea." She reached out to snag Allie's hand, practically tugging her out of her seat.

"But the dishes." Allie's sputter was made in vain.

Smith waved his hand dismissively. "Gage and I can clean up. You and Rielle go and have a good time."

Have a good time? Giving a tour of the dungeon? That was going to take a minute, unless Smith had made radical alterations. Still, she gave herself up to Rielle's enthusiasm and let the other woman lead her. Although they were about the same age, Rielle seemed more mature. Maybe motherhood, or maybe the woman's horrific past. Smith's words from last night still resonated. Rielle didn't look like a woman who'd suffered abuse, but then again, many of Allie's clients hadn't looked battered either. She was glad Rielle had found someone like Gage who made her so happy. Although she'd expected some jealousy, none materialized.

As soon as they got into the dungeon, Rielle closed the door and stepped out of her shoes. "Get out of those fucking things!"

"Oh, sure." Allie stepped from them and took a deep sigh of relief when her feet hit the cold hardwood floor. "You're right, that feels better." She startled when Rielle stepped toward her, back first.

"Gage had to zip this thing up, so I'll need your help to unzip it." She was holding her beautiful mane of white blonde hair to one side to give Allie better access to the zipper.

"Oh, sure." Because everyone who came in here had to strip? Rielle shimmied out of the dress, and big surprise, the other woman wasn't wearing panties or a bra. Kinky Dominants obviously thought alike.

"Hurry up." Rielle gestured for her to turn around. "They'll be here in a minute, and we need to be ready."

"Ready?" To her own ears, she sounded stupid, but for the life of her, she couldn't figure out what was going on.

Rielle, fingers poised on the zipper, paused, and then she burst out laughing. "Oh man, is Smith in for it. He didn't tell you, eh? Typical man. Well, here's the program for this evening—it's a foursome."

She had Allie unzipped and was tugging down the dress before she caught up. "We're what?" She was trying to hold up the dress, but if she didn't let go, the thing was going to rip. Rielle was strong.

"You don't have to do this." The other woman stepped in front of her. "We just thought it would be a way to welcome you home, you know? But I can tell the guys it's off. Or," she suggested slyly, "you can watch."

Watch?

No fucking way. She didn't want Rielle anywhere near Smith without her as intermediary. "What do you want me to do?"

Rielle's face lit. "I knew you'd be game. We need to present ourselves." She was tugging her down, but Allie shot back up.

"Wait."

"What?" Rielle's face was all concern.

She scrambled. "We have to hang up the dresses. Smith hates having to pick up after me."

Rielle's laughter was low and rich. "That's priceless. He expects you to pick up after him and yourself."

"Actually, he picks up after himself. He's fastidious, but not obsessively so." Hanging up the dresses took mere moments, and then she let Rielle lead her back to the ground where the two women knelt.

"So are there any differences?" Rielle's low voice invited confidences.

"I don't know what the room was like before, so I'm not qualified to answer that question," Allie admitted. "But—"

The door opened.

Although she wasn't supposed to look up, she did. Both men were naked, in all their masculine glory, and she salivated. Why it should be so, she wasn't sure. She'd seen both men naked before. But as a dynamic duo? That's what they were—the dynamic duo. She'd have to remember to tell that one to Rielle. Her gaze dropped, and she hazarded a glance at Rielle, who not only met her eyes but reached out to take her hand.

"A beautiful sight." Smith's contribution.

"I couldn't agree more." Gage's voice was full of amusement. "Rielle, my minx, you forgot your purse."

"Sorry, Master. I was too excited."

"A situation easily remedied. Why don't you both stand?"

Both women stood, keeping their eyes downcast.

"I want to see their eyes when you show them their treat." Smith's tone was a little husky.

Oh…he was up to something.

"An excellent suggestion. Ladies, if you please, look up."

Allie obeyed and saw a wicked pair of nipple clamps with an extra-long chain.

Gage held it out to Rielle. "You first."

Rielle turned to face her.

Okay, she was going to just clamp it on, right?

Rielle dipped her head and took Allie's breast in her mouth, then suckled for several seconds before biting lightly.

Whoa, alrighty then. Could everyone hear her heart pounding?

Rielle secured the clamp.

Ouch. Do not squeal, do not gasp. When presented with the second clamp, Allie gulped and squinched her eyebrows.

"However you feel comfortable." Rielle whispered

the words, but a hopeful light glinted in her eye.

Humbled and honored, Allie returned the favor. Rielle's breast tasted like vanilla. Intriguing. She sucked on the nipple, surprised at how quickly it peaked.

Rielle let out a little moan.

Allie felt...aroused. *Wow*. She'd never thought touching another woman who wasn't Cara would have this effect on her. Would it be the same if the men weren't watching? Possibly not.

She pulled back and applied the clamp as gently as she could. *I'm sorry*, she tried to say with her eyes.

It's okay, replied Rielle's.

Then Gage stepped forward and gave the chain a tug, and both women gasped. "Glad to see the clamps were well attached. Now go lie on the bed, on all fours."

Rielle guided them both.

Allie settled as closely as she could, leaving a bit of slack on the chain. A bit, but not much. If either of them jerked too hard, both were liable to feel pain. By malicious intent, no doubt.

The men had strolled over to the wall and were having a hushed conversation about which implement to use.

Allie couldn't catch all the words, but she suspected she was going to enjoy this, regardless.

Again, Rielle reached out to take her hand.

Feeling connected felt natural. They had Gage in common, and now they were sharing Smith. When the flogger connected with Rielle's ass, her thigh brushed Allie's, and they squeezed hands. Rielle shifted, and Allie felt the bite of the clamp on her nipple.

All the slack in the chain was gone.

Allie didn't wait long to see what implement was going to be used on her. A hand connected with her right buttock.

Then, with lightning speed, Gage switched it up, hitting left to left. Most likely Gage since he was ambidextrous and had an affinity for bare-handed spankings.

The flogger connected with Rielle's ass, and Allie winced right along with the other woman. Allie received a couple of hits, then the men chatted. A hand curved down her ass and reached around to cup her. With her eyes closed she didn't even know if Gage or Smith was touching her. It didn't matter, as long as whomever kept doing magical things with her clit.

Physical pain aroused her, but desire now took center stage. Her juices coated the hand doing wonderful things to her. Someone was pressing, rubbing, then sliding two fingers into her, hitting her G-spot. Her breath sped up as she tried to hold back against the barrage of sensations. Another hand grabbed her tender ass and squeezed hard. Pain bloomed and snaked straight to her core. She teetered so close that when Gage whispered, "Come," in her ear, she did exactly that.

The orgasm robbed her of breath, and Rielle squeezed her hand, reminding her to breathe. Then the other woman's breath hitched.

They were both in bliss.

Gentle hands guided her up to a kneeling position. The clamp was removed, and she hissed in pain until warm breath enveloped the nipple. She opened her eyes and saw a dark head at her breast. Gage. So that meant that Smith's chest was pressed against her back.

"I think this little one needs a break," Smith said.

Gage sucked for another few seconds before letting her go. "I agree. I think my slave is ready."

The word caught her off guard. She had only ever been Gage's submissive. So had Cara, for that matter. *Oh.* That exquisite necklace Rielle was wearing. The necklace she always wore. Gage had collared her. Instead of jealousy, a warmth of happiness enveloped her heart for her friend.

Smith bundled her into a blanket, and she curled into the chair.

Then the show began.

Smith lay on the bed lengthwise. He tipped his head back and gave her a reassuring smile.

Rielle settled in the V of his thighs and without ceremony, took his cock in her mouth. Smith emitted a low moan of pleasure when she swallowed him down. The woman had a look of bliss on her face as she deep-throated him. Smith grasped the sheets and arched his back, sucking in air.

Allie remembered viscerally how good he'd felt in her mouth. The memory set her insides fluttering.

Gage stepped behind his wife. What did he see? Well, Rielle fellating Smith, of course, but what else? Was he jealous? Or did he find comfort in being with people he knew so well? Had he and Smith done this before? No, not likely. And how much of this was for them, and how much was for her benefit?

Her former Dominant fisted himself a couple of times, then grasped Rielle's hips and flexed them back so he could drive into her.

Allie's inner muscles clamped. God, had she ever

seen something so erotic? She'd seen threesomes many times but never with a woman who wasn't being paid. And never with such an intimacy. An inherent gentleness mixed with downright carnality.

Rielle was clearly enjoying herself, as her moans attested. Gage grasped her hair and tugged. That movement ricocheted through Allie. She'd loved when he used to pull her hair. Nothing revved her up faster than that. Now with her hair shorn, he couldn't do that to her.

Continuing to watch, she was enraptured. The elegance and symphony to this scene entranced her. Each member of the orchestra playing their part.

Smith's back arched, and his hips flexed as he let out a low growl. A sound Allie'd heard before. It kicked her libido up a notch. Gage yanked his wife's hair up and back as he continued to slam into her. The sound of flesh on flesh reverberated around the room. Rielle's eyes closed, and she let out a low moan around Smith's cock.

The moment the other woman came, Allie reached down between her legs. Only she could ease the ache. She slid her finger through her slick folds as Gage's back arched.

He held Rielle still as he pumped into her.

The look of agony and ecstasy on his face was one Allie'd seen before. Allie expected to feel weird Cara wasn't here, but the loss wasn't as acute as she'd expected. More a dull ache in her chest than any piercing pain. When Gage's eyes opened, his gaze settled on her. He was probably having the exact same thought, and he offered a serene smile. Cara was here in spirit.

Then Rielle climaxed again, her eyes shutting against the onslaught. Still, she continued to fellate Smith as if her life depended on it. She cupped his balls, and Smith sucked in a deep breath before letting out another low growl. Within moments he orgasmed, and a long sigh escaped as he let go. Rielle met her gaze and winked. She then collapsed on top of Smith, and Gage lay down next to them. Three adults, all panting like dogs.

Allie's smile grew.

Smith angled his face back and gave her a smile. "Come join us."

She wrinkled her nose. "All those stinky, smelly, sweaty bodies? I don't think so."

"I could order you to do it."

"And I could brat."

He smiled. "And then I'd punish you." His blue eyes bored through her, and he held an arm out to her. "Come, Alessandra."

She was powerless to disobey. She dropped the blanket and went over to join them. Gage and Rielle had shifted, creating a spot between Smith and Rielle. The truth was they didn't smell bad—they smelled like sex.

Hell of an aphrodisiac.

And while Smith was strong and angular, Rielle was soft and pliant. Such a contrast, yet both warmed her from the inside out.

She squirmed.

"Did you come?" Gage was still breathing hard.

"Did who come?"

"You, Allie. Did you come when you touched yourself?"

Damn, her face was as expressive and readable as Gage's, right? "No." No point in trying to lie. "I was close, but the show was too enthralling."

"Okay." He looked at his wife. "Rielle, you know what to do."

The other woman moved so quickly Allie barely had time to register her thighs were being thrust apart when Rielle pulled back her labia and started laving her. She would've bucked right off the bed if not for Smith's hand across her belly, holding her in place. Then that hand moved up to cup her breast as Rielle sucked her clit. He tweaked her nipple, and electricity shot through her. Too much. Too many sensations bombarding her all at once.

She tried to hold back, tried to make it last, but Rielle was both unrelenting and talented. Soon, she fell over the edge, tumbling into a world of abyss and pleasure. Rielle climbed up her body to kiss her, and she could taste herself on the other woman's soft lips. Rielle's tongue was just as persistent, unrelenting, and talented, and her hand was doing all kinds of wonderful things to Allie's clit. Allie tried to reach out to stop her, but Smith and Gage each took hold of her arms, pinning them to the bed.

Allie bucked when the second orgasm crested through her. But Rielle was greedy, and she pushed her higher and higher. Fingers were working magic, and this time Gage's mouth settled on her breast. As if knowing it would do the trick, he bit her nipple.

Overwhelmed by sensation, she climaxed again. This time, she flung herself into oblivion.

Chapter Twenty-Six

Smith was proud of her. Whatever Rielle had said to Alessandra had worked because his little one had been game for anything.

He had plans for her, though. Just as soon as he was fully recovered.

Smith couldn't tell which of the women emitted the low moan. Did it matter? They'd both climaxed at least twice, Allie three times, if he didn't miss the mark.

Gage had once confided in him that when he'd met Rielle, she'd never had an orgasm. Four years as a sex slave and she'd never climaxed. Gage had taught her that she could. Then he showed her the possibility of being multi-orgasmic. Gage also let it slip that Alessandra was capable of peaking several times in a row. Jesus, the woman was responsive. Both women, he corrected himself. Between the four of them, he counted at least six orgasms, probably more.

A hand pressed to his cock, and it sprang to life, enjoying the attention. He looked down and saw Rielle's nicely manicured fingers rubbing him. He turned to face Gage who winked.

Time for round two.

"Rielle, I think it's Allie's turn."

Alessandra's eyes snapped to attention at Gage's words. Her gaze flipped back and forth between the two men.

If he sensed fear, Smith might've called it off. But her expression wasn't fear—it was nervousness. It was anticipation. It was desire and longing.

Rielle let go of his cock and rose, then moved to the dresser. Within moments, she was rolling a condom onto Gage's cock with her mouth.

Christ, that was hot.

They'd talked about this. Gage wearing a condom tonight was a must in order to make Alessandra feel safe. Now Smith knew the truth about her past, it seemed ludicrous, but he still wanted to maintain the charade. Rielle and Gage would never hear about Alessandra's activities from him.

Rielle rolled off her husband and urged Allie to crawl on top of him. Smith had a minute to watch her in awe as she took Gage into her.

Christ, that was hot too.

Then he remembered himself and rolled off the bed, taking the bottle of gel Rielle presented him. When he pressed a lubricated finger into Allie's asshole, she gasped.

"I can't," she stammered.

"Oh, you can," he corrected. "And you will."

He removed his hands and pressed his cock into her. She was tighter than she'd been the previous night, but she also knew what to expect. He pushed harder. Had she ever been double-penetrated like this at Masters' Club?

"Jesus, Smith, you're hurting her."

Rielle's voice broke through his reverie. She'd taken a place next to her husband's head to enjoy the show. Smith immediately pulled back, but not out. He ran a soothing hand up and down Alessandra's spine.

He whispered into her ear. "Do you want me to stop?"

He was prepared to do whatever she needed. He'd pull out and scoop her off Gage if that was her desire. In response to his question, her hands snaked out and clasped his hips.

"Just give me a minute to get used to this."

She said the words through gritted teeth, so he held himself perfectly still, as did Gage.

Finally, she sank down on Gage. When she pulled back, she grasped Smith's hips, and he slid into her. Then he slipped back, and she let Gage thrust into her. God, so fucking tight in there. How she kept both of them in her was remarkable.

Smith looked over her shoulder, and Gage nodded, getting the message. He reached down between Alessandra's legs and pressed against her clit. After that, just a matter of taking turns. First Allie, then Gage, then Allie again, and finally Smith.

Her orgasm was so strong it rocketed through her entire pelvis, squeezing him.

His own release was swift and powerful.

Soon Gage's eyes closed, and he held her against him as he climaxed. His grunt of pleasure seemed to push her into her second—or was that the third—orgasm. When she collapsed on top of Gage, Smith slid from her.

Rielle was soon there, urging Alessandra to roll her head onto her ample bosom.

Alessandra complied and then sighed into the cushion.

Rielle winked at Smith whose legs gave way. He tumbled to the bed on the side opposite of Gage, again sandwiching the women between them.

"I…" Alessandra gasped. "That was a first for me."

Smith only felt a negligible amount of relief. What they'd done took finesse—more than he'd shown—and if they'd subjected her to that with two men who didn't give a shit about her…

He needed to put it from his mind, or he'd go nuts. "How about some champagne?"

Rielle giggled. "I think we're all high, but I wouldn't mind a sip from Gage's glass."

"Only if we're done playing for the night." Gage's reply.

As Smith looked down at his limp cock, he smiled. "I don't think anything is going to happen."

Rielle grinned. "That sounds like a challenge to me."

"It would," said her husband. "But let's let the hosts rest. Champagne sounds great. I'll help."

"I'll come too. Hand me a pillow, Gage. Allie needs somewhere to rest her head."

Gage obliged, handing his wife a pillow.

Expertly, Rielle extricated herself and had Alessandra's head resting on it.

True to form, his little one curled into a ball. Smith snagged the comforter from the floor and laid it across her. Then he placed a kiss to her temple. Her hand reached up to brush his cheek, but she didn't open her eyes. Her lips were curled into a contented smile. If she were a cat, she'd be purring.

Gage and Rielle were necking in the kitchen when he joined them. "Seriously?"

Rielle only laughed, and Gage gave an enormous smile. "Did you notice Rielle didn't drink wine at dinner?"

Smith was slow, but then it clicked. He reached out and pulled Gage into a big hug. "Congratulations, man."

"What about me?" Rielle pouted. "I'm the one who's going to get fat and ugly."

Smith released Gage and pulled Rielle to him. "Pregnant women glow, and fat is all relative." His hand hovered around her belly, and Rielle took it and pressed it to her abdomen.

"I'm only two months along, so you're the only one we've told. We'll tell Allie." Rielle grinned slyly. "If she ever wakes up."

"Then champagne is even more appropriate." Smith pulled the chilled bottle from the fridge while Rielle brought out three glasses.

When she sold Smith the condo, she'd left everything behind except for her clothes, so she needed no directions to find the flutes.

"I have to ask you, Smith—have you found the universe yet?"

Smith was so focused on pouring he almost missed the look between Rielle and Gage. He handed Gage his glass. "I'm sorry, the universe? What are you talking about?"

Rielle grinned. "I'll be right back." She grabbed a glass. "For Allie," she said, taking a small sip. Then she headed toward the spare bedroom.

"What universe?"

Gage grinned. "You have to see this. If you knew about it, then I'd wonder about your prowess in bed."

"What the hell does that mean?"

"Okay, guys!"

Intrigued, Smith took his glass and followed Gage

toward Rielle's voice. At least this time he'd remembered to close the drapes. Four naked people would definitely set tongues wagging. Unless his neighbors were as kinky as he was. When they got to the door of the white room, Rielle took his glass from him and handed it to Gage.

"Lie down on the bed."

"Alessandra's in the other room—"

Gage pushed him. "This won't take more than a minute. Just lie down, okay?"

Acquiescing, he lay down on the bed.

Rielle flipped off the lights.

It blew his mind. "Wow. So that's the universe."

Rielle giggled. "Allie never said anything?"

"No, and neither did any of the other...women." Shit, he'd stepped in it. He sat up.

Rielle had already opened the door, flooding the room with light and taking away the universe. In the blink of an eye, she fled.

Smith looked up at Gage, who shook his head.

"Don't look at me. I've been with two women in my life, and Rielle's been with two men. Tonight we each made it three. Allie's cut from the same cloth. We don't go through partners like some people"—he looked pointedly at Smith—"go through underwear."

Smith stood and took his glass back from Gage. "It's not like that." But his protest fell flat because it *had* been like that. At least before Alessandra had come into his life. Now he wanted more than the mind-numbing affairs he'd engaged in. "And I have to talk to you about Alessandra."

"Well, we're not going to do it in here." Gage flipped off the light. "Why don't we go to the kitchen?"

"Will the women join us?"

"Hell, no. Rielle is pissed with you, and she'll be bitching about you to Allie, if she's even awake." The other man headed to the kitchen.

Smith closed the door, leaving the universe alone.

Gage turned to him when they got to the kitchen. He leaned his hip against the counter. "So what do you have to say about Allie that you don't want Rielle to hear?"

Smith looked across at his best friend. He was about to betray Alessandra, but he was doing it for her own good. "Have you ever heard of the Masters' Club?"

"What is that, a golf thing?"

"No, it's not a golf thing. Not the Masters Tournament, the Masters' Club."

Gage shook his head. "Nope, means nothing to me."

"It's a very exclusive BDSM club that meets at Kink on Wednesday nights."

A flicker in Gage's eyes. "Go on."

"Alessandra has been working there as a bottom for six months."

A tic started in his friend's jaw. "Go on."

"They're into the dark shit, Gage. I mean degrading, debasing, women-as-sex-objects kind of shit. You know, all the things bad about the lifestyle."

Something flickered and died in Gage's eyes. He felt like slime for having brought this up. He should've just kept his fucking mouth shut.

"Why are you telling me this?"

Smith was asking himself the same question. "Have you ever heard of Carl Jergen?"

257

"Sure, he's the guy running to be head of that party. I don't really follow it much because I don't subscribe to their strict morality shit...wait a minute. Carl Jergen is in the Masters' Club? The guy who wants to reopen the abortion debate and take away same-sex marriage? That Carl Jergen?"

"Yeah, the judge's judge. That's what they call him because other judges defer to him. The cops love him because he's not big on a criminal's rights—"

"The judge's judge?"

Something in Gage's tone caught Smith's attention. "Yeah, that's what they call him."

A twitch in Gage's jaw. "That motherfucker."

"Who? Carl Jergen? I thought you said you didn't know him."

"*I* don't. But I bet my wife does. He's her judge." At Smith's blank look, he clarified. "He's Mr. X."

The man who'd brainwashed Rielle so completely that when he cracked her rib, she refused to go to the police. *That* Mr. X.

"Shit." Smith's epithet was barely above a whisper because now that he'd opened this can of worms...

No going back.

"My thoughts exactly." Gage's throat worked to swallow. He took his glass of champagne and dumped it down the sink.

Smith swallowed his in three gulps, then set the glass down next to Gage's.

"What are you guys doing?" Rielle stood there, glowing with happiness. "Oh, Smith, I forgive you for all those other women. You make Allie happy, and that's all that matters."

"Where is Alessandra?"

"In the bathroom, why?"

Gage stepped forward. "Carl Jergen."

Like watching something in slow motion. The glass slipped from Rielle's hand, fell to the floor, and shattered into a million little shards. Several bounced off the floor and embedded themselves into the tender flesh of feet and calves.

No one moved. No one dared.

"What the fuck?" Alessandra's voice came from down the hall.

"Don't come in here."

"I don't plan on it. I'm going to put shoes on and then clean up this mess. Don't you guys move." Her voice faded as she went into the dungeon to retrieve her shoes.

Rielle still looked thunderstruck. Then, very slowly, she stepped back.

Instinctively, Gage started to step forward, but Smith placed a hand to his chest. "Both of you stop moving."

Gage obeyed, but Rielle didn't. She walked right through as if the glass wasn't there. She just kept on walking.

"Jesus Christ, Rielle," Gage shouted. "Stop before you hurt yourself."

Way too late for that.

"Alessandra, get Gage's shoes."

Alessandra scurried past them, wearing her own shoes, and brought back Gage's.

"Why is there blood all over the floor, and where the hell is Rielle?"

Gage grabbed his shoes and stuffed his feet into them. Like a shot, he was out of the kitchen and

259

heading to the spare room. To Rielle's old room. The room she had stayed in whenever Mr. X—Carl Jergen, Smith corrected himself—wasn't around to abuse her.

Alessandra handed him his shoes. Absurdly ridiculous. Three adults running around naked save for the shoes on their feet and one who must have a hundred shards of glass in her soles. He couldn't help himself—he started laughing.

Alessandra looked at him like he had two heads, then huffed out something about crazy people and went in search of a broom.

Rielle would need tending to, so Smith headed to the bathroom to retrieve the first aid kit. Judging by the amount of blood on the floor, a trip to the emergency room was probably in order.

Alessandra was still sweeping when he crossed the condo. The door to the spare room was open, the light on.

Rielle was on the bed, and blood was smeared everywhere.

Gage held up his hands in the universal *I mean you no harm* gesture. "Sweetheart, let me look at your feet." His tone verged on pure panic.

In response, Rielle flexed her feet, pressing them to the mattress and causing more blood to ooze.

"She keeps doing that," Gage muttered to Smith under his breath. "She won't let me get close."

Rielle's eyes were wide, her stance that of a wounded animal.

"You go left, and I'll go right. I take the arms, and you take the legs." The best he could offer. Out of the corner of his eye, he caught Gage's nod.

Then they pounced.

Rielle emitted an inhuman scream.

Once he had her arms secured, he put his hand over her mouth. "Jesus, Rielle, this room isn't soundproof."

For his trouble, she bit him.

He couldn't help himself—he jerked his hand back and lost his grip on her arms.

Gage had her legs but could barely hold on.

Making an executive decision, Smith threw himself on top of her, using his chest and arms to subdue her movements. If she screamed again, he could do nothing about that. Let the cops come. Resignation washed over him. That would just be the perfect end to this clusterfuck of an evening.

Chapter Twenty-Seven

Rielle's scream was the same sound Allie'd made just days ago—intense grief mingled with unbearable pain. With anger thrown into the mix, the sound was the perfect storm and the perfect scream. But Rielle wasn't in the soundproofed room.

What the actual fuck?

Confounded and bewildered, Allie continued to sweep up the glass. Once she finished that, she pulled out the steam mop. She was still trying to figure out how it worked when a knock sounded at the door.

Shit. She was naked. They were all naked, but since it didn't seem like anyone else had heard the knock, she went to the dungeon, grabbed a robe, and threw it on. She was just about to open the door as the caller knocked again.

Opening the door, she came face-to-face with Tarah, the security guard. Allie pulled the lapels of the robe closer together. "Can I help you?"

The younger woman glanced over Allie's shoulder, trying to look into the condo. Her stance was of authority, but discomfort flitted in her gaze as her eyes darted around. "One neighbor reported hearing a scream." She shifted and looked...uneasy. "I wouldn't bother you, I mean, I know Rielle and Gage are here, and I know...about, well, you know..." The young woman's cheeks turned cherry red.

"Oh." *Double shit.* Obviously, not everyone around here was ignorant of the goings-on in the condo. How was she supposed to deal with this? "Yeah, but that's not what happened. Someone dropped a glass, and Rielle cut her foot. That was the scream you heard."

The blood drained from the young woman's face.

"You know Rielle from when she lived here?"

Tarah nodded.

"Well, Tarah, I'll let her know you're concerned about her. I'll call you if we need an ambulance or a cab or something." Allie knew how fucking lame she sounded, but she still hadn't heard anything coming from the spare room.

Finally, the young woman looked appeased, even offering a tight smile. "I'm on all night. Tell them I say hi."

"I'll do that, I promise." With not a little bit of self-interest, Allie shut the door. She could imagine what poor Tarah thought was going on in this apartment. She likely wouldn't believe the shattered-glass story, which was ironic because it was true.

She was debating between figuring out the steam mop and going to find out what the fuck was going on in the bedroom when Gage called her name. She walked over to the spare room, pushed the door open, and gaped.

Smith was propped against the headboard with Rielle pulled tight against him, his arms imprisoning hers against her chest. Gage was holding her legs and was trying—rather unsuccessfully—to remove the shards of glass with a pair of tweezers.

"Shit, guys, she needs to go to the hospital." Too late she realized what Gage had been saying—that

263

Rielle didn't want to go to a hospital.

The woman started struggling again, and Allie held out her hands, palms up. "I just meant they might be better able to treat you, Rielle, but I'm sure we can manage." She dropped her voice. "Gage, you hold her legs, and I'll tweeze the glass."

They greeted her with three looks of relief, affirming she'd said the right thing.

Thus began a procedure that took almost an hour. The actual number of shards wasn't that great, but Allie washing Rielle's feet took time. None of the shards were that deep, and each of the punctures self-sealed. Still, Allie felt like shit when she ran a cotton ball with antiseptic along the soles of the other woman's feet.

Through the entire process, Rielle only flinched and whimpered. No more wails. No explanation, either, of what had happened.

Allie sure as shit wasn't going to bring it up, but Smith was going to explain the moment they were alone.

All she knew was one minute Rielle was plying her with sips of champagne and baby news, the next minute Allie went to pee, and then had come the crash. Why Rielle had trod through glass to come into her old bedroom, Allie had no clue.

Rielle's eyes were glassy, her face blanched white.

"Why don't I find a fresh blanket? You guys can stay the night." Since Rielle looked incapable and unwilling to answer, Allie directed the question to Gage.

Wearily, he nodded. "That'd probably be best."

"Oh, and, Gage, can you call Tarah?"

Rielle's eyes focused. "Tarah? Tarah was here?"

For the first time she appeared aware of what was going on around her.

"Yes, and I tried to convince her...well, anyway, I think she knows what goes on in here."

Gage chuckled. Dark, but also a hint of amusement. "When Rielle was in the hospital, Tarah came to get clothes for her. I suspect she found the dungeon. To save us both infinite embarrassment, I never brought it up. Tarah's a smart girl. I'm sure she figured it out."

"Make sure to tell her about the glass because I don't think she believed me."

Gage nodded.

Rielle's eyelids drooped.

With ease, Allie and Gage stripped off the comforter and maneuvered Rielle under the blanket.

Finally, with great gentleness, Smith eased her from his arms and laid her head on the pillow.

The woman's eyes closed, and she appeared asleep before he had time to retrieve a spare blanket from the upper shelf of the cupboard.

"Are you going to join her?" Allie spoke in a hushed voice.

Gage shook his head. "Not at this moment." He looked up at Smith. "We need to talk."

Allie looked back and forth between the still-naked men. "Are you insane? Whatever it is, it can wait until morning."

"No," Smith said succinctly, "it can't. Gage and I are going to put on robes, then we'll meet you in the living room."

Looking down at the robe she wore, Allie suddenly felt naked. "Is it okay if I put on the pajamas?"

He looked like he was going to argue but then relented. "You can get changed in the bathroom."

At least he was giving her a modicum of dignity because she felt suddenly exposed. Despite her previous nudity earlier in the evening, she wouldn't now be comfortable stripping in front of the men. Taking the pajamas from him, she made her way to the bathroom, but it still baffled her. Whatever had come before, it'd dissipated. The happiness, the joy, the comfort with each other—vanished. Dust in the wind.

She splashed icy water on her face and checked the time. Just after eleven. It felt like the middle of the night, instead of merely bedtime. What she wouldn't give to be tucked into bed with Smith. Maybe a quick bout of hot-and-steamy, down-and-dirty sex and then blissful sleep. She used to have nightmares when she first ran, but those had eventually stopped. Now she slept the sleep of the dead. If she dreamed, she didn't remember it.

When she emerged from the bathroom, the men's voices guided her to the kitchen. She poked her head in, finding Smith putting on a pot of coffee.

So *that* kind of night.

Time to face the music. And she was going to have to do it without Rielle's support. No guarantee the other woman would support Allie or understand why she'd felt compelled to run anyway. But at least Rielle would've been there to hold her hand.

The wait for the coffee to brew was interminable. Still, no one spoke.

Each second ratcheted up the tension until she was vibrating from nerves.

"Oh, for God's sake, Alessandra, go sit on the

couch," Smith ordered in a tone that brooked no opposition.

"I take lots of milk—"

"And sugar," Gage supplied. "More like a latté than coffee, got it." His voice was as tight as Smith's had been.

Feeling superfluous, she slipped from the room.

Chapter Twenty-Eight

"Are you going to drop his name like a bombshell again?"

Gage's hand shook as he took his mug of coffee. "We're about to give her a cup of hot coffee. Maybe this isn't the smartest idea."

"Good point," Smith conceded. "I'll get her to set it down before you drop his name."

"Maybe we should ease into it."

"Nope. Rip the fucking bandage off and let the chips fall where they may." *Let Gage sort out the mixed metaphor.* Smith still seethed with anger.

Anger at Gage for having been so indelicate.

Anger at Rielle for her stupidity.

Anger at himself for having brought the whole thing up.

Anger at Alessandra for having gotten them into this mess.

Now he had to face the consequences. He and Gage made their way to the living room.

Alessandra was curled into one corner of the couch with her back against the arm, a blanket pulled over her, almost to her neck.

When she reached for the mug of coffee, Smith gave a quick shake of his head. "It's too hot. I'll just put it on the coffee table. Give it a moment to cool." The question was in her eyes, but she made no demur, for which he was grateful.

Gage took up the chair opposite.

Smith positioned himself on the other end of the couch, angling so he could look at Alessandra. They made a weird grouping—like the Bermuda triangle. Things would go in, but would they come out? Catching Gage's eye, he gave a curt nod.

"Carl Jergen."

Alessandra tried to school her features, but she was as bad at holding in her emotions as Gage.

Smith could read them both like books. This was going to be interesting. In other circumstances, it might've been amusing, but tonight nothing was funny.

She tried again to marshal her features, but finally they crumpled, and she dropped her head, hiding her face in her hands.

The last shred of hope that he'd clung to—that maybe Trixie had been mistaken—shattered. "How bad, Alessandra?"

She shook, and he longed to pull her into his arms and soothe her pain. He was doing this ruthlessly and deserved the guilt accompanying it. "Alessandra." His tone was firm and his voice loud.

Finally, with what appeared to be Herculean effort, she raised her head. "Whatever you're imagining, think worse. How did you find out? What business is it of yours?" She looked back and forth between Gage and Smith. "Both of you should be ashamed of yourselves."

Smith brushed off the accusation. "I found Trixie. And it's my business because you're here under my roof—"

"And whose fucking fault is that?" She leapt to her feet. Sticking out a finger, she pointed it at his chest. "I tried to tell you. I tried to warn you. But no, Mr. Fucking High and Mighty thinks he knows best. Well, I've got news for you—you're not the king of the world. Your own universe, maybe, but not the world."

"Sit down." Smith made his tone firm but reasonable.

Ignoring him, she paced.

"Alessandra, sit the fuck down, or there will be consequences." Heedless of company, he'd put her over his knee in a heartbeat.

Evidently realizing he wasn't making an empty threat but a promise, she sat back down. After pulling the blanket back over her, she reached for her coffee. After taking several sips, she placed the mug back on the table. "So now you know." A deep and resigned sigh gusted out. "What do you plan to do about it?"

"Take the fucker down."

Her gaze snapped up, and her eyes widened. "You have no idea what you're talking about. He's indestructible. Nothing touches him, and he'll destroy you before you ever get within a mile of him. You have no idea who you're dealing with."

"He's just a man." Gage scrubbed his face with his hands. "Not a god. He has an Achilles' heel—his need to break women. If he gets to be leader of the party, he'll have too much power. We need to bring him down now before it gets that far."

She smiled, but the expression was sardonic and sarcastic. "And how precisely do you plan to do that?"

"Hit him where it hurts. We'll expose him for the hypocrite he is."

"Again, you're good with rhetoric and short on details."

Now his turn to smile. "We'll tip off the cops cocaine's being consumed at Kink on Wednesday nights."

"There is." She said it in a matter-of-a-fact way that unnerved him. She was preternaturally calm. Resigned. "But that won't be enough."

"We can't involve Kink." Gage's contribution.

"Why the hell not?" Smith's ire rose. "They're the ones who condone this behavior."

Gage shook his head. "Jergen is blackmailing Marie."

"Who is Marie?"

Alessandra answered the question. "Marie da Costa is Mistress Gigi. She and Master Dante own Club Kink. You try to bring down Jergen, and he'll take them down with him. Maybe even make them the scapegoats."

"Again, I'm not sure how this is my problem." He didn't give a shit who got caught in the crossfire as long as Jergen went down.

"Marie has sunk her life savings into the club. If it goes down, she loses everything. Her kids' education, her living, her retirement—they all vanish. She'll have nothing." Gage explained the issues.

Smith shrugged. "So I buy the club, and then we call the cops. I'll pay above-market value. If Marie wants to, she can open a new club in a year or two when the furor dies down. I'll back her then as well."

"Just like that." Alessandra's voice was laced with sarcasm. "There you go, playing God again."

Gage, on the other hand, was slowly bobbing his head. "This could work. The last time I spoke to Marie, she sounded desperate."

Smith turned to Alessandra. "He almost choked

that woman to death. How long before he goes too far and kills a woman?"

"What if he has already?"

Thunderstruck, he stared. "What do you know?"

She blinked repeatedly, clearly fighting tears threatening to fall. "Mimi. Her name was Mimi. They found her in Burrard Inlet about a month ago. Someone had strangled her. Two days before they found her body in the water, I'd seen her with him." She blew out a shaky breath, apparently trying to regain control but failing. A lone tear escaped. "Why do you think I kept going back? After Trixie didn't show, I overheard two men talking about how they had to find her and shut her up. God, if she talked to you—"

"Trixie was given a retirement package from me and put on a bus heading eastward. She's not a stupid woman. She won't be coming back." Smith was relieved Toby had taken care of that without delay.

Relief flooded her features, showing just how scared she was of this man and his minions.

"Don't you see, Alessandra? If we don't bring him down, there'll be more Trixies and more Mimis. He won't stop. Men like him are beyond sick. He's a sociopath." He fought to convince her.

She brushed away the tears with the backs of her hands and wiped her nose on the blanket. Hope flared in her eyes. "Do you really think you can do this? Bring him down? Because there's no halfway about this. Either you take him down or you don't try." She eyed both men. "Don't do this on my account. I ran once, and I can do it again. I can be like Trixie and disappear permanently. No one needs know."

Bullshit.

He exploded out of his seat. "There is no fucking way you're disappearing again. I...they lost you once, and you're not going to put them through that again. Look, even if you weren't involved, we'd do it for Rielle, for Mimi, and for all the girls in the future who might get hurt. Might get killed." Now his turn to pace.

Gage moved to the couch and wrapped his arm around Alessandra. "I know you're scared, Allie. I am, too—for Rielle. Jergen hangs over our relationship because she lives in fear of him. Oh, she covers it well, but there's a shadow in her eyes. It's there when she thinks no one's looking, but I see it. I don't want our daughter raised with that kind of stress just below the surface. Rielle has made such progress, working with Kennedy Dixon—I don't want all that work to go to waste."

"It won't."

All three of them whirled to find Rielle in the doorway, wearing a robe.

Gage sprang from the couch, crossed the room in three strides, and scooped her into his arms. "You shouldn't be walking. You should be in bed."

Rielle pressed a hand to his shoulder when he started back toward her old room. "I can't hide under the constellations anymore, Gage. You're right about this. If I don't face him, I'll always be afraid. I don't want to be scared anymore. I want to reclaim my life."

Gage moved to the couch and sat, settling her on his lap.

He held her so tightly Smith was amazed Rielle could breathe. He held out his hand, and Alessandra rose, taking it.

"Okay," she whispered. "Let's do this."

Chapter Twenty-Nine

In the morning, Allie woke with a hangover. Not a real hangover—she'd had one glass of wine and several sips of champagne—but one of those headaches that made her *feel* like she had a hangover. She wasn't surprised when she scented the coffee and found Smith gone. He'd been restless all night, and so had she. She figured she'd had maybe a couple of hours of sleep, but not much more than that.

After crawling out of bed, she stumbled to the bathroom.

She blanched at her reflection in the mirror. Deep, shadowed smudges under her eyes stood in stark contrast to the white skin. Not an ounce of color to be seen except the remnants of last night's makeup. She stripped out of her pajamas and let them fall to a heap on the floor. No visible reminders of the clusterfuck from last night. Just images and impressions and painful remembrances flashing through her mind like an old movie from an ancient projector. Noisy, clunky, and out of focus.

Well, maybe not everything.

The haze of the lovemaking? Vanished. The stark terror of realizing Smith and now Gage knew the truth? Gut-churning. Knowing Rielle had suffered under Carl Jergen as well? Unfathomable. He was but one man yet had wrought plenty of chaos in their lives.

Never should have gone to Kink that first night. Never should have been seduced into returning. Never should have kept going back. She still wasn't sure if the threat to her co-worker Denise was real or imagined. Obviously, she wasn't going back this Wednesday night, but what did it all mean? Had any of it been worth it?

And, above all else, could Smith take down Jergen?

Jesus, too many thoughts going around in her head. She'd better take a fast shower in case Gage or Rielle waited to use the bathroom. Normally she loved luxuriating, but today she felt no joy. The pulsating spray didn't ease muscles sore from tension. The scorching heat didn't touch the ice surrounding her heart. The water didn't absolve her of her sins or wash them away.

She dressed quickly in jeans and a sweater. Brushing out her hair took mere moments, and she again cursed her vanity. Her hair had been her one weak spot, and with it all gone, she looked gaunt and ill.

Nothing to be done. Suck it up.

With one final swipe under her eyes, she flipped off the fan and light and made her way to the kitchen. *Whoa*, she was the last one to the table.

Gage swallowed a mouthful as she sat. "It might have been rude, but we started without you."

She waved him off. "You're guests. You should eat when you're hungry."

When Smith came from the kitchen to give her a mug of coffee, she smiled. Then he plunked down a bowl of oatmeal, and she scowled. "I'm not—"

"Hungry? I don't give a damn. You look like shit, and you need to eat. Don't give me a hard time."

Obviously, somebody hadn't gotten enough sleep.

Obediently, she took a mouthful. Then another. An explosion of flavor. "What did you put in this?"

"Apple purée." With that little tidbit, Smith went back to the kitchen, leaving Allie with their guests.

Rielle met her gaze. "How are you?"

"I should be asking you that. How are your feet?"

Rielle shrugged. "They're fine. Gage put some salve on them and re-bandaged them. As long as they don't get infected, I should be fine." She shivered.

Nice, she wore a set of the clothes Smith had bought for Allie. Rielle was curvier and her legs longer, but other than that, they were close enough in size that she didn't look ridiculous.

Smith sat.

Hey, look at that—her bowl was empty.

"Now that we're all here, Alessandra, it's time for you to tell us why you left."

Allie moved to rise, but he snaked out a hand and grabbed her wrist, forcing her back down. His grip was merciless, and unless she was willing to risk bruises or a broken arm, she was staying put. "I just can't. I'm sorry, but you're going to have to accept that."

"We will." Gage's words were quiet. "If you come back."

The lance of pain to her heart robbed her of breath. What he asked seemed so reasonable and yet so impossible. "I can't do that either."

Rielle looked at her. Really looked at her.

Allie squirmed under the scrutiny.

"You've never even asked about your things."

She shrugged. "They're just things. I brought a picture of my mother with me. Nothing else matters."

"Well, we didn't see it that way." Gage spoke. "Jenna Lee and Katie Rhodes moved into your home. We made sure her rent payments went toward the mortgage. We put your personal items, including clothes, photo albums, and books, into boxes. They're in the spare room, just waiting for you. Say the word, and Jenna will move out."

Jenna was the vice principal at the school where Gage was the principal, and she'd been a friend of Allie's.

This was too much to deal with, and she just didn't give a shit. "If Jenna wants to take over the mortgage, she can have the house."

"In order to do that, you'll have to come back from the missing."

She shook her head at Gage's suggestion. "I'll sign a power of attorney. We'll backdate it, and you can claim you just found it. You petition the court to take control of my assets, and you give the house to Jenna."

"All neat and tidy." Smith's voice was laced with sarcasm and something darker.

It should concern her, but she was beyond that now.

"You just have everything worked out."

"As an officer of the court, I cannot condone creating false documents." Rielle's contribution.

Allie looked back and forth between the three others at the table, finding no support. Since Smith had let go of her arm, she shot up easily from the table. "I have to get out of here."

He leapt to his feet, but she just stepped back. "I

277

just need to go for a walk."

He appeared to relent. "I'll come with you."

She shook her head. "No, Smith, this is something I need to do by myself."

"Then I'll get you a spare set of keys, and you get a coat. It's cold this morning."

And threatening to rain. A quick glance through the now-open blinds confirmed that. She moved to the closet in the dungeon and selected a trench coat. Mme Veronique had thought of everything. When she returned to the dining room, she took the proffered keys without meeting Smith's gaze. "I'm sorry," she whispered, to everyone and no one at the same time, and then she fled.

Taking the stairs as quickly as she could, she vigilantly listened for followers. She passed the concierge without a backward glance and pushed the glass door open, hurrying onto the sidewalk. The wind was whipping, and she pulled the lapels of the coat closer together as she turned into the blustery flow. She made it two blocks before the tears came.

Chapter Thirty

For the hundredth time, Smith glanced at his watch. Rielle and Gage had left not long after Alessandra's departure, no one having anything left to say. Whether or not they were willing to accept her decision had been left in the air. They were just as capable of calling the RCMP as Smith was, and he was almost grateful they had removed the decision from his hands.

He had called Marie da Costa. She and Master Dante were going to meet him at the condo this afternoon. Smith declined to explain himself over the phone, but he suspected Marie knew what this was about. He'd reviewed his finances and figured out where he was going to find the money to buy out Marie and Dante, even scouting out a possible new location for them. Not as close to downtown, but near enough. It had more floor space, and the current tenant had both a liquor license and a strong desire to sell. A few months to renovate, and Club Kink could reopen under another name. Smith had a few in mind, but he'd keep those suggestions to himself. If this went through, Smith would leave it up to Dante and Marie to make up their own minds.

Still, Alessandra didn't return. She'd been gone for over three hours, and Smith was rethinking his decision to let her go. She'd walked out of her life once before—

who was to say she wasn't doing it again? She'd not had time to grab anything except... He beelined to the bathroom and checked the box of tampons.

Empty except for the tampons.

Damn, he should've seen this coming. He tossed the box back under the sink and was stalking to the office when a key scraped into the lock. Good, now he didn't need to call Toby.

Alessandra had come back.

When she stepped into the living room, he all but mauled her, pulling her into a hug and squeezing her tight. The band around his chest loosened more and more with each minute he held her.

"Smith, I'm soaking wet."

"I don't give a shit." His whisper was reverent. "Just let me hold you. Just one more minute."

At that, her arms reached out and went around his waist. Her grip tightened, and after a moment he realized she was shaking and crying.

He eased her away and bent to kiss her tears, much as he had that first day. "You came back."

Her brow crinkled. "I told you I would. You thought..." She let the thought trail off. "I'm sorry. I didn't mean to worry you."

"I saw your money was gone, and I panicked." He didn't care if she knew his deepest and darkest insecurities. "I thought you'd left me."

"I went to the art gallery."

That, he hadn't expected.

"I'm sorry." She ran her hand through her damp hair. "I didn't mean to worry you."

"I should punish you."

Her pupils widened, but she said nothing.

For the hundred-and-first time, he glanced at his watch. "We have company coming in three hours. That should be enough time."

Her eyes asked, but she said nothing. Instead, she let him guide her to the bathroom and slip the wet trench coat from her shoulders.

"Strip, dry your hair, go pee, and then join me in the dungeon."

"Yes, Master."

Her quick obedience was what he needed at that moment. He'd already cleaned up from the previous night's fun, feeling like it'd happened to someone else. Although he'd burned everything to the ground, maybe a phoenix could rise from the ashes.

Maybe he could banish the demon whose talons gripped the bodies of the two women he loved most in the world.

Love?

No, not love. Well, maybe with Rielle. He cared for her like he would a treasure. She was more than just Gage's wife. She was also his friend.

And Alessandra?

His breath hitched when he remembered how, just fifteen minutes ago, he'd been in a panic over the thought of losing her. Wow, the relief he'd felt when he'd heard the key in the lock. She'd been with him for just a week but had wormed her way into his life. The thought of letting her go was breath stealing. But he'd promised. They had twenty-three days to go. Maybe he could make them so good she wouldn't want to leave.

"Master?"

She stood, waiting for him in the ominous shadows.

He beckoned her inside and closed the door, leaving only the illumination coming from the spotlight over the St. Andrew's cross. He pointed, and she walked gracefully until she stood facing the cross, waiting for him to secure the manacles. When he finished, she tugged against them. She did that as if she wanted to make sure she was well and truly secured. He'd tied her down so she had no give, and he was pleased when she sighed. Methodically, he removed his clothes and chose an implement.

He didn't give her any warning as he doled out the first lash.

She screamed.

The next lash of the whip brought with it another cry. Two angry lines crisscrossed her back. Three and four were in rapid succession. The fifth hit, the hardest yet, caused her to go up on her toes. He eased off for the next few, letting them be feather-light. By the tenth, she was moaning and writhing. The eleventh whistled through the air before striking her ass.

The next one hit the top of her thighs, and he let rip another two before dropping the whip. He wiped his brow with his forearm before stepping toward her. He could smell her, and tempted as he was to delve his fingers into her and bring her to orgasm, he wanted to be in her for that first explosion.

The shackles took him entirely too long to release, and her head leaned forward, resting on the wood surface. *Press any harder, and she might leave an indentation.* When he scooped her into his arms, she came willingly.

He laid her on the bed, crawled over her, and then thrust into her. Each scream and moan during the whipping had made him harder and harder. By the last lash, he'd been ready to explode.

His need to be in her, to see her pupils dilate, to hear her scream in ecstasy and writhe in pleasure, had held him in check.

Now, though, all that restraint fled. He kept ramming into her like a dog whose mate was in heat. She'd given off that scent, and he'd reacted to it with all the finesse of a schoolboy losing his virginity.

Her fingernails raked down his back to grab his buttocks, encouraging him to sink even deeper.

He wanted to hold out but found it impossible. All the emotions from the last twenty-four hours surfaced and overflowed. He pressed home one more time and let go with a vicious howl.

****

As he lay with Alessandra curled up against him, guilt surged. "I need to ask you two questions."

Her head was on his chest, facing away from him.

He leaned forward to press a kiss to her still-damp hair.

"Okay." Her voice was quiet.

"Did I hurt you?"

She shifted to look at him, her chin pressed to his breastbone. "Of course not, what kind of a question is that?"

"Did you come?"

She smiled. "Twice, not that you would've noticed."

"So I hurt you."

"No." She meandered her hand up his arm, across his shoulder to the pulse point in his neck. "You were enthusiastic, and I appreciated it."

He swallowed the lump in his throat. "Did *he* hurt you?"

Her eyes widened, then narrowed into sharp slits. "I told you that you could have two questions. You've used up your quota."

When she pressed against his chest to rise, he let her. When she left the room, he let her.

He'd never be able to get past this. Every time he reached her, he'd wonder if his touch reminded her of those horrible Wednesday nights at Masters' Club. If he didn't get over this, they'd never be able to be truly free while together.

Disgusted, he rose and retrieved the whip. He cleaned it and returned it to its place, hanging it on the wall in a coil. Then he dressed. As much as he wanted to lure her back to bed, he had work to do. A lot, apparently.

Chapter Thirty-One

"Alessandra." Smith shook her gently, and she opened her eyes.

"What time is it?"

Predictable. He chuckled. "It's about six. You've been asleep for a few hours now." He helped her as she struggled to rise, stepping back when she swung her legs over the side of the bed.

"I've been asleep for, what, three hours?"

"Possibly more. Dinner's ready."

"I'll freshen up, then join you."

"That sounds good." He held out his hand to her, and she took it, allowing him to help her rise. Impulsively, he pulled her in for a swift, ardent kiss. Then he let her go, and she looked as stunned as he felt. When she ducked her head and left the room, he followed.

He'd made a pot of spaghetti. After the day he had, he hadn't been up for any serious preparation in the kitchen. Although his first thought was to let her continue to rest, he wanted her to sleep well later, and she never did that when she napped.

He smiled at her when she walked into the kitchen. "Will you set the table while I dish up the food?"

"Of course, what would you like to drink?"

"A beer." He paused. "Feel free to have one yourself."

She nodded, then grabbed two from the fridge.

He waited until they had consumed most of the spaghetti. "Marie and Dante were here. His actual name is Dave Martin."

Her lips curled.

"But I have to admit Master Dante suits him." He took a sip of beer. "It's all arranged. My lawyers will draw up the papers tomorrow, and their lawyers will check everything over, but the deal should be signed by this time tomorrow."

"That's good, right? How did they take it?"

"Marie cried, but from relief rather than grief from losing the club. She wanted to talk to you, but I told her that could keep for another day."

Alessandra shifted.

"Does your back hurt? Was I too strong with the whip?"

"No, Master, that's not it."

"Then what is?" His voice was clipped, but he couldn't help himself.

"It's my fault. All of it."

He reached across to take her hand. "Alessandra, he's been exploiting women for years. Someone has to put an end to it." He paused. "Marie has video."

Alessandra sucked in a breath and made a choking sound. She tensed to leap out of her seat, but he waylaid her.

"Not of you. Marie destroyed everything except the murder of Mimi Chang."

"She has that on tape?"

"Why do you think she was so relieved I was willing to take this on? A dozen times she's driven to the police station, but fear kept her from going in. I'm going in at six o'clock on Wednesday. I'll give my verbal permission for them to raid the club at eleven."

Her eyes flickered.

So Marie had been accurate about the timing. Carl Jergen always held court over his minions at eleven o'clock. Buck naked, he'd begin working over the woman of his choice. Marie had refused to say how often Alessandra had been that woman, and Smith was pretty sure he didn't want to know.

"May I clear the dishes?"

Oh. He still clutched her hand. "You may." He still didn't release her. "Do you think...I mean, do you want to play tonight?"

Her eyes were bright and clear. "Yes, please."

"Ladies' choice."

"Psychoanalyst. Only this time I get to tie you down and delve into your psyche."

He burst out laughing. "Never going to happen, my little one, but I'll offer you a compromise. Every time you give me an answer that pleases me, I'll let you ask a question."

Her nose wrinkled. "I'm not sure that's going to be fair since you tend to be critical, and answering correctly is subjective, but it's worth a shot."

"So I'll clear the dishes, and you go prepare yourself."

She nodded and grinned, practically running in her enthusiasm.

He took a deep, steadying breath. She'd made the offer, and they both knew the reason. Time to clear the air once and for all.

He didn't waste time clearing the dishes but made a detour to his office to grab a pad of paper and a pen.

He'd been accurate the last time and remembered most of what she said, but she'd also left things unsaid, and he wanted to fill in those blanks.

She lay naked and spread-eagled on the bed, a look of pure anticipation on her face. "It's Dr. MacLean," she cooed. "Here to give me my analysis for the week."

He couldn't help it—he grinned. "The doctor is pleased to see you in such high spirits. And how was your day, Ms. Soriano?" He already had one foot shackled and reached for the second.

She flexed her foot when he cuffed her. "I had a bit of a tough day."

"Well, you'll just have to tell me about it."

After mere moments, he had her secured.

As he had before, he pulled up the chair next to her head. This time he placed the pad of paper across his crossed legs. "Now why was today a tough day?"

"Because I hurt people who've never been anything but kind to me."

"And you did that because…"

Her stare went to that place in the ceiling that seemed to mesmerize her. What did she see, looking at that expanse of black? Not an inch of the room wasn't painted black. Even the hardwood was the darkest cherry available.

"My friends pushed me too far. They want too much from me."

"And what is it they want from you?"

"They want me to go back in time."

Patience. Let her come to you.

She took a deep breath. "That's not quite true. They're such wonderful friends that they'd take me as I am now, despite all the horrible things I've done."

He waited again, but it seemed nothing more was forthcoming. "And what horrible things have you done, Alessandra?"

She closed her eyes, squeezing them shut. "I'm a whore."

He winced, his stomach clenching. He'd used that word in jest before he'd known what she'd been up to. Now she was throwing it back in his face. "I'm sure you're exaggerating."

"Doctor, I'm not."

"Tell me about the first time."

"I...I went to Club Kink alone on a Saturday night. I was lonely and just wanted to lose myself. A man approached me. He offered to take me home, and I agreed. He tied me up, paddled me, whipped me, made me come, and then we fucked like rabbits. In the morning he gave me a thousand dollars. He told me to buy a slutty costume and to come back to Kink on Wednesday night and ask for Cassius."

A tic started in his jaw, and he had to consciously unclench his teeth and school his voice to evenness. "And who was Cassius?"

"The bouncer." Her fist clenched. "So I did what I was told. I went to a fetish shop and bought an outfit made of leather. I mean, the whole deal—bustier, short skirt, thigh-high boots. I was completely decked out. Cassius laughed."

"Why?"

Now her turn to laugh. Not a happy one. "Because the women don't wear clothes at the Masters' Club. I stripped out of my clothes, put them in the locker in the change room, and then stepped into the play area. Another man, Brutus, clipped a wide dog collar around my neck, attached a leash, and pushed me to my knees. He made me crawl into the room, tugging if I didn't move fast enough."

"What happened then?"

"The man was there—the one who liked to fuck like a rabbit, all quick, you know? Anyway, he was there, and he took me to the cage. I was one of eight. Six women and two men. We were the bottoms. I tried to count the number of men there—the tops—but I lost count. Then, when Caesar arrived, the games began."

"And Caesar is what they called Carl Jergen." He wished desperately for a drink.

She nodded. "But I didn't know that at first. More than a month went by before one of the girls let his name slip."

"But that first night…"

She sucked her belly in. "I was fresh meat."

Smith waited.

One minute stretched into two as emotions flitted across her face. She was playing the movie over and over in her mind.

"Let it out, Alessandra." He said it quietly but with authority.

"First, they led me to him. On my knees, of course." She paused, caught up in a memory. "I remember thinking his dick wasn't all that big, but then I realized he wasn't fully erect. Without warning, he shoved his cock down my throat." She swallowed. "You know, it's ironic. I'd never given a blow job. My college boyfriends had asked but never pushed when I said no. Being with Gage involved me watching while Cara did the work. Until Caesar, I'd never had a cock in my mouth. Imagine that. Thirty-five years old…"

He was losing her. "Then what happened?"

"Then another guy stuck lube in my ass, and I lost my anal virginity. I was so surprised I bit down. I wish I'd bitten the fucking thing off, but no such luck. It enraged Caesar, you know? He backhanded me so hard my jaw snapped. Then they dragged me off and chained me to the wall. I received so many lashes I lost count." She stuck out her tongue to wet her lips. He was about to offer her water when she continued. "Then it ended. The whipping, I mean. They left me there, just hanging. I heard sounds all around me. Cries, screams, pleasure, pain...all just a cacophony. I wanted to cover my ears, but I couldn't.

"Then someone released me, and I dropped to the ground. I thought, *this is it. It's over for me.* But it'd just begun."

She bit her lower lip between her teeth so hard he feared she'd draw blood.

"Tell me."

"They led me to the center of the room, thrust to my knees and blindfolded. The first penis stuck in my mouth was short and thick. I remember thinking my jaw might dislocate. Then someone was pushing into me. He kept pushing my knees apart and thrusting. I wasn't ready, you know? I wasn't turned on, and it hurt. Then he came, and the next guy started. That time it didn't hurt so much. The next one took my ass. He didn't come in me, though, he came on my back, and he smeared his cum all over it, pressing it into the welts from the whip. God, that really hurt. Then the other guy came in my mouth.

"Lather, rinse, repeat. That was the phrase that kept going through my mind as each man took his turn." A lone tear escaped. "I lost count, and eventually I just went away. The next thing I knew, the blindfold was off, and Brutus picked me up and carried me to the changing room. Two of the girls dressed me and told me the first time was always the worst, and it'd get better. Brutus put me in a cab, handed me five hundred dollars, and told me to be back the same time next week."

"And you did." He made a supreme effort to keep his voice clinical and detached.

"He told me they'd kill Denise Lang if I didn't."

"Who the hell is Denise Lang?"

"A psychologist I work with sometimes, back in Mission City. She splits her time between my department and Healing Horses Ranch. She has a beautiful little boy named Adam. The boy is seven. Denise is a single mother, and there's never been a father in the picture. They threatened to orphan a little young man verging on the cusp of life." The tear had streaked down her temple and now soaked the pillow. "Doctor, I have no idea how they knew about me, but they did. And not a threat, but a promise."

Jesus Christ. "So you went back."

"And the girls were right—the first time is the worst. Some of them did other things on the side because the money wasn't enough to support their drug habits. Me? I'd just lie in bed for a week, hoping to heal before it started all over again."

"What happened to the money? There's no way that flea-infested, firetrap hellhole cost you five hundred a week."

A strangled sound came from her chest. "The next day, Thursday, I'd go to the bank, get the hundreds converted into fives, and walk around Downtown Eastside, giving away the money."

My God. "And this has been going on for six months?"

When she shrugged, it pulled against the shackles. "Something like that." Then her eyes popped open, wide with panic. "I should've told Gage to warn Denise. I *told* you I had to be there on Wednesday night, but you wouldn't listen. If that little boy is orphaned, then it's your fault."

Smith couldn't imagine them actually killing a single mother, but then he wouldn't have foreseen them killing Mimi Chang either.

He put down the pen and paper. "I'm going to release you now."

Her eyes went wide again. "Did I not give you good answers? Because you promised I could ask questions if I gave good answers." She sounded like a petulant child. Like she had regressed or something.

"I need to release you so I can go call Gage." Not a phone call he wanted to make, but he wasn't willing to take a chance.

"You don't have to let me out for that."

"Do you remember what I said to you the first time? That I would never leave you alone while tied up?"

Dark brown eyes bored into his soul. "Please, Smith, just let me stay this way for a little while. You can make your call and then come back. I promise I'll be a good girl."

Every instinct screamed against this, but he acquiesced. "I won't be gone for more than a minute or two."

She gave him a dreamy smile. "I'm just going to close my eyes." Doing exactly that, her body relaxed into the bed, shackles and all.

Smith laid a blanket over her and then pressed a kiss to her temple.

The update to Gage took longer than Smith would've liked, but he had to do it. Gage knew Denise, as well as someone in the Mission City RCMP detachment. Both men felt the threat was probably an empty one but agreed best not to take chances. Smith didn't tell Gage the gory details. He wasn't sure if knowing was better or to leave it up to the imagination. He wished he could un-ring the bell, but that time had come and gone. Had he re-traumatized Alessandra? No way for him to know, but he'd needed to hear what she'd endured for the last six months.

Who counseled the counselor?

Alessandra was still when he returned. He took his time checking her hands and feet, making sure the circulation hadn't been cut off.

Was she asleep?

"Why business?"

Her voice was so soft he almost didn't hear her. Fair was fair, so he sat back down, pulling the blank pad of paper across his lap. "I loved numbers, and I loved the news."

Her eyes didn't open, but the edges of her mouth curled. "You know you're going to have to explain."

"Even as a kid I was more interested in learning how to count than in learning my alphabet." He smiled in memory. "And my mother always watched the nightly newscast with me."

"How old were you?"

"I don't ever remember not watching. Dan Rather on CBS news was a staple."

"But he's an American."

"So was my mother, and she grew up with Walter Cronkite."

Alessandra appeared to consider that. "So does that mean you're American?"

"No, I was born in Vancouver. You remember I told you my mother ran away instead of getting an abortion? She ran from California to Canada and never looked back. Eventually she applied for citizenship, and they granted it."

"But you were telling me about numbers and news."

"Right." Amazing she was so coherent. "I remember watching the news on Monday, October 19, 1987. That was Black Monday."

"You'll have to enlighten me. I wasn't even born yet."

He knew the math and was well aware she'd at least been born, but a gentleman never referred to a lady's age. Plus, she'd just told him she'd been thirty-five when she'd given her first blow job.

Wrong thought.

"The Dow Jones plummeted twenty-two percent in one day. I asked my mother to explain it to me, and she did. It stunned me all those people could lose all that money at one time. From that day forward, I learned everything I could about money."

"How old were you?" A sarcastic demand. "Five?"

"I was seven, if you must know."

She frowned. "And that makes you…?"

"Older than you are, now pay attention."

"Yes, Master."

Damn, she was a spitfire. "You've asked about six questions, so now it's my turn."

Her mouth twisted in a distinctly unladylike fashion. "Okay." Her tone was grudging.

"Tell me a story."

She shifted, flexing her fingers repeatedly.

"Tell me a story where Alessandra the social worker saved the day."

Her brow was wrinkled, but now she was squirming as well. "I don't think…"

"The doctor thinks this will help you."

Now she frowned.

But then she took a breath, and he waited patiently.

"I was one year out of school when I met Wanda. She was such a beautiful young woman. Mother of triplet boys. So overwhelmed and then her husband died. Well, he was murdered. He was a gas station attendant, working every day to help support the family. He was working one night when a robber came in. He handed over the hundred-and-twenty dollars like they'd taught him, but the robber believed he was holding back. He wasn't—they trained him to safe-drop every time he hit two hundred dollars, and, of course, he didn't have a key to the safe. But it enraged the robber. Then, bang, the gun went off."

How could this possibly end well?

"So I get a call from the neighbor that the babies are crying all the time, and she doesn't want to get involved, but she's worried."

"A good neighbor." *Or a nosy bitch.*

Alessandra nodded. "A very good neighbor. I go to pay a home visit, to see how things are going."

"Not well?"

"No, not well. Wanda says she doesn't want help, and the babies aren't being abused, so there's nothing I can do."

"But you don't give up." He had no doubt. "You're involved now."

A slow smile crossed her lips. "I call the concerned neighbor and invite her out for a cup of tea. She's a recently widowed woman whose children are all grown, but there are no grandbabies yet."

"A young widow."

"Two young widows." A slight lifting of the corners of her lips. "So I go to Wanda, and I tell her that her neighbor is depressed and lonely, needs to get out more. And I tell Thelma that Wanda is depressed and lonely. Then, voilà, neither woman is lonely anymore."

"How did the story end?"

"Paul, Luka, and Craig have a grandmother, then Wanda went back to school to become a pharmacy technician. She remarried several years ago, and they have a little girl. The boys just had their eighth birthday. I know this because I get a Christmas card from them every year."

"And what happens this year when the card gets sent back? *Return to Sender*, recipient has fallen off the planet."

"Hobbit."

A swift and certain response. He'd thought bringing back good memories might help, but she'd been teetering this whole time. He'd just about pushed her to the wrong side of the cliff.

"When did you meet Gage?" Her turn again.

"At frosh week. Gage was a year ahead of me, and he enjoyed his turn to force a freshman into becoming a man."

"How did that go?"

Smith smiled, even though she couldn't see it because she was back to staring at the ceiling. "We bonded over beer and babes."

Her look of shock was priceless. "But..."

"Oh, Gage didn't go there, but he loved to hear my adventures. It became a Sunday morning ritual. We'd drag ourselves out for coffee, and I'd tell him about the babe of the week, and he'd moon over Cara."

"Even back then?"

"They met during the same frosh week. Cara was a freshman like me. She and Gage just...clicked. But she was adamant she wasn't going to get involved with anyone."

He could see her making some mental calculations.

"So they lost their virginities..."

"You're a bright girl..."

"On their wedding night."

"And she gets a gold star." He grinned. "They were twenty-four and twenty-five respectively."

"Such restraint."

Smith nodded. "Gage really loved her, and she kept him at bay because of her medical condition."

"She worried about a recurrence of the cancer." The cancer that'd left her without ovaries or a uterus. "That's why they never had kids."

"I know."

"And it always made me sad because I thought they'd make great parents. I was right, eh? Gage is a great dad."

"How would you know? You haven't been around since they finalized the adoption." His voice was sharper than he'd intended, but the sentiment was there. Of course Gage was an amazing father—it'd been a given. Anyone who could love a bunch of surly teenagers who weren't even his own had father material written all over him. For his wife Cara's sake, he'd maintained that the students were enough, but he'd been deluding himself and lying to her.

Alessandra grimaced.

"My turn," he said sharply. "Tell me something you've never told anyone else."

Silence. Utter silence. Silence that spun out into minutes. Silence that threatened to become oppressive.

"That being a whore is better than being a murderer. At least for those five hours every Wednesday, I could escape the mental anguish. Now get me the fuck out of here."

Her voice was so flat it scared him.

She still stared up at the ceiling, unblinking.

He waited a minute before he placed the still-blank pad of paper on the bed and undid the shackles. No sound in the room except her breathing and his.

When the last manacle was released, she held the blanket against her like a shield. A barrier. "I think I'd like to sleep alone tonight."

He could try to talk her out of it. He could try ordering her. He could try persuasion, sex, money for the ranch. He could try any of those things, but he wouldn't. He'd broken her. Again.

"I'll see you in the morning." He rose. "Where are your pajamas?"

Without looking at him, she pointed to the closet

where she'd dutifully returned them this morning.

Smith retrieved them. "I have a few hours of work to do. I'm in my office if you need me."

"I won't." Flat. Emotionless.

He walked out.

Chapter Thirty-Two

Goddamn it, she'd done it again. Napped during the day. Now, at three in the morning, sleep eluded her.

Fuck Smith MacLean.

Fuck Gage Clayton.

Fuck Carl Jergen.

Men. She exhaled a lengthy breath. Then repeated the word. *Men.*

Etymologically uninteresting. Women, though, came from men. Eve had come from Adam's rib.

Not that she believed that for an instant. She was an evolutionist who believed the Bible to be a work of great literature. Right up there with *Paradise Lost*, *Ulysses*, *Hamlet*, and *Moby Dick*.

Maybe not *Moby Dick*.

Still, the minutes ticked by. She only knew three o'clock had come and gone because she'd flipped on the light to check, which was something one wasn't supposed to do because it'd mess with the circadian rhythm.

Fuck circadian rhythms.

She could read. She hadn't finished the book she'd started almost a week ago. She felt like an eternity had passed since Smith had taken her shopping. All the technology still awed her.

Flipping on the light, she reached for the phone and a pad of paper. Thank God JEAP was available twenty-four seven.

The call was answered on the second ring.

"Hello, this is Davin, and you've reached Johnson Employee Assistance Program. How can I help you tonight?"

"Davin, can you put me through to a counselor?"

"Absolutely. Have you called before?"

"No."

"Okay, I just need to open a file for you. It's all confidential, so you needn't worry that anyone at work will hear about this."

"Oh, well, I appreciate that."

He took her through the standard questions, and she followed the details she'd been given. She was twenty-five years old and worked as an insurance broker for one of Smith's companies. One of Smith's many companies, she was discovering. She wasn't even going to try to figure it out.

"Rana? Are you still there?"

Shit.

"Sorry, momentary loss of concentration."

"Well, I'm going to put you through to our counselor. His name is Hamish. Just hold the line."

Double shit.

"This is Hamish. How are you, Rana?"

"I'm…" *Shit, shit, shit. Well, fuck it.* "I'm thinking about killing myself."

****

Allie sat in one of the chairs on the balcony so she could watch the sun rising. Even here, in the concrete jungle, the sun rose. The previous day's wind had blown the clouds clear over the mountains.

Cold.

Really cold.

She'd grabbed Smith's leather jacket and every blanket she could find and was drinking coffee, but she was still cold. But a different cold. This cold came from the inside—a block of ice that had formed around her heart when DeeDee Threefeathers died.

When DeeDee Threefeathers had been murdered, she corrected. She hadn't killed the baby, but the death was on her head. And the three subsequent deaths. An entire family obliterated.

For the first time in six months, she'd found someone to talk to. She couldn't give specifics because she was supposed to be a twenty-five-year-old insurance broker, but she'd been able to conjure up the feelings of guilt that had eaten away at her for six months. She'd been able to remember her death wish and had turned that into suicidal ideation. It'd been all too easy to feel despair, and she knew, *knew* Hamish had heard it too.

They had talked for about an hour. He had started her talking about the precipitating event she had invented—she had killed a family while driving on a rain-slicked night. Not her fault, everyone told her, but she still felt responsible. Hamish didn't belittle her feelings. He acknowledged that for her, they were real.

Then he had gotten her talking about the enjoyable things in her life. Not trying to convince her she had good reasons to live but letting her draw her own conclusions. With encouragement, she admitted if she committed suicide, other people would grieve just as the loved ones of the family she killed were grieving.

Guilt. No matter where she turned. Guilt.

Hamish had talked *Rana* down off the ledge but

hadn't quite convinced Allie that life was worth living. Worth fighting for.

The wind whipped against her, causing her eyes to water. She didn't fight the tears as they fell. She remembered what it used to feel like with the wind whipping in her hair. Her beautiful hair. She'd lied to everyone when she told them she cut her hair because of wanting to disappear.

No, she'd cut her hair after that first night at Masters' Club. The men—the animals—had used her hair to lever her head in whatever direction they wanted. They'd yanked, pulled, and then come in it. She'd gone home, her hair full of cum, and hacked it off. Had shorn it almost to the scalp. If she had to go back, she wasn't going to give them another way to hurt her. She also hoped they might reject her because she looked ugly, but she realized quickly that no one cared what she looked like. They liked her because she had three holes and for no other reason.

Maybe now… Fucking vanity.

The sliding glass door opened, but she didn't turn. A fresh mug of coffee was placed next to hers, but she didn't say anything. Smith sat in the other chair, but she still held her tongue.

He sipped the hot coffee gingerly, letting the silence speak for itself. Finally, she could bear it no longer.

"You should buy JEAP. They're the best at what they do, and they should continue to expand."

"You've finished your calls?"

"Four of five, but that was enough. Even at three in the morning, they provide amazing counseling." *Damn it*, she was not going to cry. "Hamish trains his people to excel at their jobs and care about their clients. It's a hands-on management style that's so rare these days."

An uncomfortable silence.

"You spoke to Hamish at three in the morning?"

Damn it. "Yes, I did. I wasn't going to tell you, but I would either have to omit the call, which would corrupt the data, or lie about which counselor I spoke to, which might also bring everything else in the report into question."

A pause. "Bullshit, Alessandra. I call bullshit. You know very well you could've omitted the call without corrupting the sample because I told you from the beginning I wasn't looking for empirical data. I was looking for impressions. I was looking to see if they would take care of someone, really take care of someone, who is in crisis. It sounds like they did that."

She swiped at the tears that were now free-flowing. "Yes, they really care. I'm here, and that should be proof enough."

The silence that followed was profound and nerve-shattering.

"If Hamish hadn't talked you out of it, would you have killed yourself?"

"We'll never know."

Smith exploded from the chair, knocking his coffee mug to the concrete where it promptly shattered. He grabbed the blankets she'd so carefully draped over herself and threw them across the balcony. Then he hauled her up, holding her, gripping her, by the elbows. He shook her.

"You stupid bitch. You stupid, selfish, little bitch. Do you think of no one but yourself?"

Her eyes were wide, and she struggled, but still he

held on. One word and he'd release her. If she said her safeword, he'd let her go.

Right?

"You have a life, and it's worth living. You have people who care about you. If you can't find a way to live for yourself, then find a way to live for them."

She yanked an arm free, and her hand connected with his cheek. "I'm selfish? I'm selfish? Who goes around thinking he's fucking God and can fix everything by throwing money at it? Who thinks he can solve everything with numbers and graphs?"

When her hand lifted again, he grasped her by the wrist. "The first one is free, but the second one comes with consequences."

"Fuck consequences. Punish me. Beat me. Whip me. None of it matters. Don't you get that? They're dead. They're all dead." Her voice was raised to a fever pitch, and she didn't care if the neighbors heard.

The scream built within her. It welled in her chest and was pushing up through her throat.

Then Smith kissed her.

The wail died in her throat, overcome by the ferocity of his passion. His hands were everywhere—her cheeks, her shoulders, her back. He was pressing her against him, and despite all the layers of fabric, she felt his heat. His tongue thrust into her mouth, brutally punishing her, but she didn't fight. Instead, she clawed. Tried to crawl inside his skin. When he slammed her against the glass patio door, she arched. When he slid his thigh between hers, she pressed down, flexing her hips.

As he pulled back, he pressed his forehead to hers. Their harsh breaths mingled, misting in the frosty air. "I need to be inside you." He whispered the demand, biting her earlobe.

"And I need you there." All she could manage because her body was yearning for something way beyond her. She didn't want to think. She just wanted him to overwhelm her and take her away from the inside of her mind.

He gave her one more kiss, grabbed her hands, and dragged her to the latch. He took two tries to get the handle open, because his hands were shaking as badly as hers. They stumbled into the living room, Smith barely getting the door closed behind them.

He was already tugging down her pajama bottoms when she reached for his fly. Clothes flew, and soon he dragged her down to the ground. He lay on his back and impaled her, bringing her first climax.

She fought to open buttons. She wanted skin. She *needed* skin. She needed the relief that would only come when she pressed her hands to his abdomen. As she tugged the shirt aside, she placed her hands on his belly.

That pitted cold against his heat, and he sucked in a breath. He snagged one of her hands and brought it to his mouth, sucking on her fingers.

That brought with it her second climax.

Now *he* fumbled with buttons.

She brushed his hands aside, except her own were shaking. He grabbed her hips and began a punishing rhythm of thrusts that robbed her of what breath she had.

When her buttons were open, she tossed off both Smith's jacket and the top of her pajamas.

He pressed up and caught her nipple in his teeth.

She let out a keening sound, which brought her third climax. Still, he put her through her paces as he stretched her, filled her. Then he'd pull back, and she'd feel empty. She'd press down as his hips pressed up, and a bruising crush of bones occurred when they collided. Still, she couldn't get enough.

Grabbing her hips, he held her still for a moment, using her so he could pull out that last bit of friction he needed for his own orgasm. Then, as he was emptying himself inside of her, he ground his finger against her clit.

Which brought her fourth climax. "You really like the number four," she whispered, as her inner walls battered his cock.

"Bad things happen in threes, so good things must happen in fours." He barely managed a coherent reply.

When he reached out his arms, she collapsed into them. He held her against him so tightly she couldn't breathe, but she didn't care. Her bare ass and his balls were on display for the entire neighborhood, but she didn't care. They hadn't fully closed the sliding door, and the room was freezing, but she didn't care.

She didn't care about anything except holding on as if her life depended on it.

Because it did. He was like oxygen. She needed him as much as she needed her next breath.

Chapter Thirty-Three

Smith's bare ass was planted firmly on the very expensive hardwood floor, and his favorite silk shirt had been torn, but that was a minor price to pay. His arms were still around Alessandra, holding her tight to him. Her breasts were pressed to his chest, and her hips were being cradled by his thighs. He lifted his head from the ground and nipped at her lower lip.

"You cannot possibly be thinking about going another round." She pulled back, her chocolate brown eyes still glazed from passion. "Tell me you're not still horny."

"The mind is willing, but the cock is dead." That elicited the smile he'd hoped to coax from her.

"I think I need a shower."

"An excellent idea." He winced as his cock slid free of her. "I'll join you."

A good minute later they finally extricated from each other and sorted through the clothes flung around the room. As the pile on the couch grew, he caught her eye, and they laughed.

"I don't think your neighbors will ever recover."

"How about when you dared me to beat you, whip you, and punish you? I'm surprised there aren't cops at my doorstep."

Now she laughed so hard tears streamed down her face. "And I hope that wasn't your favorite coffee mug."

He waved his hand dismissively. "I'm a prick who's richer than God. I can buy another favorite coffee mug."

"No." She was still trying to catch her breath. "You're a rich prick who *thinks* he's God."

"Right, because we have to make sure we get the insults right."

That sobered her. "I was out of line."

He shrugged. "No, you had it right. I'm a manipulative bastard who uses money to get what he wants. I bought JEAP on Friday, and I've sent the hundred thousand dollars to the Healing Horses Ranch." He'd wired the remaining ninety thousand to Kennedy Dixon as soon as he'd completed the acquisition.

That stopped her cold, and all action ceased.

Oh shit.

She pointed an accusatory finger at him. "See, you go and pull shit like that, and I don't know whether to love you or hate you."

A flare lit in his chest.

In the next instant it extinguished when she snapped, "Today, it's hate." She advanced on him and poked a finger at his chest. "You never needed me to do those phone calls. I could have left days ago."

He reached out to snag the finger that was about to bruise his breastbone. "I wanted to give you a reason to stay, give you something productive to do with your time while…"

"While what? What's the plan, Smith? After the thirty days are up, what then? More negotiations? More manipulations? I'm a human being and tired of being fucked with." She dropped the pile of clothes at his feet. "I'm going to shower—alone."

He watched her go with a growing sense of desperation. She really had no idea how much danger she might be in if she left. He'd done more research the previous night after she went to bed. Carl Jergen had recently married Carla Fairhurst—widow of the recently deceased Henry Fairhurst. Carla's father had once been Premier of British Columbia, and her dead husband was rumored to be one of the richest men in the country. Smith's wealth paled in comparison to that of the widow whose husband had died suddenly and under vague circumstances. Fairhurst's body had barely been cold when his widow married Carl Jergen.

Money and power.

And now Jergen was angling to be the head of the right-wing party with the plan of being the eventual Prime Minister of Canada. The man had more hubris than the emperor from whom he'd taken his name. Alessandra and a video were all that stood between Jergen and ultimate power.

Two days. He just had to keep her safe until Wednesday night at eleven o'clock. How hard could that possibly be? He snorted softly. First he closed the sliding glass door, then he picked up the pile of clothes, fighting overwhelming weariness. She'd hate him, but he was only doing what he had to do.

If it made him a fucking prick, then so be it.

****

Three hours later he sat in his office with no great insights. After he'd showered and dressed for work, he'd given Alessandra a robe and instructions on how to turn up the temperature in the condo. He'd locked the dungeon with her clothes inside and left.

Her yowls of protest still rang in his ears.

At least she's talking to you.

Sort of.

Well, he could do one thing. He picked up his phone and sent a text. Less than a minute later, it rang.

"Hello, Rielle. I didn't mean for you to call me."

A soft laugh. "Smith, I'm sitting at home in total silence. Cara is blessedly asleep, and after much prodding I managed to get Gage to go to the school."

"Bet he didn't like that." He suspected it'd been quite a battle.

"He didn't." She sniffed. "Just because he's the Master in this relationship doesn't mean he gets everything he wants."

Fair enough. He didn't dominate Alessandra all the time, much as he wanted to.

"Why are you calling? I'm pretty sure it's not because you want to know how the baby's doing or whether or not my husband went to work." Some papers rustled in the background.

"Did I catch you at a bad time? Are you working today?"

She snorted. "Officially I only work Tuesdays, Thursdays, and Fridays. In reality I have more than enough work to keep me occupied all of the time. Legal aid work waits for no one, and there's always someone needing my help."

Man, he admired her. She and Alessandra worked to make people's lives better. He worked to make more money. Well, okay, that wasn't strictly true. His business kept hundreds of people employed and delivered goods and services to untold numbers of others. The acquisition of JEAP alone was going to help so many people.

"Why are you really calling, Smith?"

She knew him despite only having met him six months ago. "I wanted to check and see how you were doing. How are your feet?"

"They're fine." A sigh. "And you could have discovered that if you'd called Gage."

"Was I wrong to call?" Shit, had he stepped in it?

A light laugh. "You're always welcome to call—I just figured you'd be more comfortable talking things out with another Dom."

He hesitated. She made a valid point. Protocol existed for a reason. Submissives were not to be approached unless the Dominant had given express permission. But he wasn't calling Rielle today as a Dominant.

Or was he?

"I don't mind speaking to you, of course." Her voice held that husky note it often did. "But you have to know I'll relay the entire conversation to Gage. We have no secrets, Smith. We did once, but not anymore."

"Yet he didn't know who Carl Jergen was."

Shit. He hadn't meant to be so blunt.

Another soft sigh. "He didn't know the name, but he knew what was important. I never attended Masters' Club. Had I heard about it? Yes, in passing. Did I know what women were enduring? No. I honestly thought what went on was consensual. Now I see that was naïve of me. Truthfully, I was naïve about a lot of things."

"I'm sorry." The words felt woefully inadequate.

"Why? I'm not."

Smith rose to stand in front of his plate-glass

window. A stunning view of the North Shore Mountains framed the vista. The first snow had fallen last weekend, and eager skiers were already chomping at the bit. Would he ski this year? Would he do anything? Everything overwhelmed him, and this feeling of loss of control didn't sit well.

"Smith?"

"Sorry, what were you saying?"

"That I'm not sorry." The smile in her voice was clear. "Yes, Carl put me through some horrendous things, and I'm ashamed that I stayed with him four years and endured horrible abuse. It galls me that I didn't have the courage to leave. But he'd conditioned me to believe the abuse was normal in BDSM relationships, and by the time I saw the light, too much time had passed. As far as I was concerned, I'd passed the point of no return."

To Smith's recollection of events, Jergen had abandoned Rielle, and only then had she ventured to Kink alone on a Saturday night and met Gage. One grieving the loss of a Dominant and one grieving the loss of a submissive wife…they'd come together. Not easy, at least at first, but they'd built a wonderful life together.

"Can she get past this? Can I get past this?"

Well. Okay, then. Blunt enough?

"Ah." Rielle chuckled. "Now we get to the real reason for the call. I can't answer for Allie. I've been in therapy for more than a year now, and the difference is stark. I'm not the person I was a year ago when I met Gage. As for ending therapy, I can assure you that's not happening anytime soon. Saturday proved I'm not as far along in healing as I'd like to be."

Crap. More baggage he'd inadvertently brought up.

"As for you, I can't answer that. You saw Gage's reaction. Carl has been out of my life for a year and is well and truly gone, but Gage still obsesses. He doesn't think I know, but I do. Maybe…" She paused. "Maybe everything coming to a head is a good thing. I mean, if you can really nail Carl and make the suffering stop…maybe Gage and I can truly begin the process of healing."

What she said made complete sense, yet he couldn't shut down the images of Alessandra in that horrible place, at the mercy of all those men. Despite the threat of harm to her co-worker, she'd had a choice. She'd gone back week after week. Would have this past week if he hadn't prevented her. How sick was that?

"She didn't think she had a choice, Smith. She's as smart a woman as you'll ever meet, but she got caught in the trap of desperation." Rielle sighed. "Abused women have a skewed view of the world."

"Do you know why she disappeared?"

"No."

"Are you lying to me?" Desperation clawed at him.

"No." Steel. "And I'm going to forget you just asked that question. I'd have spoken up six months ago if I had any clue."

Smith closed his eyes in shame. He shouldn't have questioned Rielle's integrity. Her honesty.

"We have to respect Allie. Don't you see, Smith? She has to be the one to tell us why. Forcing the issue will only drive her further away. Oh, she might be in your condo physically, but if she doesn't feel safe emotionally, those walls will never come down."

"But they did. I mean between you and Gage."

Another chuckle. "Smith, I put the man through hell. I pushed him away too many times to count. I'll never understand the reason, but he kept coming back."

"Love." Of that he had no doubt. His friend loved Rielle as much as he'd loved Cara, his first wife. Perhaps even more because of the adversity they'd faced together.

"Maybe." A cry sounded in the background. "And now my daughter is awake and will be demanding her bottle." The sound grew louder. "You going to be okay?"

Was he? Did he have a choice?

"Thank you, Rielle, for all of it."

"Just take care of her, Smith. We all want her back, but it can't be at the cost of her life. Got to run. Bye."

The line disconnected.

At the cost of her life? Was that the price he was demanding?

Chapter Thirty-Four

By Wednesday night, Allie was ready to commit murder, to hell with the prick on her conscience. Actually, killing Smith MacLean wouldn't be a prick on her conscience—it'd be a relief.

When she'd come out of her shower on Monday, all her clothes were in the dungeon, which was locked. He'd left her with the robe on her back.

At least he had the decency to turn up the temperature.

Half a dozen times she'd dialed Rielle's number, only to stop before pressing the send button. This wasn't Rielle's fault, and the last thing her friend needed was Allie adding to her worries. So, instead, she'd spent the day pacing the condo like a caged tiger. When Smith came home that night, she pounced on him, ignoring the moment of conscience at just how exhausted he looked.

Dinner had been Chinese food, and she'd sulked through the entire meal. At bedtime, he'd dragged her into the dungeon, handcuffed her to the bed, and crawled in beside her. She'd expected him to fuck her, but he hadn't. When she challenged him on the cuffs, he told her he'd done it so he could get a good night's sleep without worrying she might bolt.

Like she was going anywhere in pajamas.

Tuesday had been a repeat with him again taking

away her pajamas and leaving her with a robe. That night, after he handcuffed her to the bed, she'd tried to turn the tables on him. Had tried to seduce him.

That'd been a bust as he turned his back and went to sleep.

Wednesday saw her grudgingly hand over her pajamas. This time she tried to be nice about it, but the response had been the same. She got the robe for her trouble.

At least he wasn't leaving her naked.

He came home at four o'clock on Wednesday and went straight to the dungeon. She remained on the couch, reading the book she still hadn't managed to finish, despite having three full days to herself.

When he dropped a pile of clothes on the seat beside her, she looked up. "I'm sorry—did you say something?"

His eyes were tired, his face strained. That pinprick on her conscience appeared again.

"Please, Alessandra, get dressed. We need to leave for the police station. The detectives are waiting for us."

Those were the magic words. She leapt to her feet. "Give me five minutes."

"Take ten." He dropped to the couch, weariness clear on his face.

More like fifteen, but she wanted to look respectable. That meant makeup and trying to do something with her hair. The results were questionable, and she wasn't sold on wearing the powder-blue business suit, but she was willing to defer to him on this one. He'd laid the groundwork for this. She was just a pawn in a gigantic game of chess, only, with this game, she didn't know the rules.

When she came out into the living room, he was on the couch with his eyes closed. Sitting next to him, she took his hand in hers. "I'm sorry." And she was.

He brought their joined hands to his lips, gently kissing her knuckles. "So am I, Alessandra. More sorry than I can say." His eyes opened. "Shall we go? We'll take my car."

They were only a few blocks away from the division, and her nerves ratcheted up more with each street they passed. "You haven't told me what my part is in all this."

"You tell them whatever you think is relevant. You confirm you saw Mimi Chang at the Masters' Club two days before she turned up dead in the inlet. You tell them about the blackmail. Tell them as little or as much as you're comfortable with."

"Will you be with me?"

"I doubt it. I'll try, but I can't promise. Marie will meet us there." Smith patted his pocket. "I have a copy of the disc, and Marie has the original." He paused. "I watched that fucking bastard kill a woman. I watched a murder on tape."

She shut her eyes against the pain radiating from him. She'd been so selfish over the past few days, not bothering to ask him about the investigation or even ask him how he was doing. Instead, she'd blithely assumed she was the wronged party. Nothing could have been further from the truth.

Hamish had pointed out that despite everything, *Rana* had survived, and that had to count for something. Maybe he was on to something. Allie couldn't bring DeeDee Threefeathers back to life, but she could reach out to the women who were going to be traumatized tonight.

As they drove the last few blocks, Smith tried to explain everything that had happened over the past couple of days.

To make it legitimate, the women were all going to be brought in for questioning that night, but he'd secured a promise none of them would be charged. He'd also made sure Marie would be exempt from prosecution because of her testimony against Jergen. Marie and her husband had also put their house on the market. Her husband had family in Newfoundland, and he and Marie had decided that it'd be an excellent time to move to the East Coast.

Master Dante was undaunted and was eyeing the deal on the space Smith secured. Club Kink might close permanently tonight, but in a few months Club Drag would be up and running, and every Saturday night would be BDSM night. Smith had an affinity for Saturday nights.

He pulled into the division parking lot and cut the engine. "It'll be okay."

She wanted to believe him. She really did. Alighting from the car, she waited for him to come around to join her. He reached for her, and she went willingly, letting him press his lips to her forehead.

Then he leaned down as if to pick up something she'd dropped and snaked his hand up under her skirt, pinching the sensitive skin on the inside of her upper thigh. As if he had all the time in the world, he rose and planted a very chaste kiss on her nose.

Allie glared at him. "What the fuck was that for?"

"Something to remember me by."

A look in his eyes, a flicker, and then nothing. Whatever had been there disappeared. The click of heels on the sidewalk had her turning to see Marie standing next to a tall, good-looking man. He was almost as tall as Smith, with light-brown skin, black hair, and deep-brown eyes.

"Alessandra, Smith, this is my attorney, Arnav Sankar. Arnav, these are the two I told you about."

The man's brow rose. "Are you two not represented by counsel?"

Smith shook his head. "Neither of us did anything wrong."

"Well, if you need legal advice, for God's sake, ask for it. You two are either the bravest or the craziest people in this town."

"Neither." Smith's voice held a modicum of menace. "Just the most determined."

****

The sun was just starting to make an appearance when Allie closed the blinds in the living room. Her eyes felt like they'd been scratched with sandpaper, and it had left all the grit behind. Her watch read barely past seven in the morning.

The raid had taken place at eleven, just as planned. By then, Allie had given her testimony on video and had been moved to a sizeable conference room. She helped a nice police officer prepare for the arriving victims. Funny, Allie'd never seen herself as one, but as five women and two men—clad only in police-provided robes—entered the room, it forced her to face the truth she'd fought so hard to deny.

She hadn't been there by choice. They'd used and abused her. She was, like the others, a victim. Some of the women were angry with her, but she knew they were more worried about how they'd pay for their next fix. She'd provided all the women with business cards for both the closest counseling center and the local detox clinic.

One of the women, Candy—whose actual name was Sasha—had asked to speak to Allie privately. The woman was so petite that the first time Allie met her, she'd thought the woman to be just a child. Now Sasha told Allie why she'd run away and why she couldn't go back. Sasha was, in fact, underage. One of the club's wealthier patrons had gotten her a fake ID, and of course, the bouncers hadn't questioned it. They also charged Cassius and Brutus, seeing as they were only glorified pimps.

Allie had arranged for Sasha to move to a woman's shelter with a promise of finding her a bed in rehab to help her break free of the meth addiction plaguing her for over two years.

One of the men—also just really a boy—had freaked out on them, and the cops had been required to put him in lockup. The entire night had been just one long never-ending nightmare.

"Are you hungry?"

Smith shook his head. "I'm going to bed."

"I'll take my clothes off."

He waylaid her. "I'm not taking your clothes. Stay, don't stay. I just don't care anymore. I'm too tired to argue. If you're still here when I wake up, then we can decide what to do with you."

God, she just sounded like some enormous burden he couldn't wait to rid himself of. She reached for him, but he slipped from her grasp, and she let him go.

****

Allie awoke suddenly, snapping from sleep to wakefulness immediately. She'd had a nightmare. But it hadn't been DeeDee she saw lying dead but Sasha. She felt just as responsible.

She still shook when she rose, having no idea the time. When she flipped on the light, her watch read one o'clock. Day or night, she had no clue.

Her bladder was making serious demands, so she opened the door, only to be confronted with darkness. She'd been asleep for almost twenty hours. Once she finished peeing, her stomach made serious demands. Locating leftover Chinese, she ate it cold and straight from the box.

After turning off the lights, she wandered over to the windows and opened the blinds. The eerie glow of the city, that pink tinge fed by the millions of lights, was striking, but the building across the way caught her attention. Those same neighbors had, just a couple of days ago, been given the chance to be witness to the mother of all fights culminating with the mother of all kisses. If Smith had wanted to take her right there on the balcony, she probably would've let him. And then the sex right inside the door.

She thought about the desperation fueling that passionate coupling. She'd wanted to escape unbelievable pain, and he'd been so angry about her having thought—just thought—about suicide. If she survived all this, she'd need counseling.

That thought brought her up short. The death wish she'd been living with for six months wasn't at the forefront of her mind. Suddenly, or maybe gradually, she was learning to let go of it. She was starting to think that maybe a future existed for her. That thought scared her more than anything. Six months ago, she'd only had the death of the Threefeathers family on her conscience. Now she had six months' experience at Masters' Club to live with as well.

She gazed out again. First, she counted the number of stories on the building across the way. Eighteen. Then she counted the number of windows illuminated. Fourteen. Fourteen other people awake at the same time she was. What were they doing? Were they insomniacs like her? Were they up because they had to be or because they wanted to be?

Had she only been here for twelve days? It felt like an eternity. Almost half her time was up. Except Smith had said he already gave the money to Healing Horses, so he wasn't holding that threat over her head. In fact, hadn't his last words to her been something like "Stay or go, I don't care"?

She'd earned her freedom. All she'd had to do was tell two police detectives about what they'd subjected her to for the last six months. It hadn't hurt as much in the telling as it had when she spilled out the story during the psychoanalysis session. Smith had made her feel safe, but it'd been gut-wrenching just the same. She had honestly believed that once he knew the truth, he'd be finished with her forever. And maybe he would've been, except for that lapse of judgment on the floor on which she stood.

God, you haven't even cleaned the floor. Yuck. Since Smith had come inside her, there probably weren't any remnants, but still she needed something to do, and she could clean. So she set about doing just that. The floors, the surfaces, dusting, mopping, and sweeping.

Then she tackled the fridge. Smith kept it tidy, but old fast-food containers abounded, and a few rotting vegetables were ready to toss. Then she pulled out the rest of the food and disinfected all the surfaces.

Next she tackled the bathroom. Smith had told her he had a woman who came in to clean every two weeks. She'd yet to meet the woman, but at the rate she was going, the woman would be able to put her feet up when she came to clean. Allie scrubbed and scrubbed and scrubbed, glad she'd put on gloves.

She was trying to outrun her thoughts, but her thoughts were still coming in staccato bursts. They were unrelenting in their overwhelming power to bring her to her knees. Then the tears came. She brushed them away with her forearms but found it of no use, as fresh ones appeared to replace them. This time, though, she wasn't grieving for the past. She was grieving for the future she might've had.

Smith had been painfully right about one thing— she had wanted a baby. She'd seen herself settling down with a husband and a baby in the suburbs. Actually, she had wanted at least two children. Growing up as an only child had made her decide that if possible, she wanted her child to have a sibling.

The child she'd never have.

Sitting back against the tub, she wrapped her arms around her waist and bent over with the blinding pain, ignoring the caustic cleaner on her gloved hands. She was so jealous of Gage and Rielle it drove her crazy. She hadn't even asked to see pictures of baby Cara. What kind of woman was she? Jealous of people who'd never done anything to her but show her love and kindness. She hadn't even called to see how Rielle was doing, didn't even know if they would bring in Rielle to testify about the hell Jergen had put her through. Hopefully not. Rielle had endured enough and had a family to focus on.

Allie had no one.

No one gave a shit about her mental health. Her true value was as a victim. Well, damn it, she'd be the best witness she could. The detectives had asked her to be as specific as possible. She'd been so nervous that details had escaped her, but now...now they were raining down on her like pellets of ice in a storm.

Scooping up the cleaning supplies took only moments. She washed her hands, all the time trying to hurry along the process. She all but ran across the condo, went to the desk in her room, and opened the computer. As it booted up, she returned to the kitchen to get a glass of water. Then she settled to type out every single thing she remembered about Hell. Mimi, Sasha, all the other girls and boys. The debauchery, the decadence, the debasement.

When she crawled into bed at six thirty, she'd spent every ounce of energy. She had nothing left.

Chapter Thirty-Five

Smith felt almost refreshed. Almost. He'd slept a good part of Thursday, spent the evening working and catching up on everything he'd missed, and then had gone to bed before eleven. He hadn't seen Alessandra the whole time until he'd checked on her. She was sleeping deeply, and as much as she probably needed sustenance, sleep had been what her body demanded, so he'd let her be.

Now, Friday morning, he was feeling human again. Then he stepped into the bathroom and was met with the smell that he associated with Gratzia, but she wasn't due until noon. So why did his bathroom smell like lemons?

Alessandra.

He did a quick check of the apartment and found it sparkling clean. One bag of garbage. After searching the fridge, he determined the bag was full of all the leftovers he'd forgotten about. He wished he'd heard Allie stirring, as he would've come out to talk to her. He would've come out to help her. But that was the thing about having a soundproofed room. It didn't just keep the noise in—it kept it out as well.

Well, nothing he could do about that now. He crossed to her room and opened the door.

She lay on her back, an arm flung over her eyes, and breathing deeply. Whatever her nocturnal exertions, she was now gone to the world.

Slipping back out, Smith went to put on a pot of coffee, then took a shower. He chose a temperature bordering on frigid to finish waking up. By the end, his nipples were erect, his balls and cock were shriveled, and his head was clear. Now just a matter of enacting his plan.

In mere moments he ruthlessly pushed away the wavering emotions and sat down to complete the task at hand. He was surveying his handiwork when his phone buzzed.

"MacLean."

"Meet me at the Starbucks on Robson at Homer. Ten minutes."

"And how are you, Mr. Driscoll?"

"Thrilled, seeing as I'm just about to get my bonus. Ten minutes."

The call was disconnected. Smith had just enough time to grab his briefcase and jacket. The walk would take him the whole ten minutes, but Toby would've known that.

Why a public meet? They could've met at Smith's office or in the condo, for that matter.

Well, he also made sure he had his checkbook.

****

An hour later, he was on his way back to the condo. Toby hadn't needed long to relay the story. A sad story, but not really Alessandra's fault. She'd made a judgment call, and it had, in the end, turned out to be the wrong one. She'd made decisions that turned out to be incorrect, but they hadn't resulted in four deaths.

They're all dead.

Her words echoed in his mind.

Now he had to find a way to get through to her. Get her to see the error in her reasoning. Yeah, that was going to be a cakewalk. Convince a very intelligent woman she was completely wrong. Show her another perspective.

He switched the latté from one hand to the other. The drink was ridiculous as a peace offering, but he had to do something. Something to show her he was serious. Serious about helping her, and serious about having her stay in his life.

And he was giving her a fancy coffee?

Nope, that wouldn't do.

He tossed the coffee in the closest garbage can and headed to West Hastings.

****

When he entered the condo, he felt the silence. Surely Alessandra wasn't still asleep. He went to the kitchen, which was empty, and then went to the dining room table. The note and envelope he'd left for her were gone, which meant she was awake. He went over to her bedroom and found the door open. The pajamas were neatly stacked on the bed, which was made. The laptop and e-reader were nicely placed on the desk.

Unease growing, he went to the dungeon. He hadn't thought to lock it this morning, and when he walked into the closet, his heart sank. The suitcase, knapsack, and all the clothes were gone.

She was gone.

And hadn't he expected that when he'd left her ten thousand dollars in cash this morning? He'd given her everything she needed to run again. The last time he made the gamble, she'd stayed. This time, she hadn't. But why leave the e-reader and laptop? Because they could be traced. Smith strode back to her room. Funny how he'd come to see it as her room.

The cell phone wasn't there. Well what the hell did that mean?

He pulled out his phone and made a call.

"Toby Driscoll."

"Can you track a phone?"

A nerve-shattering pause. "Yeah. Do you want me to come to you, or are you coming to me?"

"Come here."

"I'll be there in thirty."

The call was disconnected.

Thirty minutes? Toby expected him to sit here and wait thirty minutes? He'd go insane in that space of time.

Work. He still had his briefcase in his hand, and he looked at it like it held some kind of salvation. He strode to his office and was rounding his desk when he noticed it.

Alessandra's report.

The report she knew he hadn't needed. But like the professional she was, she'd done it anyway. He dropped to his desk and began to read.

He wasn't sure what he'd been expecting, but it hadn't been this. She was precise and detailed in each of her interactions, listing times, dates, employees, and the content of each conversation. The fourth call had been her one to Hamish about being suicidal after causing the death of a family in a car accident on a rainy night. A situation that would be rife with guilt—a non-preventable accident that had caused death and destruction.

The last call caught his attention. A woman who

had made a decision that had impacted the people she loved in ways she hadn't been able to predict. She needed forgiveness and was willing to ask for it, but what should she do if asking for absolution wasn't enough? The counselor, Hala, took Allie through the worst-case scenarios and then the best-case scenarios. They were on the phone for almost an hour, and Allie reported feeling that Hala had been both competent and compassionate.

Smith checked the time of the call. Five forty this morning. He'd been thirty feet from her and had had no idea. Of course, if he were honest with himself, he'd missed things all along. He'd been so focused on keeping her here he hadn't tended to her needs. Caught up in worries about her safety, he hadn't asked himself the tough questions.

He'd claimed he wanted to be her Dominant but hadn't thought out what that meant. Sure, he'd been with women in the past. Scened with them, played with them. But he'd never taken the step of being a full-time Dominant before, and he hadn't taken the role seriously enough.

Too fucking late.

His landline rang, and he snatched it up. "MacLean."

"Sir, it's Marvelle from the front desk. There's a Mr. Driscoll here to see you."

"Send him up. Thank you, Marvelle."

Placing the report back on his desk, he took a moment to touch it with reverence. She hadn't been obligated to complete it, but she had. That meant, somewhere in there, Alessandra Soriano the social worker was still alive.

He was waiting at the door when Toby arrived. He led the way to the living room and watched as the younger man set up a laptop. "You've got the Prey information?"

Smith handed it over. "It felt creepy installing the software…"

"Yeah, but if she ever lost it or had it stolen, then there'd be a way to track it."

"I didn't think I'd be tracking her."

Toby shrugged. "This'll take a few minutes."

"Can I get you a beer?"

Toby glanced at his watch, obviously realized noon had come and gone, and nodded.

Smith grabbed two, handed one off, and sat on the couch next to the six-foot-tall former bouncer whose wide shoulders with muscles to spare made him look ripped instead of beefy.

The night they met, Toby had been agile and calm as he handled the near-riot that broke out when one patron stabbed another in the nightclub he worked at. Impressed, Smith had then hired the man as private security a couple of times. When Toby branched out into private investigations, Smith had given him the start-up loan.

He'd repaid the money with interest within two years, and the agency was now one of the best in town. Although Toby could've pawned off Smith's case to a colleague, he'd felt the same loyalty that Smith reciprocated.

The white shirt and khaki pants he wore were in stark contrast to his dark skin. Also, Smith always secretly chuckled about the man's shaved head. The good-looking man worked so much Smith doubted he had much of a social life.

"Okay." Toby's voice pulled him from his reverie. "She's still in the downtown core."

"Any more than—" A key slid into the door lock. Gratzia. He'd forgotten today was cleaning day. Since Alessandra had done such a superb job, he'd tell his maid to take the day off. Rising, he went to the hallway.

"Look, I don't need..." His voice trailed off.

"Don't need what?" Alessandra closed and bolted the door. "Can you help me with these groceries?" She stared at him as if he were crazy. "Okay, don't help, but at least get out of the way so I can put them in the kitchen before I drop them."

"You went grocery shopping." Stupid thing to say, to be sure, but nothing else came to mind.

"And to the bank. What the hell were you thinking, leaving ten thousand dollars in cash lying around the condo? Anyway, it's safe and tucked away at an account I opened at the credit union. Seriously, Smith, get the fuck out of my way."

She pushed past him.

"Ma'am, my name is Toby Driscoll. I'm a friend of...well, this guy. Let me help you with those bags."

She handed over the bags.

Toby left the two of them standing in the hallway.

"Smith, are you okay?" Concern laced her voice. "Why don't you sit down?"

"You went grocery shopping."

"Yeah, we were running out of fresh supplies. I think you need to sit down."

He watched with a weird detachment as she reached for his sleeve, evidently meaning to pull him toward the couch.

In that moment, fear released its talons, and he hauled her against him, crushing his mouth to hers. His hands were all over her, making sure she was really there.

She pulled back, her pupils wide and her lips parted. "Look, as sweet of a greeting as this is, you've got a guest. Unless he's here for a threesome, he doesn't need to see this much PDA."

Smith couldn't help laughing. "Toby's not here for a threesome."

"But he's not averse to it," came a disembodied voice from the kitchen.

"Fuck off."

A chuckle. "I was planning on it." Toby reappeared, briefcase in hand. "I put the perishables away and will just take my laptop and be on my way."

"Surely, you can stay for a little while," Alessandra offered hospitably. "You don't have to leave on my account."

Toby grinned. "My work here is done." He tipped an imaginary hat to Smith. "Thanks for the beer." He passed between Alessandra and Smith, who still stood in the hallway, and left the condo.

She closed the door behind him and flipped the deadbolt. "Are you sure you're okay? Because you look strange. Let me get you something. Maybe some tea?"

He managed to shake his head and then reached for her hands, drawing her into the living room. Now that he could see her properly, he couldn't miss the dark smudges under her eyes. "You shouldn't have been making calls in the dead of night."

"Well, technically the crack of dawn. You saw my report? I didn't think you'd be home this early. I was planning to make dinner."

"You went grocery shopping."

Her eyes widened, and she grabbed him by the hand, all but dragging him toward the dungeon. "You need to lie down."

She kept pulling, and he decided putting up any resistance was futile.

Chapter Thirty-Six

When Alessandra pulled him into the black room, he reached for her. This time, when he plundered her mouth, she gave back as good as she was getting. Need drove him as he reached for the button on her jeans.

She broke off and stepped back. "No way am I having sex with you half-dressed again. That was just silly."

"I was desperate." He was quick with an argument. "*We* were desperate." And he felt that way again. She was here. Here. In his condo. In his life. But for how long?

"Well, I'm not feeling quite so desperate at the moment."

"Do you want this?"

"Sex? Hell yes, anytime, anywhere, but I prefer naked if it's all the same with you. And..." She looked adorably flustered. "I have to go to the bathroom. So while I pee, you strip."

It sounded reasonable, but he still pulled her in for another kiss. "You strip too."

He saw a twinkle in her eye when she responded, "Count on it."

She left, and he started removing his clothes. She was being perfectly logical—he'd already ruined one shirt this week. He removed his clothes quickly and efficiently, mindful of the seconds ticking by.

Alessandra had come back.

Where the hell were the suitcase, knapsack, and clothes? When she returned naked and a little shy, he didn't care about anything else. "Lie on the bed."

"Yes, Master."

Oh, so that was how it was going to be. Going to the wall, he snagged the handcuffs.

She smiled serenely and looped her hands through the slats of the headboard.

He secured her wrists and then slanted his mouth over hers. Hovering just an inch away, he repeated, "You went grocery shopping."

"And if this is the reception I'm going to get, I'll do it every day." Her grin was wide, and she tried to arch her hips toward his crotch.

In response, he placed his thigh between her legs, pinioning her to the bed. He looked into those deep chocolate-brown eyes. "I'm going to make you scream."

Her brown eyes flashed. "I wish you would."

Then he dove in for the kiss he'd been wanting to give her since she walked through the door. Alternating bursts of passion and tenderness. Thrusting his tongue, he demanded complete surrender. Just as she gave in, he pulled back and nipped her lower lip sensuously, with exquisite tenderness. He hadn't known what to expect, since she was usually a very demanding lover, but she seemed to revel in the sweetness as much as the spice.

He withdrew, beginning a journey of exploration with his lips, his teeth, his tongue. He moved along her jaw, down the long column of her neck. A nibble here, a nip there. A dart of the tongue and then a kiss to the pulse point. Now she rubbed sinuously and mindlessly against his thigh. Her body was readying, and Smith intended to deliver on his promise. He drew his tongue along the length of her collarbone, and she sighed.

Then he took her nipple in his mouth.

The sigh turned into a low moan, and she tugged at her restraints.

As if he had all the time in the world, he sucked, suckled, and nipped. When he pulled back, he blew a warm breath across the damp skin.

She bucked, and he chuckled.

The other nipple needed the same attention, so he shifted, making sure his thigh rubbed against her pussy.

"I'm not sure I can hold out much longer." A hoarse whimper.

"So don't." He bit down on the tender flesh of her breast.

She made some inarticulate sound, flexing her pelvis down and away from his leg. "I want you in me. Please, Smith."

"Are you begging?"

Now she chuckled. "If that gets you in me faster, then yes, I'm begging."

He'd planned a grand seduction, taking his time to repeatedly bring her to the peak of pleasure, but not letting her go over. In the end, though, he needed to be joined with her. When he put his legs between her thighs, her knees dropped to the bed, giving him all the access he could ever want. He took his time sliding into her. He tried to draw all the sighs and moans he could and smiled when she again pulled at the handcuffs.

She flexed her hips and wrapped her legs around his waist, giving him both permission and admittance.

Then just a matter of grace and ardor. He thrust, and she accepted. He withdrew, and she angled. He sped up the tempo, and she matched the intensity.

When he felt her inner muscles clench around him, he gave over to it, joining her.

****

He'd left the key in the cuffs, so a quick twist popped the lock. The cuffs clanked to the floor, and Alessandra smiled.

"You're going to have to clean that up, you know."

"You did a great job of cleaning...oh shit!" He leapt from the bed and ran to the closet, then reaching for jeans.

She propped herself up on her elbows. "What the hell...?"

"Gratzia."

"You're welcome."

He stopped mid-movement. "Not *grazie*, Gratzia."

"Okay."

"She's my cleaning lady. She should be here right now."

"Okay." A pause. "And she knows about this room."

"It's the last thing she cleans. I have to stop her." *Damn*. He threw on a sweater. "Can you...hide?"

Alessandra laughed. "You don't want your cleaning lady to know that you have sex? Seriously, Smith, have you looked around this room? I think she already knows."

"I want her to keep coming back. Good, discreet help is hard to find. Now just...duck under the sheet."

She rolled her eyes but obeyed.

He opened the door and came face-to-face with

Gratzia.

"Oh, Mr. MacLean, I wondered if you were home. I was trying to figure out what to clean." She looked panicked. "I'm not fired, am I? Did you hire someone else?"

Taking the woman's arm, he guided her to the living room. "Just an obsessive-compulsive friend who felt compelled to clean." He reached for his wallet, pulled out a hundred, and then added a couple more for good measure. "So we'll see you in two weeks?"

"Yes, sir, two weeks." Without another word, she left, and he let out a breath. He was quirky that way. He didn't want his cleaning lady to think he was a degenerate, home having sex in the middle of a workday. Of course, with what he paid her, she could think whatever she wanted as long as she didn't tell anyone.

He was about to head back to the dungeon when he made a detour to his office. Retrieving the bag took only moments. Returning, he found Alessandra lying with her thighs wide open, her labia on full display. "God, you're incorrigible."

She only laughed. "Smith, if she cleans this place, then she already knows you're a wicked, wicked man."

"Just for that, I'm going to make you clean this room. With your tongue."

Another laugh bubbled up. "So that's how you see me." Then she pointed to his midsection and made an up-and-down motion.

Smith looked down to find his fly wide open and his shriveled cock on display.

Within moments, she was holding her sides because she was laughing so hard.

"I'll have to punish you for that."

Her eyes widened in delight. "Yes, please, I've been very bad."

"First, I have to ask you something."

As if sensing the teasing moment had passed, she sat up against the headboard. "Okay, but fair's fair. You need to be naked too."

He could see her point. This had to be when they were on equal footing. The dynamic could shift later. *Would* shift later, he assured himself. It had to shift so he could find the equilibrium that'd been missing for days.

After putting the bag on the bed, he pulled his sweater over his head and shucked his jeans. Then he sat, facing Alessandra. He moved close enough that their opposing thighs touched.

"Where are your clothes?"

She arched her eyebrow and then gave him a Cheshire-cat grin. "I moved them to the other room so you won't be able to threaten to take them away."

He pondered that for a moment. She was right, of course—the spare room didn't have a lock. "Or I could just lock you in here with a bucket."

Her eyes widened, and she snagged a pillow, promptly hitting him with it. "Just try it, buster. You're not locking me in this fucking room, and you're not taking away my clothes again."

Well, that explained why his closet suddenly had more space. "If I promise to let you keep the clothes, will you promise to bring them back in here?"

She eyed him warily. "And I would do that because…?"

He reached for the bag and handed it to her.

Waited. "You look suspicious. It's not going to bite you."

She nodded, but her disquieted look didn't entirely disappear.

"Talk to me, Alessandra. What are you thinking?"

Holding up the bag, she pointed to the logo. "I'm not comfortable with you shopping at this store to buy things for me."

"But I can shop there to buy things for other women?"

That caught her attention. Her eyes stayed fixed on his. "What are we to each other?"

"Open the bag, and then you tell me."

Her fingers lingered on the turquoise paper bag with the gold embossed logo. She played with the handles. She did everything except open the bag.

"Open the bag, Alessandra."

Her eyes widened, but his message was received as she reached in for the box. She pulled it out, letting the bag fall to the bed. She snapped open the case and sighed. "Smith, it's exquisite."

"And?" Obviously, he hadn't convinced her.

She pulled her lower lip through her teeth.

He bit back the desire to order her to say something. Anything.

"Will you put it on me?"

Relief flooded his body, and he reached for the necklace. She leaned forward, and he slid the clasp into place. As he pulled back, she touched her neck. To the casual observer, it looked like she was wearing a platinum necklace with an infinity symbol. Someone in the know, however, would see it for what it was—an eternity collar.

"So…" she began and then faltered, cleared her throat. "You're asking me to be your…"

"Submissive," he supplied helpfully, all the while holding his breath.

"I like that idea, and I love the necklace." A slow smile crept to her lips. "Sorry, Master, I meant collar."

He touched the symbol sitting snugly in the hollow of her throat. "I also want to get you a real collar for you to wear when you're home. We'll keep it at the front door. You need to learn to wear less clothes. I like you naked."

"The neighbors will wonder why the drapes are always drawn."

"Or they'll know we're having sex all over the living room floor. Oh, wait a minute, they already know." He leaned forward to tweak her nipple.

Her laughter died in her throat. "Master?" He didn't answer—couldn't answer—and she pulled herself to her knees, then placed her hands against his pecs, pushing him backward.

Instead of fighting, he gave himself up and lay down, pillowing his head with his hands. He kept his gaze locked on hers but caught her movement out of the corner of his eye, so he wasn't surprised when she wrapped her hands around his cock.

"Jesus, Alessandra, your hands are cold." Still, despite any potential protestations, said cock twitched. As he grew in her hand, that Cheshire grin was back. When she leaned down to take him in her mouth, he didn't bother to bite back the moan. She'd just got him going when she pulled away. He barely had time to groan before he felt the first nip at the base of his cock. Taking her sweet time, she nibbled her way along the very delicate vein. He didn't dare breathe, lest she bite down too hard.

Relief flooded him when she deep-throated him, enveloping him in that wet warmth that promised such relief. He could take it, but he felt like sharing. He pushed against her shoulders, and she took the hint, removing her mouth from his privates.

She batted her eyelashes. "Was I not pleasing my Master?"

After pushing up on his elbows, he reached for her waist and flipped her onto her stomach. He separated her thighs with his knees and then delved his hands into her nether lips. As he had suspected, she was ready. He pulled her hips back and impaled her on his cock.

"Master was very happy with what you were doing, but he was feeling generous." He set a punishing pace and had her gasping for breath. "The question, little one, is how long can you hold out?"

"Not long." She said the words between gritted teeth.

He just chuckled, reached around her waist, and pressed his thumb to her clit. Her body jerked so hard she almost unseated him, but he was quick to thrust in again. As she came, her body clenched down on his cock so hard that now he struggled for breath. He wanted to make it good for her, he really did, but he was too far gone. A final two pumps and he emptied himself into her.

The last thing he did before collapsing was run a finger along the necklace.

****

Smith slowly pulled back to consciousness, Alessandra curled in his arms. "What time is it?"

She chuckled but dutifully checked her watch. "Just after six."

"I didn't mean to fall asleep."

Another chuckle. "I take it as a good sign when you fall asleep after sex. It means you enjoyed yourself."

He nuzzled her neck and moved the hand splayed across her abdomen up to cup a breast. "Yes, I did enjoy myself. I really enjoyed myself. Perhaps a little too much."

She turned her head to look back at him. "What does that mean?"

Propping his head up on his hand, he pressed a kiss to her shoulder. "I like proving that you're multi-orgasmic. Twice today I didn't put that particular talent to use."

Huffing, she turned away, laying her head on the pillow. "Silly man. If you think I didn't enjoy that, you need to take Sex-Ed 101 again."

Now he chuckled. "I know you enjoyed it. I'm just saying I prefer to make you come at least four times."

"At least? At least? Four is hard work, you know. I'm happy if we continue to stay at four. Most women would prostrate themselves for a man who can give them four orgasms." She sighed. "I'm grateful my Master takes my wishes into consideration, but never think one isn't enough."

"Message received." He tightened his grasp around her waist. "I need to talk to you about something, and I'm not sure how to do it."

Rolling onto her back, she gently cupped his cheek. "A couple of hours ago, you asked me to be your submissive. Trust goes both ways. You can talk to me about anything."

God, he wanted to believe her. "I know that, little one, but I'm not sure this is the right venue."

"Okay, what are the choices?"

"Well, there's casual like we are now."

"Sounds good."

He smoothed her short hair from her face. "Or there's a conversation at the dinner table."

"Where we should be heading shortly for some needed sustenance…"

"Or there's another session of psychoanalysis."

She stilled. "I thought you wanted to talk to me *about* something. Psychoanalysis is for questions and answers, not discussions."

"Can't it be both?"

The hand returned to stroking his cheek. "It can be whatever Master wants it to be."

"What if he wants a vanilla conversation?"

"Then it probably shouldn't be in the dungeon."

Which had been his thought all along. But if she balked at the dining room table, he didn't have the right to order her to obey. Here, in this room, the scales were always tilted in his favor. He wasn't playing fair, but then this was something they had to do. Not an optional thing. Not after what Toby had told him.

Her knuckles grazed his cheekbone. "You're scaring me, Smith. Just spit it out."

"Who is DeeDee Threefeathers?"

Her face lost all its color. "If you want the answer to that, then you must tie me up."

"Alessandra—"

She pulled away from him. "That's a question, and we do psychoanalysis for questions."

"Alessandra."

She held up her wrists. "Please, Master. Please."

Her desperation was palpable, and this was a make-or-break moment for them. She'd offered no outright refusal. If she had demanded he let her go, he would have, albeit reluctantly. He tried to flip this situation around and see it from her perspective. She couldn't lie when she was on the psychoanalyst's couch. Nor could she hide behind a mask of implacability because he'd see through it. Had he honestly thought they could have this discussion at the dining room table?

Executive decision made, he rose from the bed. "Lie down, spread-eagle."

Her eyes shone with gratitude as she lay in the center of the bed and spread both legs and arms.

Normally he liked to make this a somewhat sensual experience with lots of touching and caressing, but neither of them had the patience for that. Once he had all four shackles attached, he reached for his clothes. This was an important aspect of the dynamic, he told himself, even as his fingers shook. All he had to do was ask the questions.

After retrieving the pad of paper from the dresser drawer where he'd put it after their last session, he pulled up the chair. He took a moment to compose himself and then repeated the question.

"Who is DeeDee Threefeathers?"

This time, instead of the color draining, it heightened. She looked up at the ceiling, and her brow furrowed in concentration. He'd considered covering her with a blanket, but she seemed to prefer the nudity. The exposure freed her in some bizarre way, and he wouldn't question the logic behind it because there

Gabbi Black

wasn't any.

She took a deep breath. "DeeDee Threefeathers was an infant who was born addicted to OxyContin. Upon DeeDee's birth, her mother, Sabrina, agreed to enter a voluntary treatment program. They placed DeeDee in foster care." She took a breath. "I oversaw that transition. When Sabrina failed her second drug test, I made the determination we needed to look for a more permanent placement.

"Sabrina had an older sister and a mother. The sister, Daisy, lived in Winnipeg and worked as an early childhood educator. DeeDee's grandmother, Sharlene, lived much closer, and Sabrina wanted her daughter to be placed with her mother. But Sharlene had an advanced case of congestive heart failure—due to years of chain smoking—and required oxygen. She was in no shape to care for an infant, and clearly Sabrina would have access to DeeDee. Against the wishes of Sabrina and Sharlene, I determined the aunt was the best chance for successful placement as she indicated she'd be willing to give up custody if her sister was clean for six months."

Smith actually didn't know any of the details she was providing, and keeping up with the names was a struggle, but he was getting it. Grandmother was Sharlene. Mother, Sabrina. Aunt's name was Daisy. The baby's name had been DeeDee.

Alessandra, lost in a memory, offered a slight smile. "I met with Daisy when she came out to get DeeDee. Generally, we don't encourage splitting families by distance, but Daisy came with glowing recommendations and, because of her job, could take DeeDee to work with her every day. The courts

348

awarded temporary custody based on my recommendation, and Daisy flew back to Winnipeg with DeeDee."

"What happened?" He kept his tone gentle but persuasive. Coaxing. Encouraging.

"Nothing happened. Sabrina failed three more drug tests, and Daisy petitioned for permanent custody. She told me she wanted to adopt DeeDee. That was the last time I spoke to Daisy Threefeathers."

One hand clenched and released, and then the other one did the same. She was struggling with the memories and must have been playing them like a movie in her mind.

He had to bring her back. "When did you find out something was wrong?"

"When Dr. Marco Raymond called me from Mission City Memorial Hospital saying I needed to come right away, that a patient was dying, and she'd requested to speak to me." A moment passed, and then she closed her eyes. "Sharlene Threefeathers was barely clinging to life, but she had to see me to tell me what had happened. See, one ordinary Monday morning, Daisy didn't come to work at the day-care center. Then Tuesday comes and goes, and by Wednesday, the owner is getting concerned because Daisy has never missed a day of work in the four years she's been there. So, fearing the worst, the owner calls the police who agree to do a welfare check."

"A welfare check?"

"Yeah, you know, they check to make sure everything's okay. So the two cops go to do the welfare check. Daisy comes to the door and says everything's fine. When they ask her why she hasn't been going to work, she gets confused. When they ask to see DeeDee, she seems flustered. So they decide they need to go in.

"Everything is as neat as a pin, but they can't find the baby." Alessandra swallowed convulsively. "So they're looking everywhere and asking Daisy where the baby is. Finally, one officer sees a twenty-five-pound turkey in the stroller."

Smith had known this was coming, but still he felt that dread.

"Turkey in the stroller, baby in the freezer."

"How long…" He cleared his throat, struggling to keep down the bile. "How long had she been there?"

"The last anyone remembered seeing DeeDee was Friday night at the grocery store. They figure DeeDee was in the freezer for at least five days. She died of exposure, although a few more hours and she would've suffocated." Now a tear slid down Alessandra's temple to the pillow. "They did a full psychiatric workup and determined Daisy had suffered a complete psychotic break for unknown reasons. No logical explanation for it—it just happened. The psychiatrists put her on antipsychotics, and the police called Sabrina to tell her the news."

Jesus.

"The dénouement of the story was pretty quick. Sharlene had an attack upon hearing the news and went to the hospital. She was released from the hospital a day later and came home to find Sabrina dead from an overdose. The next day, after coming out of her psychotic haze, Daisy hanged herself on the psychiatric ward, even though she was on suicide watch. After receiving that news, Sharlene suffered a heart attack. Marco called me from the hospital and said I had to come right away. Sharlene took almost an hour to tell me what had happened because she was so far gone. I kept saying that they—the medical staff—should do something, but Marco said Sharlene had signed a DNR. After losing everyone, she didn't want to live.

"But she wanted to exact revenge on the woman who'd caused all the death and destruction. She held out just long enough to tell me what had happened, and then she died—right in front of me—thus completing some sick circle of Hell, sealing me in with no way to escape."

These bare facts he'd obtained. He just hadn't known the sequence of events.

Continuing, she snorted in derision. "I wiped out three generations of Threefeathers women in one fell swoop."

"Not your fault." His words were soft, non-judgmental.

She pulled against her restraints. "Then whose fucking fault was it?"

"Not yours." *Goddamn it.* He couldn't lose her now. "And the internal investigation made that determination, but by then you'd disappeared."

Again, she pulled against her restraints. "It doesn't matter what someone else says. I held that baby when she was just a few days old. I held her when she was just a month old and handed her over to the woman who was going to kill her. You know, you can't tell by looking at someone that they're going to be a murderer. I would've thought to see something in her eyes, but…nothing. Nothing that said *a few months from now I'm going to put my niece in a freezer.*"

He warred with the desire to either shake some

sense into her or gather her into his arms. "So you walked away."

"I came home from the hospital and tried to sleep, but I couldn't. I prowled around the house all weekend but couldn't find a solution to the problem." She paused as if reliving that memory. "Monday morning, I changed into a pair of jeans and a sweatshirt. I put on my hiking boots, packed a knapsack, caught a bus down to the Mission City Train Station, and took the morning West Coast Express with all the commuters to downtown Vancouver."

Stunned, he contemplated how easy it had been for her. Just hop a train and disappear. He didn't think the police had ever considered that angle. "And then?"

"I walked from the Waterfront Station to the Downtown Eastside. Not hard, you know. It's just a few miles. Then I went to the first bar I could find and got rip-roaring drunk. Not enough, though. I needed more. I took a room in one of the cheap hotels and set about planning to kill myself."

Jesus fucking Christ. He sucked in a breath, tamping down the panic. She hadn't, of course—she was sitting right in front of him. But clearly this was where the death wish had come from.

"I even went so far as to buy razor blades, but it never came to that. Saturday night I went to Kink, and the next Wednesday I went to Masters' Club. I left the hotel and found the rooming house." Now her face was almost serene. "You know the rest."

"How much money did you have with you?"

She frowned as if surprised by the question. "I kept five hundred cash reserve in my box of tampons. I took it all. I wasn't sure I'd need it all but took it just in case.

Probably a good thing I did because it's expensive surviving down there. Did you know that welfare pays just over six hundred dollars a month? No wonder people do desperate things to survive. Because it's not living," she added almost as an afterthought. "It's surviving. People survive down there."

"You never did drugs? How much did you drink?"

She laughed sardonically. "Not enough."

Then another thought. "Why did you start going to Kink on Saturday nights? I'd have thought Wednesdays would've been enough."

A shoulder lifted in a shrug. "I was lonely, and I thought maybe I could meet someone. I rarely drank, but that night I needed courage because I was going to find someone to go home with if it killed me."

"It nearly did."

A nonchalant shrug. "But then the man with the beautiful eyes was there, and everything was okay."

"Why do you call me that?"

For the first time since they'd begun, she looked at him. "All those months ago, at the party, your eyes were the first thing I noticed about you."

He snickered. "Not my hunky body, blond hair, or tight ass?"

"Well, sure, I noticed those things as well, but those eyes blew me away. You must know they're a very unique shade of blue."

He shrugged, disconcerted. "They're the same as my mother's, so I never saw them as anything but normal. I wasn't able to see your eyes that day. You were wearing sunglasses." He smiled. "When I saw them at Kink, I felt the way you did. Dark chocolate brown became my new favorite color."

As he hoped, two bright pink spots crossed her cheekbones.

"I have one more question for tonight, Alessandra, and then we'll see about giving you a reward."

Those beautiful eyes lit in anticipation, but Smith knew his last question would diminish or remove altogether that happiness.

"What will it take to get you to walk back into your old life?"

As expected, she turned to stare at the ceiling. "Can I? Go back, I mean. I'll never be able to face those people again. I don't think I'll ever be able to sit across from someone in crisis and not be seized by overwhelming panic. No." She was quiet and sure. "There's no going back."

He was willing to let it go for the moment.

After putting down the still-blank pad of paper, he moved to release her from the manacles. This time he caressed, giving long strokes.

"What's my reward?" Her voice was soft.

"Turn over onto your stomach. Lay crosswise."

She was quick to comply. The bed was so big only her feet dangled off the end. Smith went to the dresser and removed a bottle of massage oil. He wasn't an expert, but he had faith he could bring her muscles to a state of relaxation.

He started with her feet. This time she was prepared and let out a sigh before he'd worked on a single muscle. Ankles, calves, knees, thighs. As he massaged each muscle, she was sinking farther and farther into the mattress in a state of bliss. He paid extra attention to her ass. Two beautiful white globes just begging to be played with.

Relaxation. Tempting as it would be to bring her to orgasm, that wasn't the point. He removed his hands with great reluctance because he knew how important contact was. He quickly moved to her head, cushioned on her hands. He put a generous amount of oil in his hands and began another journey. Arms, shoulders, back, muscles rippling under his ministrations. The knobs in her spine weren't as prominent as they had been. Had she put on a few pounds? He certainly hoped so.

When he had covered every single muscle, he spoke softly in her ear. "I'm going to help you roll over."

She groaned but let him turn her, all the while keeping her eyes closed.

He knew a little trick of massaging temples, and she sighed. Then he added more oil and worked his way down. Cheeks, neck, shoulders. He bypassed her breasts again, choosing instead to work her sides and then her abdomen.

Finally, he sat next to her and added a little more oil. The first touch of his hand to her nipple had it peaking to attention. She moaned as he thoroughly explored. He cupped, he teased, and he tweaked. Then he trailed his hand lower, and her thighs parted in invitation. She was already damp with need, and as he ran his hands up and down her labia, her hips bucked, seeking relief only he could bring. He thrust two fingers in and began an unrelenting assault on her clit.

Her release wasn't long in coming, as the massage had just been one extensive session of foreplay. She came in slow and sustained cresting waves. Her orgasm was as languid as the massage had been.

Tempted as he was to go for more, she was already relaxing into a state of bliss and sinking back down into the mattress, letting the bed remove the last remnants of tension. She curled into a ball, placing her hands next to his thighs.

"Thank you, Master," she whispered, and then she slipped into a state of paradise.

He eased from the bed and left her to rest.

Chapter Thirty-Seven

Allie wasn't really asleep, but she just needed a moment. His lovemaking had been tender and sweet compared to the athletics before the psychoanalysis session.

She'd needed that session. Cathartic to finally let go. The last vestiges had been banished. Whether she received absolution almost hadn't been the issue. She'd finally shared the burden she carried alone far too long.

Smith hadn't turned away in disgust. He hadn't judged her or let her feel sorry for herself. Instead, he'd pushed her to face the truth. She hadn't been the one to put DeeDee in the freezer. She hadn't been the one to tie the noose, and she hadn't put the needle of heroin into the vein. Maybe she could even learn to live with the grandmother's vengeance. The old woman had been hurting and needed someone to blame. Allie wouldn't have chosen her own last moments of life to be so hateful, but Sharlene had made the choice, and Allie had to respect it.

So where did she go from here? She sure as shit couldn't go back to her old life. Even if she hadn't burned every single bridge, she couldn't contemplate sitting across from someone in need of help and not second-guessing every decision she'd have to make. But being a social worker was all she'd ever done and all she'd ever wanted to do.

She reached for the comforter, which had, as always, fallen to the ground. She turned so she could lay her head on the pillow and then pulled the cover over her head.

****

When Smith sat down next to her head and tugged the blanket from her face, Allie hesitated.

She let him, then gazed up at him. What would he ask of her now? She wasn't sure she had anything left to give.

"I've ordered pizza."

"With extra cheese?"

"Yes, my little one, with extra cheese." He smiled indulgently. "So take the quickest shower you can, get dressed, and I'll have the food ready for you."

She wrinkled her nose. "I have to get dressed? Are we going out?"

He tweaked the wrinkled nose. "No, we're not going out. I just feel like eating dinner at the table like reasonable adults as opposed to sex-starved creatures."

"What if I crawl under the table to give you a blow job?"

He guffawed. "Maybe after dessert."

"Oh, dessert." She said the words reverently. "Chocolate mousse pie." She paused. "It's a good thing your friend Toby put the groceries away."

"Toby's a good guy. Now quit dawdling. The food will be here soon."

She rose from the bed, a little stiff. Stretching, she made her way to the bathroom, pissed, and then took the shortest shower on record. She didn't bother to wash her hair nor even take time to comb it, so it still stuck out in all directions.

Who gives a fuck?

Well, maybe she did. Or maybe she should.

Two pieces of piping-hot pizza sat on her plate, and she'd eaten both before Smith ventured a comment.

"Any chance you might let your hair grow? I mean it looks fine as is…"

She scowled. "It looks like crap, and we both know it. It's going to look worse for the next six months, maybe even more. If you're willing to put up with that, then yes, I'm willing to let my hair grow."

"You might have noticed my eyes, but for me it was your hair. That riot of black curls framing a beautiful face went nicely with a smoking-hot body."

Jesus, the things he said. Part of her should be offended by the objectification, but the rest of her was thrilled he loved her hair as much as she did. "I was wearing a suit." Her tone was just a touch dry.

"A man can use his imagination, and he found a few curves under said suit." His plate was now as empty as hers. "I have a proposition for you."

Her hands went to the necklace. "I thought I had already accepted your proposition."

He laughed. "This is a business proposition."

I doubt I'm going to like this. "Go ahead." Her eyes narrowed. "I'm listening."

"I need a new training coordinator at JEAP."

What the actual fuck? "You fired Hamish?"

Smith shook his head. "Are you crazy? Hamish has been there ten years. He's one of the reasons I felt comfortable buying the company. I just gave him a raise."

"And a promotion?"

Again, Smith shook his head. "Actually, Hamish

wants to go back to the front lines. He covered several shifts last week because a bout of flu went around the office. Having spent five years in administration, he now realizes how much he missed the work. He wants to go back to counseling, his first love. I told him, by the way, that you were Rana. He remembered the call vividly and said you were very convincing."

"He didn't mind being manipulated?"

"Far from it. He liked that I was testing the competence of his workers. Well, your workers—if you accept my proposition."

"My…wait, what?"

His stare was intent. Penetrative. "With Hamish back on the front lines, we need a training coordinator." He raised an eyebrow. "We just signed eight new contracts, so we need to hire and train at least a dozen intake customer service agents and four new counselors."

"And you think I'm qualified to do that?"

"I know you are." Smith steepled his fingers. "Hamish has put together excellent training material, but you'll want to tweak it. He'll be there to back you up, but you know what it's like to mentor people. You were good at it once, and you'll be good at it again."

"I walked away from my old life. What right do I have to start a fresh one?" *But could I?* A small part of her yearned to find out, but the bigger part was scared shitless.

"Well, see, that'll actually be the toughest part of this. You're going back, Alessandra. You're going to clean up the mess you've made." Before she could argue, he held up his hand. "I'll be there every step of the way for the logistical things, but you'll need a good counselor to help you through the things beyond my capabilities." He paused. "Kennedy Dixon is expecting your call."

"Just like that?" The man who thought he was God was well and truly back.

"Yes, little one, just like that. You're going to be honest with people who ask, as I won't let you be anything but truthful. There are going to be another few changes. I'm selling this place. We're going house hunting this weekend in Mission City."

Her jaw dropped. "You don't just want me to clean up the mess—you want me to face the people I hurt every day?"

"People will be quick to forgive."

"Well, what about your work?" She was sputtering. "Your office is downtown. And what about JEAP? I need to be close to work."

Was she already accepting she'd be taking the new position? Things were moving too fast. She was in an out-of-control speeding car.

"There is such a thing as a commuter train. Plus, we'll both be able to work from home from time to time. Once you've got the additional people trained, you'll only need to go in one day a week, and, as you've seen, I'm perfectly capable of working from home. I have very competent people to take care of things if I'm out of pocket. Besides, once the baby comes, I'll want to be home."

Did he…? No, she must have heard wrong.

And yet…

"What baby?"

"The one we're going to start to try making as soon as Anthony removes your IUD."

She leapt from the table like a scalded cat. "Is there anything you haven't planned?"

He rose from the table, reaching for her. *Damn it*, she wanted to protest. She wanted to be strong. She wanted to be independent. But the comfort offered was too strong of a pull not to accept.

"Not planned, Alessandra, hoped. I want to make a life with you, and I think you want that as well."

Then, as if it were perfectly normal, he dropped to one knee. "You took my collar…now will you take my ring?" In her surprise he slipped it on her finger and smiled triumphantly when it fit perfectly.

"You barely know me." *And yet I'm not giving back the ring.*

"I spent six months getting to know you through other people. Then I've spent two very intense weeks getting to know you in more intimate ways."

"And you know about what I've done, and you still want to be with me? Are you crazy?"

He rose, still holding her hands. "Those things make you who you are." His azure eyes bored into her soul. "And since I love you, I accept that those things are part of you."

Her eyes widened and then narrowed. "You love me?" Her voice was laced with doubt. "How is that possible?"

"You'll have to ask my heart, but I think it happened somewhere between you admitting the truth about your past and you stepping into that police station. Not only did you lay your life bare, but you stayed to help those other victims. Alessandra, you're a survivor. You're the strongest person I know." He hesitated. "Unless you don't love me…"

She grabbed his biceps. *Stupid man.* "Of course I love you—that's a given. You gave me my life back. You've given me a reason to live." *Holy shit.* "You really want a baby?"

"I want our baby." He was quick to clarify. "I'm forty-three years old and never thought I'd say these things. I want to marry you. I want to have a baby with you. I want to live in the suburbs and be the best dad I can. I didn't have an example, but I suspect Gage will have lots of advice. And Rielle will be there for you."

Her eyes softened. "How is she?"

"She had her interview with the police yesterday about the abuse she suffered. The truth is there's a good chance neither of you will have to testify because the video is all the evidence they need to convict Jergen. He'll never breathe fresh air again. Oh, I forgot." He let go of her hands long enough to grab the newspaper off the coffee table.

He handed it to her. The story was on the first page of the local news section and went on for two pages. She scanned, too stunned almost to speak. Names, quotes, it all leapt out at her in rapid succession. So many people. "How did they get so much so fast?"

"Well, I spoke to the reporter, Lucille Forbes, myself. She's been working on this story for two years but could never get anyone to go on the record. With the arrest, she could get her story to print. Apparently, witnesses are offering their own stories. This won't be the only exposé. And politicians were plentiful in the Masters' Club. Along with a few titans of business, several doctors, a few lawyers, and other notables among the elite of Vancouver society." He offered her a wide grin. "I've got two of my vice presidents seeing if there are any bargains to be found buying up companies from men who are facing jail sentences."

"That's ruthless." Yet no chastisement in her voice. "I hope every one of them rots in Hell."

"They will." Reaching out for her, he rubbed a thumb under her eyes. "You look like you haven't been sleeping very well."

"I don't sleep well when I'm not with you." She smiled when he grinned slyly. "All right, I admit it. I love sleeping with you. I love being with you. With you I feel like I can do anything."

"Anything?" His voice carried a note of hesitancy.

"I'll call Kennedy Dixon, and then I'll put together a plan to reintegrate with my old life."

"We'll make a plan," he corrected her. "We're partners now."

She arched an eyebrow. "Partners?"

"Okay, maybe Dominant and submissive most of the time, but there are times when we'll be vanilla."

"Just not at this moment, right?"

No mistaking the naked desire in his eyes. "No, little one, not at this moment. Go wait for me."

She pressed a kiss to his cheek and then walked toward the dungeon, hips swinging. Clothes flew off as she contemplated all the things he might do to her. The things they might do together.

Forever.

Mind-boggling. If she'd succeeded with the razor blade six months ago, she would have missed all this. Hope had been in short supply for so long she'd despaired ever feeling it again. Now? She was filled with it. Everything felt possible, and she owed Smith for that. Her own fortitude meant something as well, to be sure, but she wouldn't be here if not for the man with the beautiful eyes.

They had the rest of their lives, and she planned to make the most of their time together.

About the Author

Even though Gabbi Black is a firm believer in happy endings, she makes her characters work for it in every romance she writes, no matter what the genre. From contemporary to BDSM, they are penned early in the morning in her home in beautiful British Columbia while her trusty ChinPoo dog and her cantankerous Himalayan cat keep her company. She also writes gay romances as Gabbi Grey.

~*~

Visit Gabbi at
www.gabbiblack.com

Also Available
from The Wild Rose Press, Inc.
and major retailers.

Amber Eyes
In Their Eyes Book One
By Gabbi Black

School principal Gage Clayton is still grieving the death of his wife and submissive, yet he can't ignore his Dominant needs. As he enters Club Kink, he's inexplicably drawn to a newly released sub with an intriguing proposition and the most captivating amber eyes. But she has disturbing baggage and her expectations prove quite a challenge, one that would necessitate a commitment he's not ready for.

Rielle Reid needs a Dom while she waits for her former Master to return. When she invites a handsome stranger to her home dungeon for a night of play, she's surprised at his gentle dominance—and her response to it. But in the light of day, his demand for equal footing confounds her. After living four years as a twenty-four/seven slave, she has no concept of how to be anything other than property.

Gage must find a way to master Rielle to free them both from the shackles of the past.

Angel's Collar

Love Strictly Tested Book One

By Anna Hague

I have it all…until he shows me more.

I didn't intentionally spill wine all over the most beautiful guy in the room, and one look at those icy-blue eyes brings on a major lapse in coherent speech. Jordan Caldera tells me his secret and wants me to join him. This is where my journey into submission begins.

So much about BDSM freaks me out, but at the same time, I can't help but be intrigued. When I imagine Jordan doing those things to me, I can't resist the adventure. Mind-blowing sex aside, my life is changing at an alarming rate and getting very complicated. Between balancing my career and my best friend's concerns, the secrets I'm keeping are killing me.

What am I willing to risk for the new lifestyle I've embraced…and the man I love?

www.ingramcontent.com/pod-product-compliance
Lightning Source LLC
Chambersburg PA
CBHW051128030726
47504CB00004B/762